DIVINE

HOUSE OF OAK BOOK TWO

NICHOLE VAN

Fiorenza Publishing

Divine © 2014 by Nichole Van Valkenburgh
Cover design © Nichole Van Valkenburgh
Interior design © Nichole Van Valkenburgh

Published by Fiorenza Publishing
Print Edition v1.1

ISBN: 978-0-9916391-3-7

To Mom,
for late-night readings of Coleridge and Tennyson,
for first inspiring my love of words.

And to Dave,
who still turns my insides all melty.

Prologue

THE BALLROOM
STRATTON HALL
WARWICKSHIRE
MARCH 10, 1808

S ebastian Carew was a man without a heart.

Not that he didn't have one in the conventional sense. There was definitely an organ in his chest that beat a steady rhythm, and friends regularly described him as good-humored and courteous.

He was by no means *heartless*.

But rather, Sebastian had quite thoroughly lost his heart years ago.

He pondered this reality as he stood in the Earl of Stratton's ballroom. Listening to bright, cascading laughter.

Not any laughter.

Her laughter.

The sound had slammed into his solar plexus, hard and swift, leaving him gasping.

Straining to see through the crowd of people, he located her gleaming head on the arm of her brother. She was smiling, brilliant, drawing every eye. Candles flickered around her golden hair, surrounding her in light.

As if some angel were sending him a sign.

Sebastian swallowed and glanced away. He wasn't sure he believed in signs, divine or otherwise.

And if there were some divine angel, it would be a decidedly ironic one with a wicked sense-of-humor.

Dwelling on *her* would only bring him heartache. And a man of his social position did not have the luxury of heartache. He should just walk away, out the door without looking back.

But against his will, his head turned, drinking her in.

He pushed against the memory of that morning six years earlier when he had topped a small hill, lifted his head into the rising sun.

And saw *her*.

Standing in the dew-kissed meadow, surrounded by wild flowers and burnished sunflare. Her back to him, blond hair hanging loose in waves down to her waist, shimmering like spun gold just as poets describe. Her arms outstretched wide, face tilted toward the sky. The goddess of morning come to embrace her realm.

The moment had seared into his soul, stretching time. The precise point which had divided his life ever after into two distinct parts.

Before her and *after her*.

When his heart had been irretrievably lost.

And now, like a helpless planet to her sun, she pulled him into her gravity, held him tethered and thralled.

Miss Georgiana Elizabeth Augusta Knight.

It had been four years, six months and—here Sebastian did a quick calculation—fourteen days since he had seen her last. He shook his head.

How *pathetic* that he knew that.

Her grandmother's estate, Lyndenbrooke, was part of the local parish where Sebastian's stepfather was vicar. Georgiana had lived with her grandmother at Lyndenbrooke for a year after her father's death.

That one glorious year in which she became everything that he knew he would never have. A highborn heiress like Miss Knight did not marry a poor vicar's stepson with nothing to recommend himself beyond a charming smile and good-natured humor.

Such were the rules of polite society.

And as one who inhabited merely the edges of polite society, Sebastian knew better than most the power of such rules.

He stared at Georgiana across the ballroom, surrounded by eager swains. She was here as a distinguished guest, whereas he had only been invited as a local gentleman and distant relation to the earl. Someone who could be relied upon to dance with every wallflower and flirt outrageously with each widow.

His lack of prospects were all that prevented her from considering him as a potential suitor. If he were wealthy and titled, then she would *see* him.

He tossed that thought around his brain. Tried to convince himself of its truth.

Tried to believe she was the kind of woman who cared about status and money.

She was not.

He watched Georgiana curtsy prettily to Lord Harward—Lord Stratton's son and heir—and his new bride. Georgiana tilted her head. Her long neck graceful, the pearls around her throat and elegant white dress proclaiming to one and all her eligible status as a wealthy debutante.

Lovely. Angelic. Always just out of reach.

Sebastian would just watch her from a safe distance. That would be enough.

But his feet had other ideas apparently, as he soon found himself threading through the ballroom toward her.

As he drew near, her head swiveled, and his heart thundered as he saw recognition dawn. One of her wide, glorious smiles lit up her face. Warm and welcoming.

It was enough to slay a man.

His emotions seesawed between excitement and dread, neither emotion quite gaining the upper hand. He swallowed, tight and hard.

There was no helping a greeting now.

"Miss Knight, it is a pleasure to see you." Sebastian performed a short bow and gave her his melting smile. The one that his mother said could charm birds from trees. Granted, mothers *had* to say such things.

But Georgiana returned the smile in full measure. She was something of an expert in melting smiles herself, Sebastian realized. The kind that turned one's insides to pudding.

"Mr. Carew, what a delight!" Georgiana curtsied in return. Her brother cocked a curious eyebrow, and she turned to him. "James, this is one of my friends from my time with Grandmama, Mr. Sebastian Carew. Remember? I believe you may have met. Mr. Carew, may I present my older brother, Mr. James Knight."

Sebastian executed another of his flawless bows, noting the resemblance between James Knight and his younger sister: golden hair, shockingly blue eyes, that same wide smile.

"Carew, eh?" Knight asked, also bending in greeting. "Any relation to John Carew, the Earl of Stratton?" Knight gestured toward the elegant silver-haired earl across the room.

"Distantly. My father died when I was a babe and my mother remarried the local vicar."

Knight nodded, his gaze casually scanning Sebastian's attire. Noting the serviceable coat which didn't fit quite as tightly as it should, the boots still shabby despite the hours spent polishing them. All the subtle telltale marks that did *not* add up to money, to prospects.

There was no judgment or condemnation in Knight's eyes, thank goodness, unlike other powerful men. But there *was* an air of dismissal. That quiet assessment which instantly placed Sebastian into a box labeled 'Not Eligible for My Sister.' A look with which Sebastian was long familiar.

The orchestra struck up the first bars of a waltz.

Don't do it. Do not ask her.

"Miss Knight, may I have the honor of this dance?"

He asked her.

Even a poor, distant relation of the Earl of Stratton deserved a moment of heaven. A tiny taste of the life he would never have.

"Of course, Mr. Carew. I would be honored." She placed her hand in his. Even through gloves, her fingers seared.

"Miss Knight?" she murmured as he led her to the dance floor. "Really, Sebastian, have we become so formal as that?"

Oh, how he had missed the sound of her voice in his ear.

"Well, I decided to have pity on your reputation and not call you 'Georgie' with everyone looking on," he chuckled lowly.

She gave him another lushly wide smile and playful tap with her fan. "Heavens, but it is so wonderful to see you after so many years. How are you, my oldest friend?"

Gutted to the core at the sight of you but otherwise fine.

Thank goodness his mouth obeyed him enough *not* to say that.

"Delighted to see you, Georgie," he said instead.

He placed his hand on to the small of her back and twirled her into the familiar down-up-up rhythm.

This made four, he realized.

Four times that he had danced with her. And this was the first waltz.

"I assume you are staying at Lyndenbrooke with your grandmother, Mrs. Knight?" he asked.

"Of course. We just arrived earlier today. Grandmama has been happy of our company before we continue on to London."

It felt shockingly right to hold her in his arms, to feel her warm breath against his chin as she spoke. Being with her had always been like this. Effortless and comfortable, without a trace of awkwardness, even now after a separation of four years. Such a pity social conventions decreed unmarried men and women could not exchange correspondence. He had to rely on chance meetings to speak with her. And for gentlemen of limited means, chance meetings were few and far between.

He saw her reflected in the mirrored walls of the ballroom. Tall and slender, white skirts swirling around them.

He had always loved her height, that he didn't have to crouch down to talk to her as with other women. Being the tallest man in the room did have its drawbacks. As it was, her head barely reached his shoulder, golden hair contrasting with his brown.

Blood pounded in his ears. It was the worst sort of agony. Having her in his arms, feeling so much like home, and yet knowing there would never be anything beyond this moment.

Why was he doing this to himself? Dancing was only going to make everything worse. He twirled her once, twice.

Georgiana stared off into the mid-distance, lost in thought.

"Still an expert at wool-gathering, I take it," he said, suppressing a smile.

Georgiana started slightly and gave him a rueful grin.

"Please tell me your thoughts, at minimum, involved a dank castle and dastardly rogue?" He arched an eyebrow.

She laughed, quicksilver and bright.

Really, it shouldn't be legal—a laugh like that. It wreaked havoc with a man's good sense.

"Remember, Sebastian, you are to pretend *not* to notice my day-dreaming? But no—no dastardly rogues this time. I was thinking about that year. It was such a difficult time for me, with my father's sudden death, my mother a little crazy with grief, and James trying to hold us all together."

As if Sebastian could forget that year. As if every minute he had spent with her wasn't emblazoned in his memory. Hiding underneath the drooping branches of that huge white willow as she spun fantastical stories about kidnapped maidens and heroic knights, her giggling laughter as he taught her to catch frogs and skip rocks, sitting in the vicarage kitchen making biscuits with his sisters, gossiping and teasing.

Yes, he remembered *everything* with vivid clarity. Too vivid.

He gave her a game smile. "Not to mention all the quilling your governess obliged you to do."

Georgiana gave an elegant shudder. "'Tis most ungentlemanly of you to remind me, Seb. Poor Miss Smith was exceptionally fond of paper filigree. Quilling is so incredibly tedious, endlessly twirling and gluing and molding all those tiny strips of paper. Do you remember that work basket she forced me to complete?"

"The one with the puffy, little lambs?"

"Precisely. It was hideous."

"Oh, I don't know that I would call it *hideous*. There is a certain elegance to lambs prancing through roses."

Georgiana froze slightly, her eyes hesitantly searching his for any hint of mockery. Sebastian tried to keep his look innocuous, but it was no use. His lips twitched upward.

"The rainbow arching over the entire scene was a nice touch," he said innocently and then ruined the entire effect by laughing.

At least he told himself it was a laugh. Not a guffaw.

"Seb, you are truly terrible!" Georgiana pursed her mouth and attempted a quelling stare. However, her dancing gaze betrayed her.

"Well, I do try. Having so many older sisters has given me a certain amount of practice."

Georgiana chuckled appreciatively and locked her playful eyes with his. Those impossibly huge blue eyes, pools of morning sky. Eyes which transported back to that year.

When they had been Seb and Georgie. Georgie and Seb.

Living in each other's pockets, finishing each other's sentences. When he had surrendered himself to her, heart and soul.

He had thought—wished, even, in his darker moments—that the connection he felt to her would fade over time.

But, no, Fate would not be so kind to him.

As they danced and laughed together, the past became present, and he allowed himself to hope. Maybe he could woo her, win her. Claim a small share of happiness for himself.

Hope. Such a foolish, futile emotion.

He twirled her again, drinking in her glorious eyes.

Maybe . . . just maybe, this time she would finally *see* him . . .

"Despite your teasing, you were so generous to befriend an awkward, chatterbox of a girl." She smiled up at him, fondly. "You made the grief of that year more bearable. I felt so blessed to have your friendship. It was like God had sent me another brother. I will always appreciate your kindness."

Sebastian felt his smile freeze.

Brother. *Ouch.*

The pain was swift, slicing deep.

She thought of him as a brother. Warm, uncomplicated filial feelings. While his for her were decidedly . . . *not.*

Well, his feelings were *warm* too. But they were about as far from filial . . .

He swallowed. He needed to change the topic. *Now.*

"Tell me of the latest on-dit." It was a question born of old habit.

She arched an eyebrow at him.

"Tell me a scandal," he'd say. "Something shocking."

"Why should I know anything scandalous, Seb?"

"Please. You love gossip like you love to breathe." He nudged her shoulder. "Probably more."

"Well . . ." She tapped her lips. Thinking. "I did overhear Grandmama talking with the housekeeper this morning about the new blacksmith . . ."

"What makes you think I still read the broadsheets, Sebastian?" she asked archly.

"The sun still rises in the east, so I am quite sure the world as I know it has not entirely collapsed. And of all people, Georgie, you would remain the same. Here, I will even give you the topic—Lord Harward and his recent marriage." Sebastian nodded his head toward the gentleman dancing across the room with his new bride.

"Oh, that has been delicious, has it not?" Georgiana grinned. Her face lit with mischief. "How wicked of Lord Stratton! Requiring his heir to marry before his twenty-seventh birthday or risk losing his entire fortune."

"And to gooseberries, no less."

"That *is* the best part of the story. I understand Lord Stratton found the whole situation entirely diverting."

"And Harward decidedly did not appreciate his father's ridiculous meddling." Sebastian gave a rueful smile.

His decidedly eccentric relation, John Carew, Earl of Stratton, had determined several months ago that his wayward son and heir, Viscount Harward, needed to marry. Being the president of the West Midlands Heritage Gooseberry Society and a decided enthusiast, Lord Stratton had altered his will. The new will stipulated that if Lord Harward did not marry before his twenty-seventh birthday, the absurdly large sum of sixty thousands pounds would be divided between three gooseberry societies: one being Stratton's own gooseberry society—the other two belonging to his longtime friends, Sir Henry Stylles and Lord Blackwell.

Good friends, all three men had spent the last twenty-five years indulging in a shared passion for the small fruit. Fierce gooseberry devotees, Sir Henry and Lord Blackwell had reportedly been giddy over the prospect of potentially receiving twenty thousand pounds each to devote to their gooseberry cultivars.

Given young Lord Harward's distaste for gooseberries and love of money, it had proved an ingenious motivation. Harward had courted and married within eight weeks. Sebastian looked over at the silver-haired Lord Stratton, standing and chatting with two widows, regal and yet sparkling with energy and mischief. The elderly earl was an unmitigated rogue.

"I heard tell that women were endlessly inventive in their attempts to woo Lord Harward. It is said that Lady Margaret Simon hid in Harward's dressing room intending to trap him into marriage."

"Have you still not learned that it is not proper for a lady to gossip?" Sebastian shook his head in mock censure, spinning her again. The strains of the waltz drifted around them.

She laughed and made a dismissive gesture with her head, easily brushing away any prick of conscience.

"Please! You asked me about the scandal first." She shot him an amused eyebrow.

He chuckled. "Indeed. My apologies."

"Besides, without gossip, what is a lady to do?" Georgiana said, matter-of-fact. "How else should we occupy our time? As ladies, we are obligated to merely pretend not to like it, that is all. Gossip is what makes the world turn round, I daresay. Secrets are far too much fun. It is the only way to be involved, to feel truly connected, don't you think?"

Ah, Georgiana. Always so utterly herself without apology.

Sebastian nodded in agreement, grinning at her. They twirled again, her body light and graceful, flowing easily with him.

"We are off in a week to London for the Season. I am somewhat fearful, as it will be my first. Will I see you there?" Georgiana asked.

He hated the hope in her eyes. As if a man such as himself had the money to spend any time in London. As if any London hostess would let one such as him through their door.

"That will be unlikely. Lord Stratton has taken pity on a poor relation and has generously purchased an officer's commission for me in the Eleventh Light Dragoons. I join my regiment in just a few days and will most likely be shipped off to Spain within the year."

"Heavens!" She missed a step as she twirled.

"Do I detect a note of concern?"

"Though I understand our men are needed there to aid the Spanish in their rebellion against the French, I should be most sorry if Napoleon's men were to turn you into a hunting target."

"Not as sorry as I should be, I assure you." He gave a game chuckle, trying for a devil-may-care attitude.

"This is no laughing matter, Sebastian. You could be killed." Georgiana's wide eyes searched his. Not amused.

"Yes, that is generally the risk a soldier runs." Sebastian shrugged.

Her eyes flared wider. Her concern more gratifying than he cared to admit. His heart hummed with it.

Pathetic. He was pathetic.

"But . . . why? Why turn to a soldier's life? Why not the Law or the Church?"

"Why not?" he countered, hating that he had to explain himself. To justify his limited life choices to her. "I should like to think I am an affable fellow, able to rub along well with others. I am not suitably serious for the Church and hardly studious enough for the Law. I am strong and not afraid of hardship and wish to do my part for King and Country. What else am I to do with my life?"

"Well . . . I mean . . ." she floundered. She regarded him for a careful moment. Stared but not really seeing.

She never *saw* him. That had always been the problem.

"Please be careful, my old friend. I should be sad if anything were to happen to you." Words spoken softly.

"Yes, I am like a brother to you, after all." Sebastian managed a crooked, sardonic smile.

"Precisely," she instantly agreed, completely missing the irony in his voice. "I could not imagine losing any of my brothers."

They twirled, the air between them suddenly weighty.

"You must promise me you will return," she said, catching and holding his eye. "I could not bear it if you did not. Please. Promise."

The memory of her face in that moment would cling to him for years afterward—concern, worry . . . *emotion* . . . all for him.

His heart hung in his throat, tangling his tongue. An odd mixture of intense elation and devastating sadness.

She *did* care for him, he reminded himself.

Just not in *that* way.

He spun her again, memorizing the lilting stretch of her neck, the warmth of her back under his gloved hand, the rustle of her skirts brushing his legs. Her subtle scent—roses and silk.

Memories that he stored for a future bereft of her. A future of guns and cannon blasts and the moans of the dying. A future filled with relentless, mind-numbing boredom and brief moments of ghastly terror. Perhaps even death.

"I promise," he said, helpless to resist anything that she asked of him. "I will return."

To you, he added silently. *I will return to you.*

Not that it mattered. Even if he did return whole and sound. Even if she did not marry in the interim. Even if his prospects improved enough for him to honorably offer for her.

Even if . . . even if . . .

Even if he were crowned king, could he ever *be* enough to capture her heart? Would she ever see *him*?

The waltz came to a close and, reluctantly, Sebastian delivered Miss Georgiana Elizabeth Augusta Knight back into the care of her brother, knowing the next time he saw her—*if* he saw her—she would most likely be the wife of some unworthy man.

Sebastian didn't know who he would be. But he knew the man would be unworthy.

Unworthy of her bright spirit. The sunlight of her soul.

For months afterward, he could still hear Georgiana's laughter across the room, could still see her backlit, the burning candles turning her golden hair into a crown.

But Sebastian knew she didn't need light behind her to be illuminated. It came from within. Radiant. Miss Georgiana Knight would take sunshine wherever she went. Bestowing her cheerful, unspoiled nature on any and every person who crossed her path.

And Sebastian also knew, with despairing surety, that person would *not* be him.

Jersey, Channel Islands
Officer's billet
December 14, 1812
Nearly five years later

Captain Sebastian Carew sat alone in his room, staring at the two letters the post had just delivered.

They could not have looked more different. One was a thin, tattered missive from his eldest sister, most likely written with the lines crossed and then crossed again to conserve paper.

By contrast, the other letter was thick, white and pristine, bearing the official mark of a prominent London solicitor.

Winter winds battered the solitary window and whistled down the chimney, licking the small fire which burned in the grate. The room was spartan: a chair, a table and low bed in one corner. A rag rug on the floor.

Such was a soldier's life. At least he had a roof over his head, an improvement over the canvas tents of the Peninsula.

Below him, Sebastian could hear the low rumble of men's voices and the clink of glasses filled with brandy as they whiled away long hours in the parlor of the officer's billet. He should join them.

But he didn't. Not yet.

It was coming on Christmas and, once more, Sebastian would spend it far from home. He wondered, as he always did this time of year, when he would see his friends and family again.

If he would ever see *her* again.

Over the years, Sebastian had kept himself apprised of Georgiana's life through letters from his sisters. She had a brilliant first Season in London but did not accept any of the numerous offers of marriage she received. Nor did she her second or third Season. He was slopping through the mud of central Spain when he learned that her grandmother had died, leaving Lyndenbrooke to Georgiana.

And yet she didn't marry. It felt like an ax waiting to fall, the end of any faint hope he still possessed.

But, thus far, he had kept his promise to her.

That crazy, impetuous promise.

For himself, it was hard to care if he lived or died.

What future awaited him? To hear news that she had married elsewhere? To scrimp and save and perhaps one day amass just enough money to sell his commission and support himself and a family, always teetering on the edge of poverty? Or perhaps even worse, marry and retain his commission, forcing his wife to follow the drum, moving with him from camp to camp?

It was no life for a lady.

Though he personally held his own life cheap, that one pledge had made all the difference.

Every skirmish with swords glinting, every battle charge into blazing guns, her words echoed through him.

Promise me you will return.

He had to stay alive, if only to spare Miss Georgiana Knight a few tears weeping for his fallen body.

It was truly pathetic when he thought too much about it.

He was pathetic.

But as long as she remained unmarried, he could hope. Could dream that impossible dream where somehow he became *more than.*

More than a captain in King George's army. More than a brother in *her* eyes.

An utterly futile dream. He knew this.

But Hope was a persistent beggar. Always hovering around the edges of his life, needing only the smallest glance of encouragement to start clamoring for a coin. Eager to purchase a place in his soul.

He looked at his sister's battered missive and declined to read it just yet. His sister was a diligent correspondent, bless her, but he never found village gossip as fascinating as she.

Instead, Sebastian carefully opened the solicitor's letter.

And gasped.

Surely, this couldn't be.

Stared. Read it again.

Felt a wide grin spread across his face, as the beggar Hope suddenly revealed herself to be an angel, granting him the deepest wish of his soul.

Sun shattered the gloom of his wintry mind.

He jumped up with a shout, bringing feet running.

"Something amiss, Carew?" asked Captain John Phillips, popping his head into Sebastian's room.

A cashiered officer, Phillips had arrived just a few weeks previously from Canada with letters of recommendation from General Brock. He was currently an unofficial member of the billet, but was considering purchasing another commission and joining Sebastian's regiment.

Phillips had proved himself an immediate friend, good-humored and always up for a lark. When Sebastian didn't immediately respond, Phillips walked fully into the room, raising an inquisitive eyebrow.

With another whoop, Sebastian threw back his head and laughed at the ceiling.

And then read the letter one more time. Just to be sure. Somewhere, his mind noted that the paper he held shook violently.

Phillips waiting patiently, a wry smile on his lips.

"Well," Sebastian began, his voice hoarse.

He cleared his throat and started over. It didn't help; his voice was still hoarse.

"It would seem that I shall now be styled as The Right Honourable Earl of Stratton."

Phillips blinked and then gave a crack of laughter.

"Good one, Carew." He slapped Sebastian on the back. "You almost had me with that Banbury tale, but you shan't turn me sweet. I intend to win my ten quid back from you tonight."

Sebastian could only shake his head, staring at the letter, the glorious reality of it all sinking in.

"No, Phillips. 'Tis most true. My distant cousin, Lord Harward, and his family were killed in a tragic carriage accident. Upon hearing the news, the old earl's heart gave out. I had always thought a large family of cousins in Gloustershire were next in line for the earldom, but there have been other deaths the last few years and, well . . . as it turns out, I am the next heir."

Phillips snatched the letter from Sebastian and quickly read it.

"It says you need to report to London immediately and present yourself before the House of Lords, something about the will needs to be addressed, but you have full possession of all properties, real and otherwise . . . It goes on and on."

Sebastian knew his face looked stunned silly. He could see the expression echoed on Phillips'.

"Well, well, well . . . Lord Stratton. Imagine that." Phillips chuckled, deep and low. Then made a deep, somewhat mocking, bow. "If your right honorable lordship will permit me some impertinence, I think this occasion calls for a celebration."

Laughing, Sebastian shook his head and allowed himself to be led downstairs, listened to the huzzahs and shouts of congratulations from his fellow officers. Grinning all the while, his joy and relief almost palpable.

Fate had suddenly given him options. He was no longer penniless. He could provide for his parents and sisters. Ensure that his nieces and nephews had advantages he never did.

He was an *earl*. A peer of the realm.

His life suddenly held social status, security, purpose.

Possibilities. *Hope*.

Visions of Georgiana danced through his head.

At last! He could finally do something to earn her regard. He could *act*, instead of just longingly wish.

The joy of it fizzed through him. Champagne bubbles exploding in his chest.

It wasn't until he woke the next morning that Sebastian remembered the letter from his sister. Friends continued to move in and out of his room, congratulating him. The entire officer's billet had been turned into an impromptu party, celebrating Sebastian's good fortune.

In between laughing jests from fellow officers, Sebastian gingerly opened his sister's missive and decoded the words written across each other.

One phrase haunted him for months to come.

Oh, did you hear about poor Miss Knight? The one who inherited Lynden-brooke? It seems she is now consumptive and has been sent off to some special-ist doctor in Liverpool. No one expects her to survive the winter. 'Tis such a shame. She was such a pretty, vibrant thing.

Somehow, no one in the crowded room heard his heart freeze and then crack, shattering into a thousand pieces. This seemed almost impossible, as the sound thundered in Sebastian's own ears.

Later, Sebastian would ponder the cruelty of the moment.

Fate handing him the means to finally reclaim his heart and then brutally crushing all hope in the same day.

The irony of Georgiana passing away when Sebastian had survived so much.

He tried to imagine her as a consumptive: emaciated, pale, racked with cough. Dying.

But all he could see in his mind's eye was a girl, twirling, lost in a flame of golden sun, holding his heart in her brilliant light.

Chapter 1

The letter arrived on a Tuesday.

Brittle, yellowed, moth-eaten with age.

Georgiana Knight immediately read it, letting the thrill of the words pour through her, absorbing their implications.

The letter seemed innocuous enough at first glance. The direction was clearly inscribed in a looping calligraphic hand on the outside.

Haldon Manor
Herefordshire

Neat and plain. Just as any letter written in 1813 should be addressed.

Georgiana instantly recognized the handwriting—knew it as well as her own, because indeed it was.

Her own.

Which really summed up the problem entirely. As Georgiana was most decidedly not in 1813. Never had been. And she had not written this letter.

At least, not yet.

How Georgiana had come to find herself in the twenty-first century—rather than the nineteenth, the century of her birth—was a long story involving an old oak tree, a time portal in her cellar, her brother, James, and her own near-death from tuberculosis. Modern antibiotics truly worked miracles.

With her health restored, she had spent the last year adjusting to the twenty-first century: mastering the terror of motorway driving, resisting the time-sucking vortex of Facebook, earning a green belt in taekwondo and reconciling to wearing tight jeans.

And now this letter arrived, written in her own hand.

Georgiana stood in the kitchen of Duir Cottage—once the dower house for Haldon Manor, the nearby estate where she had been born—staring transfixed at the letter nestled in a protective plastic sleeve, still warm from the sun-heated post bag. Silence drummed through the cottage, broken only by the sudden tumbling of ice in the freezer. She startled, remembering only then to breathe.

Swallowing, she strolled to the overstuffed sofa in front of the fireplace and sat. Well, *flopped* actually, if she were being honest with herself. Her mother—God rest her soul—would be appalled.

She stared at the letter again. Goosebumps shivered up her arms, the plastic sleeve trembling in her hand.

The quixotic letter made her *quiver*.

When was the last time anything had rendered her breathless?

It was just so unexpected . . . so enigmatic . . . so *thrilling*.

Georgiana nearly giggled from sheer exhilaration.

Setting the letter down on the sofa, she picked up the brief note that had been enclosed with it:

Ms. Knight,

We were sent this letter from the Society of Genealogical Good Samaritans. As we know you have some connection with the original Knights who owned

Haldon Manor, we are forwarding the letter in hopes it will mean something to your family. If you do not wish to keep it, please send the letter to the local museum in Marfield for storage in their archive.

Sincerely,

Charles Ellwood
Director of Operations
Haldon Manor Hotel and Spa

Nothing else.

Her tablet suddenly binged, followed quickly by a chirp from her laptop and a wolf whistle from her phone. Alerts always came in threes.

A text from James.

Ready for your date?

Georgiana swallowed and shook her head even though her brother and his new wife, Emme, were half a world away—in a place called Bali, was it?

Emme's brother, Marc, was working on another martial arts film there, and they had joined him on the movie set for a couple weeks. After that, they planned to travel around the south Pacific for a while. James forever itched to see what lay beyond the horizon.

James and Emme wanted—begged, actually—Georgiana to accompany them on their travels. But she always felt like a third wheel, a spectator on the edge of James' life, watching her brother blissfully in love.

Not exactly the most enjoyable way to spend one's time.

Besides, unlike her brother, she didn't necessarily yearn to see the world. She just wanted her passage through life to matter. To be more than mere existence. She had been making plans, trying to fit her nineteenth century upbringing into twenty-first century life.

But then this letter had to arrive and muddle everything.

Bing. Chirp. Whip-woo. Another message.

I know you're there, Georgie. You check your phone like it's crack.

Georgiana grimaced. *Pavlovian* was the word Marc used to describe her incessant social media use. He had tried to explain once what it meant, something about dogs and salivating. She still didn't get it. The wolf whistle was his doing. Marc found it hilarious for some reason.

She pondered the letter. It was riddled with two hundred years worth of moth holes and water damage. But her own handwriting was unmistakable. Slanting, loopy, hurried. She re-read the fragmented words:

[. . .]
[. . .]ber [. . .] 1813

Beloved keeper of my soul,

Oh, my darling love! [. . .] my own affections. You and only you rule my heart. [. . .] forgive me? [. . .] hole in my heart the shape and size of you. Your beating heart might as well be my own.

I came [. . .] Wretched, wretched fool [. . .] your love. [. . .] comfort me with the warmth of your embrace. Whisper those words of adoration [. . .] profound love that comes from deep within a woman's soul. Darling, suffer me no more to pine [. . .] Wrap me in the light of your love.

[. . .] heart ever your own,

Georgiana Knight

Georgiana swallowed hard, feeling the shock of it again.

And then she giggled. Gleefully.

The letter gave her *goosebumps*. Every. Single. Time.

Smiling, she sank back into the couch, letting the wonder of it fizzle through her blood, tucking her bare toes under herself.

She *loved* someone! Or had? Would?

And quite passionately too. *Beloved keeper of my soul . . . a hole in my heart the size and shape of you . . .*

Who knew she could be so poetic?

But what did this portend? Was she to return to 1813?

Well, the letter implied that she *did* actually return. She most certainly couldn't write the love letter from her couch here and now. She had to *be* in the nineteenth century to write it.

She shook her head. Wasn't this one of those space-time conundrums that Emme talked about? If she chose not to pass back through the portal, time would unravel? Or, at the very least, history would alter and she would wake one morning to find the world ruled by knife-wielding sharks?

Which meant she *had* to return, didn't she? For the good of *humanity*, if nothing else?

Just the thought caused her heart to simultaneously climb into her throat and sink to her feet.

How impossible!

But for a chance to truly love like this . . .

Her emotions were a cacophony of conflicting thoughts. Like bickering children, each demanding attention.

She was twenty-four years old and had kissed six men. Five of those kisses had been stolen during her three London seasons—and, yes, she did still count the one from that excessively drunk dandy, even if his kiss had been more of an accidental stumble into her lips.

A kiss was a kiss, right?

Though none of those kisses had been of the toe-tingling, knee-melting variety one read about in novels.

She also tallied four proposals of marriage. Well, at least what she considered to be marriage proposals. It was astonishing how vague men could be about it.

But she had not experienced fierce romantic love, not enough to commit her life to another's, not as this love letter described.

Though, now she did have Shatner.

Shatner. Kisser number six. Her twenty-first century boyfriend of several months—the man of Intense Stares and Brooding Charm, despite his odd name. His parents were huge fans, apparently (*Star Trek* not Priceline). Whatever that meant.

She did care deeply for Shatner. Or, at least, her heart beat a little faster when he touched a hand to her back. And she did enjoy his kisses. She liked the *thought* of him, of who she could be with him.

Was that love?

Bing. Chirp. Whip-woo.

Seriously, Georgie! Are you kissing Shatner or something? Talk to me.

Giving a decidedly unladylike grunt, Georgiana grabbed her phone, and laying the letter on the couch, snapped a photo of it.

This came in the mail today. She attached the image.

Sitting back, she debated how quickly James would reply. What would he make of it?

As with any letter written in the early nineteenth century, it wasn't in an envelope but was instead a single sheet of paper, folded and tucked to create its own enclosure, the address written on one side, the message on the other. The single sheet had been unfolded and pressed flat in the plastic.

So achingly familiar, a poignant reminder of the simplicities of home.

Of course, there was a particularly pesky moth hole right where the addressee's name would have been, preventing her from knowing to *whom* she had written the letter. Frustrating that. But *Haldon Manor, Herefordshire* was clearly legible. Holding the letter up to the light didn't reveal anything more.

She turned the letter around in her hands and then noticed something odd on the outside edge.

A small squiggle. More than just a stray pen mark. Clear and deliberate.

21

She brought it closer to her eyes, examining. It resembled a rather stylized number four, swooping and open on top. Or was it the number twenty-one, where the two and the one were overlapping each other in such a way as to resemble a four, the two a little higher than the one?

It was in an odd place, on a part of the paper that would have been tucked and folded away. Unseen.

It was unusual . . . unexpected.

Georgiana flipped the letter over and reread it. Again.

And then leaned (slouched) against the back of the sofa, curled her legs in their loose pajama bottoms up against her tight t-shirt and stared at the beamed ceiling.

Why, oh why, *knowing* that she would read this letter, did she not leave herself a clue? Or at the very least, have written the name of her supposed beloved on the existing part of the letter?

It was utterly maddening. Or was it? Maybe that small symbol *was* the clue that she left for herself.

She pondered it for a moment.

No, it was still maddening. *Fascinating.* But maddening.

Who was he, the man who inspired such devotion from her? Shatner?

Or was it someone else? Scouring her memories, she couldn't recall any gentleman from the nineteenth century who had garnered her interest, particularly as she had been so sick. Was the mystery man someone she had yet to meet? An enigmatic man whose brooding gaze promised hidden secrets.

Briefly, Georgiana imagined it all too clearly.

Going through the portal in her cellar and entering the front door of Haldon Manor. Arthur—her stodgy, but still beloved, middle brother left behind in 1813—gasps in astonishment to see her whole and healthy. Marianne, his wife, runs to her, sobbing into her shoulder. Arthur draws them across the great hall and into the drawing room, Marianne still weeping.

And there, rising from the sofa, an unknown man. Dark maybe, tall definitely, dressed in tight breeches and an immaculately cut coat. All worn with a devil-may-care attitude and intense smile. Looking a little bit like Shatner. She smiles back at him, curtsies, and extends her hand in greeting. He grasps it, raises her knuckles to his warm lips—

—her phone buzzed, loudly.

It had taken James less than five minutes to call.

"So, is there anything in your past you would like to share with me?" Exasperation laced his voice. "A hidden love interest of which I have been unaware?"

"Heavens, James! What a thing to say. You know that there is no such person—"

"Really? Because this letter would indicate otherwise."

"Truly! Did you even note the date, James?"

A pause.

"The date alone should tell you that I have not written this letter. At least not yet."

"Georgie, you cannot seriously be considering returning to the nineteenth century." His tone a mix of frustration and weariness.

"Well, the existence of this letter definitely implies that I *do* actually go home, at least for a while."

"Georgie—"

"Which is precisely what makes it so . . . so fascinating, do you not agree?"

"I am inclined to call this letter many things. *Fascinating* is not one of them. My list consists of words like *worrisome, impulsive, alarming.*"

She could practically *hear* him shaking his head.

"James, I haven't done anything yet, so please leave off scolding me."

"Consider this scolding preemptive. I know how obsessive you are about mysteries, particularly romantic ones. You can't let them go. And then it's all any of us can do to rein you in—"

"Pardon? I am hardly a flighty mare in need of a firm hand on the *reins*—"

"Georgie, if you didn't go running off helter-skelter at the first sign of something mysterious—"

"Honestly, James, you are starting to sound a little bit like Arthur."

Silence. And then . . .

"That was a low blow, Georgie."

"Stop, James. Arthur isn't that horrid. You must admit that the letter is, at a minimum, *intriguing.*"

Another pause.

"Perhaps," he conceded, "but there is no guarantee this letter means anything at all. It is just as likely to be a lark from your over-fertile imagination."

"Of course, I realize that."

She hadn't.

It was a stinging slap to think that the letter might not reflect actual emotions.

Drat! Would she write a fake love note?

She grimaced. Yes, yes she would.

"Georgiana, I thought that you had adjusted to being in this century. You have Shatner now. You have seemed excited about him, about his work and what you could do together."

She and Shatner had met several months ago at the annual show of the Gooseberry Lovers International Brotherhood, which went by the incongruous acronym GLIB, where he had been the keynote speaker. Attending the gooseberry shows had become a bit of an obsession for Georgiana as they reminded her of the simplicities of home.

She had been admiring the gooseberry trophy—a large silver bowl on a pedestal which was said to have been in use since 1798—when

Shatner approached and introduced himself. She made some wry comment about GLIB; he chuckled appreciatively and had said something, well . . . glib. She laughed and the rest was history.

A solicitor turned philanthropist, Shatner helped establish and oversee orphanages in impoverished areas of the world, always running off at an hour's notice to help those in need.

Which reminded her.

"Shatner! Oh dear, what time is it? I think I'm late!"

"You look so lovely tonight," Shatner D'Avery said for the fifth time. He leaned forward in his chair and took Georgiana's hands in his across the table. A waiter hovered nearby, filling their wine glasses. "I always love that color of blue on you, darling."

Georgiana smiled at the compliment. After getting off the phone with James, she had loosely curled her long hair and dressed in her favorite cream lace maxi skirt with a shimmery aqua blouse.

They had driven down to Bristol for the evening and were seated front and center in one of *those* restaurants. The kind where people went to see and be seen. Where atmosphere and energy were more the centerpiece than the food served. The room hummed.

Shatner matched her smile and brought her hand up to his lips for a slow kiss. He had very nice lips.

He looked particularly smart tonight: dark brown hair worn a little long and stylishly mussed, attractive stubble on his face, Italian suit immaculately cut to his frame with a crisp white shirt underneath, open at the collar. Lean and confident, he fixed her with his gray eyes.

Their fingers twined together. She studied them on the table, interlaced. His hands were the only part of him that didn't quite match. Belying his suave persona, his hands were small, thin and often clammy. It was an odd contrast.

For her part, Georgiana was determined to stay focused on him. No mental side-trips to the Land of Fascinating Old Letters where Sherlock Holmes himself would appear—a la Benedict Cumberbatch with that divine coat—and take the letter from her trembling fingers, stare at the moth-eaten words, assess the odd number four shape, look her intensely in the eye and bend in even closer to her . . .

. . . aaaaaaaaand she was doing it again. Sigh.

Focus. She could focus.

"How fare your gooseberries?" she asked.

"Thriving. Now that the shows for the year are over, the next meeting of GLIB isn't until October."

He smiled again. That consumingly confident smile that fixated all his energy on *her.*

That smile which said, *You matter to me.*

It *nearly* made her toes tingle.

And clammy hands were a small price to pay for such intense smiles, right? No one was perfect.

"And when do you leave on your next trip?" she asked.

"Tomorrow."

"Jakarta?"

"No, Namibia."

Georgiana blinked. She hadn't a clue where Namibia was located.

He noticed her puzzled look. "It's just north of South Africa."

Ah, South Africa. That helped a little. As it was Africa and, well . . . south.

As usual, she always felt a little out of her depth with Shatner, somewhat unsure. Maybe because Shatner always seemed so sure about what *he* wanted.

Which was what she loved best about him. A man of action, of purpose.

"Will you be working with orphans there too?" she asked, pulling her hand back from his moist caresses.

Keeping her squarely in the center of his Intense Look, he leaned in and talked to her about adoption and schools and clean water—his gray eyes boring steadily into hers, ignoring the crowded room, the eyes watching them. All that drive and energy focused down to a single pinpoint of purpose.

Georgiana found it incredibly attractive. Loved that she was the center of it, too.

"I would love to join you sometime. The work sounds so rewarding," Georgiana said as the waiter laid her dinner plate in front of her.

"Perhaps." Shatner shook his dark head. "Though it would mean taking a break from your Bosom Companions of the English Regency reenactment group, and I know how much you adore *pretending* to be a Regency lady." He gave a rueful, teasing smile.

Georgiana just barely managed to keep a frozen grin on her face. Would she have to *pretend* to be a Regency lady if she returned to the nineteenth century? How much had spending a year in the twenty-first century changed her?

Not that poor Shatner knew—she hadn't told him about her 'history.'

"Of course, you look adorable in those old dresses. It almost makes it worthwhile to suffer through a meeting. *Almost.*" He winked at her.

Shatner had attended one Bosom Companion meeting where he had cracked heads with Mrs. Withering while attempting an awkward bow, spilled tea on his ill-tied cravat and then loudly questioned Miss Cartwright's choice of embroidery design. He had not been well-received.

Afterward, he had emphatically declared that he would not attend another meeting. It was the closest they had ever come to a quarrel. Though he sweetly supported her involvement.

Or, at least, tolerated her attendance.

But how could she explain to him the importance of those Bosom Companion meetings? That small connection to her past life.

Dressing up like a lady once a month, taking tea and gossiping. Feeling like *herself* for just a couple hours.

She even had an entire wardrobe—day dresses, ball gowns, spencers, pelisses, fetching bonnets and the like—all made from wonderful twenty-first century fabrics. She had worked for months with a costume designer from Cosprop in London.

Though Georgiana had sworn off traditional undergarments. Anyone who thought a whalebone corset was romantic *obviously* had never spent a day tightly laced into one. And whoever had invented spandex deserved a knighthood.

"I'm not sure about you coming with me on these trips," Shatner was continuing, cutting into his filet mignon. As usual, his tone sounded non-committal. "The places we visit are so dangerous, not to mention barely sanitary. Can you imagine living without running water and electricity for weeks on end?"

Well . . . yes, now that he mentioned it . . .

"Shatner, I think I can tolerate a little unpleasantness. My personal comfort is nothing compared to the needs of others."

He gave another of his wry smiles. "Dearest, Georgiana, always so no-nonsense. It's like you are practical to your core." He saluted her with his wineglass.

Did he truly mean that? Did he see things in her others did not?

It must be all that focused staring. He saw through to her soul.

Maybe she *was* practical. Or, at least, with him she could become practical. It would be a good trait for working in orphanages in Africa.

Visions of half-clothed children crowded in.

A crumbling school room surrounds her, plaster falling off the walls of the room where she teaches. A fellow teacher walks through, dripping praise for her pragmatism, her soberness. Her students' wide, bright smiles look up at her, to her. She releases them from their schoolwork and watches them leave, running down the dusty road.

Suddenly, from the trees, a lion looms, growling, threatening. The children freeze in terror. Without hesitation, she jumps into the nearest Jeep, racing to put the vehicle between the children and the lion, yelling at them to get back. She fumbles behind herself for a rifle as the lion stalks closer. Finds the gun, lifts and sights along it—

"I can see the gears in your head working. You are dreaming of helping these children, aren't you?" Shatner held the wineglass loosely in his hands.

Sort of. Georgiana nodded weakly.

He set the wineglass down, his focused gaze lingering on her. "When will James return home? I have some papers from my solicitor for him to look over regarding his donation."

"I am not sure precisely, but he is looking forward to being involved with your charity."

"Exactly! We are excited to have him on board. His money will do some much needed good."

He smiled and reached for her hand again, eyes intense as usual.

"I so enjoy spending time with you, Georgiana. I know I'm a bit of a romantic, but I would love to see our relationship develop into something more . . . more permanent and lasting." His eyes were warm and his hands were only the tiniest bit clammy wrapped around her fingers.

Georgiana felt her breath catch. How sweet!

And then . . . *wait*—

Was that a marriage proposal? Or . . . what was that? What was he asking her exactly?

And why could men *never* be clear on this point?

She chewed on her lip, pondering. It seemed fairly marriage proposal-ish. What smacked more of marriage than a 'permanent and lasting' relationship? She would count this, she decided.

So that made five. Five marriage proposals.

"Georgiana, what do you say?" Shatner had that half-smile on his face. That look which said he was sure of her answer. Whatever the exact question had been, it obviously meant that he wanted to be more serious with her.

Georgiana paused, the words stuck in her throat.

Yesterday, she would have been ecstatic over such a declaration. But, now . . . how *did* she feel?

That enigmatic letter had caught her off-guard, the strong emotions it described. She didn't know if she felt them for Shatner. She admired his intensity, his focus and passion, the work he did with his life.

But love? That had never been spoken between them.

Shatner noticed her hesitation and froze slightly, giving her a puzzled look.

"We've been seeing each other for months, Georgiana. I quite adore you and thought that you were coming to adore me too. Was I wrong?" His eyes pleaded with hers. He was so darling, so sincere.

She felt like a heel.

She stared at their hands, fingers twined together. Too many decisions.

"No . . . I mean . . . It's just . . . I don't know," she said helplessly. "I adore you too, but I think I just need a little time to think it over. It's a big decision, and there are . . . issues that I need to resolve once and for all."

"Issues?" He looked at her blankly.

Poor, dear man. How could she ever tell him the full truth?

It's not the idea of you I'm struggling with. It's my two hundred year old past that concerns me.

Curse that silly letter with all its doubt-inducing allure. Kind, sweet Shatner deserved better than this.

Georgiana took a deep breath and gave him a trembling smile.

"Just give me a little time, Shatner. I'm sure I will come around."
The tension in his body eased slightly, and he nodded confidently.
"Yes. Yes, I am sure you will."

Chapter 2

Time was running out.

Becoming an earl was supposed to solve problems, not create more.

Sebastian pondered this as his carriage rolled to a stop along the country lane. Out the window, he could see a hired post chaise teetering in the roadside ditch, its bright yellow paint splattered with mud. The postilion had managed to unhitch the horses and stood appraising the mired carriage.

A flash of pink muslin greeted Sebastian as he stepped down.

"Gracious, Lord Stratton! How fortuitous you have happened along."

Sebastian watched Lady Ambrosia approach him, clutching a small white dog to her chest, blond curls bouncing under her jaunty hat.

His emotions see-sawed, bouncing back and forth. Irritation at her relentless persistence. Reluctant admiration for her clever maneuvering.

She gave a simpering smile meant to make her seem helpless and in distress. In need of his rescue.

She wasn't.

"Indeed. What a remarkable coincidence." Sebastian couldn't help his ironic tone.

"M'lady," said Captain Phillips, stepping down behind Sebastian, lips twitching in amusement.

Phillips had proved himself a loyal friend, acting as something of a man-of-business turned paid companion. There really should be a word for it, Sebastian mused. A gent who traveled and assisted another gent, particularly when faced with situations like this one.

Lady Ambrosia shifted the small dog in her arms, ensuring that both men could clearly see her thin pink muslin gown with its plunging neckline. Sebastian was not quite sure in what situation the gown would be considered proper. He was equally sure, however, travel along a quiet country lane was *not* one of them.

Of course, if gossip were to be believed, propriety had never been Lady Ambrosia's strong suit.

Pretty and vivacious, she had married decidedly up in the world only to find herself recently widowed—Lord Ambrosia's aged heart not being equal to the challenge of a young, scandalous wife. Widowhood should have had a sobering effect, but Lord Ambrosia's money had quite rejuvenated her. She looked decidedly ten years younger, more debutante than widow.

"As you can see, we are quite in distress." She gave a tittering laugh, gesturing toward the mired carriage, looking at Sebastian through her eyelashes. A few blond curls had been strategically dislodged and now tumbled about her shoulders.

Sebastian found himself reluctantly admiring her performance.

Though, really, he had hoped it would take her longer to find him. He and Phillips had left London stealthily enough, heading to Stratton Hall in Warwickshire.

Hoping to leave the chaos that had ensued in London behind them.

"I am so relieved to have a knight show up just in time to rescue me," she continued, breathlessly. "I know Mr. Snickers is most relieved too. He was quite nearly shivering in his little tunic just before you arrived."

She emphasized the point by giving the little dog a strangling kiss, allowing Sebastian to see that Mr. Snickers sported a pink knitted shirt the same exact shade as her frock.

"Yes," Sebastian agreed, even more dryly. "It would be a tragedy of epic proportions if . . . Mr. Snickers were to quiver in his, uhm . . . tunic."

Phillips covered his crack of laughter with a hasty cough.

Lady Ambrosia smiled brightly. Bending over, she set the dog down, purposefully giving both men a generous eyeful of her bosom in the process.

Subtly was also *not* one of her fortes.

Sebastian gestured to his coachman and footmen to help the postilion get the carriage back on the road. It looked to be sound, definitely more 'purposefully driven' into the mud than 'accidentally fallen.'

"Bless you. I do hope I can find a way to properly express my thanks for your kind help." Lady Ambrosia gushed as Mr. Snickers, blue tunic and all, toddled over to inspect Sebastian's polished boots. "As I mentioned in London, I know oh-so-many eligible young ladies. I should dearly love to be your guide during this . . . difficult . . . time."

Ah, yes. This again. Sebastian pasted on a smile.

"I thank you for your concern, Lady Ambrosia, but as I have said, I do believe I have the matter well in hand."

He gave her a short bow and then stepped aside to confer with his men about the mired post chaise.

From the corner of his eye, he saw Phillips offering the lady his arm. "Come, my lady. While Stratton assists your men, allow me to regale you with tales of my service in Canada under General Brock."

For her part, Lady Ambrosia gave Sebastian a longing look and then pasted a vapid smile on her face and took Phillips' offered arm, obviously unhappy with the arrangement but helpless to do anything. Just as Phillips intended.

It was his assignment, after all. Block any and all ladies from getting too close to Sebastian. Phillips cheerfully referred to himself as Sebastian's chaperone. Sans matron cap and smelling salts, of course.

They had just harnessed the horses to pull out the stuck chaise, when a jangle indicated the arrival of another carriage along the road. Sebastian turned in time to see a blur of muslin and bonnets approaching them.

He barely suppressed a groan. So much for leaving London surreptitiously. From the heads bobbing out of the carriage window, Sebastian identified Lady Michael Burbank and her brood of four daughters.

Four very well-connected, very silly, very *unwed* daughters.

As the younger son of a duke, Lord Michael Burbank's family were received everywhere. But everyone knew that with his pockets-to-let and steep gambling debts chasing him at every turn, Lord Michael's daughters needed to marry well. And fast.

The carriage bore down upon them, a hurricane of lace and ribbon. With a sigh, Sebastian stepped back into the road. Phillips was at his side in an instant, being a most vigilant chaperone. Lady Ambrosia hovered off to the side with her dog.

"Lord Stratton, Captain Phillips. What a delight to see you!" Lady Michael said from out her window. She glanced down at Mr. Snickers and then up at the dog's owner. "And Lady Ambrosia, naturally."

The two ladies eyed each other like wary cats, hackles rising.

"Lady Michael." Lady Ambrosia gave a stiff bow and simpering smile. "How lovely to see you and all your Miss B's." The bonneted heads of the Miss Burbanks bobbed inside the carriage.

Sebastian could never keep them straight, each girl being a copy of the next. Their names were even variations on a theme: Mica, Michelle, Micayla, Michaelina. Lord and Lady Michael had proved decidedly unimaginative when it came to child naming.

"Indeed." Lady Michael gave Lady Ambrosia a scathing perusal. "What a lovely gown. I was unaware they made mourning gowns in pink nowadays."

Sebastian saw Phillips biting back a laugh out of the corner of his eye.

Lady Ambrosia's smile froze, eyes narrowing. "What brings you here, Lady Michael? Such a burden to find husbands for four daughters. Do you often scour the hedgerows of Oxfordshire for eligible men?"

Lady Michael's gaze turned arctic. "At least I manage to keep my carriage on the roadway."

Lady Ambrosia stiffened, causing Mr. Snickers to growl.

Before things could become more heated, Sebastian stepped forward. "How delightful to hear that your carriage is in excellent repair, Lady Michael. We shall not hinder your journey." He moved to wave on the coachman.

Lady Michael's eyes acquired a hint of desperation. "A moment, my lord. Perhaps you would be so kind as to settle a disagreement between Miss Michelle and Miss Mica." She gestured toward two of her daughters inside the carriage. "Michelle thinks that lilies make the best subject for paper filigree, but Mica quite disagrees and insists that it is roses. What make you of this conundrum, my lord?"

As a specimen of absurd questions, it was truly superb. Inane and completely frivolous.

Sebastian forced himself to see the humor in the situation. The ladies hunting him down, all leaning toward him, waiting gleefully for his pronouncement on lilies versus roses.

It was either hilariously funny or terribly, terribly sad.

And, as with most aspects of life, Sebastian chose to laugh.

And so, he made a point of looking up at the sky as if thinking. "Lilies or roses? Are those my only choices? Personally, I have always been partial to lambs. What say you, Phillips?"

"Lambs? I am afraid I must disagree with you, my friend. For me, it has always been unicorns." Phillips' lips twitched.

Ah, he was truly the very best of friends.

Lady Michael looked back and forth between them, eyes wide.

"Lambs or unicorns?" she repeated faintly. And then rallying asked, "What would complement them more, lilies or roses?"

She was obviously not going down without a fight.

"Have you considered adding cherubs to your list of choices?" Phillips asked solicitously.

Sebastian just managed to stifle a chuckle.

Before long, all the ladies had piled out of the carriage and were fluttering around the roadside, shades of blue and yellow and pink.

It was utterly absurd.

By unspoken rule, Phillips engaged them in conversation while Sebastian directed the men in righting the yellow chaise.

"Bless you, Phillips," Sebastian said as they resettled into his own carriage after sending both sets of women on their way. "Honestly, there is not enough money in Christendom to adequately thank you. It just keeps getting worse."

"I predict that ladies will be falling out of trees next. Anything to ensnare you. You really do just need to get married, you know," Phillips laughed good-naturedly.

Sebastian snorted. "I'm trying, my good man. I am most definitely trying."

Phillips gave a grunt of agreement. "You have so little time left. Just under two months, right?"

Sebastian nodded in agreement. "A point the ladies all well know."

Sebastian looked out of the carriage window, the trees passing slowly along. He had officially been earl for nearly eight months now. Which in and of itself was a good thing.

The problem, of course, lay in the old earl's will.

Sebastian, along with the rest of aristocratic society, had been surprised to learn that the eccentric old earl had neglected to alter his will after the former Lord Harward married.

The will still required the heir to the earldom to marry before his twenty-seventh birthday or forfeit sixty thousand pounds: twenty thousand pounds each to three gooseberry societies—one the earl owned—the other two run by Sir Henry Stylles and Lord Blackwell respectively. He had never met either Sir Henry or Blackwell, but their devotion to gooseberries was only rivaled by their fierce competition with each other. They had apparently had a falling out several years previously over some gooseberry slight. Judging by the correspondence he had had with each man, the little fruit could inspire strong passions.

Sebastian had thought it all a merry joke until his solicitor pointed out the earldom could ill afford to lose sixty thousand pounds. Most of polite society considered Sebastian's immediate marriage to be a necessity. As he would celebrate his twenty-seventh birthday on the eighth of October, time was running out.

A fact not lost on Lady Ambrosia, Lady Michael and other eager matchmaking mamas desperate to trap him into marriage. London had rapidly become intolerable with ladies following him everywhere, popping up at the most inopportune moments. Calling at odd hours of the day. Constantly accosting him during his rides in Hyde Park. One particularly enterprising young miss had even hidden herself in his carriage.

Thankfully Phillips had been there to help. As a cashiered officer, Phillips had no current ties to the army. Therefore, he accompanied Sebastian back to London and had proved himself a most useful friend ever since.

Phillips had proposed the ingenious solution of acting as Sebastian's chaperone. Being caught alone with a young lady almost guaranteed a marriage. It was marry her or face her angry father/brother/guardian with pistols at dawn. Having already experienced enough violence for a lifetime, Sebastian wished to avoid either scenario. Phillips, always at his side, ensured that no young debutante managed to get Sebastian alone.

Besides, Sebastian had long ago decided whom *he* wanted to marry. And no over-eager debutante would stand in his way.

He loved Miss Georgiana Knight, had always loved her and—now that he was an earl—was finally eligible to honorably court her.

From all reports, she was ill and, most likely, dying. She only cared for him as a brother.

But brotherly feelings aside, it gutted him to think of her wasting away without him at her side. Sick or no, he would relentlessly woo her, somehow persuade her to marry him and spend what little time they had together, ensuring that whatever life she had left was as comfortable as possible.

As far as plans went, it was an excellent one.

Now if he could only *find* the lady in question.

For someone supposedly dying of consumption, Georgiana Knight had proved remarkably agile at hiding from him.

As soon as he had cashiered out of the army and returned to London to assume the earldom, Sebastian had written James Knight, inquiring after his sister's health and discreetly asking for permission to formally court her.

Arthur Knight had written in reply, informing Sebastian that his brother, James, had been killed in a carriage accident while on the road to visit their sick sister in Liverpool. Arthur welcomed Sebastian's interest in his sister.

But, regretfully, her health is such that she cannot permit visitors.

Months passed. Becoming a new earl had been overwhelming, so many things to learn, so many decisions to make, so many people suddenly looking to him. Sebastian quickly found himself drowning in duty, commanding a small army of servants and tenants, taking up his seat in the House of Lords. The demands on his time were such that he couldn't drop everything and chase across England, tracking Georgiana down. Despite the fact that was *all* he wanted to do.

Fortunately, Phillips again saved the day, taking over the responsibility of sending out letters and inquiries. After several pointed letters back and forth with Arthur Knight—letters which took an inordinate amount of time going and coming—they had finally learned that Georgiana was in the care of a physician named Dr. Carson in Liverpool, a renowned specialist in the treatment of consumption.

Sebastian, himself, had written Dr. Carson separately, but the man had been circumspect, citing patient confidentiality. Phillips had then taken the extreme step of hiring a man to investigate the good doctor's practice, but Phillips reported that their man had not been able to confirm or deny Georgiana's presence in Liverpool. All the while, events managed to keep Sebastian in London: the ongoing war with Napoleon required his insight as a former soldier, legislation needed to be passed through Parliament, piles of legal papers demanded his attention.

At times, it felt as if Fate were standing in his way, preventing him from finding her. Everything he tried came to naught.

It was utterly maddening.

Everyone he questioned agreed Georgiana's health had been failing for nearly two years now. She had lost weight and had developed a rattling cough. There was no suggestion from any quarter that she had left to cover an unwanted pregnancy or unequal marriage. Sebastian didn't doubt she was genuinely ill.

Parliament had *finally* closed for the season, allowing Sebastian to escape London at last and devote all his energies to pursuing Georgiana in earnest.

"For the thousandth time, Phillips, it just makes no sense. Why does Knight resist telling me of Miss Knight's exact whereabouts? Why the secrecy?" Sebastian gazed out the carriage window, fingers drumming his thigh in frustration.

"I agree. 'Tis a pity that Dr. Carson hasn't been more forthcoming. It is as if Miss Knight has fallen off the planet. I have not been able to find a trace of her anywhere."

They rode in silence for a minute.

"It seems unlikely that she is no longer . . . living?" Sebastian shied away from the word *dead*.

Phillips nodded almost reluctantly. "It would be odd of Knight to lie about her death. But, it is hard to know his true motivations. Perhaps the manner of her death was disgraceful in some way, and Knight wishes to protect the family honor . . ." Phillips' voice trailed off.

Sebastian swallowed. It was his worst fear.

That Georgiana was already gone, his chance with her lost before it had even begun. He didn't care if Georgiana was dying, if she was emaciated and feeble, her body wracked with ragged coughing. He just wanted to see her again, to hear her voice.

Sebastian stared sightlessly out the window. Wildflowers dotted the lane, poking their heads out from the grasses, a riot of late summer color. Reds, pinks, yellows followed by bush after bush covered in small icy blue flowers.

"Here, Seb," Georgiana said, handing him poppies and daisies. "These will do."

"What about some of those cornflowers?" He pointed to the cobalt stems dancing farther out in the meadow.

She glanced at the flowers and then turned back to him. "To match my eyes?" she asked, shamelessly fluttering her eyelashes.

"No. Cornflower is not the right color. Too dark," he returned drolly. "Your eyes are definitely more forget-me-not blue."

"Not larkspur or bluebell?"

"Not in the slightest. Forget-me-nots. Two little flowers of them."

She matched his wry smile. Nudged him with her shoulder. "And will you ever?"

He gave her a questioning eyebrow.

"Forget me?" she asked, teasing.

He stilled, her words a lance to the heart.

"No." A pause. "That's what 'forget-me-not eyes' mean. You don't ever leave them behind."

He ran a hand over his face and turned away from the window.

He was nearly at the end of his tether, unsure and helpless as to what to do next.

Two months. He had just shy of two months left. What time did Georgiana have?

He needed to *find* her. Soon.

He refused to leave her behind, to forget, to move on with his life.

But time was, indeed, running out. For both of them.

Chapter 3

What to do?

Georgiana felt herself sliding into a morass of indecision. It beat a steady tattoo in her head.

Whattodowhattodowhattodowhattodo.

The letter had thrown her life into confusion. It was proof—wasn't it?—that she did indeed return to the past and soon.

Like a tourist. She could take the air, wear a high-waisted dress, embroider some flowers. Discover what her letter was all about.

But . . .

What if she returned to 1813, and then then portal didn't let her come back to the present? What if she fell in love and decided to stay in the nineteenth century? What if she never saw James again?

That thought made her want to stay put. How could she risk being parted from James? Being nearly eight years apart in age, their relationship had always been part brother/sister and part father/daughter. With the death of their parents, James had assumed responsibility for raising her, for guiding her into adulthood. He was so very dear, and she was closer to him than anyone else. Just the mere *thought* of life without him made her eyes sting.

But to not return at all . . . would she tear apart the fabric of the universe if she didn't go back?

Honestly, proper young ladies should not be faced with such difficult questions, as etiquette books did not cover these topics.

The fair maiden, when presented with a paradoxical time travel enigma which threatens the very foundations of humanity, should endeavor to listen to the tender admonitions of the gentle muse . . .

It was probably just nerves. Dinner with Shatner on Tuesday had rattled her. Committing herself to a more serious relationship with him was a big decision. She had watched enough American sitcoms to know this. Of course she would find it difficult.

She had promised Shatner she would think over his proposal and call him while he was in Namibia.

Georgiana pondered this on Wednesday as she drove to taekwondo, shopped at Co-operative Foods and studied modern culture by reading a celebrity mag. She also took three quizzes on Facebook. Answers: Lydia Bennett, executive chef and 89% British. For dinner, she ate her favorite low-mien takeaway and then slumped on the sofa, watching the BBC *Sherlock* into the wee hours of the morning. Again.

She tried to assess the situation with Shatner, but it was hopeless. All her concerns about him were wrapped up in her inscrutable letter.

Oh, that letter!

It was like the holy grail of mysteries, an unbearable siren calling to her. Circe to Odysseus.

A church steeple to lightning.

A white t-shirt to ketchup.

Sherlock would take one look at it and divine all its secrets, she was sure. But, alas, she was no detective.

Not for lack of trying, however.

She had taken a photo of the odd number four-ish symbol and plugged it into Google image search. Google had pulled up page after page of spindly floor lamps. Decidedly less-than-helpful.

Wasn't Google supposed to know everything? What was the point of living in the twenty-first century if she couldn't get an immediate answer to every nagging question?

The letter teased her. She read it over and over, her breath repeatedly snagging on those simple words: *my darling love.*

Who did she adore like that? Did she mean those words for Shatner? She wasn't sure she felt that way about him yet. Perhaps spending time in the past would solidify her affections for him.

But why did she return to 1813 to write a love letter to Shatner? It all made no sense.

She knew from past experience that a good list could solve most problems.

So sitting at the rough-hewn kitchen table, bare feet tucked underneath her, tablet and the plastic-covered letter in hand, she made a list of all the clues she could deduce.

My Mysterious Love Letter

She looked at her title for a moment and then decided to replace all the 'o's with heart emoji.

Much better.

From there, she studied the contents of the letter. The moth holes and generally terrible poor condition of the paper didn't give her much, but after a few minutes, she did have some items listed.

1. *The letter bears my signature and most certainly appears to be my handwriting.*

2. *The date and my own memory indicate that I have not, as of yet, written this letter.*

3. *Though with what is legible from the date (—ber . . . 1813), I write it sometime between September and December. Which means that I could leave for the past any time now.*

4. *The letter implies that I fall in love, so much so that I long for this mystery man's embrace. And I call him 'darling.'*

5. *I say 'forgive me.' Have I done something that needs forgiveness?*

She pondered that for a minute. She regularly did and said things which required forgiveness, so that part actually wasn't too surprising. Half the letters she wrote included an apology of some sort.

She turned the letter over and examined the outside.

>   *6. There is an odd mark on the outside that looks like a swooping letter four. It seems deliberate. But what does it mean and why?*

>   *7. I wrote the letter to Haldon Manor (where I usually live when in 1813). Am I not at home when I write this? If not, who would be at Haldon Manor while I was away?*

She studied her list, particularly the last point. Why *did* she put the direction as Haldon Manor? Perhaps she did write it to Shatner and then Arthur was supposed to deliver it somehow?

It made no sense.

The letter was a torment. She *hated* not knowing.

She didn't call Shatner.

On Thursday, Georgiana pondered curiosity and wondered why God had cursed her with it.

She even trekked down to the cellar in Duir Cottage and sat in front of the time portal. It seemed innocuous enough. A huge slab of stone standing upright on the wall opposite the narrow wooden stairs. Sitting crossed-legged on the dirt floor in pajama bottoms and tight t-shirt, she felt the heavy air, the thrum of some unseen force. The portal was potently alive.

Once hidden under the roots of an ancient oak tree, the portal had been inaccessible for millennia. But the death of the old oak had uncovered the portal, making travel through it possible. This particular portal was connected to a point two hundred years in the past, tethering 2013 and 1813 together.

Georgiana knew that, for the portal, time was not a river but a vast ocean—a sea where the life of each person who had ever lived existed simultaneously as rippling concentric rings on its surface. Past and future being eternally present. Jasmine—Emme's best friend and a bit of a mystic—had told her this much. Where the rings of one person's life touched those of another, the universe provided a link, a pathway that could be traversed. So if the path of one's life required a trip through the portal, then the trip would be possible. If not, the portal would not work.

Worst of all, due to the cosmic forces at work, she couldn't research the letter. Georgiana knew from experience that the universe prevented one from seeing things that pertained to one's own life. She had tried multiple times to see information about her past. But something always got in the way. The person she needed to talk to was out sick for the day or the required documents couldn't be found.

There was always some impediment.

Emme claimed it had something to with protecting the space-time continuum. It was often hard for Georgiana to get her mind around it.

But one simple fact was obvious: receiving the letter indicated that her destiny was still linked to someone in 1813. But who? And why?

After climbing out of the cellar, Georgiana watched *Pride and Prejudice* again, smugly pointing out each and every historical inaccuracy. Honestly, real nineteenth century ladies *always* wore gloves. Though Colin Firth plastered in a wet, muslin shirt was a delicious twenty-first century perk.

She read another celebrity mag and took a few more Facebook quizzes. Answers: Watson, adventurous personality and slim leg Hudson jeans.

She still didn't call Shatner.

On Friday, Georgiana woke up with a firm resolve.

It was time to bring in the heavy artillery. She needed answers, and there was only one person who could help with a time travel, love conundrum such as this.

She texted the letter to Jasmine.

"I *knew* that something was in the works for you. I just knew it!" Jasmine said, her American accent exuberant and startlingly loud on the phone. Jasmine was always excited. And loud. "Your star charts have been pointing toward an enormous change for months, but it's been shrouded in this fog of mystery. I mean, I just thought it was related to Shatner and his travels, but now this letter arrives and, all I can say, is, uhm . . . wow! Are you so thrilled?"

Finally! Trust Jasmine to get into the proper spirit of the thing.

"This letter is killing me, just . . . *killing*!" Jasmine added for emphasis.

Georgiana laughed. "Yes, it's been tying me into knots. I am at a loss as to what to do. Obviously, I am supposed to return to 1813, and the letter itself is thrilling, as you say. But the consequences worry me. What if I return and then can't come back?"

"Hmmm, that is a legit concern. The portal isn't something you can travel at will. You can only go through if the expanding ring of your own life is intertwined with another's—"

"Exactly! But if I don't go back, what will happen? Will I shred the space-time continuum? Will we all wake up one morning with webbed feet and eating flies because I chose not to—"

"Oh please!" Jasmine laughed "No offense, Georgie, but I don't think you're that important to the universe. I mean, of course, you are important, but you travel the portal for *your* own good, your own happiness."

"But I'm worried to risk it, to be parted from James and Emme and everyone else here. If I don't return, won't something terrible happen?"

"I honestly don't know. This letter indicates your circle is still linked to someone in the past. You can chose to ignore that connection and, at some point, the link will break—"

"Break?"

"Well, it's probably more of a rip. When your circles come apart, the division will tear through the fabric of your life. Cause some kind of damage." Jasmine sounded excessively sure on that point.

A shiver shot through Georgiana. "I can't say I like the sound of that."

"Agreed. Obviously, I have never seen a situation like this, so I can't say what the exact damage would be. It's entirely possible that it means you remain single for the rest of your life. Like choosing to ignore the path of your destiny kinda pulls you out of circulation, as it were."

Georgiana swallowed. To remain single? For the rest of her *life*?

"Okay," she said after a moment. "So deciding to remain here is *not* a good idea. Do you have any thoughts about the letter?"

"It's definitely fascinating." Jasmine clicked her tongue, as if thinking. "My only question is why the Jupiter sign? I didn't know you took a serious interest in astrology too."

Georgiana froze.

"Pardon me, the what?"

"The Jupiter sign, ya know, king of the Roman gods and all that."

Georgiana knew who Jupiter was. She did know her ancient mythology better than most. She hadn't been born in 1789 for nothing.

At Georgiana's silence, Jasmine continued. "That odd number four looking design is the astrological sign for Jupiter. It's an extremely old symbol, found in some of the earliest Greek texts."

Georgiana felt her eyes widen. This whole mystery just kept getting better and better.

There was now an astrological symbol involved too. The thought made her toes *tingle*.

Jasmine continued, "Personally, I think it's a stylized letter zeta from the Greek alphabet."

"Zeta? It's a zeta?" Georgiana was quite sure she was babbling just a bit. She pulled her thoughts together. "Representing Zeus, the Greek equivalent of Jupiter?"

"Exactly. Though some say it's meant to look like a stylized thunderbolt or an eagle's wings—"

"An eagle?"

"Yeah, eagles were always associated with Jupiter and Zeus."

An eagle! Just when she didn't think her letter could get any more interesting. Georgiana grabbed her tablet and looked at her list. She added another point.

> 8. *The odd symbol on the outside could be an ancient symbol for Jupiter (planet or god) or a zeta for Zeus, both associated with thunderbolts and eagles. If that is what the symbol represents, why is it in my love letter?*

She surveyed her new entry with satisfaction. If she could put aside her worries over being parted from James, the entire situation would be euphorically intriguing.

Jasmine sighed. "Oh, Georgiana, I'm so happy for you. This is going to be so awesome!"

Awesome. Right. That was an *excellent* way to view it.

"I don't see the connection with the rest of your letter, though," Jasmine said. "I mean, Jupiter is the king of the gods. The god of power and rule. He has little to do with love. How does it all tie together? I cannot *wait* to hear what you find out about this in 1813."

Georgiana laughed. "Assuming, of course, that the portal allows me to return to the twenty-first century."

Jasmine made a dismissive noise.

"Don't worry, Georgiana. The universe has your best interest at heart. It wants you to be happy. You will end up where you are meant to be."

When phrased like that, Georgiana's decision seemed so fatalistically easily.

Of course, Jasmine regularly made ridiculous things sound sensible. It was a bit of a gift with her.

Or was it a curse?

"Seriously, Georgie. Just enjoy the ride and trust the process. All will be right in the end."

Saturday arrived and Georgiana still hadn't called Shatner.

But she had made a firm decision.

James was not happy about it.

"Georgie, don't listen to Jasmine. You don't have to return."

"But if I don't return, who knows what will happen. It's my destiny. Besides, the letter presents so many delicious questions—"

"You and your mysteries. Is it time for a *Sherlock* detox again? You don't have to return to 1813 to find a perplexing secret to unravel."

She stared at him on her phone screen; Skype calls were her favorite. James wore a body-hugging t-shirt and loose khaki shorts, eyes vividly blue in his tanned face. He and Emme were still in Bali. Blurry palm trees swayed behind him.

He scrubbed a hand through his bright blond hair, shaking his head.

"If I somehow arranged for you to have dinner with Benedict Cumberbatch, would you stay?"

Georgiana stilled. Mmm, that *was* tempting.

"James, this isn't about solving some random mystery. This is *my* mystery. Something from my own life—"

"But if you go back . . . you nearly died of consumption. What if you returned and—"

"Yes, returning is fraught with danger. But then so is staying here. I could die just as easily in a car accident."

He gave a wry smile.

"True that. I *have* experienced your driving and—"

"James, stop! My driving has improved immensely."

He waved his hand.

"And what if you return and Arthur has told everyone that you died? It seems he has already told everyone in 1813 about my supposed death in a carriage accident. Remember the parish entry we found? It has to be significant if the universe allowed us to see such a small detail about our own lives. Arthur can only hedge for so long about you too. Everyone back home thinks you have gone to Liverpool to be treated for consumption. At some point, Arthur needs to resolve that story. What if you return home only to barge in on your own funeral?"

Georgiana paused, chewing on her cheek. She hadn't considered that possibility.

Unbidden, she pictured herself walking into the parish churchyard.

A crowd of men surround a simple wooden coffin, each wearing a black band around their upper arm. Arthur stands next to the vicar, trying to look desperately sad despite knowing that the coffin is filled with rocks instead of her lifeless body. Arthur raises his head and they lock eyes. She sees that instant when jubilant recognition sweeps him, joy which suddenly turns to alarm as his eyes drift down to her supposed coffin. The vicar raises his head and sees Georgiana as well and then gasps in horror. At that, everyone turns around. Someone cries "Ghost!" and points a shaking finger at her . . .

"Georgie. Georgiana! C'mon. Stay with me."—James snapped his fingers—"Stop imagining your own funeral. It would be ghastly, trust me. Not romantic at all."

Really? Because the way it was playing in her head was actually quite delicious . . .

But she had enough sense *not* to say that to James.

"I promise not to go near the churchyard until I've talked with Arthur. How does that sound?"

James heaved an enormous sigh. The sound he made when exasperated.

"What about Shatner? Are you giving up on him?"

"No! Of course not."

"Do you love him?"

She paused.

"I don't *not* love him. I like the idea of our life together."

James let out a heavy gust of air, shaking his head. "Georgie, in my experience, if you have to think about whether or not you love someone, you don't love them. When you are truly in love, you *know* without a single glimmer of doubt."

She mulled the idea through briefly.

"Is that always the case, James? I think that sometimes love just grows, and it takes a while to realize it."

He made a skeptical noise, shrugging. "Love can take a while to blossom, perhaps. But once you're in the middle of it, you just *know*."

"Well, maybe the universe wants me to return to 1813 so I can understand my own heart. I clearly am in love in this letter. This might be how I come to realize the depth of my attachment to Shatner—"

"I suppose." James made a dismissive gesture. "So visit 1813 and then you come back and decide to marry some guy who heads off to Namibia and then—"

"Pardon, James? I haven't mentioned that Shatner is going to Namibia."

A long, drawn out silence.

She stared at him on her phone screen, noting the gentle breeze buffeting his hair.

"In fact, he just barely informed *me* of the matter." She fought to keep her voice calm. "I cannot *believe* that you are monitoring Shatner. Have you hired someone to track him?"

Another pause.

"Maybe." James groaned and hung his head.

"James, how could you trust my judgment so little? I feel so . . . so betrayed."

He lifted his head and ran a hand through his hair again.

"Heavens, Georgie. You're overreacting. This has nothing to do with not trusting your judgment. I just want to make sure that everything is on the up and up with the man I am entrusting with my sister and my money."

Georgiana sucked in a deep breath, forcing herself to calm down. James just cared for her. He had always been the very best of brothers, her closest friend and confidant. Even if that closeness drifted into over-protectiveness from time to time.

"I am not fourteen years old anymore, James. You need to let me live my life."

James sighed. "I think that it is normal to want to go home, to return to the life you had before this time travel adventure. But if you are not able to come back to me—"

"Of course, I know that is a risk, James. But I need to understand why the universe sent this letter to me. Who I am still linked to in the past—"

"Georgiana, please, don't go back." He looked away. Swallowed. Brought his gaze back to her. "After Emme, you are the person I hold nearest to my heart. Please don't leave me, Georgiana. I nearly lost you once. I don't want to lose you again . . ." His voice trailed off, eyes bright.

Georgiana blinked back the raw burning in her throat.

"I'm so sorry, James. Trust me, just this once."

He let out a long breath of air. The pause lengthened.

"Of course I trust you, Georgie," he finally said, scrubbing his hand through his hair as he did. "Just, please, find a way to come back to me."

"Yes," she whispered. "I will. I promise."

In the end, she never did call Shatner.

Chapter 4

Really, Knight, this endless going around and around grows tiresome. I cannot believe you have no knowledge of your sister's exact whereabouts," Sebastian said, trying to keep frustration out of his voice. Failing to do so.

Sebastian sat in Arthur Knight's drawing room at Haldon Manor, the whitewashed interior gloomy from the rain pattering against the mullioned windows.

Like thieves, Sebastian and Phillips had stolen from Stratton Hall in the dead of night, traveling quickly by horseback, telling no one of their destination. In so doing, he hoped the husband-hungry ladies would take a week or two to find him.

He and Phillips had arrived at Haldon Manor the night before. Arthur Knight had been surprised to see them but had immediately recognized the social advantage of having an earl under his roof. Arthur had insisted they stay at Haldon Manor instead of the Old Boar Inn in nearby Marfield. Though grateful for the hospitality, Sebastian needed Arthur to provide detailed answers to a few, very *basic* questions.

Well, it was really only one question: Where is your sister?

Sebastian had been surprised to find Arthur did not greatly resemble his brother or sister—his hair more sandy-brown than golden, his eyes decidedly gray instead of blue.

Even more, Arthur seemed tensely wound. A far cry from Georgiana's sunny smile and impulsive nature.

Being at Haldon Manor was a painful juxtaposition of joy and heartache. There were reminders of Georgiana everywhere: the fine painting of flowers done in her hand, that work basket decorated with quilled lambs and roses she had completed under the strict tutelage of her old governess, the small miniature portrait on the fireplace mantle. The entire house echoed her presence.

Currently, he sat staring at a larger portrait of her on the drawing room wall. Obviously done several years previous, she sat serenely in front of a curtained window, embroidery in her lap. The artist had expertly captured the golden sheen of her hair and width of her smile, but the image lacked the vibrancy of her eyes, the energy of her presence.

It was a hollow imitation of the real woman.

Arthur sat across from him, straight and proper in his chair.

"I should like a little honesty between us," Sebastian continued. "I have made it abundantly clear that my intentions toward your sister are honorable. I fully intend to do everything in my power to persuade Miss Knight to be my countess. So I ask you again, where is she?"

He didn't even try to keep the irritation out of his voice. Speak firmly and expect results—being an army captain had taught him that.

Arthur shifted slightly, as if the question made him uncomfortable.

Normally, Sebastian was unflappable. Steady and pleasant in any situation. His good cheer had sustained his men through many a long march against Napoleon. They may have cursed his eternal optimism, but they leaned on it nonetheless.

Unfortunately, dealing with Arthur Knight was slowly eroding all his charm reserves.

"As I have said, she is still in Liverpool, and we pray Dr. Carson will affect a miraculous cure—"

"Enough." Sebastian waived his hand dismissively. "We both know Miss Knight is not in Liverpool. I have made careful inquiries, and I see no evidence that she is currently seeking treatment there, despite your assertions. Again, Knight, please. Have faith in my honor and discretion. I want what is best for your sister just as much as you do. Why hide her from me? I will care for her, regardless of her circumstances."

Arthur's face tightened, his eyes widening slightly. Something flickered across his face. Fear? Worry?

Arthur stood and walked to the window, looking out onto the dripping terrace, hands clasped behind his back, struggling against some emotion. He ran a ragged hand over his face and his shoulders slumped, as if making a decision. Shaking his head, he turned back around.

"Unfortunately, the situation is not so simple, Stratton. You are correct. My sister is not in Liverpool. To be perfectly honest, I do not know exactly where she is."

Sebastian raised a skeptical eyebrow.

"You have . . . *lost* your sister?" His tone dripped disbelief and censure.

"Well—I—uhm . . ." Arthur nodded his head, dejected. "Yes."

"You have *lost* her? Like a misplaced glove?"

Arthur at least had the decency to blush.

Sebastian was not done. "Pardon me, but in my experience, knowing the whereabouts of one's sister seems like the foremost obligation of a brother. I, myself, have five older sisters and have yet to lose one of them."

Arthur could only sigh in weary agreement, hand waving helplessly as he sank back into a chair.

"She was so ill, you see. She had taken a terrible chill and was at death's door. She hadn't long to live. So . . . James took her to receive some . . . special treatment that only he knew about. He just whisked her away and then he himself was . . . uh . . . killed. So you see, I have had a devil of a time trying to sort it all out."

Arthur Knight was a terrible liar. Of that fact, Sebastian was sure.

His *story* was a honeycomb of unanswered questions. Only his concern for Georgiana rang true.

"My condolences on your brother's death, by the way. I met him on a few occasions, and he seemed a most amiable gentleman. I know he and Miss Knight were close. His death must have been a shock to her."

"Yes, it was, I am sure."

Arthur shifted, uncomfortably.

"By everyone's account, Mr. James Knight was killed last fall, over ten months ago. Your sister has been . . . lost . . . all this time?"

Arthur nodded, staring sightlessly at the floor.

"Again, Knight, it seems excessively careless. One might misplace a boot or even a book, but an entire *sister*? Some might call *that* downright criminal."

Arthur sighed and lifted his gaze to Sebastian's. "Hopefully, you can see, Stratton, why I have been hesitant to bring it out into the open. It has been difficult."

Sebastian blinked. *Difficult* seemed a decided understatement.

More like appalling. Horrifying.

"When did you last hear from her?" Sebastian asked.

Arthur's shoulders slumped even more.

"I haven't," he said glumly.

"Not a word?"

"Nothing. I haven't a clue if she still breathes. She was . . . very ill last I saw her." Arthur swallowed, shaking his head. "I . . . don't know what to say. I would greatly welcome an alliance between our families. But Georgiana *was* at death's door. I cannot lead you to hope that she will suddenly appear, recovered and whole. Very few escape the white death once it has such a hold."

Sebastian's heart snagged, his breathing suddenly unbearably tight.

He had known she was decidedly ill. All reports had been unanimous on that point. But, as he hadn't heard anything definitive about her death, he had still held out hope.

The word cut through him over and over.

Hope. Hope. *Hope.*

How long could he cling to the tiniest scraps of her?

"Is there any clue, anything at all, in the late Mr. James Knight's papers to indicate where he might have taken Miss Knight?"

"No," Arthur said, curtly. Perhaps too curtly. He was obviously still hiding something. "There is nothing, no help for it. Trust me, I have exhausted every avenue. It seems that our only option is to wait and hope."

Sebastian let out a shaky breath at the word again.

Hope.

He had nourished that beggar for so long. But with so little to sustain it and time running short, he wondered how long hope could last.

Four days later and Sebastian needed to make a decision.

Arthur had provided no further information and seemed decidedly despondent over the situation. As her brother, he wanted to believe Georgiana was alive but had little hope of it.

Today Sebastian had stolen out alone for an early morning ride across Haldon Manor's fields. Should he wait here for another day or two, just to see if he could glean any more information?

With sinking heart, Sebastian recognized there was most likely no more information to be had. The logical course would be to admit defeat and give up Georgiana for good. After so long, why wouldn't she have contacted her brother if she were still alive?

He had discussed options endlessly with Phillips the night before. Phillips was of the opinion that they should wait. There was time yet, and did Sebastian *want* to marry someone who wasn't Georgiana?

The answer to that was an emphatic *no*. She was the only woman he had ever wanted.

But . . .

The earldom was in need of those funds. And it was hardly sensible to endanger the livelihood of thousands because his heart ached for a woman who may or may not be alive. There *was* a greater good to consider here.

He should probably just return to London and get on with finding himself a suitable bride. It was a dreadful prospect, but better to choose a bride himself than allow meddling women to do it for him.

It had been a lovely reprieve to be tucked away at Haldon Manor, but any day now Sebastian anticipated women like Lady Michael and Lady Ambrosia to catch up with him. Somehow, despite all his efforts, they always managed to find him. As he rode, Sebastian kept glancing around, half-expecting women to come bursting from the trees at any minute.

Which really put a damper on everything, as it was one of those rare summer days when all of England broke free of its regular gloom and burst out in glorious sun. Sunlit mist still swirled lightly on the ground, and the golden morning light turned lingering dew drops into a thousand dancing gems.

Making the world fairy-kissed.

Normally, Sebastian would have stopped to revel in the sheer unabashed exuberance of it all. Nature at her most unapologetic.

He imagined Georgiana here as a girl, riding across these fields, gathering wildflowers in this meadow, just as she had in the meadow near Lyndenbrooke. He could almost hear her bright laughter.

Forget-me-not.

The ache in his chest burned with each breath. In and out.

Would he ever be free of this obsession with her?

Sebastian cut through the woodlands, passing the shuttered-up dower house—Duir Cottage according to the plaque beside the front door—and then continued out over the fields, turning back toward the gabled roof of Haldon Manor.

Trying somehow to come to grips with saying goodbye to her. To chasing away all the hopes and dreams he had built.

To reconstruct a world without Georgiana Knight in it.

The prospect felt . . . overwhelming. Like severing a limb.

Gah! He was becoming maudlin.

Shaking his head to clear his increasingly morose meanderings, Sebastian topped a small rise.

Lifted his head into the rising sun.

And saw *her*.

Standing like an apparition in the dissipating mist. Facing away from him. Golden hair a mass of curls pinned to her head, tendrils escaping and clinging to the back of her elegant neck.

As if some divine angel had reached into the recesses of his heart and conjured his deepest longing.

Sebastian closed his eyes, forcing his vision to clear. Surely it was just a trick of the light, a cruel heartbreaking impossibility. She would be gone when he opened his eyes.

No.

She was still there.

He blinked.

No. Still there.

Tall and slender. Her body a suggestion of womanly curves. Arms wide, turned away from him toward the rising sun, her white muslin dress trailing in the damp grass behind her.

Sebastian tried to swallow past the searing pain in his chest. Shook his head. But the vision—*she*—remained.

He was being mawkish. It was *impossible*.

She had been *dying*. Alone. In some unknown place.

This was just some terrible coincidence. This blond woman would turn around, and he would realize his mistake.

He had been thinking about *her* and so now saw her everywhere.

That was all.

But then she lifted her face higher to the sun, drew in a deep breath and laughed in delight.

That bright cascade of sound. Bell-like and clear.

The laugh which Sebastian would know anywhere. The sound that carried him through cannon-fire and the cries of men dying. The sound he would hear ringing through his ears as he drew his last breath.

Impossible. It was just so utterly . . . It was . . .

His throat tightened.

Was she real? Was this a dream?

And, if so, could it please never, ever end?

Quietly dismounting and dropping his horse's reins, Sebastian walked toward her, watching the warm sun illuminate the edges of her, tangle through her golden hair, skim the back of her elegant neck. The light filtered through the mist eddying across the surrounding field.

Had he somehow conjured her? Had she truly died and was now returning as a ghost to haunt him?

That would be his luck, wouldn't it? To be haunted by Georgiana Knight, to never be left in peace.

Again and again, he blinked. But each time he opened his eyes, she was still there.

Back to him, arms open, embracing morning, swaying from side to side.

An utterly inconceivable dream.

His horse snorted behind him and she startled, turning around.

They froze, staring intently at each other. A part of his mind registered the surprise in her wide eyes.

Somehow, the reality of her exceeded the beauty of memory.

Her eyes pools of winter-blue sky. Hair golden and perfectly curled around her chin. Her face sculpted, older now, reflecting the maturity of womanhood.

No trace of illness clung to her—she glowed, vibrant and whole.

He stared, greedily drinking her in.

She had to be a ghost.

"Sebastian?" She tilted her head at him, puzzled.

"Georgiana," he said in return, dazed.

Slowly, that wondrous, wide smile spread across her face.

The smile that Sebastian loved most. The one that brought the sun with it.

It was almost more than he could bear.

His throat closed tightly, making swallowing difficult.

"Have you come to haunt me?" he asked, heart thundering in his ears.

Her smile froze.

"Pardon?" Confusion skittered across her face.

"Are you a ghost?"

Confusion rapidly transformed into panic. "A ghost? No . . . not . . . I mean, uhm, oh dear . . ."

Her brow furrowed. "Do you expect me to be a ghost?"

Sebastian paused. For a question, it was . . . odd.

"Not . . . necessarily," he said slowly.

She took a step toward him. Assessing.

"Are you dead?" he continued. "Did you *die* wherever your brother took you?"

Georgiana held eerily still, her eyes wide and questioning.

Definitely panic-stricken.

"I am not . . . sure?" How could that be a question?

Yes, definitely odd.

She took another step toward him.

Sebastian opened his mouth to speak and then shut it again, hopelessly bewildered.

"Do *you* think I died?" she asked after a pause, eyes still wide.

She took another step toward him.

"I should certainly hope you did not," he answered.

She blinked, processing his statement.

"Good . . . I should hope that I did not die . . . either," was her cryptic reply.

This had to be the oddest conversation of his life.

"Why are *you* here, Sebastian? Did you come to attend my funeral?"

A beat.

"No."

She nodded. His reply seemed to relieve her. Maybe.

They stared at each other for a moment, at an impasse.

"How can you not know—"

"I am . . . I am quite convinced I am not a ghost," she interrupted, taking a few more steps toward him.

They were now only separated by a few feet. He could see the wind ruffling the curls next to her face, the damp seeping through the bottom of her gown.

"Are you sure?" he asked. "How would you know that you are not a ghost?"

She stilled again. And then cocked her head.

"Is this a metaphysical question, Seb? Like if a tree falls in the forest, does it make a sound? Because I am most assuredly real." She took another step.

Sebastian stood his ground, watching her close the last few feet between them.

"Proving I am truly physically here is quite simple."

She looked real enough. He could see her chest rising, her breath slightly visible in the cool morning air. She looked older. Not the young woman he had last seen nearly five years before. Her eyes more seeing; her body more the curved roundness of true womanhood.

"Let me show you," she said as she stopped in front of him.

Gently, she reached out and took one of his gloved hands in both of hers, firmly pressing it between her palms.

"There, you see, I am quite solid."

Quite. Her hands were more than solid.

Scalding where they touched him. *Searing*, actually.

She lifted her impossibly blue eyes to his and, for an instant, Sebastian nearly drowned in them.

Her eyes had always defied description for him. A thousand shades of blue flecked with white, rimmed by a darker blue around the edge of her iris. She was close enough for him to see the few freckles on her nose, the downy hair next to her ears backlit in the sun.

It was almost too much. More than he had ever dreamed over the last few months. He had fully expected to attend her funeral or, at the very least, find her as a weak invalid.

But this . . . having her before him whole and healthy and sound . . .

How was any man to resist?

He grasped her hand in his and tugged her to him. Convulsively wrapping his arms around her, engulfing her in his embrace.

It was compulsory. As if his arms were helpless to do anything else.

Georgiana Knight held all of him in her thrall.

The sudden sheer *solidity* of her shocked him.

He had never held her this close.

He sighed, pulling her even closer. Bless her. She didn't stiffen in his embrace but instead slid her arms around his waist, giving him a tight hug, laying her cheek against his chest.

Hope crashed through him, relentless in its intensity. Wave after wave. Unbearable bliss choking.

She was *alive*! Most definitely solid and real and un-ghostlike. And he was *embracing* her.

The rushing sweetness of the moment stole his breath. She was so . . . warm and so . . . soft and so . . . *warm*.

It was dreadfully unpoetic. But true nevertheless.

Unbidden, he dipped his face to her hair, his lips lightly brushing her head. She smelled of roses and sunlight.

See, she would make a poet in him yet.

She was the perfect height, just as he had always known she would be, her head tucking neatly under his chin. She felt so *right*. Like he had been created for just this purpose. To hold Georgiana Knight and keep her safe. Beloved. He closed his eyes, breathing her in.

It was as if for one brief second, all the stars of heaven aligned.

Everything in the universe exactly where it belonged. The stars in the heavens, the moon in the sky, and Georgiana in his arms.

She pulled away and he allowed her to step back from his embrace. But he caught her hands in his. Determined to keep her close.

She would not be *lost* again.

He smiled down at her, not caring that his grin was punch-drunk silly.

"Georgiana," he said and then laughed. "We had all thought you dead . . . and then to find you here and cured . . ."

He stopped, his voice cracking.

"Sebastian, my dearest, oldest friend! I cannot tell you how pleased I am to see you." She grinned up at him, wide and lush.

"Not nearly as pleased as I am to finally *find* you. You look so . . . *well*."

She pulled their joined hands wide and ran her eyes up and down him, inspecting. "You look well yourself. I am so glad to see you returned from the war, safe and sound."

"Yes," he nodded, "yes, I did return, just as I promised I would."

He stared at her, still unable to trust the reality of his eyes. She was so much the same. Being with her felt effortless, like the intervening years had never happened. Sweet, sunny Georgiana.

Would she vanish? Could this dream truly last?

Dare he hope to have her as his own?

"I am sure you must have heard the news by now . . . everything that has happened to me. The broadsheets speak of little else," he continued. "So, please . . . you must put me out of my misery and agree to be my wife."

Chapter 5

Georgiana froze. Literally robbed of breath. Blinked.
The shock was jarring.

Exhilarating.

But jarring, nonetheless.

"Pardon me . . . but what did you just say?" she managed to gasp.

She had come through the portal with her trunk to find Duir Cottage all closed up. Which was both good and bad. She had hoped to see Arthur first and ascertain what exactly he had told everyone about her. Running into Sebastian beforehand definitely complicated things.

Though how wonderful to see her old friend. She studied him, hands still clasped together. He looked the same and yet different.

Taller. Broader. More mature.

Unruly chestnut-brown hair peeking out beneath his beaver skin hat, closely trimmed sideburns cutting partially across his cheeks lending his face a saturnine look. Eyes the same chocolate brown.

But his face had lost the roundness of youth and was now all angular planes from his strong cheekbones to square jaw. Maybe not typically handsome, but certainly striking. Interesting.

He was definitely bigger. Broader. *Wait* . . . Hadn't she already thought that?

Well, he *was*. He fairly towered over her.

For his part, Sebastian looked flustered. Off-balance. His eyes wide and intense.

Had he really just asked her to *marry* him?

"I'm sorry," he said, squeezing her hands tighter. "I'm making a muddle of this. I am asking you, Georgiana, to let me honor you for the rest of my days. To have a place at my side as my wife."

He gave her a hopeful smile, sweet. Sincere.

Georgiana stared.

What was it with her and lame marriage proposals? Why couldn't she find a man who could do the job properly?

Fall down on his knees, profess undying love and actually *ask* her the question.

Not that she wanted *Sebastian* to do such a thing.

She had only just arrived, fresh from the twenty-first century. She had Shatner, orphans and a mysterious love letter to consider. Marriage to an old friend was hardly in the cards.

She floundered. What to say?

"Is this some sort of jest?"

Sebastian paused. "Surely, you, of all people have read the broadsheets. My needing to marry should come as no surprise."

Broadsheets? When had Sebastian ever been a subject in the newspaper rags? He was an impoverished gentleman of no real consequence. Granted, an agreeable and self-effacing gentleman but never anything more.

"Why should you be in the broadsheets, Sebastian? Has your vaunted charm finally brought you notoriety?"

"You truly don't know?" He gave a startled laugh. And then performed a small bow. "Allow me to introduce myself. Lord Stratton, at your service, Miss Knight."

Georgiana felt her jaw drop.

Literally sagged open. It was an interesting sensation.

But now that he mentioned it, his clothing far exceeded a simple gentleman's wardrobe.

How could she have forgotten how much she enjoyed the sight of tight buckskins and a linen overcoat?

His overcoat hugged his shoulders and fell straight nearly to the ground, clean and perfectly tailored. A white, crisp cravat peeked out from his dark green coat and expensive silver buttons winked on his subtly striped waistcoat.

"Lord Stratton," she managed faintly. "How? . . . Well, obviously, the old earl and—heavens, Lord Harward too!—must have—"

She was stuttering.

Sebastian nodded his head. "Yes, it was a terrible tragedy."

Sebastian was an earl. An *earl!* She could scarcely process the thought. And he had just asked her to be his *countess.*

At least *his* proposal of marriage had been clear enough for her to definitely count it. Not precisely a question and not done with much panache.

But a sixth marriage proposal, nonetheless. She added it to her mental list.

Sebastian tucked one of her hands into the crook of his arm and collected the reins of his horse, gesturing for them to walk toward the house.

Her heart quickened upon seeing the peaked gables of Haldon Manor, the sight achingly familiar. She had dearly missed the old Tudor home, with its mullioned windows and clinging wisteria. She knew that it would burn down at some point in the next decade or so, as the Haldon Manor in 2013 was from a later period. A great, rambling Victorian Gothic building that had been converted into a hotel and spa in the 1950s. But, of course, she had struggled to find out anything concrete about the fate of the current house. The universe, as usual, preventing her from seeing things that pertained to her own past or the ones she loved.

As they strolled, Sebastian recounted events for her, including the odd conditions of the late earl's will. That the earldom would lose sixty thousand pounds to the gooseberry societies run by himself, Sir Henry and Lord Blackwell if he did not marry before October eighth, his twenty-seventh birthday.

"How relieved I am to find you whole and healthy," he said. "What a merry chase you have given me! I was about to tear England apart to find you."

She gave a surprised laugh. "Heavens, you have been looking for me?"

"Most emphatically. Even Arthur did not know of your whereabouts."

"Really? He knows that I had gone to Liverpool for treatment."

"Liverpool?" Sebastian cocked a skeptical eyebrow at her. "Give over, Georgie. I know you were never in Liverpool. Arthur told me that James had taken you off somewhere else. So where were you exactly?"

Oh dear. She hadn't prepared for this kind of question. He looked at her expectantly, his eyes rich and warm in the morning light.

Georgiana swallowed and then laughed a little nervously. She most certainly couldn't tell him the truth.

Well, you see, Seb, I have just returned from the year 2013 through a time portal.

Kind old friend or no, Sebastian would have her committed to Bedlam.

"Unfortunately, the nature of my treatment is a bit of a secret. I am not sure how much I am allowed to disclose. But you did terrify me for a moment there, calling me a ghost. I haven't been able to communicate with Arthur as I would like, so he does not know of my recovery or my coming."

That lame answer would have to satisfy him. But just to be sure, she changed the subject.

"So you have to marry in just over six weeks' time? The gossips must be having a heyday with all of it."

He laughed, good-naturedly as ever.

"Yes, I am sure many a London newspaperman squealed like a little girl in delight over the whole situation. It has been relentless fun for the broadsheets. But the underlying facts are quite serious. If I don't marry, the earldom will be nearly bankrupt. It's not something I can allow to happen. So you see, Georgie, I need to marry. And quickly. Please say yes."

His eyes pleaded with hers. She didn't know which was worse: questions about her whereabouts or dodging marriage proposals.

This was *Sebastian*, her oldest friend. But she had never considered him as anything more than that. He was just . . . Sebastian.

She shook her head. "Seb, I am so sorry, but I've only just returned. I empathize with your situation, truly I do, but I am not really in a place to consider marriage to you. This is just too sudden. We are dear friends, yes, but it does not necessarily follow that we should marry."

He blinked, taken aback. Georgiana was well aware that few women in England would refuse the charming new Earl of Stratton.

He nodded slowly. "We *are* good friends. The best of friends. Most marriages are founded on much less than that. I think we should rub along quite well."

Georgiana bristled. "That might be well and good enough for you. But I want more than to merely 'rub along quite well' with my husband." She tried to tug her hand free from his arm.

"I cannot imagine being married to anyone who is *not* my dearest friend," he countered, keeping her hand firmly through his arm.

Georgiana frowned. When had Sebastian become so strong? His arm was like steel.

"True, but I want more than mere friendship out of a marriage. I want love. The kind of love that makes your knees wobbly and your insides all melty—"

"*Melty?* I am quite sure that Johnson's *Dictionary* would disagree with the adverbial use of melt to describe—"

"Sebastian—"she warned.

"Yes, *dearest* friend?"

"I don't love you in *that* way, and I am quite sure that you don't love me—"

"How can you be sure that I am not hopelessly, madly, *meltingly* in love with you?" His dark gaze danced.

Georgiana nearly rolled her eyes. "Please, Sebastian. I am sure you do love me, in a sisterly sort of way. Just as I love you like a brother. But we both merit better than to just settle for each other. You deserve someone who adores you, Seb."

Sebastian looked at her mischievously. He most certainly didn't appear to be a man in love.

And then he smiled. That easy, boyish grin that lit up his face.

He winked at her. "Well, then, I just need to make myself adorable, don't I? I will win you yet, Miss Georgiana Elizabeth Augusta Knight. Consider yourself forewarned."

In the end, Georgiana's arrival at Haldon Manor was exactly as she had imagined.

Arthur staring at her in astonished, relieved joy. Her sister-in-law, Marianne, bursting into noisy tears and throwing her dark head onto Georgiana's taller shoulder, blaming most of her outburst on her burgeoning belly. Sebastian beaming throughout it all, a confident gleam in his eye.

The entire scene had a dreamlike quality. Or perhaps the past year had been a dream, and Georgiana was only now awaking to reality.

Yes, being home was wonderful and yet . . . not . . . all at the same time.

Adjusting to being a lady again might take some time, despite all her insistence that the last year hadn't changed her.

She had hugged (hugged!) Sebastian Carew. Who was now The Right Honorable Earl of Stratton.

Sebastian was an *earl!*

The Earl of Stratton!

She added twenty exclamation points to that thought.

A lady didn't casually embrace an earl in greeting. Even *if* said earl was an old friend. She hadn't been gone so long as to forget that obvious bit of etiquette.

Though he was shockingly solid. The Sebastian of her memory had still been part boy, excessively thin and wiry.

She remembered seeing him at that ball at Stratton Hall right before he left for the war. He had been larger then, but she had been too distracted by her upcoming first season in London to really pay much attention.

But now . . . all trace of the boy was gone. His wide shoulders towered over her five foot seven inches. She was used to the much leaner, shorter Shatner who only topped her by a half a head. The kind of man who matched her size instead of making her feel small and dainty in comparison.

But Sebastian was so much larger now. Vividly, she relived the embrace, the width of his chest underneath her cheek, the smell of leather, wool and clean soap surrounding her. The controlled strength of his arms.

In that brief instant, she had felt precious, protected.

At home.

Surprising, really. But after pondering it, Georgiana decided it was only to be expected.

She definitely *was* at home. Back at Haldon Manor, returned to her place in society, to familiar faces.

After all the exuberant greetings, Arthur maneuvered a chat with her alone.

"So we agree, then, that you were in Italy for your cure from consumption?" Arthur asked, confirming the story they had decided upon.

He looked at her questioningly from behind James' desk.

No, wait.

It was Arthur's desk now, Georgiana realized. All of this had become his with James' supposed death.

The room looked the same. The imposing desk situated in front of large, paned windows, morning light pouring in, outlining Arthur's brown head. Heavy blue velvet curtains framed the window, complementing the warm highlights in the dark paneled wood and bookcases that lined the rest of the walls. A strong, masculine room.

"Of course," she replied. "It makes sense, and I have visited Italy in 2013, so I can most likely talk credibly about it."

Distinctly, she conjured her supposed convalescence in one of the many hillside towns dotting the coast south of Rome. She *had* spent several weeks in such a place with James and Emme last winter. But now, she transferred it all to 1813.

An aging villa with sweeping views of the Mediterranean, glittering under impossibly blue skies. The scent of jasmine and lemon trees hanging in the heavy summer air. Nuns, acting as nurses, softly move in and out of her room, bringing draughts to soothe her lungs. Suddenly, a shout interrupts the calm. A tall, dark man bursts past a nun, calling Georgiana's name . . .

"Georgiana. Georgiana!" Arthur's voice cut into her reverie, his fingers snapping. "I see that you still live with your head in the clouds."

Georgiana shook her head. "Sorry. So sorry. Italy is a good story. It will work."

Arthur nodded his head in satisfaction, sitting back in his chair.

Georgiana longed to do the same. To slouch back into her chair and get comfy. But being a lady meant having aggressively erect posture. And so she sat primly in her seat, upper back aching from the strain of remaining so straight.

Had she truly once sat for *hours* like this?

Silence hummed for a moment.

Unbidden, Georgiana found herself listening for James' footsteps. His endless energy still echoed from room to room. It was as if nothing had changed and yet everything had.

He was gone. Gone from this life—this world—never to return.

"Did you have a funeral for James?" She couldn't stop the question. It just popped out.

Arthur had refused to hear anything about 2013 beyond a general statement that James and Emme had married and were well. It was as if he wanted to believe that she really had just been seeking treatment in some far-off place in 1813. Her brother definitely struggled to accept anything that pushed against the strict boundaries he set for himself and his world.

"Yes," Arthur nodded. "I put it about that he died in a carriage accident."

"Does he have a grave marker?" She nearly winced at the question. It tempted fate.

"In the parish churchyard." Arthur nodded again.

Even though she *knew* that James was alive and well in 2013, the news still felt unsettling. To Arthur and everyone else in the nineteenth century, James was dead, for all intents and purposes. It was unlikely that Arthur would ever see his brother again.

She would never see James again either, if she was forced to remain.

"So you have not decided if you will stay with us for good?" Arthur asked quietly. "All this assumes, of course, that the portal will allow you to return to 2013."

Georgiana let out a shuddering breath.

There was *that* small factor too.

"As I said, Arthur, I'm just here to understand how and when I write this mysterious love letter, to ensure that history flows as it should. It has been so . . . *captivating* to contemplate why I might write such a thing and—"

"Captivating? Did you just describe that letter as *captivating?* Honestly, Georgiana. That letter brings to mind words like *alarming* and *troublesome.* Please assure me that you will keep a steady head on your shoulders. I would hate for you behave in such a way that would damage your reputation—"

"Please, Arthur. As I said, I intend to return to 2013 and James, if possible. So my reputation here does not overly concern me."

Arthur stared at her, his gray eyes speculative, fingers drumming on the desk.

"Well, forgive me, but I hope that you change your mind and decide to stay here. Marianne and I should be glad of your presence, particularly as you will be an aunt sometime before Christmas."

Georgiana managed a fond smile. She did love Arthur, truly she did. And the thought of becoming an aunt *did* make her a little giddy. It wasn't Arthur's fault he wasn't a kindred spirit to her, like James.

"I am very happy for you and Marianne, Arthur, but—"

"There are other compelling reasons for you to remain with us," Arthur was continuing. "Lord Stratton's presence here is not idle. He has been writing me for months, asking about you and your condition. In fact, that is the main reason I did not announce your 'death.' He has already requested my permission to pay his respects and, as you can imagine, it has been readily granted."

Arthur had a pleased-as-Punch look on his face. Obviously, her acceptance of Sebastian was a foregone conclusion.

She held up a stalling hand, shaking her head. She had only been home for *three* hours, and Arthur was already trying to arrange her life.

"Arthur, I *literally* just said that I do not intend to remain in this century. So there is no need to play matchmaker—"

"Matchmaker? I am hardly arranging this marriage, Georgiana. I am merely stating that when Lord Stratton asks for your hand, I hope you will appreciate the great honor he does you and accept him."

Georgiana felt like holding her head in her hands.

Three hours! And here she found herself, thrust into the middle of this entire debacle.

It would have been funny, if it just wasn't so . . . *not.*

"I must tell you honestly that I have already politely refused Lord Stratton's most kind offer of marriage and—"

"I am sorry. You have what?!" Arthur's voice rose quite dramatically at the end of the sentence.

"I have refused him."

"But . . . but . . . why? He is offering to make you his countess. You would be Lady Stratton. How can you think so little about the honor of this family—"

"Please! I have just returned after a year-long absence, and suddenly you want me to drop everything and bury myself in family honor?"

"Georgiana, James may tolerate your eccentricities in 2013, but here—"

"Stop acting all lord-of-the-manor, Arthur—"

"In this century, I am the head of this family and—"

"You are being positively medieval—"

"—I expect you to respect—"

"Don't you dare throw guilt back at me. How could you be so uncaring about my feelings? To assume that I would marry where I do not love? Not to mention, my life with James and my prospects there—"

"I thought you had more sense than this, Georgiana. Has gallivanting around the future made you completely numb to the responsibility you bear to this family?"

His words stung.

Georgiana sat quietly and counted slowly to ten.

And then thought the better of it and continued right on to twenty. *Honestly!*

She took in a deep breath.

"Arthur, I must tell you immediately that I am already involved with a gentleman in 2013. I have no intention of becoming involved with someone here too."

No matter *what* her enigmatic love letter foretold, she mentally added.

Arthur sat for a second, absorbing the information.

"You have changed. You were not always so headstrong," he finally said.

"I must beg to disagree, brother. I have always been this headstrong. In the past, I just chose to bite my tongue."

Another pause. Another long stare.

"I see. And what is this suitor like? A gentleman, I assume? I trust that James has made all the proper inquiries into his family and finances? Will he be able to support you in the style in which James and I have raised you?"

Such a typical, nineteenth century statement. As if she were a prized possession to be passed from brothers to husband.

Though she could hardly *say* such an impertinent thing to Arthur.

"I would like to think that I am more than just a prized possession to be passed from brother to husband," she said, as she was in the mood to say impertinent things.

Arthur needed to understand that he could not walk all over her, as if she were a small, stubborn child.

"I had hoped you would outgrow acting like a small, stubborn child," he replied.

Ah.

Apparently Arthur was in the mood to say impertinent things too.

They pondered each other in tense silence, his fingers drumming loudly on the desktop.

After a moment, Arthur's shoulders slumped. "James and I love you, Georgie. We only want your happiness. I would hate to see you hurt. I have worried about you for so long. I would like to have a reprieve from the emotion, if possible."

Trust Arthur to make her feel like a heel. She *hated* having to apologize.

"I am sorry to cause you any concern, Arthur, but this is the rest of my life you are playing with. I would like to be able to decide my own path."

A commotion erupted outside, and then loud voices echoed from the great hall. An instant later, a footman tapped on the study door.

"Come," Arthur called.

"Sir, a number of visitors have just arrived. Mrs. Knight requests your presence in the drawing room."

Chapter 6

They had found him.

Somehow, despite all his precautions, they had tracked him down. Really, the British army had to look no further than husband-hungry women to find masterful spies.

Sebastian sighed as he watched Lady Michael Burbank and her brood of Miss Burbanks flutter into the drawing room of Haldon Manor. Unsurprisingly, Lady Ambrosia followed behind them, making nuzzling noises to Mr. Snickers (sporting a yellow and black striped tunic) in her arms.

Apparently they had all just arrived in Marfield, taking rooms in the Old Boar Inn and, of course, immediately set out to call upon Mr. Arthur Knight and his distinguished guests.

"Cheer up, old man," Phillips murmured from his side. "I am here in your hour of great need."

Sebastian almost smiled at that. He knew that Phillips considered it no great hardship to spend large amounts of time flirting and telling dashing tales of his escapades as a soldier in Canada.

Bless him. He was the best of chaperones.

The ladies had just all performed their curtsies—Lady Ambrosia nearly spilling out of her dress in the process—when Georgiana and Arthur reappeared.

Sebastian's heart did a triple skip seeing Georgiana again, her golden head and infectious smile. It was just such a *relief*. She was whole, healthy. *Alive*.

How like Georgiana to come back, seemingly, from the dead. A plot twist worthy of a gothic novel.

He remembered his actions in the meadow and forced himself not to cringe. For heaven's sake, he was an *earl* and former army captain, not some green lad. And, yet, around Georgiana his mouth sped ahead of his brain.

Had he actually proposed? And a terrible, bungled proposal at that? He had just been so happy to see her, flourishing and well—the words had sprung free without thought.

He was an idiot. Though he had long known *that* fact.

He needed to woo and charm her. Turn her affection for him into something more. Something that—as she put it—made her knees wobbly and her insides liquid . . . liquidy . . . liquidish?

Regardless, somehow, some way, he would become *that* for her.

She glanced his way while being introduced to the newly arrived callers. Georgiana was already acquainted with Lady Michael and her daughters as they all had met in London several years previously.

A smile tugged at her lips as the ladies all pretended to be delighted by her sudden reappearance.

They weren't.

Lady Michael and her daughters sank onto a long divan, all seated primly in a row. Lady Ambrosia with Mr. Snickers availed herself of a chair by the fireplace where Sebastian and Phillips stood. Marianne sat in the chair opposite Lady Ambrosia, a hand draped across her swelling belly, Arthur standing beside with a hand on her shoulder. Georgiana sank into a smaller chaise opposite Lady Michael.

"Indeed, we are all most heartily thankful for Miss Knight's recovery." Sebastian beamed at her and took the opportunity to seat himself at Georgiana's side on the chaise. Not so close as to imply anything improper, but most certainly close enough to show interest. He gave her his most doting smile.

No sense in hiding his intentions.

Naturally, no one in the room misunderstood what was going on.

Lady Michael swallowed loudly.

"Miss Knight, how fortunate we are to find you so recovered." Her tone so very, very dry.

Georgiana flashed her renowned smile. "I am most relieved to be here, Lady Michael."

An awkward silence ensued.

Lady Ambrosia cleared her throat and turned to Marianne. "Is your brother in residence, Mrs. Knight?" she asked, turning her shoulders to expose even more of her bosom.

Marianne's brother—Timothy, Viscount Linwood—resided at the family seat nearby, Sebastian recalled. He had come to know Lord Linwood over the past few months, being nearly the same age and working together in the House of Lords.

From what Sebastian recollected, Linwood had opposed his sister's marriage to Arthur Knight. Linwood had found Arthur's prospects, as a younger son, lacking. However, somehow Marianne had convinced her brother to relent and support her marriage.

It was said that Linwood had not taken James Knight's early demise too hard, despite their long acquaintance as near neighbors. James' death meant that the substantial Knight estate had passed to Arthur, making him a man of decided consequence and more worthy of Marianne's hand.

Of course, that was *not* why Lady Ambrosia had inquired after Linwood. After Sebastian himself, Lord Linwood was one of the most sought after bachelors of the *ton*.

Marianne smiled wanly, not missing Lady Ambrosia's intent. "Why, yes, Timothy will be at Kinningsley all autumn."

Instantly, all the Miss Burbanks went profoundly still.

Like a pride of lions, all jerking to attention and turning their heads toward that irresistible prey: an unmarried man of consequence.

"Oh, how delightful, Mrs. Knight. I was unaware your brother lived so close." Lady Michael's hands fluttered against her chest, her eyes instantly glassy with delight. "We shall have to make a point to call upon him, shall we not, my dears? It will not do to have poor Lord Linwood languishing without female company."

All of her daughters nodded their heads in unison.

Sebastian *almost* felt sorry for the man. But anything that tempered Lady Michael's enthusiasm for him was a welcome diversion.

He glanced at Georgiana, catching her stifled smile. He held her gaze for a moment, basking in the humor that sparkled between them.

Mr. Snickers wiggled off of Lady Ambrosia's lap and began to sniff his way around the room, bearing a striking resemblance to a lumbering bumblebee with his tail wagging above his yellow and black striped tunic. The little dog paused at the lamb and roses quilled work basket near the fireplace.

"What an interesting basket. Is this your work, Miss Knight?" asked one of the Miss Burbanks, turning to Georgiana. Mica, he thought. Or was it Michaelina?

Sebastian watched as Georgiana blinked at the basket, her eyes widening. Obviously, she had hoped to never see it again.

"Yes—yes it is. I had a governess who was quite accomplished in paper filigree and insisted I learn the art."

Here Georgiana gave a polite little laugh.

"Miss Knight is a most accomplished quiller," Sebastian said with a guileless smile.

Georgiana shot him a warning look, her expression freezing.

Sebastian tried to keep his expression innocent but, as his smile morphed into a roguish grin, he was not sure he succeeded.

"How charming, Miss Knight," Miss Mica/Michaelina said. "I know we all simply adore paper filigree. You must join us. Why I daresay we could spend the entire day quilling." All the Miss Burbanks nodded their heads at this.

"Indeed? That is . . . remarkable. Did you know that Lord Stratton is a tremendous admirer of quill work?"

Georgiana turned and beamed at him, shifting slightly to press her foot down on the top of his boot. Not enough to do any damage, but enough to make her point.

He grinned right back, his smile definitely mischievous now. If she thought he found her teasing annoying, she was *far* off track.

The ladies' heads were almost like a line of kittens, flashing back and forth between Georgiana and him.

She turned back to the ladies. "I hear Lord Stratton's favorite subject for filigree is fruit," she deadpanned.

"Fruit? Really?" Sebastian only just managed to keep from laughing.

"With faces on them. Particularly gooseberries."

The Miss Burbanks all nodded in unison, obviously already composing paper filigree in their heads. Sebastian saw an army of smiling gooseberries in his future.

"Ah, Miss Knight, you know me too well. I look most forward to seeing your own charming *fruitful* example."

He trapped her hand resting on the sofa. With a languid smile, he raised her knuckles to his lips in a careful salute. Her eyes widened in warning.

"You are all politeness, Lord Stratton," she said, tugging her hand free.

"No, merely truthful."

"You should know that I am only skilled in rendering lemons."

"Perfect."

"Truly? Oblong, boring, acidic. Lots of yellow."

"Lemons are the most romantic fruit of all."

"Lemons? I think that most poets would beg to disagree with that assessment." She folded her hands primly in her lap.

"Oh, I think not."

"Many would consider the pomegranate to be the most romantic fruit."

"There the masses are wrong."

"Not oranges or strawberries? Even the humble gooseberry is more likely to inspire amorous feelings."

"No. It is most decidedly lemons."

"Indeed? I had always considered them to be quite sour."

"Exactly so, Miss Knight. Therein lies their charm."

She cocked a quizzical eyebrow at him. He let his slow smile creep across his face, hoping it was as disarming as some claimed it to be.

He leaned toward her and whispered, low and quiet for her, and her alone, to hear.

"I find lemons make my lips . . . pucker."

Georgiana caught her breath at that, the tiniest of catches expanding her ribs, the slightest flaring of her eyes.

She did not, however, blush.

Which was somewhat odd. The Georgiana of his youth would have flushed bright pink at such a statement.

Instead, she gave him a quelling look and pressed her heel into his foot again.

Sebastian turned back to see the entire room staring at them. Phillips, Arthur and Marianne grinning good naturedly.

The rest of the ladies . . . not so much. Lady Michael and Lady Ambrosia seemed ready to spit daggers, and even Mr. Snickers had a mean little look in his eye.

The sooner he convinced Miss Georgiana Knight to marry him, the better.

GEORGIANA'S BEDROOM
HALDON MANOR
EARLY MORNING HOURS ON AUGUST 28, 1813
BIRTHDAY IN MINUS 42 DAYS

. . . Wrap me in the light of your love . . .

That impossibly enigmatic letter.

Arthur had been quite dismissive of it. *Troublesome* indeed! Neither of her brothers had demonstrated a proper appreciation for the profundity of its mystery.

Georgiana tossed a photocopy of the letter onto the counterpane—she had left the original in 2013—and collapsed back into her pillows piled against the headboard.

After maintaining lady-like posture all day, she felt the tiniest bit naughty slouching on her bed.

She reached for her tablet and pulled up her *My Mysterious Letter* list, pondering it for a moment.

Who did she love to such depth? And when?

As she had noted in her list, the letter was dated -ber 1813, which meant it would be written sometime between September and December. Given that it was now pushing the end of August, she could write the letter at almost any time.

If only she felt that kind of emotion for someone.

. . . love that comes from deep within a woman's soul . . .

Shatner. She cared about him—his focus, his energy, his drive—but did she care *that* much? Perhaps being away from him would make her heart grow fonder.

Or absence could make the heart wander.

She chewed on the inside of her cheek and pondered the state of her heart.

It felt . . . oh, who was she fooling?

Her heart felt whole and entirely her own. Perhaps she just wasn't made out for romantic, gushy love like poets described. She felt happy when she was with Shatner, and she loved the idea of the life they would have together.

That probably described love for her. Other people just waxed more rhapsodic about it.

So what about her letter then? Did she write it as a lark as James had suggested—a joking expression of poetic love?

She briefly saw herself seated in Arthur's study, pen in hand, composing the letter.

Someone else strolls to her side, leaning over, helping her come up with the lines. Someone with broad shoulders and dark hair, his low voice laughing as they write the ridiculous words of love together . . .

Georgiana groaned. Yes, she could see it all too clearly. Perhaps the letter truly was just a lark.

Sighing, she added that point to her list:

9. Could I have written (will I write?) the letter as a joke?

The clock on the mantle chimed once. Was it already one o'clock in the morning? Georgiana pursed her lips and looked around her room, the place that had always been her sanctuary.

The two windows stood open, allowing a cool summer breeze to stir the pale green bed curtains. No fire burned in the hearth, but the room was lit enough by a decidedly anachronistic solar lamp sitting on her bedside table. Much brighter and less sooty than candles.

The large trunk she had brought through the portal stood open at the foot of her bed. Marc had the ingenuous idea to place the trunk on casters, enabling her to wheel it through along with herself.

Georgiana had chosen the trunk because it looked quite period, but its contents were anything but nineteenth century. She might be returning from her adventures in the twenty-first century, but that didn't mean forgoing all the perks of modern life.

Aside from the solar lamp, Georgiana had brought her phone and tablet, as well as extra batteries and discrete solar chargers for them. She had loaded an external harddrive with a ridiculous amount of information, everything from medical textbooks to music to dress patterns. She even had night vision goggles. All the tools necessary for sleuthing out an answer to her mysterious letter.

She had the trunk fitted with a false bottom, enabling her to hide all her futuristic anomalies from servants. And she knew of a small window in the attic which would be the perfect stowaway place to recharge all her small solar batteries.

However, the bulk of her trunk she had dedicated to clothing, all the dresses and accessories made for her Bosom Companions of the English Regency meetings. Even if she didn't find love, she would be the best dressed young lady in Herefordshire. Right now she was wearing a lovely nightgown of the softest Egyptian cotton with yards of lace. The kind of lace that abounded in 2013 but would be obscenely expensive in 1813. A matching dressing gown lay draped at the end of her bed.

But how to go about investigating her letter? The Jupiter sign was an utter enigma. What did the symbol mean in the context of the letter? It wasn't as if she could go around showing the symbol to people, asking for their opinion.

Or could she?

Georgiana pondered for a minute. That wasn't such a terrible idea actually. A small wondrous smile touched her lips. It was just so *exciting*. The whole situation made her feel all bubbly.

And Sebastian? What to do about him?

He really was her dearest friend. Kind and cheerful and just . . . *Sebastian*.

Every time she looked at him, she saw the gangly boy who had nothing better to do with his time but sit under that old willow tree, its branches dipping down into the river.

"The Mysteries of Udolpho," he said, taking the novel from her hands with a raised eyebrow.

She grabbed for the book, but he turned his shoulders to her, his long arms keeping it out of reach.

"Sebastian . . ." she warned.

He laughed and thumbed through a few pages. "Let's see. Dastardly guardian. Creepy decrepit castle. Please tell me the story involves copious amounts of swooning—"

"You are terrible." She lunged around him and snatched the book back, her long braid hitting his arm. "There is nothing wrong with swooning if the situation merits it."

He laughed harder. A full on guffaw really.

"Please! Georgiana Knight, I cannot imagine a situation that would induce you to swoon."

She glared at him, trying to control a smile which threatened to undermine the sternness of her look.

"If I were the heroine of a gothic novel, I am sure swoon-worthy moments would arise with shocking regularity—"

He shook his head, chuckling incredulously.

"I am sorry to be the bearer of bad news, Georgie, but gothic heroines are regularly praised for their exemplary and obedient natures. I can think of many words to describe you, but for some reason obedient is never on the list—"

"What a thing to say! Of course I am obedient. In what way am I not?"

He gave her a wry grin and then tapped the cover of her book.

"Case in point. Does your grandmother approve of this reading material?"

She opened her mouth to reply and then shut it.

"Touché," she said with a nod. "But what Grandmama doesn't know won't hurt her. Besides, who is going to tell?"

Sebastian smiled. Slow and decidedly mischievous.

"Oh no. Just no, Sebastian." She knew that look too well. "You cannot seriously be thinking—"

"How delightful." He leaned toward her. "I love nothing more than holding a secret over you."

She stared at him for an instant and shook her head. "Is it to be blackmail then?"

He chuckled. "You were wanting your life to be more like a gothic novel. Blackmail seems like a good place to start."

It was just like Seb. It had taken her a month's worth of pin money to buy his silence. Which he had used to purchase more dreadful novels for her. Just to have additional things to hold over her head.

Everything was a joke to him.

When other boys heckled him about hanging around her, he brushed it off. It was the same way he laughed away their teasing over his step-father's sermons, his sister's flirtatious beaus and his mother's eccentrically large hats.

He was the boy with an irrepressible sense of humor who looked at the world as a grand lark. Nothing ruffling him.

Which was both good and bad.

He was easy-going to a fault. Nothing captured his emotions, focused whatever passion he may have. He was a good sort but lacked the emotional depth to make him truly interesting to her as an adult.

She gave a puzzled little frown.

Yet there was no sense of boy about him anymore. Sebastian fit comfortably into his own skin, shouldering power and authority like a well-worn coat. Becoming an earl had changed him somewhat. Or maybe it was serving in the army? Hadn't he said something about rising to the rank of captain?

She was honest enough with herself to admit that the Georgiana of a few years ago might have married him. For someone in 1813, his reasons for proposing marriage were sensible and logical.

But she wasn't that Georgiana any more. Not entirely. Facing death and spending time in the twenty-first century had changed her too much.

Without the old earl's silly will in the way, Georgiana was quite sure the issue of marriage would never have been brought up between them.

And even if she were to tell Sebastian about the last year of her life (and that was an enormous *if*), he would never fully understand her experiences there. A part of her would always be separate from him. Not that Shatner knew about her nineteenth century origins. Was she doomed to always keep a part of herself from any potential suitor?

It was *not* a comforting thought.

With a sigh, Georgiana tossed her tablet onto the counterpane and turned off the solar lamp, plunging the room into darkness. Weak moonlight drifted in through the open window.

Pushing to her feet, she looked out over the rolling hills, lumpy in the dim light. It was wonderful to be home but, without James here, the house felt empty.

No, not empty. Just hollow.

It was an odd kind of death in a way. Gone and yet not. Georgiana found herself suddenly swallowing against tightness in her throat.

She stared out into the darkness. The night was eerily quiet, broken only by the far off lowing of a cow. No light pollution glow from Hereford on the horizon. No hum of machinery or cars on the motorway. Just the faint chirp and rustle of natural things.

A soft breeze swished through the trees and stirred the hedges. Suddenly, a slight movement to the right of the garden caught her eye. Peering into the darkness, Georgiana thought she saw a moving shape. Squinting, she tried to make it out.

Without hesitation, she turned back to the room and dug into her trunk, pulling out her night vision goggles with a low cry of triumph.

How exciting to be able to use them so soon!

Giddily, she turned them on. Instantly, night became clearer shades of green-gray.

Training them on the garden, she skimmed around until she located a person furtively moving away from the house. The figure was wearing dark breeches, stealthily darting from bush to bush, crouching against the garden wall. Obviously intending not to be seen.

Even with her night vision goggles, she couldn't make out the person's features. The figure paused next to a flower urn on the garden wall and slipped something that flashed white under the violets in the pot. And then with a suspicious glance around, the person melted farther into the garden, disappearing from view.

A shiver of excitement shot down her spine. At *last*. Something to investigate.

With an eager grin, Georgiana turned back to the room, drew her dressing gown over her nightgown, grabbed a flashlight and dashed out of her bedroom.

Chapter 7

The great hall
Haldon Manor
A few minutes later on August 28, 1813
Birthday in minus 42 days

Honestly, this just needed to stop.

Sebastian rubbed a weary hand over his face as he quietly crossed the great hall of Haldon Manor aiming to return to the guest wing and his bedchamber to hopefully (maybe) get some rest.

He had awakened from a deep sleep to find a cloaked figure slipping into his room. Fortunately, he had recognized Lady Ambrosia before mistaking her for an intruder and tackling her to the ground.

This made three.

Three times that she had stolen into his bed chamber in some ridiculous attempt to entrap him. Twice before with Mr. Snickers and now tonight without her dog.

It was a poorly thought out scheme. As a widow, she could not force a marriage by being caught alone with him. Her persistent presence only served to make him more wary of female-kind in general.

Of course, he had never cataloged *intelligence* as one of Lady Ambrosia's strongest assets, either. He could only assume she had some sort of seduction in mind, not that he allowed her to remain long enough to find out.

He had firmly escorted her out a side door with some choice sharp words, most of which involved the legal ramifications of trespassing and a not-so-subtle threat to haul her before the magistrate, the tense whiteness of her face oddly gratifying. Maybe the seriousness of his tone had sunk in.

He had watched her disappear into the night, headed back to her room at the Old Boar Inn. Thank goodness Knight wasn't housing her in Haldon Manor itself. Now all he wanted was a soft bed and undisturbed rest.

He padded quietly through the great hall, pulling his banyan a little tighter over his chest. Faint moonlight streamed across the parquet from the floor to ceiling bay windows to the right. As he neared the far end, he heard the rustle of fabric and slippered feet on the staircase ahead of him.

Not again.

Suppressing a groan, Sebastian darted behind the curtains lining the large windows. Why couldn't they just leave him be?

Peering out, he saw a slim figure glide through the doorway, her white dressing gown glowing in the dim moonlight. The long, golden braid instantly identified her, even though a subliminal part of him had already known.

Georgiana.

His heart whispered over her name.

Without thinking, he stepped out and grabbed her arm. She let out a small shriek and whirled on him with surprising speed, yanking down to break his grip and taking a swipe at his head with a cylindrical object she held.

Grinning, Sebastian ducked and let go of her arm, taking a quick step back and holding up his hands to show he meant no harm.

Her pale eyes flashed in the moonlight which shimmered through the window behind him. Her chest rose quickly in surprise. Like a kitten, bristling at some imagined threat.

She looked outrageously gorgeous or, well . . . at least gorgeous in her outrage.

"Sebastian," she squeaked, swatting at his shoulder. "You nearly startled me out of my skin!"

"That was uproariously amusing," he chuckled.

Her breath was still coming fast and hard, but she managed a little laugh.

"Seb, stop! My poor heart nearly tumbled out of my chest."

Still chuckling, Sebastian leaned into her. "Never fear, my dear. Had that happened, I would have happily caught your heart and held it close to my own for safekeeping."

Even in the dim moonlight, he could see the slight roll of her eyes.

"Give over, Sebastian. Is there ever a time of day when you are not an incorrigible flirt?"

Sebastian paused, as if pondering the thought.

"No," he said, feigning reflection, edging even closer. "At least, not where you are concerned."

She shook her head and, with a disbelieving lift of an eyebrow, took a pointed step back from him.

Clever girl.

"Was that you I just saw creeping through the back garden?" she asked.

He gave a puzzled look. "Me? Heavens, no."

"Well, I saw someone creeping around the garden from my bedroom window and—"

She stopped as he shook his head.

"What is it?" she asked, looking genuinely puzzled.

"Do you mean to tell me you saw someone out your window and immediately ran to investigate?"

"Of course. Why ever not?"

Sebastian nearly groaned. "Did you even stop to consider that it might be dangerous? That it might have been better to wake a footman and have him investigate?"

Georgiana's mouth opened as if to say something and then a faint frown skittered across her face.

"No, actually, I didn't," she finally said. "Though there is no enjoyment in waking a footman. Why should I let someone else have the thrill of chasing down a culprit in the dead of night?"

Right. How could he have forgotten about *this* aspect of Georgiana's personality?

Unbidden, memories flickered.

Georgiana leaning perilously over the edge of the Lyndenbrooke gatehouse, hand outstretched, tongue pinched between her lips. "Can't you see it, Seb? That little piece of paper there? I bet it's a love note. Now if I could only reach it . . ."

Georgiana whispering to him following church services. "I promise on my father's grave, the shape hovered *in the air. Hovered! We definitely need to investigate . . ."*

Georgiana beckoning to him at the back gate, eyes lit with mischief. "I saw him again, that large scarred stranger who was chatting with Mrs. Young. I followed and found that he's staying with the blacksmith. Meet me by the water trough at midnight. I have a plan . . ."

Sebastian shook his head, taking in a deep breath. She had always been far too eager to jump into trouble, taking him with her.

"Honestly, you and your mysteries—"

"Yes, well, I did see someone acting strangely in the garden just now and—"

"I am sure it was only Lady Ambrosia, as I am returning from escorting her outside."

His whispered words echoed in the quiet room, the implication hitting them both.

Georgiana's eyes widened, inquisitive.

"Indeed. I was unaware that she was your type. Was she wearing breeches by any chance?"

"No, just a muslin gown with her signature decolletage—"

"Does she visit you often at night?" Her voice a wonder of irony.

Again, not a trace of blush on her cheeks.

Sebastian felt the shock of her comment sink in. She *had* truly changed.

"It's not what you think." He managed a small startled laugh and briefly explained Lady Ambrosia's persistent problem with being-where-she-wasn't-supposed-to-be.

With a smile, he shook his head. "I was unaware that treatment for consumption also involved an expansive education in the ways of the world."

Georgiana was silent at this, merely staring at him.

"I am four and twenty, Sebastian. Hardly the child you knew. I have lived life. You mock it, but I have survived a terrible illness and . . ." She paused, holding on to her braid and staring past him at the moonlit window behind.

He pondered her for a second.

"And your brother's death. James," he finished for her. "I am so sorry for your loss. I know you were close."

She gave a brave smile at that, bringing her gaze back to him. She blinked once . . . twice, eyes bright.

"Yes," she said, swallowing, "James was always the best of brothers to me. I miss him terribly. It's hard to imagine a life without—"

She shook her head and let out a slow breath. Cleared her throat.

Changed the topic.

"Is this a constant problem for you? Women lying in wait in your bedchamber?"

Sebastian gave a rueful smile. "Well, somewhat. My hand in marriage is highly valued in *some* circles, particularly as I have less than two months to marry. Knowing this, enterprising women constantly try to entrap me somehow. Thank goodness Phillips is a most effective chaperone."

Georgiana laughed, just as he knew she would. That bright, cascading sound that bubbled from within.

A man would sell his immortal soul for a lifetime full of such laughter.

She instantly covered her mouth to muffle the sound.

"Poor Captain Phillips. He is a good friend, though pity he isn't here right now. I am sure that our current situation is quite perilously compromising."

She gestured at the space between them, barely even an arm's length.

Sebastian let out a surprised gust of air. "Yes, that is true. But there is a decided difference, you see. I actually *want* to marry you. So I have no problem with this."

He mimicked her gesture, again bringing attention to the short distance that separated them.

With a start, Georgiana backed up a step, her eyes widening. Swallowed.

"True," she whispered.

There ensued a fraught moment when neither spoke.

"You know it would never work between us, Sebastian."

Her whispered words hung between them.

"Because you want someone who turns your insides all melty?"

"Yes," she nodded, taking another step backward. She eyed the staircase to the family bedrooms through the doorway to her left.

"And you think I could never be that person? The one who makes your heart melt?"

He *had* to ask the question.

"You are a dear friend, Sebastian. However, I am sure that I don't turn *your* insides all melty."

The statement caught him off guard.

She definitely did something to his insides. Though he wasn't sure he would describe the feeling as *melty*.

More scorching and pervasive. Like hunger and ache and longing all jumbled into one heady concoction.

Powerfully potent.

Unfortunately, Georgiana took his silence to be agreement.

"You just want to marry me because you must, and I am convenient," she continued.

Sebastian shook his head. "I have spent a good deal of time tracing your whereabouts, Georgiana. That does not exactly make you *convenient*—"

"You know that's not what I meant." Her tongue gave a quiet disapproving click. "You are in this situation where you have to marry, and I seem like the least vile of all your current options."

Sebastian stared at her, wondering briefly how she would react to a confession of deep, abiding love.

Would she believe him? Would it draw her closer to him or send her running in fear?

He pondered for half a second.

Fear.

Given her reactions, he was definitely siding with *fear*.

She looked impossibly lovely in the moonlight, slippered feet peeking out from under the lace trim of her dressing gown. Bright hair glimmering. She fingered the end of her long braid.

"Nothing about you is vile, Georgiana," he said quietly.

"Fine praise indeed." She gave a short, ironic laugh. "Of course, I must again insist that a general lack of *vileness* is not exactly a recommendation for marriage. I bid you goodnight, sir."

She bobbed him a polite curtsy and, turning, walked quickly up the stairs.

He wanted to say a good many things more, mostly expressions of adoration and love.

Patient. He could be patient. Slow and steady would win the race.

He was not going to rush his fences again. He would carefully woo her. There was time yet.

Georgiana crouched on the stairs until she heard Sebastian's footsteps move through the great hall and fade into the guest wing.

Was *everyone* out and about tonight?

She was quite sure the figure she had seen in the garden had *not* been him. Sebastian had been wearing a heavy banyan tied tight at the waist, while the figure in the garden had clearly been in a coat and breeches.

But still. It was all very odd.

Unexpected. *Thrilling.*

Moving quietly, she skirted back down the stairs, through the great hall and then the drawing room, darting through the french doors which led to the terrace and down into the walled garden.

To the pot on the wall. Where the figure had slid something small and white.

On tiptoe, she slipped a hand underneath the violets, patting the loose dirt until something more solid brushed her fingertips.

Grabbing, she pulled it out.

Folded foolscap. A note.

Giggling behind her free hand, she studied it. It was far too dark to read, and she didn't want to risk someone seeing her flashlight from the house. Quickly, she retraced her steps.

But as soon as she quietly closed her bedroom door, she turned on the flashlight and, fumbling in eagerness, wrenched the note open.

> *I have heard the warning thunder and understand the lightning bolt can harm those who do not heed the eagle's cry. Your servant awaits.*

She stood still for a moment.

And then laughed, hoping she didn't sound too maniacal.

Perfect. The note was *perfect*.

Everything one could want. Coded and yet somewhat specific. Vaguely menacing.

It was *exhilarating*.

If she were excessively lucky, the words *lightning bolt* and *eagle* would be cryptic references that somehow tied in to the Jupiter mark on her letter. Jasmine had said that lightning and eagles were both associated with Jupiter. It was too much of a coincidence that this note now surfaced with those exact words.

Giddy, she launched herself onto her bed with a decidedly unladylike bounce and grabbed her tablet. First, she laid the slip of paper on the counterpane and took a photo of it for reference. Then she went back into her list and added the text of the note as an entry:

> 10. *"I have heard the warning thunder and understand the lightning bolt can harm those who do not heed the eagle's cry. Your servant awaits."* Could this be related to the Jupiter symbol?

Giggling with delight, Georgiana collapsed back onto her pillows. Now how was she supposed to sleep?

Chapter 8

The drawing room
Haldon Manor
Mid-morning on August 28, 1813
Birthday in minus 42 days

Well, well, well, m'dear child," Sir Henry Stylles boomed as Georgiana entered the drawing room the next morning. Primped and corsetted and feeling very much like a nineteenth century lady again.

She smiled at the jovial middle-aged gentleman who instantly crossed the room to greet her. Sir Henry looked much the same as he always had: portly, flushed cheeks, eyes sparkling with good humor. His signature salt and pepper mustache stretched impressively across his face.

"How vastly pleasing to have you returned to us!" he boomed again.

Sir Henry always boomed. His voice only had two volumes: loud and louder. He bowed over her offered hand, mustache wafting as he did.

"Well, well, well," he repeated, still holding her hand and patting it. "You were at death's door last I saw you. Never thought to see you again, m'dear."

Tact was also *not* one of Sir Henry's strong suits.

"Thank you, Sir Henry." Georgiana planted an affectionate kiss on his cheek.

Enthusiastically, Sir Henry clutched her hand and beamed at her, his eyes suspiciously bright. He cleared his throat rather loudly.

Despite his eccentricities, Sir Henry was a dear friend of the family, more like an uncle than a neighbor. His mustache was as lustrous as ever, large and expansive, looking for all the world like some furry creature had taken up residence on his upper lip.

However, his face was a little more careworn. A bit of an adventurer in his youth, Sir Henry had never married, preferring instead to devote his energies to his greenhouses and collections of exotic items at Sutton Hall, the nearest estate to Haldon Manor.

Releasing Sir Henry's hand, Georgiana noted the other people in the room. Sebastian stood near the fireplace looking immaculately put-together in a blue coat, expertly tied neckcloth and tan breeches which hugged surprisingly muscled legs; the skinny legs of teenage Sebastian were a thing of the past. The man must employ a talented valet. Chestnut hair styled carelessly in a short Caesar cut with hair swept down onto his forehead, sideburns jutting forward across his cheeks.

He gave her a signature Sebastian smile—not too broad but one which radiated laughter and good humor.

One of his elbows rested on the mantle, his hand hanging loosely over it. A strong, sculpted hand with long fingers and broad palm.

A hand that somehow managed to be sensitive and yet screamed *male* in one fell swoop.

What a silly thought. Georgiana gave her brain a shake. He was just Sebastian. Nothing more.

Captain Phillips hovered protectively at his friend's side, sticking valiantly to his chaperoning duties. Arthur sat on the divan with Marianne, looking radiantly pregnant with dark curls framing her petite face.

Surprisingly (or perhaps not so surprising), Lady Ambrosia occupied the chair opposite them, cuddling the tiny Mr. Snickers, who sported a red knitted sweater and was being surreptitiously fed small treats from her reticule.

Georgiana narrowed her eyes slightly. Really, the woman had no shame. Escorted out of the house the previous evening and here she was again, her blond head looking innocently around the room, looking for all the world like a nineteenth century Marilyn Monroe impersonator.

As usual, her pink muslin day dress was cut decidedly too low for propriety. Rather than donning a fichu and tucking it in to mask the low neckline, Lady Ambrosia had wrapped a shawl around her shoulders instead, the barest nod to modesty.

But as the shawl kept slipping accidentally-on-purpose every time she moved, it did little to conceal her 'assets,' managing to draw more attention to them.

It was all quite cleverly done.

Yes, Lady Ambrosia definitely bore some watching.

Georgiana made her curtsies to them all and settled down on the chaise next to Sir Henry, back straight and lady-like. Hopefully, her poor body would soon readjust to hyper-erect posture. How long before massage would become acceptable for a lady anyway?

"I heard tell of your miraculous return last night, Miss Knight, and had to come over first thing to see if the reports were true. And here you are, right as rain." Sir Henry chuckled. Or rather, his mustache bounced up and down in a jovial sort of way.

"Yes, I am most delighted to be returned to my family. The doctors achieved a most miraculous recovery."

"Indeed, my dear. My mind is most curious as to how such a cure was effected." Sir Henry looked at Georgiana expectantly.

A sly grin touched Sebastian's lips. "Yes, Miss Knight. Please tell us exactly how you came to be wondrously cured." His eyes fixed on her, full of teasing irony.

Georgiana shot Arthur a fortifying look. They just needed to stick to the story they had agreed upon.

"Yes. Right," he said, his voice wooden, as if reciting words. "Dr. Carson of Liverpool felt that our damp English air was part of the problem and contributed to Georgiana's ill health. So he recommended a

Mediterranean cure at a sanatorium in Italy which seems to have done the trick." He shifted in his chair.

Georgiana barely controlled a grimace. Arthur truly was a most terrible liar.

"Goodness gracious, child! You have been all the way to Italy, have you? I cannot fathom how you made the difficult journey with your health, fragile as it was. Not to mention the French naval blockade." Sir Henry's mustache bounced quizzically.

Georgiana swallowed.

Drat. She had forgotten about the blockade. Perhaps Italy hadn't been the best choice after all.

Though . . . who could contradict her story?

"Well, I hadn't much choice, Sir Henry. As you well know, I was so desperately ill that any chance for a cure was welcomed. Staying on English shores meant certain death. However, we were fortunate our ship was not accosted going or coming. It also explains why I was unable to relay any correspondence to my family. I am so sorry for their worry." She gave Arthur an apologetic smile.

In for a penny and all that . . .

"But hasn't the war with Napoleon extended into Italy as well?" Lady Ambrosia asked, her eyes a little too innocently wide. "How frightening for you."

Georgiana fixed her with a hard look.

Yes, Lady Ambrosia did bear watching indeed.

"Yes, my lady. However, I was in the more southern climes where the war has not reached. Being tended to by nuns."

They regarded each other for a moment.

Lady Ambrosia gave a simpering look and shrugged. "'Tis amazing you were cured at all, given the reputation of Continental doctors."

"I must beg to differ, my lady," Arthur replied, stiffly. "Georgiana received the most modern care possible. Medicines and knowledge that we do not have here in England. It was truly miraculous."

Ah, poor Arthur.

Even the truth sounded like a lie.

Sebastian nearly chuckled at Arthur's stilted story. It wouldn't convince a child.

As a soldier, Sebastian had been to Italy. With the Italian city-states constantly at each other's throats and Napoleon's incessant fighting redrawing the peninsula's political map every other month, it was hardly the place to send a well-bred, consumptive, English miss. Nor was it a likely place to find a 'miraculous' cure. Even in the more stable south.

But what were they lying to cover? All accounts made it very clear that Georgiana had been desperately ill. And if she had truly traveled to Italy and been healed there, why not share more specifics so all could benefit? And if she didn't go to Italy, where *had* she spent the last year?

It made no sense.

He wanted nothing more than to pester her immediately with further questions, divine where she had spent the last year.

However, before Sebastian could say anything, Lady Ambrosia stirred in her chair, obviously intending to drag the room's attention back to herself.

"Well, regardless, we are all a flutter over your return, Miss Knight," she said in her most lisping, lilting voice. And then smirked as all the male heads in the room turned in her direction.

Sir Henry, in particular, seeming to notice Lady Ambrosia for the first time. She gave a simpering smile and shifted again, allowing her shawl to slide down to her elbows. Sir Henry's mustache twitched appreciatively. She did have a fine bosom.

Sebastian squelched a resigned grunt.

With her constantly slipping shawl, not-so-subtle maneuvers and wool-enshrouded yippy dog, Lady Ambrosia was not unlike a one-woman traveling circus.

Generally entertaining in small doses but gratingly irritating in larger quantities.

By Sebastian's estimates, Lady Ambrosia had definitely moved into irritating territory.

Lady Ambrosia continued, "Given the dangers which lurk for all gentlewomen, I had feared for your safety. How terrible if you had gone the way of poor Miss Franklin in Wales."

"Heavens! Poor Miss Franklin. That was a horrid case." Marianne leaned toward Lady Ambrosia. "Outside Brecon last year. September was it not? Such a tragedy. That unfortunate girl, missing for several days and then to find her body below the castle walls." She placed a protective hand over her expanding waistline and looked duly upset.

"They say she lost her footing and fell," Arthur chimed in, patting his wife's hand comfortingly.

"Yes. 'Twas most unusual," Lady Ambrosia agreed. "I was in the neighborhood at the time, visiting an aunt in Brecon. Miss Franklin had told no one she was going for a walk to the old fortress. She must have slipped somehow. The stones were said to be worn and slippery with moss."

"Surely the tragedy must have been felt throughout the neighborhood," Marianne said.

Lady Ambrosia gave her shawl another twitch. "Indeed, madam, you are correct on both accounts. My aunt was most dismayed by the events. Poor Miss Franklin was quite the budding artist. She had painted a commendable watercolor of the prospect from my aunt's drawing room. Of course, I consider myself to be something of an artist as well, so I felt Miss Franklin's loss quite keenly." She pulled a handkerchief from her reticule and dabbed at her eyes.

There ensued a small silence.

"Well, we have had quite enough of dismal talk." Marianne rose to her feet and walked to a table behind the divan. "Lady Michael was kind enough to show me several new paper filigree techniques yesterday, and I am eager to try them. Will you join me, Georgiana?"

Sebastian smiled as Georgiana's face instantly adopted a frozen look. He was quite sure quilling was the last thing she wanted to do.

It was too much to resist.

"Yes, please do join in, Miss Knight. Whilst you work, I promise to sit here and compose compliments for whatever marvel you create." He flashed her a wicked grin. "You know I adore lambs."

Eyes narrowed, Georgiana rose from her seat. Sebastian gave her his most innocent face which he could only hold for a second before slipping back into a teasing smile.

He had no worry that she would get back at him. He was looking forward to it, in fact.

Georgiana followed Marianne to the table, took a seat and started sorting through the thin paper strips.

Sebastian gazed at Georgiana, wearing a morning dress that he was quite sure his sisters would describe as excessively smart.

Made of flowing off-white muslin, there was a contrasting subtle vine pattern somehow woven through the fabric in a different shade of white. A long aqua-blue shawl with a subtle yellow and orange floral pattern draped over her arms as she reached for pins to hold her designs.

For someone who had supposedly just recovered from consumption, she had a remarkably *au courant* wardrobe.

The rational part of his mind recognized that Georgiana was not the most beautiful woman he had ever seen. Her eyes a little too wide set, her mouth too generous, her forehead a titch too high.

But how could a woman's attraction simply be laid down to physical appearance?

Georgiana's zest for life lit a fire within her. She bounced with energy. Life was simply *more* when Georgiana was around.

Brighter. Sweeter. *Alive.*

She shot a glance at him from beneath her bent head and then turned to Sir Henry.

"Sir Henry, Lord Stratton has expressed an interest in gooseberries. I understand that Stratton Hall boasts ever so many varieties from the late earl, but his lordship is at a loss as to how to best maintain them." Georgiana looked back to Sebastian as she spoke, everything in her body language saying this was her way of getting back at him. Sebastian raised a quizzical eyebrow.

Sir Henry instantly perked up, mustache quivering.

"Gooseberries are a most worthy opponent, Lord Stratton. The old earl would be pleased to learn of your interest." Sir Henry rubbed his hands together. His mustache looked nearly gleeful.

Ten minutes later, Sebastian was fully aware there was nothing in the world Sir Henry loved quite so much as gooseberries. He took his duties as the president of the Greater Herefordshire Old Gooseberry Society most seriously.

Additionally, Sir Henry was also one of the four founding members of the Royal Gooseberry Show—established under the good grace of

King George himself—which had just held its fifteenth annual show. Where, yet again, Sir Henry had presented the heaviest berry and had come away with the coveted gooseberry trophy, a silver oval-shaped bowl that was meant to look like a gooseberry cut in half.

From the mischievous looks that Georgiana kept shooting his way, she expected him to find Sir Henry's gooseberry monologuing tedious.

But it was strangely . . . *fascinating*. The varieties, the tender care, the science behind it. So much passion focused on such a humble little fruit.

"I have great hopes of my new Hereford Blush variety," Sir Henry said after debating the nuance of gooseberry tint with himself for at least eight minutes. "They are a lovely rose color, and I have been developing the plant for several years. It combines the sweetness of Conquering Hero with the red coloring of Whinham's Industry. At the last meeting of the Greater Herefordshire Old Gooseberry Society, Mr. Johnston declared the Hereford Blush to be the most spectacular gooseberry he had ever seen."

"Remarkable, Sir Henry," Sebastian said without a trace of irony.

"And when do we get to taste your new rose-colored gooseberry, Sir Henry? A large gooseberry is well enough, but the taste of them is most important," Georgiana said.

"Yes, yes, my dear. I could not agree more. To that point, I actually had my cook create the most delightful gooseberry fool this morning and brought it straightway here as a welcome home gesture." Sir Henry looked to Marianne. "Perhaps, Mrs. Knight, you would be good enough to have a footman bring it in for Miss Knight's inspection?"

Marianne gave a gentle smile. "Of course. It was quite the sight, I do assure you, Georgiana." She gestured a footman over and made the request.

"Gooseberry fool made with Hereford Blush gooseberries?" Sebastian nodded. "How delightful! Not only am I exorbitantly fond of gooseberry fool, but given that the Greater Herefordshire Old Gooseberry Society may soon be the recipient of twenty thousand of my hard-won pounds, I should like to know it will be put to a good cause."

"Yes, my lord, indeed it would be. In fact, I should dearly love to show you exactly what I would do with the money. John Carew—may his soul rest in peace—was a terrible rascal, leaving his will as he did. It has put all of us in a terrible fix. Cannot understand what he must have been thinking."

"Indeed, Sir Henry, I could not agree with you more," said an excessively cool voice from the doorway.

All heads turned as a decidedly aristocratic figure pushed his way past the footman holding the door. The newcomer stopped just inside the door, the better to glower at the room.

"Though it pains me greatly to agree with you about anything," the gentleman continued. "All of Stratton's money should have been left entirely to *me*. Instead, I now find myself having to share it with an inept amateur such as yourself."

"Lord Blackwell." Sir Henry named the visitor, imbuing the word with scathing contempt, mustache bristling in disdain. A look Blackwell haughtily returned.

Lord Linwood, Marianne's older brother, followed Lord Blackwell into the room, bowing to the company and handing his hat and gloves to the waiting footman. His face a mask of cool indifference, as usual.

Everyone rose to greet the new guests.

"Brother! Welcome," Marianne said smoothly, crossing and standing on tip-toe to give Linwood a fond kiss on the cheek. "How lovely to see you. Though I had assumed you would call this morning to witness Georgiana's miraculous return yourself. And Uncle Bertie, what a delight!" She turned to Blackwell who continued to exchange hostile looks with Sir Henry. "I have not seen you since Mama's funeral nearly two years past. Please allow me to present you to my husband and visitors."

Sebastian studied Lord Albert Blackwell. Ah, so this was the other gooseberry enthusiast who stood to gain from his misfortune. What a specimen he was.

Disdaining the subdued men's clothing made popular by Beau Brummel over a decade earlier, Blackwell clearly still favored the ostentatious fashions of his youth. Which, judging from his lined face and stout figure, must have been decades past.

His peacock-blue velvet frock coat edged with silver embroidery and matching waistcoat and knee breeches contrasted sharply with bright white stockings and heeled shoes with sparkling silver buckles.

Additionally, Blackwell sported a white, powdered wig with a puffed, pompadour front and rolling side curls, all drawn back into a queue and tied off with a matching blue ribbon.

All in all, he looked as if he had just arrived from the French courts of Marie Antoinette circa 1775.

Recalling his manners, Blackwell managed to give Marianne a polite smile and minced into the room, balancing precariously on his heeled shoes. Instead of bowing at the waist as was currently common, he placed one leg forward, bowing low over it as he greeted each person in the room. He presented Lady Ambrosia with a particularly appreciative look. Her shawl had 'slipped' again to hang loosely around her elbows.

Next to his uncle, Linwood looked coolly reserved in an *au courant* dark green cutaway coat, tan breeches and glossy Hessian boots, his dark hair cropped short. Nearly as tall as Sebastian himself, he nodded a polite greeting.

Sebastian found Linwood a difficult man to read. He was arrogant and often cold, but Sebastian knew of few other peers who took their responsibilities so seriously. Working with him in the House of Lords over the past few months had been satisfying, despite Linwood's haughty reputation.

"Uncle, what brings you to Kinningsley?" Marianne asked as they all sat down. She resumed her place at the work table with Georgiana. "Timothy neglected to tell me of your arrival." Marianne shot an accusing look at her brother, who merely raised an eyebrow. It was the most emotion Linwood ever showed.

"I was scarcely informed myself, Marianne," Linwood said in clipped aristocratic tones. "Uncle Bertie merely showed up on my doorstep yesterday evening—"

"'Tis easy enough to see why I am here," Blackwell interrupted, flicking a spot of dust off of his velvet sleeve and adjusting the froth of lace extending past the embroidered cuff. "This whole business that wastrel Stratton set in motion—oh I beg your pardon, my lord, I was referring to the late earl, not yourself." He nodded to Sebastian. "This business has got us all worked into a lather. I have come to ensure no one sabotages the proceedings." He directed a pointed look to Sir Henry.

"How dare you, Blackwell!" Sir Henry's mustache quivered with righteous anger. "It is more likely that I should be here to ensure that no perfidy occurs—"

"Perfidy! If anyone will stoop to low means, it would be you—"

Sebastian could not contain a startled laugh. He held out a calming hand. "Gentlemen, please. I am at a loss as to how you think there will be any underhanded dealings in this case. Either I marry or I do not. That is the beginning and end of the matter. I fail to see how either of you could influence the outcome."

Sebastian watched the two older men glare at one another, their raised hackles practically visible.

He glanced at Georgiana, which was a mistake. She had her lips pinched tightly together, eyes wide and sparkling with incredulous laughter.

Blackwell gave a disdainful sniff and went back to adjusting his lace. "Well, Sir Henry, you would do well to remain at home and tend to your precious gooseberries as heaven knows that is the only way you will defeat me during the next competition—"

"Bah! You are just jealous the trophy still remains in my possession," Sir Henry huffed.

As if on cue, a footman entered the room carrying a large silver pedestal bowl ornamented with curling, filigreed handles, gooseberry fool mounded high above its rim. Sebastian could see flecks of green and red peeking out from the frothy cream. At Marianne's gesture, the footman placed the bowl on the table where she and Georgiana sat working. Georgiana examined it with interest.

Blackwell gasped in outrage. "Really you have stooped to new lows, Sir Henry, flaunting the gooseberry trophy cup in such a manner. If you think such a display will sway Stratton in his decision to take a bride, you must be entirely mistaken."

Sir Henry gave Blackwell a slow, perusing look, scathingly assessing his clothing. "Well, perhaps if you spent half as much time doting over your gooseberries as you do your ancient tailor—"

"How dare you! At least I can manage to keep my lip clean shaven instead of indulging in whiskered histrionics. Your mustache, sir, is a disgrace to polite society—"

Sebastian stifled a bark of laughter, turning it into a cough only at the last second.

"Sir Henry, who is Lord Tangert?" Georgiana suddenly asked, gesturing toward the silver bowl. "I see your names are engraved here on the bottom as the founders of the Royal Gooseberry Show: Sir Henry Stylles, Lord Blackwell, Lord Stratton—meaning the old earl, of course— and then Lord Tangert. I was unaware that there was another founding member of the Royal Gooseberry Show."

Blackwell drew in a hissing breath. Sir Henry's mustache stood nearly on end.

"We do not speak *his* name," Sir Henry said, his voice taut with emotion.

"Indeed. Such traitors are beneath our notice." Blackwell adjusted his cuff again with a sniff.

"The blackguard! Using a hollow needle to inject water into his berries to make them heavier. And then once he was exposed, starting that ridiculous Gooseberry Lovers International Brotherhood."

Both men glowered at the thought.

"Well, at least there is *one* gooseberry society in England who does not stand to take my money," Sebastian offered into the silence.

No one appreciated his attempt at levity.

Blackwell sniffed. "Indeed. Tangert was outraged when the old earl cut his gooseberry society out of the original will, leaving money to just his own society, myself and Sir Henry here. You should have seen the look on his face when he found out. He turned so red I feared his head would near explode."

Sir Henry nodded. "Tangert never could dismiss the slight. More the fool."

"Agreed, Sir Henry, agreed."

"Fortunately, Tangert did have the decency to be lost in the wilderness of Newfoundland with his younger son—"

"Jack, was it? Utter scapegrace like his father," Blackwell interrupted.

"Yes, Jack. I understand they were trying to find the fabled giant golden gooseberry of Labrador. As if such a thing actually exists!"

Blackwell harrumphed. "Nearly bankrupted the barony in the process. Golden gooseberry indeed."

"And now his elder son, the present Lord Tangert, persists this ridiculous Gooseberry Brotherhood." Sir Henry waived his hand dismissively.

"At least the Prince Regent has barred them from our Royal Gooseberry Show," Blackwell replied.

"Thank heavens, Bertie," Sir Henry's mustache bounced in approval.

"Indeed, Henry, it has all been such a disgrace." Blackwell shook his head in disgust.

Both men regarded each other for a moment, surprised to discover that they were still comrades.

"It has been a long time, Bertie, since we had a good chat. Shall we lay down our weapons? Perhaps you would like to try some gooseberry fool. I understand that luncheon is in order?" Sir Henry turned a questioning eye to Marianne, who nodded her head in agreement.

Blackwell pondered this for an instant and then let out a long breath.

"Perhaps a chat is in order, Henry. Though I find your mustache ridiculous."

"Duly noted, Bertie," Sir Henry said with a nod. "And for the record, your sense of style is still truly absurd."

Chapter 9

A scratching noise at the door woke Georgiana from a deep sleep. Blearily, she turned over in bed, dragging her phone from underneath her pillow. It was two thirty in the morning.

Coming more awake, Georgiana sat up and pushed aside the heavy bed curtains. From the light of her phone's lock screen, she could see a white square on the floor in front of her bedroom door.

A note of some sort.

Slipping out of bed, she quickly scooped up the folded paper and switched on her phone flashlight.

You will send Lord Stratton away. He is destined for another.

That was all. She turned the paper over, examined it. Nothing more.
She scrunched her nose. What a *ridiculous* note.

Please.

As if *she* were Sebastian's keeper and could control his movements.
As if she were pursuing *him* and not the other way around. As if she were
even a threat.

And then adding insult to injury, the warning note was so . . . *tepid.*

Ugh. How disappointing.

The first menacing note of her life, and it would hardly deter a
mouse, much less herself, were she determined to win Sebastian.

Which she was *not.* But still.

What amateurs!

With a faint frown, Georgiana opened the door to her bedroom and
shined the light down the hallway.

Empty.

Honestly, how was it possible for so many people to have access to
the house at night? Quite appalling.

She closed her bedroom door, pondering what to do next.

The whole situation was absurd. The sort of debacle she and Sebastian would laugh themselves silly over, were they not its principle players.

Which only emphasized the ridiculousness of anyone sending her
intimidating notes about Sebastian. It was almost worth being cozy with
him just to annoy whoever had sent it.

Which begged the next question: Who *had* sent it?

Pondering, she tapped the note against her lips. Perhaps one of the
Miss Burbanks, though Lady Ambrosia was also a likely suspect.

If so, they could *definitely* use a few lessons on clandestine subterfuge.
Honestly, Mr. Snickers in his little sweaters was more fierce than this
note.

She had been back almost five days, and the ladies continued to visit
with shocking regularity, finding endless reasons to flaunt their charms.
Sebastian took it all in good-natured stride, remaining courteous even
when Miss Mica insisted he help her glue quilled paper circles to a pic-
ture frame.

And he had not renewed his offer of marriage. Had he given up on
that too? If so, the man was easy-going to a fault.

Tapping the note against her lips, she leaned against her bedroom door, the wood chilly against her back. Mentally, she compared Shatner and Sebastian, so vastly different from each other.

Shatner with his penetrating gray eyes—the focused intensity when he talked about his interests and work, the sound of his voice sending shivers up her spine. He was a man of action, of purpose.

When his partner had called about flooding in their orphanage in Honduras, Shatner had hopped a plane the next morning and gone himself to fill sand bags and repair the damage. He had texted her every couple of hours with updates, going on endlessly about how much he loved his work. It had melted her heart to see his steadfast devotion. And along with all his charity work, Shatner could rival Sir Henry when it came to discussing gooseberries.

Well, Sebastian had his own gooseberry woes too, she supposed. Why did everything seem to come down to gooseberries with her? Was it proof that the universe had a sense of humor?

But, in the end, Sebastian was . . . just *Sebastian*.

She remembered the shooting contest that Lord Stratton had hosted every year. Sebastian had practiced for months, shooting targets behind the vicarage with his Baker rifle. It had been a different side of Sebastian, focused and determined. He had talked incessantly about the prize: ten guineas and a new pistol.

However, the day before the competition, Sebastian got into a terrible fight with Jack Carpenter who had taunted Sebastian about participating in a *man's* competition. Sebastian had come home sporting a fierce black eye. And then, the next day, he had shown up at Lyndenbrooke instead of going to the competition. Georgiana herself had taken a severe chill and had been forced to stay home. Abandoning the competition, Sebastian sat with her throughout the day, keeping her company.

"Seb, you should go," she'd said between coughs, voice hoarse. *"I am well-enough and a maid will check on me every hour or so."*

"Nonsense, Georgie. You can barely speak above a whisper."

"Truly, I will be well soon enough." She tried to lift her head off the pillow, with little success. The room kept spinning.

"You shouldn't worry, dear friend. The competition means nothing compared to your—"

"But, you have practiced so diligently and 'tis such a shame—"

"Hush, Georgie. You will tire yourself. Think nothing more of it. Get some rest."

Georgiana had found the entire incident disheartening. How could he abandon a dream over a little teasing from dumb Jack Carpenter?

Just look at his decision to marry her! She was convenient and comfortable, and so he had sought her out. The path of least resistance. That had always been his way. No hidden depths or passion.

She pondered it for a few minutes longer. She needed to be fair to Sebastian. He had been extremely kind listening to Sir Henry rambling on and on about gooseberries. She would give him that much. He took patience to new levels. It was ridiculous and yet, somehow, oddly endearing.

Standing in her nightgown and bare feet, she shivered and read the note again. Perhaps whoever had sent it was still around.

With a smile, Georgiana threw on a dressing gown and stole out of her room. Turning off the light from her phone, she tucked it into the pocket of her dressing gown. She knew Haldon Manor well enough to move around without a light. Besides, the moonlight streaming through the windows was sufficient to light the way.

She crept down the stairs and across the great hall, jumping when her bare feet hit the cold flagstones of the large room.

Shoes! Why did she always forget to put on shoes? Though barely September, the stone floor was *freezing*.

Grimacing, she continued across the great hall. Glancing inside the drawing room, she noticed the french doors leading to the back terrace were slightly ajar. Creeping quietly into the room, she peered around. Empty.

Puzzled, she walked over to the doors, intent on closing and latching them firmly. Really, someone needed to speak with the butler about ensuring the house was better locked each evening.

But as she swung the doors closed, she saw something glowing. The terrace led to the garden surrounded by a medieval wall and there, on the old wall, something stuttered and winked at her.

She squinted. Why it looked like . . .

She paused. Surely it couldn't be what she thought it was. It must be some simple trick of the moonlight.

And her mind, always yearning to see something fantastical.

Cautiously, Georgiana crept out of the door and darted across the (cold) terrace for a closer look. Just to put her overactive imagination to rest. But as she drew near, she realized it was indeed what she had first suspected.

The Jupiter sign. Glowing. On the wall.

The electrical thrill started at her scalp and then cascaded downward, twitching arms, hands, legs, toes in its wake.

The whole sensation was *utterly* delicious.

She clamped a hand over her mouth, stifling a giggle. She darted looks left and right.

No one.

And yet, here was the sign, clearly drawn on the wall with a green luminescent chalk of some sort, looking like a loopy, undecided number four.

The glow wavered slightly and started to fade. Obviously, it was not meant to last. Quickly, she pulled out her phone and snapped a photo of the sign, if only to prove to herself this wasn't just a hallucination.

A scent reached her, a smell similar to a struck matchstick, slightly acrid. She frowned for a moment. It was odd.

First a threatening note and then the Jupiter symbol on the garden wall.

Now she *did* giggle, loving the way excitement zoomed up and down her spine.

Ah, it was just so *magnificent.*

But who was responsible for it all? And were they one and the same person?

Despite her cold toes, Georgiana made a circuit of the garden, but saw no one and nothing else suspicious. When she returned to the garden wall, the Jupiter sign had faded entirely away.

She slipped back to her bedroom and collapsed on her bed with a contented sigh.

Grabbing her tablet, she made another entry:

> *11. Saw glowing Jupiter symbol on garden wall tonight. Could it be a signal of some sort? And for whom?*

Sinking back into her bed pillows, she shook her head. Again, how was she supposed to sleep with so many ideas chasing each other around her head?

Too many more nights like this would make her a zombie.

Now wouldn't *that* be delicious.

Georgiana woke several hours later to sun streaming and birds quarreling loudly outside her window.

Had she only imagined the events of last night?

Rubbing sleep out of her eyes, she reached for her phone under her pillow. There was the photo with the Jupiter sign, clear as could be.

An electrical zing shot down her spine again. Gooseflesh pebbled her arms.

Who had drawn it? Why *that* symbol? What did it mean?

And why *here*?

Haldon Manor was tucked on the border of Wales in rural Herefordshire, for heaven's sake.

Rural Herefordshire.

It was like saying one lived in the section of Seven Dials that even those *from* Seven Dials considered a slum.

It was the backwater of nowhere. *Nothing* ever happened in Herefordshire, particularly the *rural* parts.

She pondered all the possibilities again.

Pirates?

Unlikely. The ocean was over fifty miles away in any direction.

French spies? They were at war with Napoleon after all.

No. That also seemed unlikely, per her first point. She was in *Herefordshire*.

Smugglers?

No. Again, that needed the ocean.

Thieves?

Not likely. If they were merely thieves, they would have robbed the house instead of leaving the sign.

Georgiana tapped a finger against her lips. *Think, think, think.*

Well, such things were nearly always messages. In this case, it could hardly be a warning as the symbol had been painted to disappear. So it had to be a directive of some kind to someone else.

She *could* deduce that the symbol was related to the note she had intercepted in the flower planter. The references to lightning and eagles definitely called up Jupiter. It seemed logical that both messages had been intended for the same person.

But who? And why?

What did the sign of a large planet and the king of the Roman gods have to do with Haldon Manor?

Fizzling glee skittered through her again as she buried back under the counterpane. How wonderful to have such a mystery to solve!

Fanny, her maid, opened the door and backed into the room carrying a breakfast tray with a pot of hot chocolate and fresh scones. Again. Just as she had every morning for the past week. Georgiana had been torn between the guilt of another person waiting upon her and delight at being so pampered. After doing for herself for so long, it was nice to be taken care of.

As Fanny set the tray down on the bedside table, Georgiana noticed a small, square package next to the pot of chocolate. Reaching for the package, Georgiana bid Fanny a cheerful good morning as the girl curtsied and left.

Georgiana hefted the parcel in her hand. Though, really, it seemed to be more of a present, tied with pretty ribbon and a bouquet of delicate wildflowers secured in the center. She inhaled the delicious scent of small forget-me-nots and lavender.

Inside, she discovered a small box—the kind one used for trinkets or pins. The box had been constructed with a recessed top and sides and was now covered in paper filigree. The quilling was simple, merely twisted circles of paper, but different colors had been used, resulting in a design. The top featured a red heart set into a pink background, while the sides had butterflies and flowers.

Well . . . maybe.

She examined the box more closely. It was hard to tell what the sides were meant to be. The quilling was quite sloppy and haphazardly done. Puzzled, she opened the box.

A note lay curled inside.

Dearest Georgiana,

Look to what you have reduced me. As a devotee and admirer of the finer arts of paper working, I beg of you to stop this horror. Please agree to be my wife, and I promise you a life free from quilling and its abuses against good taste everywhere.

Yours in this dire hour of need,
Sebastian

Georgiana laughed. She couldn't help it. Trust him to always make her smile.

She studied the box again, imagining poor Sebastian affixing all the little circles. How utterly ridiculous.

And did a paper filigree marriage proposal even count? Assuming that multiple proposals from the same person counted.

Which they most certainly *should.* A proposal was a proposal, right?

That said, quilling and serious marriage proposals should *never* go hand-in-hand. Talk about abuses against good taste.

She pondered, tapping a finger against her lips. No, she would count it, even if Sebastian meant it more as a silly jest. So, this made proposal number seven.

But why did men find it so hard to phrase a proposal of marriage as a question? Why did they always try to just slip it in?

She saw Sebastian again in her mind's eye, standing in the drawing room of Haldon Manor. Buckskins tucked into polished Hessian boots, shoulders broad in his immaculately cut coat. Giving her that wry grin that said he never took the world or himself too seriously. Lifting her hand to his lips, soft and warm against her knuckles. Briefly, she wondered if his lips would feel as soft against her own . . .

She blinked. Where had *that* thought come from? Georgiana shook her head.

It was just the clothes. Every man was more swoon-worthy in buckskin. She really needed to convince Shatner to be more serious about attending her Bosom Companions of the English Society meetings. Seeing him regularly in a tight coat and breeches would probably be enough to send her over the edge into full-blown love.

Shatner. Drat.

Shouldn't she be thinking about him more? What kind of a girlfriend was she anyway? Shatner was still very much part of her heart.

Home was nice, seeing Arthur, being a lady again. But without James, the nineteenth century wasn't the same. She didn't feel tethered to it anymore.

They say 'home is where the heart is,' and her heart was most definitely *not* in 1813. She would solve this little mystery and then return to 2013 and James and Emme and, yes, Shatner. It was the only solution she could see.

Chapter 10

S ebastian waited all morning for Georgiana to make an appearance. He was not at all confident his poor paper filigree proposal would be effective. But after nearly five days of saying nothing, he needed to broach the subject again, desperate to continue his argument for marriage.

She held his heart more than ever. Every glance, every touch, every look drew him deeper under her spell.

Lady Michael and her daughters had come calling, followed shortly by Lady Ambrosia. They were all now ensconced in the drawing room of Haldon Manor, oohing and aahing over bonnet ribbons and paper filigree designs. Lady Ambrosia considered herself to be something of an artist and was decidedly *not* circumspect in asserting her opinions.

Sebastian was quite sure there existed other unmarried women who were not so vain and silly. He just had yet to encounter them. It was like there was a fortress about him, staked all round with signs which read 'All Those with Sense Keep Out' and 'Intellect Not Allowed.'

Honestly, even his good-humor had its limits.

Listening to Miss Michelle argue about the vagaries of coral-colored versus peach ribbons with Miss Micayla brought him nearly to the breaking point.

Begging leave to attend to correspondence, he had quit the drawing room and gone in search of his true quarry: Georgiana.

Which was fortunate, in the end, as Georgiana had collected flowers from the garden and then taken a gig and driven into Marfield. He finally ran her to ground in the parish churchyard.

Tethering his horse next to her gig along the low stone wall, he studied her as he walked up the gravel path. She knelt on the ground in the graveyard, back to him, carefully arranging flowers on the grave before her. A sage green pelisse hugged her shoulders, and she had removed her straw chip bonnet with its matching green ribbon, resting it on the ground. The overcast day hinted at the chill of approaching autumn but somehow made the colors of the green grass and flowers in her hand more vibrant.

Coming closer, Sebastian noted the grave marker:

In loving memory of
James Richard Knight
Born May 23, 1781
Died Oct 15, 1812
Aged 31 years
Beloved son and brother

Ah.

Sebastian paused. The scene encompassed a world of sadness and loss.

"Oh, Seb, there you are. He has come! Just as he said he would." He looked up from his spot under the willow tree to see Georgiana beckoning eagerly, her face lit like a beacon. In her excitement, she grasped his hand, dragging him along.

Reaching the gate of the kitchen garden at Lyndenbrooke, she released him and dashed through. Sebastian watched a blond man in his early twenties walk around the vegetable beds, a huge smile on his face.

"James!" Squealing with delight, Georgiana hurled herself into the man's arms. Chuckling, he swung her around. Half laughing, half crying, she covered her brother's face in exuberant kisses.

Darling Georgie. Sebastian knew she had been waiting weeks for this moment.

"Have mercy, Georgie," James cried.

"It is what you deserve." She emphasized the point with one last noisy kiss. "Don't you dare leave me again."

Still chuckling, he hugged her close. "Never, dearest little sister. That I promise."

Georgiana lifted her head as Sebastian drew near. She gave him a barely-there smile, swiping at the tears on her cheeks with gloved hands. Wordlessly, Sebastian dug into his overcoat pocket and handed her a handkerchief.

"Thank you," she whispered, wiping her eyes.

Her pain gutted him, made him ache to sweep her into his arms and soothe it all away.

As if grief were so easily dismissed. As a soldier, he had been on a first-name basis with Death for far too long.

One never got used to it.

He offered her a hand and helped her stand, her fingers reassuringly warm in his. She dabbed her face a few more times and handed him back his handkerchief.

"I am *so* sorry," he murmured, pocketing the square of linen. "I know how close you were to him."

She smiled again. That sad travesty of a smile that didn't touch her eyes. Nodded.

"Yes," she sniffed. Swallowed. "How impossible to imagine a world without James. With him gone, it will never truly be home." She took a deep, stuttering breath.

"Did you—?" He gestured toward James' gravestone.

The words dangled unspoken between them.

Did you know about his death?

Slowly, she nodded again, looking down.

"Yes, I knew." A pause. "Being here at his grave makes it seem so real though. He truly is *gone*. He will never experience 1813 or 1814 or

1815 . . . and so on." She rolled her hand as she said this, expressing the passing of time.

There was really nothing to say. There never was. Sebastian hated feeling so helpless, not knowing how to comfort her.

Side-by-side, they stared at James' grave.

Silence hung, broken only by the chirping of birds, thoughtlessly cheerful and full of life.

After a minute, she straightened her shoulders and stood more erect, as if making a decision and rallying her spirits.

His plucky Georgiana. She had never been one to wallow in what could not be fixed. Bending, she picked up her bonnet from the ground.

Sebastian took her hand and threaded it through his arm, gesturing toward the path that wound around the church.

"Come," he said, "walk and allow me to cheer you."

She gave a half-hearted grin, the sorrow retreating from her eyes. And then laughed softly.

"Shall we begin by discussing your sadly lacking quilling skills?" she asked, giving him a sidelong look. The teasing tone of her voice warmed him.

"Ah! I take it you received my small token of *esteem* this morning."

She arched a rueful eyebrow, swinging her bonnet loosely from the fingers of her free hand.

"Esteem? Is that what you are calling such a . . . monstrosity?"

"*Monstrosity*! Georgiana Knight, you wound me." He kept his face carefully nonchalant, studying her reaction. She didn't appear to be on the brink of accepting his suit. "We could just agree to call it *art*, instead," he offered, leaning in to her.

Georgiana shook her head. "Well it was a work of . . . something. I'm not sure that *art* is the word I would use, however."

He chuckled affectionately. They reached a stile at the end of the churchyard. A path meandered beyond, disappearing into a stand of trees. Clouds crowded the sky but didn't quite threaten rain. He took the two steps of the stile and then turned to help her over.

Once on the other side, she readily wrapped her hand through his elbow again. The warmth of her gloved hand seeping through his jacket and shirt, branding him with her touch.

"I know my paper filigree skills are indeed lacking, particularly in comparison with your own." He stole a more serious glance at her. "But the note which accompanied the box . . . surely, such a sentiment cannot be labeled a *monstrosity* . . .'"

She had That Look—the one he had seen far too many times on his sisters' faces. The one that said he was being particularly vexing.

She sighed.

It was *not* a good sigh.

Most definitely not an I'm-going-to-marry-you sort of sigh.

He had been a soldier long enough to know when to cut his losses and beat a respectable retreat. Consider a different way to breach the defenses. Save his skin to fight another day.

"Sebastian, you know I care deeply for you, but—"

"Wait, stop right there. I liked that sentence. Now let's just continue it without the *but*, shall we?"

"Sebastian, you must—"

"No, again, you have it wrong. I greatly prefer sentences like 'Sebastian, my dearest love, I care deeply for you *and* . . .' Why don't you give that a try?"

Georgiana nudged his arm with her shoulder as they strolled into the grove of trees.

"My dearest *love?*" She did a decent mimicry of his voice.

He raised an eyebrow and looked at her expectantly.

"Honestly, Seb, that filigreed box is much more likely to *kill* love rather than inspire it." She gave her head an exasperated shake. "You are utterly incorrigible, Lord Stratton."

"And you, Georgiana Knight, can be a cold, cruel woman." He clicked his tongue. "That box represents nearly . . . *hours* of my life and here you sit, mocking it."

Her lips twitched, suppressing a smile.

"Yes, forgive my manners." Georgiana cleared her throat and adopted a decorous expression. "Lord Stratton, the filigreed box was extremely lovely, and I greatly appreciate the time and sentiment you put into its creation. However, I have never considered a quilled marriage proposal sufficient inducement to accept an offer—"

She burst into laughter, completely ruining the seeming sincerity of her statement.

Sebastian shook his head in mock pain, hissing through his teeth.

"Cold, Georgiana. That was so cold. Practically frigid." He shivered for good measure. "I shall retire my quills and give up any dreams of filigree greatness."

"Oh, Seb. Is that a promise?" She laughed harder. That glorious sound.

If she thought that her manner of refusing him would cool his affections, she was sadly mistaken. She looked up at him, eyes dancing and impossibly blue.

Heavens, but she was lovely. How had he lived so many years without her?

Sebastian wondered if he would ever tire of just looking at her. The expressions that skittered across her face, the way her smile always brought light into even the cloudiest of days.

It was as if the years passed and the world around him changed, but Georgiana Knight remained ever the same. Always bright and cheerful, full of energy and zest for life.

As they laughed together, he found his eyes drifting down to her lips. They had always beckoned him, plump and pillowy, the bottom lip slightly fuller than the top. It seemed impossible that he could find himself even more drawn to her now than he had years ago.

Sensing the air change between them, Georgiana's eyes instantly took on a more guarded look, and she turned her attention forward, breaking the moment.

How to sway her, to launch a convincing attack? To make her truly consider him?

"Quilling aside, Georgie, I do truly want to marry you—"

"Enough, Sebastian." She shook her head and heaved a deep sigh. "I know you need to marry and, for whatever reason, you have decided that we will suit. But the reality remains there is no romantic love between us and—"

"How do you know that I don't love you?" Sebastian asked, unable to stop the words from escaping. His heart thumped heavily in his chest.

"Please, Seb. Let it be. As I keep saying, we have only ever been like brother and sister to each other."

Sebastian swallowed and drew in a fortifying breath. "Successful marriages have been built on considerably less."

"Perhaps . . . but I want more from my marriage than just filial affection."

"Why do you resist marrying me, Georgiana? You have admitted that you *do* care for me, and I most certainly care for you. Why not take that affection and work on it to develop something deeper and more lasting?"

Sebastian tried to keep the begging tone out of his voice. With little success.

She gave a shake of her head and looked sightlessly into the surrounding trees. They walked in silence for a few steps. Somewhere, sheep baa-ed in the distance. A gentle breeze ruffled her golden curls.

"It's not that simple, Sebastian. My *life* is not that simple. I want more from my husband than just polite regard—"

"But Georgiana—"

"Please allow me to finish, Sebastian." She squeezed his arm, silencing him. Took a deep breath. "There is another man. That is what I have been trying to say. I met someone about five months ago while recovering from consumption. He is a wonderful person, and he has asked me to consider spending the rest of my life with him."

The bottom fell out of Sebastian's world with those words.

Unexpected. Like being shot with a bullet.

At first, one only registered the resounding crack of gunfire. Felt the force of the impact.

The pain took a second to catch up.

Ah, yes, *there* it came.

Searing and fiery.

His chest constricted. How had he not seen this coming?

Georgiana was a beautiful, vibrant woman. Not to mention an heiress. A full half of the men of Britain—probably more—would welcome a life with her. Why had he assumed that no one had yet captured her heart?

"Do you have a formal understanding with this man?" He was proud of the steadiness of his voice. It hardly wavered, despite the numbness of his lips.

She paused. "No, not yet. I asked for a little time to think about it. To decide."

A wave of relief washed through him.

How *pathetic* to feel hope over such poor odds.

But still. He had *not* come this far to give up.

"Do you love him?"

Again, that pause.

"I honestly don't know." Georgiana twisted her mouth. "How do you know if you are in love?"

"Well, I seem to remember a friend who once described love—quite authoritatively, mind you—as a generally liquid internal feeling. I believe 'melty inside' were the exact words used." He glanced at her.

She swung her bonnet from its ribbons, lips pursed. Pondering.

"True. But how much *melting* is enough?" she asked.

"Forgive my presumption, but in my experience, if you wonder if you are in love, you most certainly are *not*."

She gave a humorless smile.

"Yes, that is what Ja—uhm, a friend said. But I am not so sure. Perhaps love just grows over time. You sound quite knowledgeable on the topic. Have *you* been in love before?" She shot a look at him.

He laughed.

The *irony* of such a question.

How to reply? "Perhaps—"

"Ha! So you admit to being in love with someone!"

Drat!

"I admit nothing and—"

"Did she fall for another and break your heart? Is she now married?"

Blast. That arrow hit too close to the mark.

Georgiana's eyes danced with excitement. She was like a bloodhound to the scent when it came to another's secrets.

Time for a diversion.

He gave her his game smile. "As I have said more than once, I have only ever been madly in love with you, my dear." He pulled her arm a little closer to his body.

As he predicted, she rolled her eyes and nudged his shoulder.

"Stop, Seb! The joke is becoming stale. You tell such bouncers. Are you ever serious?"

"I am *always* serious, dearest Georgiana."

More serious than she would ever know.

She made a frustrated sound in the back of her throat and looked heavenward. Most likely praying for patience.

"But we were discussing *you*," he said. "Does this paragon of manliness have a name?"

For some reason, the question gave her pause.

"Naturally. But I don't see any reason to tell you. The poor man could do without the Earl of Stratton harassing him."

"Ah, fairest Georgiana, you wound me! I would hardly harass the man—"

"Really?"

"Pay him off, perhaps. Have him badly beaten. But harass—"

"Sebastian!"

"Come now, I jest. Tell me his name, Georgiana. Please. Just so I can hate him."

She pressed her mouth closed and shook her head.

"No. You will not be nice. My lips are sealed." She fixed him with a stern look.

He gave a wry grin. "Well, be warned. Until you come to a formal agreement with this gentleman, I will continue to press my suit—"

"Enough!" She pulled him to a stop along the lane, removing her hand from his arm. "Sebastian, I want us to remain friends, but if you continue to pester me about marriage, I am afraid that our friendship will suffer. Please, promise me you will stop."

"Georgiana, what is wrong with me pursuing you? Why would you—"

"Promise me, Seb. Please." She lifted her impossibly blue eyes to his, deep and pleading.

He thought quickly. He had no intention of abandoning his pursuit of her.

When the solution came, it was startlingly simple, yet utterly brilliant.

He was instantly absurdly proud of himself.

"Very well," he agreed, hoping his face looked appropriately solemn. "I will stop pestering you about marriage, but I would ask a favor in return."

Georgiana gave him a skeptical look, clearly not trusting his motives. Wise woman.

"I found out today that Captain Phillips must leave tomorrow to attend to some business."—Phillips didn't know this yet, but being a good sort, he would readily go along with the plan—"However, without Phillips, I will be decidedly chaperone-less. I was hoping to persuade you to do gooseberry for me."

"Do gooseberry? As in, hover around you and ensure that nothing untoward happens? Protect you from the fairer sex?" Her gaze became even more doubtful.

"In case you haven't noticed, Georgiana, I am a matrimonial *prize*." He leaned toward her, placing a self-righteous hand to his chest. His voice dripped with wounded vanity. "Someone has to protect my virtue, and, seeing how Captain Phillips is leaving, I was hoping you would be kind enough to exercise your sisterly affections and protect me from being hopelessly compromised."

"By sticking to your side like glue? Yes, that would do *wonders* for both our reputations—"

"If my virtuous, lily-white character means nothing to you, sister dearest—"

"Virtuous? Lily-white?" and then, "*Sister?!*"

"Exactly! With your sisterly-ish feelings for me, you would be the perfect person to stand by my side and keep any who would despoil—"

"Sebastian, you have got it all wrong. The whole purpose of doing gooseberry is to be a lax chaperone, looking in the hedgerows for fruit while you get sweet on your lady love. Such behavior is hardly going to maintain a *lily-white* reputation for either of us—"

"Purity, my dear. Purity of soul and deed. All I ask is for you to do a little gooseberry—"

"If I never hear the word gooseberry again—"

"I thought it was *marriage* you wished me to stop speaking of, but if gooseberries will do the trick too—"

"Enough, Sebastian!"

She folded her arms across her chest and glared at him, tapping her foot, trying to maintain a posture of anger. But her lips kept twitching to control a smile, ruining the whole effect.

She was utterly adorable.

Sebastian grinned widely, mischievously.

"Fine," she agreed. "I will do what I can to ensure that you are not left alone, but you must promise you will give up this ridiculous idea of us marrying."

Sebastian barely managed to control his look of triumph. They regarded each other for a moment.

She held out her gloved hand.

"Are you in agreement?" she asked.

"Yes, indeed," he said, engulfing her smaller hand in his and giving it a firm shake and then tucked it right back into the crook of his elbow.

Oh, yes, despite the overcast skies, his day had just brightened. There might be a rival for her affections, but he would not give up his fight, not until he watched her walk down the church aisle to marry another man.

And in the meantime, he needed to inform Phillips that he would be making an unexpected trip to London.

Though Sebastian didn't have any names, it was time to start investigating Georgiana's story more thoroughly, divine where she had spent the last year. With Phillips' help, perhaps a Bow Street Runner could get to the bottom of it. Check the passenger lists and find the ship she arrived home on. Discover the identity of this mystery man.

Somewhere there had to be information as to where she had spent the last year.

And he intended to turn Britain upside-down to find it.

Chapter 11

Georgiana stood beside her bedroom door. It was the dead of night, and someone had left a threatening note. Again.

For the *third* time.

There had been another note two days earlier, similarly slipped under her door while she was out riding with Sebastian and Captain Phillips, right before the latter had taken his leave of Haldon Manor.

That note had been vaguely sinister but otherwise disappointing:

Something bad may befall you if these warnings are not heeded.

However, the note tonight seemed more promising.

You have been repeatedly warned. Send Lord Stratton away or the consequences will be dire.

It was the same handwriting as before, but there was something below the script. Holding her phone flashlight steady, she examined it more closely.

Was that a drawing of a dagger with *blood* dripping off it?

Georgiana smiled as all the hairs on her arm stood on end.

Finally a letter to give her gooseflesh. At last. Third time was the charm.

Now she just needed to track down the culprit. As usual, shining a flashlight down the hallway revealed nothing.

It was rapidly becoming preposterous. Who was leaving all these notes? She most certainly couldn't be expected to return to bed *now*.

Which meant investigating in the middle of the night. It was becoming quite the habit.

Only this time, she would be properly prepared.

Five minutes later, Georgiana cautiously opened her bedroom door. Dressed in dark jeans and t-shirt topped by a moto jacket, she had stuffed her long braided hair into a black beanie. She also carried a rucksack with her night vision goggles, a flashlight, pepper spray and a taser. Just in case.

She felt decidedly detective-ish.

Or was it ninja-ish?

She shrugged; either was perfectly acceptable.

The moon, full and bright, sent beams through the windows and providing enough light that she didn't need her beloved night goggles.

More's the pity.

A quick perusal showed the family wing sadly lacked intruders. From there, she made a thorough sweep of the first floor of the house.

The library and Arthur's study were empty, and the drawing room french doors firmly locked. No one hid behind the curtains in the great hall. Billiard balls cast long shadows in the game room, but nothing else was amiss.

The house seemed decidedly tucked in and asleep for the night. Nothing stirring.

At least her admonitions to the butler and housekeeper had been heeded. Everything was securely locked.

So how had someone gained entry?

She ventured into the guest wing. Though the thought of chaperoning Sebastian was ridiculous, she also wanted to ensure all was well. She saw it all too clearly.

Lady Ambrosia slowly opens Sebastian's door, Mr. Snickers wriggling in her arms. Another cloaked woman creeps down the hall, while a third woman drops stealthily from a hole in the ceiling. All nearly vampire-like in their quiet intensity . . .

Of course, that was just her vivid imagination. No one was there. The hallway of the guest wing stretched empty before her, punctuated by bands of moonlight streaming through the open doors of unoccupied bedrooms. Decidedly loose women and vampire free.

Georgiana stopped every ten feet or so to listen, but all she heard was the sound of her own breathing and the house itself, wood creaking as it contracted after the heat of the day.

She continued, peering into several of the vacant guest rooms but saw nothing amiss. Just tidy rooms, breathless and waiting. Not unlike herself.

Pursing her lips, she entered the rose bedroom—the last bedroom in the wing and the only one with a partial view of the walled garden. It was so named not for the color of its draperies (an uninspired gray), but instead for the profusion of roses which dotted the room: a pair of rose painted vases on the fireplace mantle, the rose painting above the bed, roses twining through the rug on the floor.

Imagination had never been her mother's strong point.

Nor, despite its excellent vantage over the surrounding park lands, was it the sort of room one assigned to a visiting earl. *He* was firmly ensconced in the blue bedroom across the hall with its large mullioned window and commanding view of the gravel drive and approach to the house.

Not that it mattered.

The rose bedroom was empty, everything neatly in its place. Just as the rest of the house.

How frustrating.

Georgiana tiptoed over to the window and, depositing the rucksack on the window seat, dug out her night goggles. Even when viewed as an eerie shade of green-gray, the garden was still. Though she could barely see the section of wall where the Jupiter sign had been written, she could tell there was nothing there tonight.

No one was about.

It just figured, didn't it? Her life was always on the *cusp* of mystery.

Never firmly immersed in the middle of it.

Sighing, she stowed the goggles back in her rucksack on the window seat and bent to zip the bag.

The faintest slip of sound shushed to the right.

Suddenly, vice-like arms grabbed her from behind, wrapping around her upper arms and chest in a crushing grip.

Gasping, Georgiana went into instant defense mode, her taekwondo training from the past year instinctively coming out.

Without a second's hesitation, she leveraged her weight backward, twisted clockwise and used her right leg to hook her attacker's left leg and throw him to the ground, catching him by surprise.

However, her attacker was tall, quick and obviously used to hand-to-hand combat.

As he fell, he clutched her upper right arm, dragging her down with him, spinning her around.

A fraction of a second later, Georgiana found herself on her back on the floor, immobilized beneath a large male body with strong hands pinning her arms to the hard wood.

She fought him for a second, but he was far too substantial and muscled to budge.

She twisted her head toward the window. If only she could reach her rucksack and the taser inside it.

"Release me now or I'll scream loud enough to wake the dead," she hissed, bringing her face back to him and struggling to free her arms. "How dare you attack me in my own home!"

The man went intensely still, most likely realizing he held a woman, not a man, pinned to the floor.

"Bloody hell!" he whispered hoarsely.

Their combined breathing echoed in the dark silence.

Georgiana froze, acutely aware of his heavy weight on top of her, the smell of leather and wool and clean soap surrounding her.

She knew that smell. That voice.

"Sebastian!" she whispered, relief flooding her body.

The moonlight streaming through the window outlined the shadow of him above her. He shook his head back and forth and then lowered it.

"If I release you, are you going to take another swing at me? I would prefer that none of my various parts receive any further damage," he whispered in her ear, his breath puffing against her cheek. He vibrated with leashed power.

Georgiana swallowed. When had Sebastian become so strong? And so . . . fierce?

He was just . . . Sebastian. Good-humored, funny, often obnoxious. But *fierce*?

"Let me up," she said, pushing against his hands. "You're hurting my arms."

Without any apparent effort, he sprang upright and, reaching down, pulled Georgiana to her feet. He did not, however, release her arm. His grip was tight and unyielding.

"Georgiana, are you mad?!" Even in the faint light, she could see his scowl.

Scowl? Since when did Sebastian ever scowl?

This night was proving full of surprises.

"Sebastian! How you startled me." Georgiana tugged on her arm, testing his grip. He merely grasped her more tightly.

"You will be the death of me, woman. How could you go creeping around the house dressed like—" He drew her closer to the window to inspect her clothing in the moonlight. "—like a common thief? And in breeches, no less."

Georgiana grimaced and twisted her arm in a quick half circle, simultaneously pushing against his forearm, efficiently breaking his hold on her. Taekwondo was proving all sorts of useful tonight.

"What the hell?" he hissed and grabbed her forearm again. Holding her harder this time.

With a grunt, Georgiana leveraged her weight forward and then promptly yanked her elbow upward toward her shoulder, again quickly breaking his grip. Simultaneously, she grasped his hand, twisting it out and pulling downward on his thumb, forcing him to the side.

As before, the fast, unexpected nature of her attack caught him by surprise.

Righting himself, Sebastian held out his hands. "Enough, Georgie! *Pax.*"

She folded her arms across her chest and tapped a foot against the floor, staring at him. Half lit by the moonlight, his face looked decidedly confused. Georgiana was quite sure Sebastian had never experienced tae-kwondo before, soldier or no. That said, she was also quite sure he could defeat her if he was truly determined.

When had he become so strong and . . . large?

Dangerous.

Georgiana wrapped her arms tighter around her chest as a shiver chased down her spine.

She was cold. That was all. The tingling she felt had *nothing* to do with Sebastian.

Nothing at all.

He was *not* thrilling to her.

He shook his head and placed his hands on his hips. Which made his shoulders look even larger.

He was dressed in a loose shirt unbuttoned at the throat and stuffed into breeches. Hair mussed, chin stubbled and unshaven. His sideburns cut sharply across his cheeks, giving his face a menacing look.

It should be *illegal* for a man to look like that. All sweeping romantic clothing and leashed power.

"What the . . . Where did you . . . I mean, dash it all Georgiana, you fight like a soldier. Where did you learn how to do this? You cannot tell me such maneuvers are now part of a lady's traditional education."

Georgiana grimaced and looked out the window. How could she respond? She couldn't tell him the truth. What would be believable?

She needed to think.

Silence.

"Another second and I would have put a knife into you," he said, taking a step closer to her, forcing her eyes back to his. "Blast! This isn't some sort of game. One of your little fantasies. I have seen war and death and such ugliness . . ." He took in a deep, steadying breath. Even in the dim light, she could see the muscles in his jaw working. "Where did you learn this? Why are you roaming the house in the dead of night? And what, in heaven's name, are you wearing?"

She let out a frustrated huff and chewed on her cheek.

Think, think, think. She needed a good story.

But for once, her mind was blank.

This hulking man in front of her scrubbed all coherent thought from her brain.

The low light cast him into sharp relief, highlighting the width and breadth of him. Catching the drape of the white shirt over his shoulders and chest. The pulse of his breathing in and out.

He had lived nearly a decade since she had truly last known him. This fact struck Georgiana forcefully now. Tonight, the good-humored boy had vanished and, in his place, was this powerful, threatening man of action.

Hostile letters, glowing symbols and now a hunky guy had cornered her in a darkened bedroom. She took back everything about her life only being on the cusp of mystery.

Ah, what a fantastic week!

Wait . . . Had she just considered Sebastian *hunky*?

The air in the room suddenly felt too close, too charged.

"Talk to me, Georgiana. How did you go from Death's door to possessing the skills of a trained assassin in little more than a year? I'm not letting you out of this room until I get some answers." He folded his arms across his chest. Even in the low light, she could see the muscles in his upper arms flex.

All in all, it was a little mesmerizing.

Oh, who was she kidding? It was more than just a *little* mesmerizing.

Georgiana shook her head, trying to clear it. She needed to *stop*.

This was *Sebastian*. Not some dark, mysterious guy she had just met. This was her old playmate, her friend. The person she loved like James or Arthur. *Brotherly* affection.

Nothing more.

But he says he wants to marry you, a tiny part of her brain whispered. *All this gorgeous male-ness could be* yours.

Georgiana quickly pushed *that* traitorous thought away. And ignored the goosebumps covering her arms.

"I will wait all night, if I must," he said after a moment.

She still had no good answer. He had effectively turned her brain to mush.

So she said the first thing that came to her.

"Well, why are *you* out and about at this hour?"

If she had learned anything from all her television watching it was this: the best defense was almost always a good offense.

The smallest smile touched his lips. "I heard someone creeping about and came to investigate. Nice try. Now answer my questions, if you please."

They stared at each other for a heartbeat.

"Someone slipped a threatening note under my door," Georgiana finally said. "I wanted to find the person who did it."

Sebastian let out a heavy breath and closed his eyes, pinching the bridge of his nose.

"And, again, it did not occur to you to wake a footman or notify *anyone* that there might be an intruder in the house?"

"I am a grown woman, Sebastian! And if someone threatens me, I feel that I have the right and ability to investigate—"

"In the middle of the night? In breeches?"

Sebastian was, once more, shaking his head, hand still pressed between his eyes.

Georgiana almost rolled her eyes. "Well, of course! A skirt would have been far too confining, not to mention noisy—"

"Of course." His voice a wonder of sarcasm. "Foolish me for not realizing. So the only logical thing to do, at that point, was to don pantaloons and prowl through the house?"

"Exactly!"

He gave a frustrated grunt and lifted his head to stare out the window. The muscles in his jaw jumped in the faint light.

Why had she never noticed his magnificent jawline? Like chiseled granite. Would it feel hard if she reached out and touched him?

She blinked.

Honestly, this was getting out of hand. The sooner this conversation ended, the better.

Maybe.

"Georgiana, I have half a mind to march you down to your brother's bedchamber and allow him to deal—"

"You are not striking the proper tone here. I thought you were supposed to be the master of charm, the easy-going earl, always with a ready quip—"

"There is nothing humorous about this. I am a *soldier*, Georgiana. Trained to hunt and kill. And when I see clandestine figures in dark breeches, I assume that something nefarious is going on."

"Yes, something nefarious *is* going on—"

"Georgiana, you are giving me a headache." He went back to massaging his forehead with his fingers.

"Sebastian, you are entirely overreacting. It is perfectly normal to investigate when mysterious people leave one threatening notes in the middle of the night."

"And the hand-to-hand combat maneuvers you have so skillfully demonstrated for me?"

"Well, a woman does need to be able to defend herself."

He stood, still shaking his head in the moonlight.

"Instead of sneaking about on your own, why didn't you wake me for help? Again, I'm a *soldier*. Fighting is what I have been *trained* to do."

Oh.

Silence.

"I . . . uhm . . . didn't think of that, actually. That might have been a good idea."

She chewed the inside of her cheek. *Not* mesmerized by how the barely-there light skittered across his hand as he pressed his fingers between his eyes.

"Are you deliberately trying to drive me into an early grave?" His voice a weary sigh.

Sebastian nursed the bridge of his nose for another minute. She was talking in circles. Purposefully trying to confound him. He felt torn between kissing her witless and strangling her.

Somehow he had forgotten this was how Georgiana *regularly* made him feel.

"Calm down, Seb. I am a perfectly capable swimmer. 'Tis not my fault the skiff sank. Though I am quite disappointed the lake monster turned out to be simply a submersed tree."

"Oh Seb, don't be ridiculous. The common English adder isn't that venomous. How could I be Cleopatra mourning Marc Anthony without a snake?"

"Heavens, Seb, you are completely overreacting. The roof tiles were only slightly slippery from the rain. Besides, now your sister thinks the vicarage is haunted! Isn't it diverting?"

He drew in a ragged breath, trying to calm his shaking nerves.

Blast!

He had seen the dark figure stealing down the hallway and had come prepared for battle. Every instinct tense, his heart pounding. Instead, he had found himself on the floor on top of a decidedly female form.

And then to realize that it was *Georgiana.*

His brain was still trying to deal with the shock.

The soft warmth of her body, the thrum of her pulse under his hands.

The sheer *smell* of her—roses and fresh air and something elusively Georgiana.

He had hugged her, to be sure, several days ago in the meadow, but that had been nothing to *this.* The entire experience seared into his brain.

He was utterly rattled.

He could have seriously hurt her. A part of him still wanted to throttle her.

Again, where had she *been* for the past year? He knew enough of combat to realize that someone, somewhere had trained her to fight. But why? And when?

This man that she possibly loved?

She had seemed so much the same old Georgiana that he had known: insatiably curious, imaginative, sunshine.

And yet, somehow, she wasn't. He should have realized she would change too. Heaven knew the past several years had changed him. War had a way of doing that.

That said, Miss Georgiana Knight was most certainly hiding things from him.

Important things, if he knew her.

"You mentioned something about a note?" he asked, lifting his head to look at her.

That was a mistake.

She was impossibly lovely. Moonlight raked through the window, illuminating her hair which had slipped out of the dark cap she wore and was now coming out of its braid, giving her an impish, disheveled look. Her leather jacket was cut short and seemed to be edged with metal in the front. And the breeches . . .

The less he thought of *those*, the better. Where had she found this absurd outfit?

Too many questions. Far too many.

"Oh, the note." She twisted and pulled a piece of foolscap from behind her. Did her breeches have pockets behind?

No. He was *not* going to think about her breeches. No, he was not.

She extended the foolscap to him and then laughed softly, pulling it back.

"There's no light. You can't read it. Basically, it says that unless I send you away, something bad will befall me. It's actually fairly feeble as far as threats go, but it does include a drawing of a bloody dagger this time which is an improvement, I must say. The notes before this one were positively infantile—"

"I'm sorry. Did you just say notes? Plural?"

Georgiana blinked.

"Did I forget to mention that?"

Sebastian shook his head, not trusting himself to speak.

"Well—yes—this is the third note, you see. I received two others earlier this week, but they weren't nearly as menacing. I mean, this one at least gave me gooseflesh. The dagger was a nice touch and—"

"Dagger?!" Sebastian was quite sure his voice rose an octave. It was *not* his most manly moment.

"Yes, as I said earlier, this note included a dagger—" His wide eyes clearly alarmed her. "—Not a real dagger, of course. Just a hand-drawn one. The blood dripping off it was a bit much. It all seems a little amateurish—"

"Amateurish? Georgie, any threat of physical violence—"

"A good menacing note needs to have a ring of specificity to it—"

"And a dagger doesn't do that for you?"

"Well, *no*, quite frankly. Now pin the note to my bed frame *with* a blood-soaked dagger—*that* would give me chills for days."

She shuddered just to emphasize the point.

Sebastian pressed fingertips against his temples. She was maddening. She was killing him—slowly but surely shaving years off his life.

"Georgiana, did it not occur to you to *tell* anyone about this?"

More and more, Sebastian wanted to pound his head against the wall. Nice and slow.

Or strangle her. That thought was also proving attractive.

"Well, if the notes had smacked of a professional, I most certainly would have said something," she continued. "I don't know why you are so upset. I mean, it's not as if you and I are betrothed, so the threats are entirely unfounded."

Ah, back to *that* were they.

"I still intend to marry you, if only to stop—"

"You are *not* my protector, Sebastian. I am practically betrothed to someone else—"

"Of course, this nameless mystery man who is *such* a paragon of virtue—"

"Shatner cares deeply about me and—"

"Shatner? That is his last name? Shatner."

There was a small silence.

"Shatner is his first name, Sebastian. Shatner D'Avery."

Startled, he laughed. "Who names a child Shatner?"

A smile touched her lips. "I know, it's a terrible name, but Shatner is a wonderful person, and I would appreciate you not mocking him."

Sebastian paused. "Shatner D'Avery. Can't say I have heard of anyone by that name."

Georgiana laughed—a hollow, little sound. "You don't exactly move in the same circles," she said dryly.

Sebastian cocked an eyebrow.

"What do you mean? Is he not a gentleman?"

Georgiana let out an irritated puff of air. "Of course, he is a *gentleman*. He is a solicitor in London and does charity work. Just not a high and mighty earl—"

"Wait, he is a solicitor? You are considering marrying a solicitor?"

Georgiana stared at him, eyes pensive with a look that was vaguely . . . disappointed.

"Of all people, I would think *you* least likely to get caught up in ideas of rank and importance."

"I don't care if you marry a farmer, Georgiana. I am just surprised that a solicitor would capture your attention. That seems far too staid. I would have thought a pirate more to your taste."

She gave a knowing chuckle. "Well, he is a decidedly dashing solicitor."

Sebastian held up a staying hand. He did *not* want to hear Georgiana rhapsodize about Shatner D'Avery.

"Enough," he said, glancing out the window. "Whoever left you that note must be long gone. Let me escort you back to your bed chamber."

Georgiana made a disgusted noise.

"Heavens! I can most certainly make my way back to my bedchamber on my own."

"I am well aware of that fact. However, you are just as likely to go traipsing through the gardens. Come."

Despite her breeches, Sebastian placed a hand in the small of her back and walked with her back to the family wing.

All the while, pondering Shatner D'Avery. He had no recollection of ever hearing about a D'Avery family. It seemed unlikely she had met him in Italy, if she had indeed ever been in Italy.

All in all, it just did not add up.

But it was decidedly useful information to pass along to Phillips and the Bow Street Runner in London. And maybe finding this D'Avery fellow would also solve the problem of where exactly Georgiana had spent the last year.

Chapter 12

A week. It had been a *week*.

Georgiana wrapped yet another minuscule paper ribbon around her quill, securing the end with a drop of glue to prevent the tight spiral from unraveling.

A week since she had received her last threatening note. Two weeks since seeing the glowing symbol on the garden wall. Nearly three weeks since returning to 1813.

And she was no closer to understanding the mysterious love letter than when she arrived.

And now it was September—she could write it at any moment.

If only she knew why. And to whom.

She pinched the quilled circle tightly on each side, morphing the circle into a marquis, diamond shape.

Twisting and molding tiny strips of paper had to be the most *ineffective* way to manage frustration. The entire process was an exercise in self-control. But she had no choice.

Done. She was almost done.

"Your design is most interesting, Miss Knight," said Miss Michaelina Burbank at her elbow. Or was this one Mica? Another Miss Burbank lifted her head across the table and studied her work.

"Is it supposed to be the number four?" she asked. Georgiana was quite sure that she was Miss Micayla.

"Yes." Georgiana nestled the small diamond shape into place within her design. "Or something very like it."

The ladies exchanged a conspiratorial look and then went back to their own paper filigree. Marianne smiled indulgently from across the table. She was ornamenting a tea caddy with butterflies. Georgiana subtly flexed her shoulders, working out the stiffness in them. Though, thank goodness, she seemed to have redeveloped her back muscles. Lady-like posture wasn't proving quite as much a strain.

Every day for the past week, Lady Michael had come with her brood. She had quickly capitalized on Marianne's love of paper filigree, and now all the ladies sat about rolling thin strips of paper for hours on end, squeezing and teasing the small paper rolls into a variety of shapes.

It sounded *much* more exciting than it actually was.

Georgiana was going mad.

But the ladies kept coming, even Lady Ambrosia most days. Everyone hoping for a Sebastian-sighting so they could all flaunt their various charms in his direction. Lady Ambrosia being a particularly adept charm-flaunter.

Georgiana had been diligent in her chaperoning duties. Which meant, much to her dismay, many hours spent quilling and listening to the Miss Burbanks' bickering. All to ensure Sebastian was never left alone with any other woman.

For his part, Sebastian had been his old good-humored self, endlessly teasing and charming, regularly reducing her to laughter. No more prodding over her whereabouts for the last year, no more proposals of marriage. All traces of the dangerous, fierce stranger gone. Georgiana was starting to think she had greatly exaggerated the intensity she felt that night when he had tackled her to the ground.

All in all, her week had been placidly boring.

After the promising dagger note, she had been expecting *something* to happen. But nothing had and Georgiana felt antsy.

So she had decided to be bold.

Today was the perfect day for it. Sebastian had left for Bristol yesterday on some business and wouldn't be back for two days, so she didn't have to worry about the ladies taking him by surprise. In fact, Marianne had specifically invited the ladies for dinner today, mostly to prevent them from scurrying after him.

Sebastian's absence had nothing to do with her dullness, she decided. It was just the lack of *anything* exciting that had her in doldrums.

Then again, she kept expecting to hear his voice at her ear commenting on Mr. Snickers' choice of knitted tunic (orange stripes today) or to turn and give him a knowing smile when Miss Mica went off on how divine Marianne's purple quilled butterflies looked with their gilded edges.

All right, so perhaps she *did* miss him in an affectionate sort of way. She missed James, didn't she? So it was perfectly acceptable to miss Sebastian, too.

As a sister *should* miss a brother.

She chewed on her cheek and wrapped another paper strip around her quill.

And she did *not* think about tall, muscle-bound men towering over her in moonlit rooms.

At least not *too* much.

Lord Linwood and Lord Blackwell had come to call and sat with Arthur chatting about horses.

Well, Blackwell and Arthur chatted. Linwood, taciturn as ever, nodded every now and again but did not join in the conversation. In lieu of Sebastian, the Burbank sisters had taken to casting their lures out to him, constantly asking his opinion on this or that.

Given the shortness of his answers, Linwood was not amused to be part of their games.

Blackwell was in fine form, wearing a satin dark pink jacket with white embroidered flowers along its edges and a contrasting white waistcoat, the queue of his powdered wig sporting a matching pink bow. The silver buckles on his high-heeled pink shoes glinted in the afternoon light.

He bore an eerie resemblance to Hello Kitty. In a demented, eighteenth century sort of way.

Georgiana had to stifle a chuckle every time she looked at him. It was the best part of her day so far.

Which, given that she was spending it quilling with the Miss Burbanks, was not saying much.

Georgiana finished the last three small rolls of paper and nestled them into her design. Surveying the completed piece, she was pleased to note the Jupiter symbol stood out quite well against the background.

Go big or go home? Wasn't that what Marc always said?

"Are you finished then?" Marianne asked, gesturing toward Georgiana's board.

"And what, exactly, is your design supposed to be, Miss Knight?" Miss Michaelina queried, leaning closer to examine it.

"I am not entirely certain myself. The design just seemed pleasing." Georgiana shrugged.

Miss Michaelina furrowed her brow, obviously not liking Georgiana's vague response. Georgiana pursed her lips. The whole point of the design was to see who *else* would recognize it. Not to give others ammunition.

"May I?" Miss Michaelina asked, lifting the design into her hands and studying it for a minute.

"Lord Linwood," she said, turning to the gentlemen seated across the room, "would you be so kind as to offer an opinion on the design that Miss Knight has done?" She crossed over to them and held the design for Linwood to see.

As predicted, he cocked an unamused eyebrow. Georgiana forced her face to maintain a careful mask.

"How . . . interesting," he said after a moment, his tone implying that it was anything but.

"May I?" Arthur asked. Miss Michaelina dutifully passed the piece to

Arthur, Blackwell glancing at it as well.

Both men wore puzzled expressions.

"Well, Georgie, you have stumped us all," Arthur said, handing it back to Miss Michaelina who then returned it to the table.

Georgiana shrugged and stood. "I believe I will take a turn around the garden while it finishes drying," she announced, tugging her shawl around her shoulders.

"Charming idea, Miss Knight," Blackwell said. "May I join you?"

Georgiana watched as Blackwell used his walking stick to push to his feet, teetering on his heeled shoes, pink bow bobbing in his white powdered hair.

Hello Kitty. Truly. It was almost uncanny.

Pressing her lips together to keep her giggle inside, Georgiana wrapped her hand around his arm and allowed him to lead her out of the french doors and across the terrace.

They walked sedately, Blackwell making polite inquiries about her health. Georgiana slowed her pace to match his mincing step. She was suddenly grateful that heeled shoes for men had gone out of style around 1795.

Walking into the walled garden, his shoes crunched along the gravel path, punctuated by the tap of his silver-tipped walking stick. From the corner of her eye, Georgiana could see Blackwell studying the sky and the overcast clouds chasing across it.

"The weather has been quite fine lately, but I wonder if we are not due for a spot of rain," he said after a little pause.

"Indeed," Georgiana murmured.

"I thought earlier I perhaps heard some warning thunder, though I did not see a lightning bolt and nothing came to harm." He was still studying the sky.

Georgiana went incredibly still. Had he truly just said that? Those lines almost *straight* from the mysterious letter she found tucked in the flower pot on the wall.

I have heard the warning thunder and understand the lightning bolt can harm those who do not heed the eagle's cry.

What to say?

There was really only one possibility.

"That is a relief. I understand lightning can harm those who do not heed the eagle's cry."

Blackwell's head instantly swung back to her. A small smile tugged at his lips, and he heaved a sigh of relief. He glanced calmly around them.

"Thank goodness, I have found you at last," he said quietly after a moment, stopping to examine a rose bush. His agitation only evident in the tap-tap-tap of his walking stick against the gravel.

Somehow Georgiana managed to keep a straight face. Inside, however, she was doing one of those crazy dances Marc performed when his beloved Broncos scored a touchdown.

Now how to reply?

"Yes, I am happy to finally meet you." Suitably vague but inviting further confidences.

Blackwell nodded, as if the answer pleased him.

"The paper filigree was genius, the perfect sign," he agreed. "Thank you. My nephew delayed my departure last week, and so I arrived too late to see the prearranged signal. I was told the signal would fade if I were too late. I apologize."

Georgiana could only assume he meant the glowing symbol on the garden wall. She felt like jumping up and down and clapping her hands with glee.

Of course, this entire discussion, though providing some answers, was also creating more questions.

A lot more questions.

She nodded conspiratorially. "You must forgive my impertinence, Lord Blackwell. But how do I know you are to be trusted?"

He turned quickly toward her and then looked apologetic.

"Of course, of course," he murmured. "I am a mere amateur with this. Lord Zeus was right to send you. He said he would send his best agent to help me. But, naturally, you need to see the mark."

Lord Zeus? Of course! Zeus, Jupiter's Greek name. Her eyes widened in surprise, but she recovered quickly.

It was sensational, astonishing. *Electrifying.*

She was sure every hair follicle on her body stood on end.

Who *was* Lord Zeus?

With a glance toward the house, Blackwell pushed on the silver handle of his walking stick. The top of the stick swung free to reveal the Jupiter—no wait, Zeus mark—burned into the wood. Georgiana nodded appreciatively. Blackwell snapped the tip back together.

"You have taken me by surprise, Miss Knight." Blackwell gestured for them to continue their walk. "Though I should have suspected. A most brilliant ruse, saying you had gone off for treatment for consumption. Genius, truly. I can only imagine the things you have done for Lord Zeus."

"Yes, my experiences of the past year have been decidedly beyond the scope of most young ladies."

Somehow she managed to say the sentence with a straight face. Blackwell merely tugged on his lacy sleeves and shot her a self-satisfied look.

"Well, I am most absurdly glad you are here. You have been doing your assignment admirably. I never suspected you."

Her *assignment*?

Somehow, this just kept getting better and better.

Blackwell was continuing on. "It will be a pleasure to watch a master at work. I admit, when Lord Zeus gave me the task of preventing Stratton from marrying before his twenty-seventh birthday, I felt all hope was lost. How was it to be accomplished? But, as you well know, Lord Zeus can be most persuasive. Without the money from Lord Stratton, well . . ." He stared off into the distance and then swallowed. "There were some indiscretions in my youth. We all have our secrets, don't we?"

Georgiana nodded in agreement. So Blackwell needed the money from Sebastian to pay off Lord Zeus? He was being blackmailed.

"I am here now to ensure all goes smoothly, Lord Blackwell," she said in her most soothing tone.

He breathed a visible sigh of relief.

"I am most glad to hear it," he said. "If I may ask, what is your current plan of attack?"

Drat.

Georgiana drew in a sharp breath and pondered the greenery, as if deciding to share a secret. In reality, her thoughts scattered trying to find something, anything to say.

What *was* her plan of attack?

"Of course, I do not assume you must take me into your confidence," Blackwell said in a rush. Bless him for coming to her rescue.

"Naturally. I assure you, Lord Blackwell, I have the entire situation well in hand."

He let out a breath. "You have been doing an excellent job of distracting Lord Stratton from the other ladies. I can guess you intend to pretend to fall for his advances, string him along and then jilt him at the altar. Is that correct?"

Ah. That sounded like a *splendid* plan.

How kind of Blackwell to suggest it.

Georgiana nodded, suppressing a smile.

"You are most perceptive, my lord." Time to fish for more information. "If I may ask, when did you last see Lord Zeus?"

Blackwell drew in a hissing breath.

"You have actually *seen* him?" he asked, his eyes widening. "I have only ever received letters and visits from his man of business, if you could call him such. Heavens! I had not realized you were so highly valued. I thought no one ever saw him, that his identity was completely secret. Thank you for your help. I know my very life depends on the success of this enterprise. Lord Zeus is not kind to those who disappoint him."

Georgiana only barely suppressed a shivery shudder.

"Well, we shall do our best, shall we not, to ensure success?" she said, giving a comforting smile. Blackwell managed a tentative grimace in return.

A crunch on the gravel behind them announced the footman, informing them that luncheon was to be served.

Georgiana contemplated Blackwell over cool cucumber soup and roasted partridges.

She was officially a double-agent!

And she had thought a silly drawing of a bloodied dagger to be thrilling. This was utterly *stupendous!*

If only Sebastian were back. What would he make of it all?

Gah! But she wanted to talk to him right now. How long before telephones would be invented?

After all their guests had departed, Georgiana escaped to her room. Pulling out her tablet, she added the whole episode to her *My Mysterious Love Letter* list.

12. *The note I found in the garden is a code for identifying a secret organization run by someone named Lord Zeus. Lord Blackwell has connections with Zeus and displays the Jupiter/Zeus symbol on his walking stick. Who is Lord Zeus?*

13. *Blackwell implied he is being blackmailed by Zeus and needs money to pay him—money Blackwell must not currently have.*

14. *Consequently, Blackwell must prevent Sebastian from marrying, thereby ensuring Blackwell receives twenty thousand pounds of the gooseberry money. He will then use the money to pay off his debt to Lord Zeus. Or something like that. Lord Zeus is aiding him in his efforts to do this.*

15. *I am now officially a double agent. Eeek!*

So many questions. Who was Lord Zeus? Why did he want Sebastian's and then Blackwell's money? Did Lord Zeus have a personal vested interest in this too?

And perhaps most important of all:

Who was the agent Lord Zeus *had* sent?

Chapter 13

On the lane near Duir Cottage
Haldon Manor
September 15, 1813
Birthday in minus 23 days

"Meet me at noon along the road by the second bridge," she had whispered while leaving the breakfast room, her breath a teasing whorl around his ear.

He was not one to disobey.

Sebastian walked quickly down the long drive leading to Haldon Manor. He had barely seen Georgiana since arriving home late the previous night, but he was most anxious to chat with her. Which was good, as she seemed eager to speak with him.

He had spent the last few days trying to chase down more information about Georgiana's year away. Nothing had been forthcoming.

Phillips and the Bow Street Runner had been unable to find her name on any ship passenger list. Nor did inquiries produce a pseudonym that matched her description.

It was literally as if she had disappeared the previous summer and then reappeared just a few weeks ago.

And then there was the elusive Shatner D'Avery. All inquiries hit a dead end with him too. It was clear that either the man courted Georgiana under a false name or did not, in fact, exist at all.

Sebastian was inclined to believe the latter. Given her reticence to speak of D'Avery, Georgiana had obviously made him up in an attempt to dissuade Sebastian from courting her.

But why? Did she really dislike the idea of marrying him that much? His pride smarted at the thought. He knew he had his faults, but was he truly so unlovable?

He had sent Phillips after a couple more leads which might yet yield answers, but he had little faith. Phillips had begged to return to Haldon Manor with him, obviously tired of the futile chase. But Sebastian wanted to cover every possibility.

The easiest task would be to get an accounting from Georgiana herself. As far as he was concerned, she had some serious explaining to do. And, this time, he *would* get answers.

He actually didn't care what her answers were. He just wanted them to be honest ones.

Even though he had only been gone for little more than three days, he had missed her. How was it possible she had become even more vital to him? More important to his happiness than ever?

And what was he going to do when she married someone else? Lock himself up in Stratton Hall and become an eccentric dedicated to gooseberries like the previous earl?

Coming around a curve in the small road, he saw her, framed by trees, pacing across the bridge.

Lovely. So lovely.

Her white walking dress seemed to be made of flowy fine muslin but with a subtle sheen he had never known muslin to have. A teal-blue velvet spencer sat atop the dress, ending just below her ribcage, the color perfectly matched the embroidered ribbons in her jaunty bonnet. The jacket hugged her body, revealing womanly curves that the girl he knew had never had.

She was still slender, but no trace of the girl clung to her.

Their relationship was on a precipice. She was keeping secrets from him, and he needed answers. With his birthday less than a month away, time was short.

A week. He had given himself just one more week to win Georgiana Knight.

Somehow he had to convince her to *see* him. To look into his soul and notice something worth having.

If he was unsuccessful, he would need to consider the other marriage options before him. One of the Miss Burbanks, perhaps?

His future suddenly floated before his eyes, full of tepid discussions over paper filigree. Not to mention Lady Michael as a mother-in-law.

He barely suppressed a shudder.

His boots scuffed along the path, and Georgiana turned at the sound. Her wide, glorious smile spread resplendently across her face.

His breath caught.

Sunshine. Even on this gray, English day.

A treacherous part of his heart whispered that the warmth of her welcome was unique. That her light shone for him.

Traitorous, wicked heart.

Wanting and needing. *Hoping.*

He took a fortifying breath as he came nearer to her.

"Sebastian." She hurried forward, her smile somehow broader still. Stopping in front of him, she clasped his hands. "I am so glad you have come. I have so much to tell you!"

Even through both their gloves, the heat of her grasp scorched.

"Wonderful," he replied, "as I wish to speak with you, as well."

She took a step sideways and looked past him, along the lane toward Haldon Manor.

"Did anyone follow you?" she asked.

"Ah, ever concerned about my spotless reputation, my little chaperone." He winked at her.

She rolled her eyes. "Please. I just have so much to talk about. I don't want to be interrupted."

Still holding one hand, she pulled him off the main road and onto a smaller lane that Sebastian knew led to the shuttered dower house.

"Have a care, Georgie," he said, unable to stop his grin. "What will people think if they see you dragging me into the woods? 'Tis shocking."

Deliberately, he leaned his weight backward a smidge. Just enough so that she had to lean forward to keep him coming along with her.

Grasping his hand even tighter.

"Oh stop! You know it's no such thing!" she laughed but continued to tug him along behind her.

"Upon my honor, Miss Knight, this begins to seem somewhat compromising." He mock-fanned with his free hand, as if waiving off a fit of vapors. "You are proving yourself a terrible chaperoner."

Shaking her head, Georgiana stopped and faced him. Eyes full of laughter, the blue of her jacket mimicking their color.

"Chaperoner? I am quite sure that is *not* a word." She arched an eyebrow skeptically.

He held her hand even tighter between them and drew her another step closer to him, her skirts brushing against his boots. He leaned down, as if telling a secret.

"Indeed? I understand the remarkably dashing new Earl of Stratton has made the word fashionable and—"

"Remarkably *dashing*? Really?"

He nodded, eyes innocently wide. "Have you not heard? I thought you read the broadsheets?"

She pursed her ever-so-kissable lips.

"Impossible man," she muttered and turned, continuing to drag him along the lane.

He smiled broadly at her back, genially going along with her.

"I am just saying you need to be a better gooseberrier, is all," he said after a moment.

"Gooseberrier?" She glanced back at him. "Is that another word the—uhm—*dashing* Earl of Stratton has decided to inflict upon polite society?"

He feigned astonishment. "Why, yes, indeed it is. You are most perceptive, Miss Knight. If you were to meet the man, I am sure you would agree he is the most debonair—"

"Enough, Sebastian," she laughed, stopping in the road.

She still held his hand.

"Please be serious. You did make me promise to tell you if anything new happened, right?"

Sebastian instantly stilled.

"Have you received more notes? More threatening drawings?" He tugged on their joined hands, pulling her closer to him. Wanting to draw her all the way into his arms.

"No, no more threats, but the most interesting development." Her words slowed, and she glanced down at their joined hands.

Before she thought to pull away, he smoothly transitioned her hand to the crook of his elbow and gestured for them to continue walking.

"Tell me," he encouraged.

"Have you ever heard of anyone called Lord Zeus?"

He frowned. "No, I haven't. What has happened?"

He listened as she breathlessly relayed her story: seeing a symbol on the garden wall, quilling the symbol onto a board, having the odd conversation with Blackwell and his disclosure about Lord Zeus. And then, finally, Blackwell's assumption that she was in league with this Lord Zeus to stop Sebastian's marriage.

By the time Georgiana finished, all the hair on his neck stood on end.

"Isn't it just so exciting?" she asked, practically skipping along beside him.

They had come upon a large opening in the trees. The dower house sat in the middle of the meadow, encircled by a low, stone fence with a stable behind. A small oak, newly planted, stood in the side garden to the right.

He stopped in the lane and pasted on his sternest look. "No, Georgiana, it is not exciting. It is terrifying. You seem to have stumbled upon a deep game Blackwell is playing with some shadowy figure who is obviously up to no good."

"Exactly!" She bounced up and down on her toes, her eyes lively.

Maddening. *Lovely.* But utterly maddening.

"Georgiana—" he began, resisting the urge to hold his head in his hands. "Look, you cannot get further involved with this. I have half a mind to bundle you off to one of my estates far away from here and keep you safe until—"

"Don't you dare! This is the most fun I have had in ages, and until I get to the bottom of why this whole Lord Zeus thing matters—"

"Matters? It doesn't matter. It has nothing to do with you. Or it *had* nothing until you went and inserted yourself into the mess—"

"What makes you so sure this has nothing to do with me? Maybe it does. Maybe I have things that prove—"

"What things? What do you have?"

She froze, eyes impossibly wide. Caught.

"Georgiana, you are keeping far too many secrets from me. I need there to be some honesty between us. Please."

She swallowed and darted a glance at the dower house.

Silence.

"Look, I don't know where you have been for the past year, but we both know it most likely wasn't Italy. You are here and whole and for that I am grateful, but I just want to know the truth.

"Seb, I haven't lied—"

"Enough. I don't care what your answers are. Truly I don't. Please. Trust me. Confide in me."

Slowly, he gave her his melting smile. That lazy, smoldering expression his sisters assured him was lethal to the hearts of young ladies everywhere.

It was the last weapon in his arsenal.

How he hoped it would work.

Had he always smiled like that? Georgiana wondered.

Slow and warm, spreading like honey.

That smile took charm to a new level.

It did something to her knees. Not exactly melty, though they were most certainly a little more relaxed. Somewhat wobbly.

That smile chased all coherent thought from her brain.

"I have been to Italy," was all she could muster.

He nodded, the smile still pasted on his face. All charm and ease, as usual.

"Italy. You have already asserted that in the past." He nodded. "Would you care to elaborate more? How did you find the journey? What ship transported you?"

He rolled his hand. *Go on.*

She paused and glanced at Duir Cottage. She hadn't realized this was her destination.

That she would have to tell him everything.

The house hadn't changed much over the intervening two hundred years. Golden stone with a gabled roof and peaked front door. Ivy starting to grow up its walls.

It stood where once an ancient oak tree guarded the time portal. The tree was no longer, but its wood had been used to construct the house. The front door paid homage to the old oak with a stylized tree carved into its warm surface. The branches of the etching curved sinuously across the panel, bending and twisting.

Suddenly, she *wanted* Sebastian to know. The thought surprised even her. She wanted him to understand her and what had happened over the past year. Wanted to pull her phone out of her stays and take a photo of him, wanted to march him down to the cellar of Duir Cottage and let him feel the powerful thrum of the portal.

He was her friend. He would believe her, right?

He noticed her studying the cottage. With her hand still tucked into his elbow, he led her over to the stone fence surrounding the house.

Calmly, he removed his gloves and then his beaver hat, dropping his gloves inside and placing his hat on top of the fence.

Unbidden, Georgiana watched his hands as he did this. Long fingered and elegant, yet broad through the palm. Strong. She could see the callouses on his palms, evidence his life had not always been one of ease.

And when had he become so striking?

His brown eyes pools of warmth, side whiskers cutting narrow and thin across his cheeks. Hair a light chestnut color, glinting with hints of red and gold. Broad shoulders filling out his tight green coat. Spotless white cravat at his throat.

Georgiana was quite sure every member of her Bosom Companions of the English Regency reenactment group would go into a collective swoon at the sight of him.

She barely repressed a sigh herself.

This was just Sebastian, she reminded herself. Not a handsome leading man from a BBC costume drama, no matter how much he looked the part.

He leaned back and half sat on the stone fence, bracing his hands to either side, legs extended in front. Lowering himself just enough to be more eye level with her.

He lifted a questioning eyebrow, mistaking her silence for reticence.

"Georgie, please. You could have been on the *moon*, for all I care. I just want truth."

She studied him. That small freckle next to his left eye. The slight curl in his hair as it fell on his forehead in the Caesar haircut he favored. The shadow of stubble already touching his cheeks.

"And if I say I was on the moon?"

"Is that the truth?"

She smiled, a mirthless, sad little thing. "No, but the truth is no less strange. Are you sure you want to know?"

His gaze turned wistful. "I just want honesty between us."

She stared sightlessly at Duir Cottage. Where to begin with her tale?

"Shall I tell you my guesses? Will that make things easier?" he asked.

He surprised a laugh out of her.

As if!

"Please, be my guest, Sebastian. I assure you, the truth has probably not occurred to you, but I'm curious to see what you think."

His expression was decidedly skeptical. "Well, I cannot say I have a clear idea of where you have been. I do, however, know what is *not* true."

"All right. Let's start with that."

"Shatner D'Avery—ridiculous name, by the way—does not, in fact, exist."

"Of course, he exists."

"Georgiana, please, give it a rest. I thought we had agreed to be honest with each other." His voice ever so quiet. "There is no solicitor in London who goes by the absurd name of Shatner D'Avery. I had a Bow Street Runner look into it."

She stared at him, her stunned eyes eloquent.

"You did what? Why would you do *that?*" Her voice climbed with each question.

"Because I wanted to see who you would choose to marry. I guess I wanted to assure myself this D'Avery fellow was worthy of you."

"Despite all your affection, I am *not* your sister and—"

"Does Arthur know about this D'Avery?"

"Naturally."

"And has *he* inquired after the man?"

She stared at him.

"Honestly, I cannot for the life of me understand what this has to do with anything, Sebastian."

"This is your *life* we are talking about, the man you are supposedly considering marrying, and yet every time I try to get a straight answer—"

"What do you want to know? Yes, I had consumption. Yes, I was gone for a year. Yes, I was cured by miraculous medicine. Yes, I visited some remarkable places: most of Europe, including Italy, America, the Bahamas. I even made it as far as Thailand—I mean, Siam—"

"Enough, Georgiana!"

He pushed off of the wall and came to his full height. Held up a hand, cutting her off.

Suddenly he was the menacing man from the rose bedroom: tall, broad, pulsing with barely leashed power.

All traces of the charming, happy-go-lucky boy gone.

He stared at her—dark, brooding—eyes intent.

Her breath caught.

"Give it up, will you please? We both know you could not have traveled to so many places in a single year. Europe is in chaos, torn apart by war. A boat to Siam alone would take well over a year there and back. Not to mention the French naval blockade. Why do you not tell me—"

"The answer is difficult. It's hard to explain—"

"Try. I'm an intelligent man. Use small sentences if you must."

"Sebastian—"

"If there is to be any hope of a future marriage between us, there needs to be honesty—"

"Pardon? Sebastian, let me repeat one more time. There is *not* going to be a marriage between us. After all my refusals and protestations, why do you keep *hoping* this will happen?"

He flinched at those words, something close to pain flickering in his eyes.

"Give over, Georgie. Am I so abhorrent you cannot stomach the thought of being with me? That you feel the need to make up absurd stories and a fictional betrothed to keep me at a distance?" With a deep breath, he ran a drained hand over his face, pinching the bridge of his nose again.

"No—Seb, that is not it at all. I am telling you the truth—"

"You would be a *countess*, married to a man who will do everything to ensure your happiness—"

"How can you know what will bring me happiness? I am a grown woman, not the thirteen-year-old girl you knew!"

He raised his head and fixed her with such a . . . *look.*

Fierce and intense.

"Yes . . . well, life changes us all, Georgiana. I am not that sixteen-year-old boy. Consider me a battle-toughened soldier. One who has endured a decade of life without you and, yet, still fights on."

Her old friend vanished. Utterly gone.

And in his place was this man of power. An *earl.* A man who had commanded troops in the army. A man who sat in the House of Lords and oversaw thousands of servants and tenants.

She stilled, her throat tight.

He reached out a hand and brushed a stray curl off her cheek, his fingers grazing her face.

His touch *scalded.* Robbed her of breath.

Georgiana felt the axis of her world tilt. He was so much the same and yet so different.

So strong, so sure. Dangerous.

Thrilling.

That last thought terrified. Not the good kind of terrified that tingled her spine and made her giggle.

Terrified terrified.

Because he couldn't be *this* man.

One who made her feel tingly. Hitched her breath.

Sent bubbles floating through her blood.

He was . . . Just. Sebastian.

Nothing more . . . right?

Because if she felt like this about Sebastian, then life suddenly became much more complicated with worrisome, difficult decisions. Feelings which could lead to having her heart split across centuries.

Something she promised she *would* not do.

A dreadfully possible impossibility.

They stared at each other for a long minute, breath sounding loudly. His dark eyes liquid, fathomless. Consuming.

A glimpse into his soul.

She was surprised to find it a cluttered place. Full of contradictions and darkness and pain she didn't understand.

She felt like she was surveying him for the first time.

Truly *seeing* him.

And what she saw . . . well . . . was beautiful. It was that simple.

He was gorgeous.

All of him.

Her gaze dropped to his mouth.

How would his kiss feel? To have the breadth of those large shoulders surround her and hold her close?

To *know* tangibly he breathed only for her?

Her breath snagged.

His gaze had turned ferocious, consuming. The dark man who trapped her in moonlit rooms.

Unbidden, she drifted toward him. Closed the remaining space between them.

"Georgiana?" he whispered as her skirts swept against his legs.

His hand brushed her elbow, searing through the layers of fabric, and then wrapped around her waist, drawing her nearer still. Swallowing her up in his arms.

She placed a hand on his chest. Slowly rose onto tiptoes, eyes fluttering closed.

She could feel his breath on her cheek.

On her lips.

So close.

So impossibly close . . .

"Yoohoo! Lord Stratton!"

A bright chipper voice broke through the surrounding forest. Followed by the yipping of a small dog.

Shattering the silence.

Startled, Georgiana jumped back, her chest heaving, eyes saucer-wide.

Sebastian swore and glanced toward the sound.

"Blast! That impossible woman—I cannot endure—"

"Go." Georgiana grabbed his hat and gloves off of the wall and pushed him toward the cottage. "I'll deal with her."

He stared at her for one more moment, eyes drifting down to her mouth, his chest rising as quickly as hers.

She shoved his hat into his chest and made a shooing motion with her hands.

"Go!"

Chapter 14

Lady Ambrosia burst from the trees along the lane, a billow of pale-green low-cut muslin, golden hair peeking out from underneath her bonnet. Mr. Snickers wiggled in her arms, his matching green knitted shirt bunching around his neck.

Georgiana folded her hands at her waist and tried to slow her pounding heart as Lady Ambrosia drew near.

Had that really almost happened?

She would probably *still* be kissing Sebastian without Lady Ambrosia's timely interference.

Or was it not-so-timely?

She couldn't decide.

Kissing Sebastian . . .

His powerful arms around her, the racing pulse of his heart under her hand. So warm, so safe. She swallowed and tried to clear her brain.

She had a *boyfriend.* Did that count for nothing? Was she really the kind of woman who would commit herself to one man and then kiss another?

With an inward sigh, she recognized she very well might be.

What did that say about her? What did that say about her commitment to Shatner?

She was an awful person.

Part of her wanted to march into Duir Cottage, through the portal and leave this confusing mess of emotions behind.

Of course, the other part of her wanted to send Lady Ambrosia on her way and pick up with Sebastian where they had left off.

Dratted man was too handsome and charming for his own good.

Gah! She needed to *stop*!

This was Sebastian, her friend.

Even if she *was* the sort to kiss around, Sebastian deserved better than to be so trifled with.

She fixed a weak smile on her face.

"Well met, Miss Knight," Lady Ambrosia said, stopping in front of her and then glancing around. "Heavens! I thought I saw Lord Stratton with you too. I had a most important question to ask him."

"As you can see, I am currently quite alone." Georgiana kept her expression vague and unassuming.

Lady Ambrosia brought her gaze back to Georgiana and pursed her lips, studying her.

"What is your game, Miss Knight?" she asked.

Georgiana's eyebrows inched upward.

"Game, my lady? I cannot say I have any game—"

"Come now, there is no need to be coy with me. You have Lord Stratton panting after you, and yet you continue to keep him at arm's length. It is a dangerous dance you play."

"Truly, I do not understand your meaning, Lady Ambrosia. Lord Stratton is merely an old friend." Georgiana pasted on her most vapid look.

Lady Ambrosia's eyes narrowed.

"I wonder very much if I haven't been mistaken about you, Miss Knight," she said after a minute.

A beat of silence.

Lifting her head and studying the gray clouds, Lady Ambrosia continued, "I fear a storm. I thought perhaps I heard thunder and saw the threat of lightning earlier."

Georgiana stared at her, a sudden suspicion forming. "Indeed," she replied. "Perhaps a lightning bolt will strike us, much as the eagle's cry . . ."

Georgiana paused, watching Lady Ambrosia's expression pale as the words sunk in.

Bullseye.

It seemed she had found the original 'helper' sent by Lord Zeus.

Lady Ambrosia's jaw tightened. The woman did have some pluck.

"Lord Stratton is my task, not yours," Lady Ambrosia lifted her chin.

"Perhaps." Georgiana coolly nodded her head.

Silence hung for a moment, stretching the tension.

"But is it perhaps possible Lord Zeus has become disillusioned with your abilities?" Georgiana asked.

Lady Ambrosia sucked in a hissing breath. It had been strictly a guess on Georgiana's part, but an accurate one, it seemed.

Lady Ambrosia licked her lips nervously, glancing about.

"What has he said about me? Please, you must tell me."

The poor woman was suddenly terrified. Even little Mr. Snickers trembled in his green sweater.

Was Lord Zeus as scary as all that?

Georgiana smoothed her face, not wanting to reveal anything.

"Unfortunately, I cannot say, Lady Ambrosia. As you well know, Lord Zeus does not countenance those who break his confidences."

"Oh dear, oh dear, oh dear," Lady Ambrosia murmured, lifting Mr. Snickers and burying her distress in his neck.

The woman's anxiety was so real. Georgiana felt a twinge of something that smacked suspiciously of guilt.

She hadn't meant to upset her. "Come now, there is no need to worry so."

Lady Ambrosia lifted her head, her eyes filled with horror.

"Worry? I am hardly worried, Miss Knight. I am terrified. You know what *he* is capable of. We could both so easily end up like that unfortunate Miss Franklin, tossed off a castle wall. Lord Zeus does not tolerate failure of any sort."

Georgiana blinked. The conversation had suddenly gone to a dark place.

Kill them?

"I had so hoped my artistic skills would continue to be of use to Lord Zeus, just as Miss Franklin's were. She only ran into trouble when she refused to help him any more. Oh dear, what are we ever to do?" Lady Ambrosia cuddled Mr. Snickers even tighter.

"Must something be done?"

Lady Ambrosia grabbed her arm.

"Of course! You musn't fail us, Miss Knight. You must *stop* Lord Stratton from marrying. Please. My life . . . *your* life depends upon it."

Sebastian peered surreptitiously out the front window of Duir Cottage. Lady Ambrosia was still talking with Georgiana, clinging to her arm.

How long would Lady Ambrosia keep her?

Georgiana shook her head and replied to some question.

Stepping back from the window, he began to pace the floor of the front parlor.

Lovely Georgiana. Dearest, sweetest Georgiana. So close! It had been so close.

And she had come to *him*. At last.

He had seen the change in her, the instant he had touched her petal soft cheek. Her eyes had narrowed, focused. As if *finally* truly seeing him.

His blood had shouted hosannas through his veins.

And then her eyes dropping to stare at his lips until he thought he would go *mad*.

He could still see her, closing the distance between them, placing her hand firmly on his lapels, the rise of her body against his chest as she stretched on tiptoe to meet his mouth . . .

And then that woman had to appear.

Blast!

Would he ever get the moment back?

He paused in front of the small fireplace, placing a hand on the mantle, staring sightlessly at the barren grate.

And what about that ridiculous nonsense with Lord Zeus? He needed to get her away from here, if only to protect her. He made a mental note to send a Runner to inquire after Lord Zeus.

How much wasn't she telling him?

"Georgiana!" A voice shouted.

A man's voice—muffled and yet distinct.

Puzzled, Sebastian cocked his head. The sound seemed to be coming from the back of the house. Was Knight calling his sister?

Sebastian walked down the central hallway with its L-shaped staircase and through a door into the kitchen and scullery. An enormous fireplace dominated the left of the room. He peered through the back door but could see nothing.

"Georgiana!" The voice called again, this time accompanied by the sound of knocking. However, the voice had moved and now came from the front of the cottage. Had someone walked around the house?

He moved back out into the hallway and into the front parlor. Pushing apart the curtains, he could still see Lady Ambrosia gesturing to Georgiana. Neither of them had moved.

"Georgiana!" Again, coming from the back of the house.

What—?!

What was going on? Was he hearing things now too?

He walked down the hallway, stopping midway.

Waited for a moment.

"Georgiana Knight, so help me!" The words were muffled but still clear.

And coming from neither the front nor back of the house, but a closet under the stairs.

Again, he heard the knocking.

That was . . . odd.

Was Georgiana now keeping prisoners? Was that part of what she hadn't told him?

Sebastian resisted the urge to roll his eyes skyward, pleading for patience.

He wouldn't put it past her.

Opening the door, he peered inside. It was a typical closet, full of linens and bottles.

The pounding seemed to be coming from underneath the floor. Pushing aside a basket of sheets, he noticed a trapdoor leading, most likely, to a cellar.

"Hello? Anyone there?" he called.

Nothing.

But the pounding continued. Faint, as if far away.

But definitely coming from the floor.

How could that be?

Sebastian pushed more baskets out of the way and wrested the trap door open. A simple staircase descended into the gloom.

"Hello?" he called again.

Nothing.

Or was there nothing?

Squinting into the darkness, something faintly flickered.

Carefully, he descended the stairs, his boots hitting packed dirt. From what he could see, the cellar was small, only a couple paces wide with a ceiling so low he had to duck his head.

Blinking, he tried to focus on the barely-there light. It was only just discernible but seemed to be coming from the wall directly ahead.

A certain heaviness settled on him. The air felt weighty. Charged.

Odd.

Frowning, he took a step and then another. Something seemed to tug him forward. The room suddenly went darker, and vertigo swamped him. He felt like he was falling, falling, falling.

Gasping, Sebastian reached out a hand, managing after a second to brace himself on the side wall.

Shaking his head, he stood for a few seconds, gulping in deep breaths, trying to clear the dizziness.

What had happened there?

"Georgiana!" the voice called again. This time much nearer. Clearer.

And coming from upstairs.

How——?!

Thoroughly confused, Sebastian turned and walked back up the stairs and into the hallway, his head still spinning.

Everything felt a little off-kilter. Like the world had tilted on its axis. Disconcerting.

Someone was pounding on the front door.

"Georgiana! Open this door! I know you're home. Your damn car is in the driveway!"

The solid oak door trembled, fists buffeting it.

Pausing, Sebastian stared.

A short bar secured the upper part of the door. Had the bolt been there before?

Rattled, he drew it back and opened the door.

To a different world.

A man stood on the stoop. Medium height and lean, dark brown hair hanging over his ears, face stubbled as if it hadn't seen a razor all week. Gray eyes snapping in anger.

They stared at each other for the space of a heartbeat. The warrior in Sebastian immediately bristled.

"Who the bloody hell are you?" the man asked after a moment. "Where's Georgiana?"

It was impossibly rude.

The man's accent indicated he was a gentleman. His clothing, however, defied categorization.

He was wearing some kind of dark blue pantaloons with a simple white shirt without buttons and a tight-fitting short brown leather jacket. And were those dark spectacles resting atop his head?

Donning his authoritarian face—the one which had sent enlisted men running in the army and servants scurrying to do an earl's bidding—Sebastian ruthlessly surveyed the insolent man, letting his gaze wander slowly from head to toe.

"May I help you?" Sebastian asked in quelling tones.

With a cocky lift of his eyebrows, the man returned the arrogant perusal in full measure. And then gave a deliberate, mocking smile.

"You must be one of Georgiana's Bosom Companion friends. Nice." He gestured toward Sebastian's coat. Sebastian resisted the urge to smooth his waistcoat and straighten his jacket.

Instead, he asked, "And you are?"

"Her boyfriend." The man stared at him, cool and collected.

Boyfriend? The word made no sense.

Allowing his lip to curl slightly, Sebastian gave the man his most haughty nod.

"Indeed. The Right Honorable Sebastian Carew, Earl of Stratton, at your service." He paused allowing his title to sink in. What was the point of being an earl if one couldn't occasionally fling it about?

Instead of being properly cowed, the man guffawed and rolled his eyes.

"Ooooh, pardon me, *your lordship,*"—he waved his hands to his side, as if astounded—"but I'm here to see Georgiana."

He moved to step around Sebastian.

Without thinking, Sebastian blocked his path.

"Miss Knight is not at home," he said icily.

"*Miss* Knight?" The man laughed, as if Georgiana's name were a great joke. "Seriously, you need to get with reality. I swear all this reen-actment stuff goes to the head."

Sebastian wanted to haul him up by his scruffy jacket and shake him.

No, that wasn't true.

He *wanted* to beat him to a pulp.

He settled, instead, for jabbing a hostile finger into the man's chest, forcing him back.

"You, sirrah, will take yourself off. As I have said, Miss Knight is not at home and—"

"Georgiana!" the man said in relief, looking over Sebastian's shoulder.

Sebastian swiveled to see Georgiana herself standing behind him, a strained smile pasted on her face. She looked at Sebastian and then at the man on the stoop, giving a nervous laugh.

"Shatner," she said, moving around Sebastian and out the door.

The man instantly wrapped her into a tight embrace.

An embrace that Georgiana returned.

So *this* was the mysterious Shatner D'Avery.

This was who she preferred over him. This scrawny, belligerent, impolite *man*?

Sebastian was quite sure D'Avery did not deserve the label gentleman.

"Georgie, where have you been? I've been crazy waiting to hear from you, luv," Shatner murmured to her.

Sebastian was going to be ill, toss his accounts right here in the front garden. After coming so near to kissing her less than an hour ago, his heart slammed back to the ground with a thud.

It hurt like hell—hitting reality this hard.

Shatner pulled Georgiana away from him, surveying her muslin dress with its teal-blue velvet spencer and the jaunty bonnet on her head.

"Is this one of your Bosom Companion meetings?" he asked. "I've been banging on your door for the last ten minutes at least. Why haven't you returned my texts? I nearly *called* you, I was so desperate!"

Uncomfortable, Sebastian looked past them and, for the first time, really took stock of his surroundings.

The house was the same and yet completely not. The front door seemed unchanged with its sinuous carving of an oak tree. But the yard had altered. The stone fence was worn and covered in moss and a huge oak tree arched over the house. Ivy chased across the cottage's golden stone and the front garden was a riot of roses, lavender and wildflowers.

Even more oddly, two carriages sat along the gravel drive, all shiny metal and gleaming glass, with small wheels which left the vehicles perilously close to the ground. Where were the horses to pull them? Sebastian glanced around, but he could see no stables nor any sign of a groom or coachman.

It was surreally odd.

"So who's your friend?" D'Avery's question brought Sebastian back to them.

Shatner stood with one arm wrapped possessively around Georgiana's waist, snugging her tightly against his body. For her part, Georgiana had her arm wrapped around him and a smile planted firmly on her face.

Sebastian couldn't tell if she was relieved or panicked.

She did not, however, seem to mind that Shatner's hand was now making small, caressing circles on her hip.

Jealousy tasted metallic and bitter, choking in its potency.

Sebastian wanted to punch D'Avery, if only to wipe the smirky smile off his face.

"How silly of me!" Georgiana said, stepping out of D'Avery's embrace and moving to hold his hand instead. "Shatner, this is an old childhood friend, Sebastian Carew. Sebastian, this is Shatner D'Avery."

They eyed each other. Sebastian knew he should say something polite in greeting.

He *knew* he should. But he didn't.

The pause lingered a little too long.

"Nice one, saying you were an earl," D'Avery said into the silence. Turning to Georgiana, he continued, "He said he was an earl. Is he part of your reenactment group?"

Georgiana's eyes widened, and she gave an uneasy laugh edged with consternation.

"Something like that," she replied and then glanced at Sebastian with a pleading look. "Would you mind giving me a moment, Sebastian?"

Yes, he *did* mind and he most certainly didn't want to leave her alone with D'Avery.

But being a gentleman to the core, he gave them both a stiff little bow and turned back into the house.

As he did so, he heard Shatner say, "That guy is awesome, with the bowing and everything—"

Sebastian shut the front door. If only to muffle Shatner's incomprehensible comments.

He rubbed a hand over his face and, closing his eyes, massaged the bridge of his nose.

What was going on here?

He still felt dizzy and disoriented. Like a nightmare where everything was familiar and yet not.

Opening his eyes, he surveyed the hallway. It seemed the same. Soft, worn oak covered almost every inch of the walls. The entryway was paneled in the honey-colored wood, as was the parlor to the left of the central hallway.

But it was different. The floors were worn and not level. Odd fixtures hung from the ceiling. He walked down the hallway and glanced at the still open closet, trying to understand.

What had happened? He had gone down into the cellar, felt dizzy and then come back up.

That was all.

And yet somehow everything had changed.

He moved farther down the hall and into the back where the kitchen and scullery had been.

The room was altogether transformed. He blinked and glanced back into the hallway, just to convince himself he was in the same house.

He was.

Turning, he surveyed the room.

The enormous fireplace still dominated the left side of the space, but that was the only recognizable feature. Instead of work baskets and cook pots, high wingback chairs now flanked the fireplace, facing an overstuffed sofa. A large, rough-hewn table with chairs stood in front of him. The entire back half of the house sported large windows that opened onto an overgrown back garden, flooding the room in light.

But, beyond that, he was at a loss.

The right of the room gleamed in marble and steel. A large pale marble-topped cabinet sat in the center of the space, and there seemed to be some sort of spigot over a sunken basin, but everything else was unknown and baffling. Large metal cabinets dotted the room, and strange objects cluttered the marble.

Bewildered, he walked around the table and took a seat at the opposite end so he could see down the hallway. Loosened his cravat and settled his head in his hands.

Waited for Georgiana to return and explain what in blazes was going on.

The front door opened and shut. He heard Georgiana's footsteps along the hallway and looked up as she entered the room.

They stared at each other for a tense moment. She took in a deep, shuddering breath—eyes shuttered and unreadable.

Georgiana broke first, shaking her head and walking to the table, stopping opposite him.

Lifting her left wrist, she undid the buttons of her kid glove, but her hands trembled, slowing her progress. Buttons undone, she tugged on each shaking finger. The leather whispered as she drew it off her hand and tossed it onto the table. She turned to her right hand and repeated the process, drawing the glove over her fine-boned fingers.

Then, she slowly untied her bonnet and set it on the table next to the gloves. Her blond hair shook loose a little, a few curls tumbling to frame her face.

Next, she unbuttoned her teal-blue spencer and, shrugging out of it, laid it next to her bonnet. Agitation evident in her rigid shoulders, in her tight breathing.

She sat down—slumped, actually, in a decidedly unladylike manner—into the chair at the opposite end of the table, lit in a pool of sunlight from the windows behind Sebastian.

She looked impossibly lovely in her flowing muslin dress, golden hair teasing around her face, blue eyes bright.

Like the woman he loved.

But he was not sure he *knew* her.

Not anymore.

Silence.

A sudden series of chirps and whistles shattered the quiet.

Bing. Chirp. Whip-woo.

What the—?!

With a grimace, Georgiana reached into her stays and pulled out a thin, rectangular object about size of her hand. Shaking her head again, she touched its surface. The noises instantly stopped. She laid the object down on the table.

Sebastian swallowed and lounged back in his chair, legs wide. Slouched, just like her. Drumming his fingers, giving her his most earlish stare.

He could wait her out.

She regarded him and then exhaled. Leaned forward to place her elbows on the table and sent her fingers into her hair, as if trying to hold some emotion inside.

"Heavens, what a horrid mess," she murmured, rubbing her neck, as if it ached.

She reached up and pulled out a hair pin, dropping it with a *ping* onto the table.

Two more followed. *Ping, ping.*

Still running her hands through her hair, she sighed. "Oh Seb, I am *so* incredibly sorry. What a horrid situation." She shot him a glance through her eyelashes.

Ping, ping, ping.

He continued to drum his fingers, not trusting himself to speak.

"Sebastian, I don't know—" she stopped and pulled a final pin out of her hair.

Ping.

Her glorious mass of golden hair tumbled loose, cascading across her shoulders and down her chest. With a weary sigh, she continued to massage her head.

Was the woman *trying* to drive him mad?

Vividly, he saw her walking into D'Avery's arms, resting with a hand casually around his waist.

Who *was* this woman? The one who let down her hair and slumped in chairs?

Where were they? And where was the Georgiana he knew?

She swallowed and fixed him with her blue, blue gaze.

"So remember what you said about the moon? How you wanted to know the truth?"

He nodded. A painful, stunned motion.

"Well, for the record, this is *not* the moon. But it is not far off."

She let out a long breath. Spread her arms wide, eyes soulful and intent.

"Let me be the first to welcome you to the future. Welcome to the twenty-first century."

Chapter 15

S ebastian's eyes widened at her statement.

Or, more aptly, bulged out of his head.

Whatever he had been expecting, Georgiana knew time travel was most definitely *not* it.

"Par—Pardon me?" he stuttered, shifting in his chair. "Is this yet another of your flights of fantasy, Georgiana?"

His dark eyes were shuttered. All traces of good humor and cheer gone.

In their place was the Earl of Stratton.

Intense, brooding.

Jaw clenched, side whiskers cutting across his cheeks, giving his face an almost devilish look.

He vibrated with leashed power.

Unbidden, she saw him again at the front door, staring at her and Shatner with hooded eyes. Bristling with aristocratic hauteur and confidence.

Seeing the two men together had been . . . surprising.

Shatner had seemed so small in comparison. And not just in stature.

She swallowed, forcing such thoughts away.

It had been *nice* to see Shatner. He was a *good* man.

Sebastian stared at her for another moment and then, shaking his head, he stood up and began to pace, his tense energy reverberating through the room. His large body *filled* the space, looking somehow completely at home in his tight green coat and elegant ivory waistcoat, boots clicking against the wood floor.

"I'm so sorry, Sebastian. I most certainly never expected you to get caught up in this mess. If it helps, I meant to tell you today. It was why I led you to the cottage . . ."

He looked around the room, taking in the kitchen with its stainless steel fridge and industrial gas range. The microwave blinking the time.

Then stopping, he turned to stare at her, resting a hand on the kitchen island, tapping fingers again.

"Do I know you?" The deep bass of his voice rumbled through her.

Georgiana gasped, her heart snagging in her throat.

Of all the *questions*—!

"Of course, you know me. We have both changed, Sebastian, but I am still the same intrinsic person."

His dark gaze snared her, emotions skittering across his face. Confusion, hurt . . . and something else deeper and more fathomless.

A beat.

"Are you? Or is the girl I knew just a facade?"

She blinked. "I am still Georgiana, Seb. I am sure your experiences as a soldier have changed you but—"

He snorted. "What an understatement—"

"Exactly. We were practically children the last time we knew each other. Both of us have experienced . . . *life* over the last decade. And the last year, in particular, has most definitely changed me. It's one of many reasons why I have resisted your persistent offers of marriage—"

He laughed at that.

A harsh quick sound. Devoid of any humor.

He turned his head, took a step toward the window. His jaw tensing, quivering.

Silence.

"Have I been a complete damn fool?" he asked after a minute. Voice hoarse. He leaned forward, hands braced on the counter under the window. Back to her.

She paused.

"No—not a fool—"

But she had hesitated a fraction too long before responding.

He made that sound again.

The laugh that was not a laugh.

His head hung forward, shaking back and forth.

Georgiana was not entirely sure if he was laughing or crying.

Perhaps a bit of both.

"You are *not* a fool." Georgiana stood and walked over, leaning on the opposite side of the kitchen island. "How could you have anticipated this reality? I have *lived* through it and can still scarcely believe it."

He seemed so . . . bereft. She ached to reach for him. To offer some sort of comfort. To feel his arms around her.

To have him understand.

"Sebastian, I was dying . . . No nineteenth century medicine could save me. It was my only option . . . coming here. The only way left to save my life."

"How—How did it happen?" His voice a choked whisper.

He lifted his head and turned around, facing her and planting his hands on the island. The expanse of cold, glittery marble between them.

Symbolic that.

He fixed his gaze on a point beyond her. Away. Refusing to look at her.

She stared at his hands resting on the hard white stone, fingers in agitated motion.

Long elegant fingers, broad palm. A hand that promised strength and kindness.

"There was an ancient oak tree on this spot that had guarded the portal since Roman times. But oak trees don't live forever and—and the portal was uncovered. James had this house built to protect the portal. I never intended to come here. That was not part of my plan. But I was so ill . . ."

She shifted her gaze to the windows behind his shoulders, remembering those awful and yet miraculous weeks over a year ago.

"I was barely conscious through the entire process. I have fleeting memories of the vertigo of the portal and then people everywhere, shouting orders. Sticking me with pins, whispering soothing words. I woke up in a white room with machines beeping all around, tubes poking in and out of me. It was not pleasant, but at least I felt no pain. I lay in that bed for a couple weeks while twenty-first century medicine worked a miracle."

She gave a small, little laugh. He still looked away, but his hand had stilled on the counter.

"I had been so ill, you see? *No one* expected me to live. Especially not myself. I had reconciled to the idea I would never marry, never have a family, never . . . never experience . . . romantic love. Never have a life full of hope and choice and options—"

"Oh, Georgie." He abruptly shifted his gaze, dark eyes drilling into hers. "I was prepared to offer you all of that. I fully expected to find you ill and dying when I came in search of you. I wanted to make the time you had remaining magical, to give you whatever bit of happiness I could . . ." He choked again and looked down at the counter, at the stone that separated them.

Unable to resist, Georgiana reached across and captured his hand in hers. He wrapped fingers around hers, engulfing her hand.

Warm and strong. True.

"Thank you." Her voice barely a whisper.

They both stared at their twined hands.

"I would have, you know. Married you. If you had found me ill and dying, if I had lived long enough. If I hadn't come here." A stuttering breath escaped her. "You were always the best of friends. So kind and thoughtful—"

He let out a short burst of air. His shoulders shrugged. Swallowed.

He traced the back of her hand with a single finger.

"But, being here has changed everything. I am whole and healthy and anything is possible again. James is here with Emme and—"

"Wait—James?!" His head snapped to attention. "Your brother James is here? He is not dead?"

"Oh, yes, did I not say that first? He deliberately left 1812, deciding instead to spend his life here. The future suits him better, and his wife, Emme, is from this century. Duir Cottage is actually his home now. Arthur placed the gravestone in order to provide closure and ensure he inherited the Knight estate as James' heir. James will never return to the past."

The news seemed to unsettle Sebastian. He stared again at their hands still entwined on the countertop, rubbed his thumb between her knuckles.

"So your brother is here, too." He did not look up from their hands. "James—the person you always claimed to be closest to in the whole world . . ."

She nodded. "Yes, he is here. Happy and whole. And with him choosing to stay here . . ." Sebastian raised his head, locked his eyes with hers. She licked her lips. "I cannot imagine leaving him and returning to live permanently in the nineteenth century . . ."

Her voice drifted into a whisper. His gaze snared her.

His eyes, in that moment . . .

Georgiana was quite sure she would always remember that look.

Haunted. Gutted.

As if she had *died*. Was dead to him.

Unbidden, it echoed through her too. Felt it all too keenly, as if he had wrapped her in the pain of his soul.

The tightness in her throat suffocated.

"I am so sorry, Sebastian. I know you need to marry and soon . . .

that you considered me your simplest option. I tried so hard to help you understand. I should have told you everything sooner. I just didn't know how to make you believe me . . ."

He dropped her hand and turned sideways, looking away, swallowing every now and again. Taut.

She couldn't bear it.

"Sebastian," she murmured and walked around the island to him.

Wanting—no, *needing*—to comfort him.

Without thought, she slipped her arms inside his coat, wrapped her arms about his waist and rested her cheek against his chest.

Holding him to her, *willing* him to give her some of his heartache.

His arms reflexively crushed around her, gathering her to him, burying his face in her hair. Her hands rested on his back, and she could feel his muscles twitch under his waistcoat, could hear the bellows of his lungs as he fought his emotions.

Why did his pain gut her so?

She melted into his warmth, his strength. Breathed him in, wool and starch and clean soap.

The smells of home.

But then he stiffened, brusquely pulling back and pushing her away.

"Enough." His voice hoarse and rough.

He took a step back, ran a shaking hand over his face. Placed his hands on his hips, staring at the floor.

Silence.

Then, he let out a long, shuddering breath. And lifted his head to look at her.

His jaw was still clenched, but he had mastered himself.

Taken all his emotion and reeled it back inside. Closing himself off.

Gave her his game, boyish Sebastian smile.

A smile that masked everything and gave nothing.

Had he *always* been able to do that? To hide himself like this?

How little she truly knew him.

But, suddenly, she wanted to know him so much more. Ached for it. To understand all the emotions that bound him.

"Enough, Georgiana. I appreciate your honesty with me throughout all of this. You insisted from the beginning there was never to be anything between us. I was wrong to doubt your understanding of the reality of the situation."

"Sebastian—"

He held out a staying hand, giving his head a sad shake.

"No, I understand. You have a life here and you want to stay. To be with James and his new wife, to continue your relationship with Shatner . . . To be with someone you view as more than just a *brother*." He imbued the last word with *such* irony. He took a deep breath. "I am sure, however, that you appreciate that this cannot be my life. I need to marry within the next few weeks. I am an earl and have tremendous responsibilities, a position within the government. Being part of something so much larger than myself . . . It is a worthy goal for my life."

"Sebastian, I am so sorry—"

"My dear, it is for the best. This battle weary soldier knows when to lift the flag of surrender. A clean break, as it were."

Swallowing, he grasped her hand and bowed, elegant and proper, over her knuckles.

But before releasing her hand, he raised it to his lips. Pressed a hot, scalding kiss on her fingers.

The shock of his warm mouth—Georgiana nearly gasped.

"Adieu, Miss Georgiana Elizabeth Augusta Knight."

With a smile, he released her hand and turned for the hallway and the stairs leading to the cellar.

Stunned, Georgiana felt her mouth move. But no words came. She watched him disappear down, and then her entire body came to life.

"Sebastian—" she cried, running across the kitchen, skittering down the steep cellar stairs.

Only to run into his solid chest in the darkness.

The portal pulsed and hummed in the dim light.

But it was closed.

For now, there would be no return.

For either of them.

Chapter 16

Sebastian followed Georgiana up the stairs and into the same strange room they had just left.

After his theatrically dramatic exit too.

It just figured.

He couldn't escape Georgiana Knight so easily.

Some diabolical god must find perverse joy in his misery, tethering him to her like this.

"Sebastian, I am so sorry," she murmured, turning to face him. "Obviously, I never meant for things to go like this. Look, take off your coat and boots. Be comfortable. I'm going to change my clothes, order Chinese takeaway and make us some tea. Then we can talk, okay?"

"Okay?"

She froze.

"It means . . . all right. Everything will be all right." She gave him a smile. Too bright, forced. "You'll see. Some low mein and a pot of Earl Grey will make everything better. Trust me."

"I haven't a clue what such things are . . ." He swallowed, still fighting a strange combination of hysteria and terror and loss.

"Tea. Tea and food." She gave that small smile again.

Walking over to the large table, she picked up the palm-size rectangular object and started touching its surface again, staring at it intently.

The afternoon sun poured through the window behind her, setting her edges aglow. Her hair hung loose down her back, rippling waves of silk, golden in the light.

So desperately like the first time he had seen her.

The irony was nearly suffocating.

Now what was he to do? Watch her be wooed by D'Avery? Pretend he was *happy* for her in this new life?

How could everything have changed so quickly?

She glanced up at him.

"Smart phone." She indicated the object she held and then turned her attention back to it.

He nodded, even though it made no sense.

Smart phone? What did *that* mean? It didn't look particularly stylish to him. It was an unremarkable silver rectangle.

Perhaps it was meant ironically?

He was still staring at her.

"Ordering takeaway," she explained, not looking up. As if that helped him understand.

It didn't.

"Can I do something?" he asked.

"Oh—no. Just make yourself comfortable and—"

"I'm sorry. I didn't phrase that right. I feel as if I might lose my mind at any moment." His jaw clenched. "Please give me something I *can* do. Some *limited* nineteenth century task?"

She stared at him for a second, her mouth an 'O' of surprise. And then nodded.

"A fire," she said, gesturing toward the large fireplace. "A fire would be lovely. There should be wood in the box to the left there. Matches are on the mantle. They're the long sticks in the tall box. You can strike them against the stones to create an instant flame. No tinder box needed."

She smiled too brightly again and walked toward the stairs.

"You'll see. Everything will be okay," she repeated. They must say that word a lot in 2013—*okay*.

She left, skirts swishing up the stairs.

He glanced around the room and then, with a sigh, shrugged out of his coat, folding it carefully over the back of one of the table chairs.

Next, he untied his cravat. And then slowly unwound its long length. Deliberately, carefully.

Unraveling himself with each sweep around his neck.

All his hopes. Every wish gone.

Would he ever be put back together?

He placed his neckcloth on top of his coat but opted to leave on his waistcoat. Walking over to the sofa, he sat and contemplated his boots.

Taking them off without the assistance of a valet was tricky at best. Besides, taking off his boots felt like he was surrendering to this century. To the thought of settling in for a long stay.

Something with which he was not *okay*.

The boots stayed on. For now.

Taking a deep breath, he set about doing what he *could*: build a fire.

He stacked kindling, followed by a few larger pieces. And then the— what had she called them—matches? Long and thin, they were coated in a red substance on one end. Selecting one, he scraped the tip along the flagstones lining the fireplace, jumping when it flared to life with a hiss.

Impressive.

Five minutes later, he had the fire roaring. Satisfied, he sat back on his heels, watching the wood crackle. An island of comfort in this strange new world.

For nearly a decade, Georgiana had been his lodestar, the one brilliant shining guiding force by which he steered all his dreams.

That impossible possibility.

But now . . .

It felt as if his life had been a house of cards. A collapsed illusion.

A loud buzzing sound emerged from the front of the house.

"I'll get it," Georgiana called, her feet pounding down the steps.

The front door opened, and he heard the murmur of voices. And then Georgiana sailed into the kitchen, a bag clutched in her hand, staring at the rectangular smart phone thing.

He instantly stood, as any gentleman should when a lady entered the room.

Not that she noticed, as she was still intent on her 'smart phone.'

But she had changed her clothes . . .

Sebastian sucked in his breath with a hiss.

Her hair tumbled down her back, now combed and loosely curled. She wore a foamy-green skirt that skimmed the ground but hugged her body more tightly than would have been considered proper in 1813. On top, she wore the same type of simple, unadorned white shirt that Shatner had, clinging to her slender form. Without buttons, how did one put on a shirt that tight? Over it all, she had a gray jacket-ish, wrap-ish thing that hung loosely to her hips.

Her feet were bare, toes peeping cheekily out from under the hem of her skirt.

It was all hard to describe. Simple and yet impossibly alluring.

Georgiana walked around the counter and lifted a handle on the spigot, causing water to instantly gush out into the basin. Blinking in surprise, Sebastian watched as she picked up what looked to be a shiny tea kettle off the counter and filled it with water. Then she set it down on a round circular object. A light at the base of the kettle lit up.

Odd.

She turned around and saw him staring.

"Everything will seem incredibly different until you get used to it," she said, apologetically. "The twenty-first century is a place of tremendous contradictions. Nearly magical machines and amazing freedom mixed with a complete lack of social niceties and decorum. James fits right in." She gave a soft laugh as she grabbed two oversized tea cups from the cabinet.

"And you?" He had to ask the question.

She shrugged and pulled a yellow box labeled 'Earl Grey Tea' out of a drawer.

"I don't know." A pause. "James is here. And I do love so much about the twenty-first century. Women are freer. We can do everything a man can do: hold a job, vote, attend university, travel alone, hold political office and so on. I never realized how few my choices were in the past."

She reached into a drawer and pulled out a large bag labeled 'sugar.' Surely a bag of sugar that large would be an extravagant luxury. Or was it?

Georgiana continued. "Aside from marriage, what options does a well-bred lady have in nineteenth century Britain? Respectable work is limited to being a governess or companion. If she is very lucky, she might have an independence, like I received from my grandmother. But any woman who marries, instantly becomes her husband's property. She isn't even seen as a separate *person* under British law. Just an appendage of her husband."

He walked around the sofa and into the kitchen. "Any gentleman would always consider his wife's feelings—"

Georgiana waived her hand. "Of course. But problems arise because there are no social systems in place when men *don't* behave as they ought. A man can beat his wife and children for no reason whatsoever, as long as he does not use a stick larger than his thumb. But were he to beat a stranger in the same manner, he could be held liable before the law. How absurd is that?"

All the air sucked out of his lungs. He knew what she said was truth, but still—

"Is this what you think of me? That I would do such a thing?"

She blinked. "No—no, of course not. But to live in a time where my children would be subject to such laws and social mores . . . Where death from easily treatable diseases is common . . . It's hard to get used to the idea again, I guess."

Her eyes pools of blue, her smile so very wide. She was still his Georgiana.

But *not*.

She had taken his neat little world, shaken it around in a box labeled *Nuance* and then dumped the pieces out into a morass of confusion and complexity.

Her gaze turned concerned. He couldn't decide if the pity in her eyes comforted or alarmed him.

The light popped off on the kettle, and Georgiana dropped a couple mesh bags into it.

Tea.

"Come," she said, taking his arm and directing him back to the sofa in front of the fire. "Sit. We'll enjoy the wonderful fire you have built, and I will tell you my entire tale while we eat some lovely Chinese takeaway."

A few minutes later, she had him situated on the sofa, holding a fork and box (box!) of food with a cup of steaming tea on a small table at his elbow.

She curled up on the sofa next to him, twisting her body to face his, tucking her knees underneath her and slumping. The diaphanous material of her skirt stretched and pulled, covering all of her except her bare toes, which peeped out at him, like the pink noses of so many mice.

It was not at all ladylike.

But it suited her, this new Georgiana, and had the ease of much practice. She had obviously sat just like that many times.

He inspected his food. Chinese takeaway. It was noodles with vegetables and smelled of soy. He perked up. He liked soy sauce and curries in general. Not everything was so different it seemed.

They ate in silence for a few minutes. The food was lovely, just as promised.

"So, where is James?" Sebastian asked.

"He and Emme are in Bali. Or are they on to Fiji now?"

"Fiji?" Sebastian thought through everything he knew. "That is . . ."

"It's an island country in the middle of the South Pacific. Pretty much on the opposite side of the planet from here." She lifted up the smart phone and touched it. Again. "I messaged him, but it will still be an hour or two before sunrise there, and he won't call until he wakes up. But I am sure James will want to talk—"

"Wait. You can send him messages? Talk to him? I don't—"

"Smart phone." She held up the object in question.

What was so remarkable about that silly rectangular box?

"Yes, you seem ridiculously attached to it. Does it ever leave your person?"

Georgiana laughed. "Stop! Now you're sounding like James. Honestly, it's worth living in 2013 just to have one of these."

He held out his hand, motioning for her to give it over.

With a wide smile, she set her box of takeaway down and slid next to him. Tucking her shoulder against his. Her body a ball of warmth at his side.

"Look," she said and touched the phone. It lit up with words and images. "Emme swears the history of all civilization has had the creation of this one device as its end game."

A half hour later, Sebastian reluctantly had to agree. The device was miraculous. It could order you food, tell you the weather days in advance and play weeks worth of music. Remarkable.

He kept looking for something, some reason why Georgiana should be dissatisfied with her life here. Any glimmer of hope to which he could cling and convince himself there might still be a way for them to be together.

Yet every minute he spent here, the more utterly futile it became.

She would never be his. Not now. Why would she return to a life in 1813 with him, assuming that were even possible? And if he were stuck in the twenty-first century with her, how could he even begin to create a life for them here? What could he possibly offer her that was *more* than what she already had?

The sooner he accepted that fact, the better off he would be.

Of course, convincing his wayward heart of the reality of his situation . . . *That* might take some time.

"Tell me your story," he said, handing the phone back to her. "I want to understand everything you have been through."

He expected her to move away. To retreat from him, just as she seemed to have retreated from her childhood and the world to which she was born.

But she didn't. Instead, she snuggled into him even more, wrapping her hands around his arm and resting her head on his shoulder, her body soft and heated through his thin linen shirt. She smelled of sunshine and roses and Georgiana.

Sebastian nearly laughed at the irony of it.

To have her here, so close, relaxed and nestled against him.

How many lonely evenings had he had this very dream? Sitting with her curled up against him, talking and laughing together?

And now—*now!*—it happened.

When events had destroyed his understanding of her and the world.

She only held him out of pity. To console him when everything had turned upside down.

She sighed into his arm. Or had she breathed him in?

And did he want to know the difference?

"Yes, let me explain." In her soft voice, she told her story. The time portal and how it worked. Her miraculous recovery in a hospital, the joy of being whole again. And then a new world to discover.

She described traveling with James and his wife, Emme. There were impossible seeming things in her story. Flying through the air above the clouds in a machine called an airplane. Riding in and then actually driving a car—a carriage which didn't use horses and instead was self-propelled through a fuel called gasoline.

Through it all, she stayed tucked up against him. Knees folded into her chest, bare feet peeping out.

Had he ever seen her toes before today? He didn't think so—even frolicking together at Lyndenbrooke as children, she never went barefoot.

But now he found himself fixated on her toes. Watching them bounce as she animatedly described thieving monkeys in India. Curling up as she described buildings in New York City which stretched to touch the clouds.

How could he not have known her toes were long and slender, like her fingers, with her second toe extending farther than all the rest? Each little nail a symmetrical half moon. The pinky toe on each foot shyly ducking underneath its neighbor.

They *offended* him—those treacherous little toes.

In their innocence, they represented everything he *didn't* know about her.

Like a fool, he had believed himself in his own house but then walked through a familiar door and found an entirely different world lay on the other side.

Everything changed.

Her toes stilled as she recounted meeting Shatner D'Avery and gave a brief outline of their history. D'Avery wanted to move their relationship into something more serious. He seemed like a decent sort: charitable, devoted, nice.

Sebastian loathed him.

Ridiculous D'Avery probably knew all about her toes.

"So what prompted you to return to 1813? It seems like your life here has been quite settled."

Sebastian gave his brave smile. The one that didn't touch his eyes.

Georgiana pulled away and looked at him.

Pityingly.

Sebastian swallowed. What else did he expect?

He *was* pitiful.

"Let me show you," she murmured, unfolding herself off the couch and wandering into the front parlor. The sudden loss of her body heat startled him. He missed it immediately.

She returned and sat down away from him—unfortunately—handing him a letter inside some sort of clear protective covering.

"This arrived via post about the middle of August."

Sebastian looked at the letter and examined the signature first, hissing in a breath, head rearing back in surprise.

"How—What—this seems to be your own handwriting, Georgie. But the date . . . How is this even—"

"Exactly!" Georgiana studied him with a rueful look. "I got this letter—which I *still* have not written, might I add—with a date and the mysterious content. How could I not be curious? You know me."

Did he?

Sebastian gave a weak smile and then actually read the letter.

The words ambushed him, jumping out . . . *a hole in my heart the shape and size of you* . . . gutting whatever shreds of hope he had clung to . . . *Comfort me with the warmth of your embrace* . . .

She *loved* someone. Enough to plead: *Wrap me in the light of your love.*

A gasp echoed in the room. He was embarrassingly sure it had been his.

Who could she love like this? Surely it would never be himself.

Pitiful.

"I know—it was a shock for me too. It's just so enigmatic, don't you think?" Georgiana patted his arm.

"Who?" was all Sebastian could manage to say.

"I honestly don't know. I don't feel these things for anyone. At least, not right now. But once I received this letter, I realized I must return to the past this autumn. It seemed like a sign that I needed to go home, at least for a visit." She gave a lost little laugh and shrugged her shoulders.

He shook his head. "Visit? You found yourself in the center of a real-life two hundred year old mystery and jumped at the chance to solve it, more like. Visit, indeed."

Only Georgiana.

"Can you blame me, Seb? How could I resist such a letter? I'm fairly certain it's not an actual love letter. I probably made . . . will make? . . . the whole thing up. I don't feel this way about Shatner, at least not yet. Besides, he doesn't even live in the right century to receive the letter."

He should have felt at least a *flicker* of hope at her statement. But despair had firmly settled in, determined to build a fine house in his soul and stay a while.

He had known a girl. A girl who smiled sunshine and lived laughter.

But this person curled up on the end of the sofa was now a woman, full of complexity and ambiguity and love that the girl could never have understood.

With *toes* he did not know.

What was he to do? Was his love for her nothing more than affection born of long habit?

Without Georgiana Elizabeth Augusta Knight as his guiding star, what would his life become?

Chapter 17

Sebastian stared at the letter. Georgiana felt like snapping her fingers in his face to break the tension.

He was not dealing well with any of the events of the last couple hours. Granted, few could travel two hundred years with aplomb and grace.

He sucked in a deep breath and then handed the letter back to her with a faint smile.

"Intriguing," was all he said, his deep aristocratic voice blending with the hushed pop of the fire.

He held her gaze for a moment, liquid pools of chocolate night. Now shuttered. Asking everything and revealing nothing.

He seemed to be coming undone, nonessential bits of him being stripped away. First his coat and cravat and now his charm and endless good humor.

Unraveled.

What had she expected? The old Sebastian she knew?

She liked old Sebastian. He was uncomplicated and charming and simple to understand.

But now she found herself building him anew, reconstructing him from the ashes of the boy.

A somber stranger—so large and powerful—who fascinated her.

The boy had been a cherished friend. Nothing more. But this new man . . .

He held her spellbound. And she was honest enough with herself to admit there was nothing platonic about it.

The thought both excited and frightened her.

He turned to stare at the fire and relaxed back into the sofa. The sun had set and the room deepened into gloom. Firelight flickered across his face, casting all the crags and crevices of its surface into sharp relief: the strong line of his nose, the darkening stubble on his chin, the angular cut of his side whiskers. Muscles moved underneath his fine linen shirt.

Vividly, she recalled the warmth of him, wrapping her hands around his arm and tucking herself against his side. Feeling the flex and subtle movements of his tendons under her cheek. Some unknown part of her desperate to learn everything about him.

How could she not *long* to curl into his strength?

A series of beeps broke the silence. Georgiana grabbed her phone.

A Skype call.

"Georgie!" James greeted her, holding his own phone between his hands. He shook his head, hair tousled and still sleepy.

Hearing her brother's voice, Sebastian turned, raising his eyebrows.

"Good morning to you too, James," Georgiana said. James smiled at her and ran a hand through his golden hair, making it stand even more on end.

"I didn't expect to see you for weeks, maybe even months. It was wonderful to wake to your text." James stifled a yawn and adjusted the loose white shirt he wore, his eyes remarkably blue in his tanned face. "*Please* tell me you are back for good."

"I don't know. I still haven't written that letter." Georgiana shrugged. "You look like you've been spending time on the beach. I don't remember your hair ever being quite so blond. Where are you?"

James smiled wryly and swiveled his phone camera round, slowly panning the scene. He sat on the edge of a bed, draped in white netting. On every side, the building opened up to reveal crystalline turquoise waters, ocean waves lapping.

"Fiji." James sighed the word. "It's the most unreal place. Did you know you can rent a cottage *on* the ocean? I don't think Emme will ever leave."

"That's true," Emme called from somewhere out of the frame. "This place is uh-mazing!"

"It looks warm." Georgiana flexed her bare toes, which were starting to feel the nip of the brisk autumn evening.

"It is," James said with a laugh. "You should join us. You could be here in just a day or two."

Georgiana sighed. "Maybe, but things are a little problematic and—"

"Ah, Georgie. How did I know you were going to say that? So what's up?"

With a rueful look, Georgiana tapped her phone screen and switched from the front to the back facing camera, showing James the man sitting on the sofa next to her.

For his part, Sebastian merely inched his eyebrows upward and folded his arms across his chest. The sidelight from the fire bathed him in moody, golden light.

He looked dashingly impressive.

"What the devil? Who—?!" James exclaimed and then sat up straighter, suddenly becoming less a beach bum and more a nineteenth century gentleman.

Sebastian somehow managed to raise his eyebrows even higher.

"You can see me then, Knight?" he asked.

"Georgie, turn the dashed phone around so I can speak face-to-face with your gentleman caller."

Sighing, Georgiana switched back to the front facing camera and handed Sebastian the phone, scooting to sit next to him again, hips touching. She had been looking for an excuse to do so anyway. The man made an excellent heater.

At least, that is what she told herself.

Sebastian stared at the phone screen, obviously trying to merge the image of a rumpled, half-dressed James with the man he had met in the nineteenth century.

James gave Sebastian the same assessing look. "You look familiar, sir," he said.

"Yes, we have met once or twice. Lord Stratton, at your service." Sebastian nodded his head.

Poor Sebastian. Georgiana was quite sure it was the oddest introduction of his life. What was the expected protocol? Did one bow to a smart phone?

"Stratton?" James' forehead wrinkled. "But—what of the earl and Lord Harward—I don't remember—"

"James, this is my friend, Sebastian Carew. You remember, the vicar's stepson who lived near Lyndenbrooke." Georgiana leaned into Sebastian so her face showed on the screen too. "Well, Lord Harward and his family were killed in a carriage accident which caused the poor old earl to expire from shock. All resulting in Sebastian inheriting the earldom."

James nodded, as if trying to piece it all together. And then he gave them both a decidedly arch look.

"And why are you *here*, Stratton, if I may ask?"

Georgiana felt Sebastian's lungs deflate, air rushing out. "I . . . experienced some confusion and accidentally went through the time portal. Georgiana—uh, Miss Knight—was kind enough to follow me."

Taking the phone from his hand, Georgiana cuddled closer to Sebastian. Despite the fire, she could feel the evening chill seeping in. He was so *warm*.

James smiled, his eyes not missing the fact that Georgiana and Sebastian were huddled together on the sofa.

"Forgive the old-fashioned nature of this question, but may I ask what your intentions are toward my sister?"

Sebastian instantly stiffened.

"James! How dare you embarrass Sebastian by asking—"

"My intentions are most honorable, Knight. And I must say that your question, to me, is anything but old-fashioned," Sebastian said, his voice a wonder of irony. "However, your sister has already repeatedly refused my many offers to make her my countess."

James grimaced. "Pity. I had always heard you were a decent sort,

Stratton. Give her time. Though heaven knows she would try a saint." He shook his head.

"Pardon me, James. I am sitting right here." Georgiana waved her hand in front of the screen.

"Oh, I know," he replied without a trace of apology.

"Yes, she can be a sore trial," Sebastian agreed.

"It's her fascination with mysteries," James commiserated.

"Exactly. And the endless curiosity."

"Excuse me. Yoo-hoo. Still here." Georgiana waved her hand again.

"She has no fear. She actually *likes* being scared." A smile teased the edges of Sebastian's face.

James shuddered. "Imagine trying to raise her. It was ghastly."

"You poor man." Sebastian clicked his tongue without a trace of sarcasm. "You have my deepest sympathies."

"Still here."

James nodded. "I've often wondered if my hair is truly blond or just shot through with white from her antics."

"No wonder you are a man of such upstanding character."

"Precisely." James scrubbed his hand through his hair again. "The refiner's fire and all that."

Both men suddenly grinned widely at each other.

"I hate you both so much." Georgiana tried to keep her expression mock-severe.

James laughed and looked at her. "Are you sure you won't accept his offer, Georgie? Assuming Stratton still wants your troublesome self, of course."

Sebastian shrugged. "I *have* been reevaluating my offer."

Georgiana's stomach instantly dropped. Was he serious—?

"Wise man," James agreed.

"I am generally considered a fount of wisdom." Sebastian made a show of piously examining his fingernails.

James sighed. "'Tis a pity. Arthur would probably wet his breeches with glee over the thought of an alliance with the Earl of Stratton."

"It's entirely possible he already has," Sebastian deadpanned, head still down.

James let out a crack of laughter. "Damn, but I like you, Stratton."

"The feeling is mutual, Knight." Sebastian grinned, lifting his head.

"Like the brother I never had," James said wistfully.

"Dang, that was cold, James," Emme's voice called. "Though funnier if Arthur were here."

Sebastian laughed. In a flash, he was that boy Georgiana knew. She could feel the tension ease out of him.

"Knight, your sister has run me ragged these last few weeks. At the rate she is going, she will either get herself killed or—"

"Or you will kill her yourself?"

"Precisely."

"Yes, that is the Georgie we all know and love."

"Are you both quite through?" Georgiana fixed them with a hard look.

Both men stared at her, eyes wide and innocent.

Emme suddenly stuck her dark, curly head into the frame. "They're bromancing, Georgie. You might want to give them a moment. Let them work it out of their systems."

Emme sat down on the bed next to James and slowly surveyed Sebastian, tossing Georgiana a decidedly arch look—a look that clearly said *Emme* did not find Sebastian wanting.

"Okay, seriously, Georgie. What *have* you been up to?" James fixed her with his sternest I-am-your-older-brother stare.

With a grimace, Georgiana started at the beginning and told them everything. Her letter, the glowing Jupiter symbol, the threatening notes, Miss Franklin's untimely death.

Somewhere between the Jupiter symbol on Blackwell's walking stick and Lady Ambrosia's terrified warnings, Georgiana realized her toes were no longer cold. Sebastian had wrapped one of his large hands around them. A strong, blessedly dry hand.

Curiously, his warm fingers on her toes did funny things to her stomach. And her breathing, making it difficult to keep a coherent train of thought.

Swallowing, Georgiana finished the story, recounting everything from her final conversation with Lady Ambrosia.

"Georgiana Elizabeth Augusta Knight." James hung his head

between his arms, shaking it back and forth. "Wow! I'm feeling such a strong urge to strangle you right now."

"I would be more than happy to do the honors, Knight," Sebastian offered, giving Georgiana's toes a hard squeeze.

James groaned. "So, let me get this straight. You pretended to be an agent of Lord Zeus to both Blackwell *and* Lady Ambrosia. This Lord Zeus who, I might add, has shown no compunction whatsoever in murdering other meddling young ladies. What did you think he would do once he found out about your duplicity? Pat your head and laugh at the good joke?"

"Hear, hear," Sebastian agreed, his voice deep and rumbly.

"Naturally, James, I could not have anticipated death would have been—"

"Georgie, you have made yourself a wanted woman."

She swallowed.

It figured it would happen to her eventually. And it was still the tiniest bit thrilling. Well, it was actually *excessively* thrilling, but given the way Sebastian and James were staring at her . . .

She wisely held her tongue.

"What are we to do with her, Knight?" Sebastian pinched the bridge of his nose.

"Nothing." James shook his head at her. "You say the portal is closed. So Georgie isn't going anywhere."

Georgiana opened her mouth to speak, but James cut her off with a sweep of his hand.

"No, Georgie. Even if Stratton here decides to return—which I don't see what would keep him in this century given his responsibilities in 1813—"

"Agreed. I intend to return as soon as the portal allows it," Sebastian murmured.

James nodded his agreement. "However, you—Georgiana—will stay. I don't care that you haven't written that letter yet. I won't risk your life over this foolishness."

Silence.

Waves sloshed soothingly. The fire popped cheerily.

"For the record, I am truly sorry." Georgiana chewed her cheek. "I obviously did not mean for the charade to go this far. But why am I here?"

"Georgie—"

"We are not going to argue—"

"No, hear me out." She held out a pleading hand. "Why did the portal work? Why were we able to come through and, yet, now can't return? We know the portal only works when one's life path necessitates a trip through time, when people and events are linked. Given that, would it not seem logical there is something we need to accomplish? Or at least something Sebastian or I must do here?"

James arched an eyebrow at her.

"That's actually not a bad point," he said after a second

"There must be something we need to research or divine here—"

"Yes, but the universe is notorious for not allowing you to see things from your own life, remember?" Emme interjected. "How can you do any research?"

They all pondered that thought.

"Well, we can at least try," Georgiana shrugged. "It will give us something to do."

"Agreed." James ran a hand through his hair again. "Emme and I will cut our trip short and head home in a day or two. I've been regretting not flying back to see you anyway. I'm glad you are here to stay. Welcome home, sister dearest."

After ending the conversation with James, Sebastian was surprised Georgiana stayed tucked against his side, head resting on his shoulder. He still had his hand wrapped around her unknown toes.

Night had long ago settled. The fire burned low. She sighed, body rising against his arm.

The silence *should* have felt uncomfortable.

It didn't.

Sebastian shook his head and tilted it back to rest against the top of the sofa. How could he ever have imagined the events of this day?

That letter? The one that had teased her into returning to the past?

He sucked in a painful breath at the thought.

He hated him. The man to whom she wrote those words. Whoever he proved to be.

She had lived so . . . much.

Why, in all his campaigning as a soldier and responsibilities as an earl, had it never occurred to him Georgiana would experience her *own* changing journey?

He chuckled, running his hand over his face.

"What?" she asked, muffled.

"You are truly a ghastly chaperoner."

He could feel her smile.

"According to the *dashing* Earl of Stratton?"

"Precisely. The remarkable-and-in-no-way-pathetic Earl of Stratton."

She laughed in his arm.

She did not, however, *contradict* his assessment.

He sighed and slumped even lower into the sofa, extending his still booted feet toward the fire, crossing them at the ankle.

"So what are we to do now?" he asked.

"What do you mean?"

He gestured at them, nestled together. The silence of the empty house around them.

"In 1813, being *this* alone with a gently bred young lady would necessitate our betrothal."

She let out an exasperated puff of air.

"I'm not saying that will happen, mind you," he quickly corrected, holding out a staying hand.

He wasn't in the mood to hear her go on about how *un-marriageable* he was.

Not again. Not tonight. Not ever, actually.

"I'm just pointing out that this situation is compromising," he continued. "We disappeared at the same time in 1813 and there will probably be talk."

She shrugged. "Please. It is what it is. You heard James. I am not going anywhere, so it seems unlikely I will return. Besides, Arthur cares mightily about family honor, and he knows about the portal. He will put two and two together and cover for us. Running off with you would be a terrible scandal, so he will concoct some plausible story. Something about my aunt in Shropshire suddenly needing my help and you returning unexpectedly to Stratton Hall."

"And us here?"

He couldn't help it. He had to ask the question.

"What do you mean?" She pulled back to look at him.

He gave a charming smile. "Well, I am quite *dashing,* and you have spent the evening cuddled next to me . . ."

She didn't deny it.

"I was cold, Sebastian. And you have warmed my toes." For emphasis, she wiggled her feet which were still nestled under his hand.

Treacherous little beasts, those toes.

"Besides," she continued, "we *are* good friends. And in the twenty-first century, good friends who share a house are called roommates. It happens all the time and no one finds it untoward."

She nudged his shoulder.

"Come, roomie." She unwrapped herself from his side and stood, holding out a hand. "It's getting late and tomorrow will be Monday, so we will be able to start hunting for information. Besides, I am *so* ready for a shower." She tugged him to his feet. "Let me show you the marvels of twenty-first century plumbing."

He allowed Georgiana to drag him upstairs and walk him through using the water closet and wash basin with instant hot water.

And then there was the shower.

How had he lived so long without such an amazingly marvelous thing? He stood under the streaming fountain, letting the warm water wash over him. Wondering if the next few days would prove as overwhelming as the first.

With smart phones and hot showers, what could he possibly offer Georgiana that compared?

The girl he knew was long gone. Georgiana had changed, altered through the sheer business of living.

Would he love the woman she had become as much as the girl she had been?

And heaven help him if he did.

Chapter 18

Duir Cottage
September 16, 2013
Birthday in minus 22 days plus two hundred years

Monday dawned bright and clear. The crisp air strongly hinting of autumn even though the leaves had not yet started to change. Georgiana stared at the ceiling for a moment before getting out of bed.

She tried hard not to over-think the situation with Sebastian.

She *tried* not to. With varying success.

After going to bed, she had lain awake debating if he had been serious in his conversation with James. That he was reevaluating his offer of marriage.

Trying to decide how she felt about it. A part of her was relieved at the thought.

But there was also a piece of her heart that wanted to weep.

It was all most confusing.

Tumbling out of bed, Georgiana dressed in a long maxi skirt and loose sweater again. No need to shock Sebastian's sensibilities too much. Though she did put on some light make-up. Thank goodness Duir Cottage boasted two separate bathrooms. Sharing a bathroom with him would make their current situation even more awkward.

First things first. Sebastian was going to need some twenty-first century clothing. At several inches over six feet, he topped James by nearly half a foot, but perhaps there was something in James' clothing that would work for a few hours. Until they managed to drive to Birmingham and acquire a wardrobe for him. She dug through the warmer clothing in James' dresser, coming up with an outfit that would hopefully work.

Clothes in her arms, she trudged downstairs to find Sebastian kneeling in front of the hearth, making another fire. He wore his breeches and shirt from the night before, wrinkled and rumpled. His hair was still wet, a testament to his fascination with the shower. And he had put James' shaving kit to good use. Appreciatively, Georgiana watched him apply a struck match to the kindling wood, muscles visibly moving under his fine linen shirt.

He really was a marvelous specimen of manhood.

"Good morning." Sebastian turned around, tossing the burning match back into the fire. "I thought we could use a fire. And I boiled water for tea." He gestured toward the electric kettle on the counter with a sheepish grin. "I felt absurdly proud of myself for remembering how to do it."

Georgiana laughed. He was Charming Sebastian again this morning. Boyish and at ease.

Charming Sebastian she knew. Could deal with.

It was Intense Sebastian that messed with her breathing and made her toes tingle.

As long as *he* didn't make an appearance, her heart would, most likely, make it through the week unscathed.

Besides, it was only her toes he made tingle. Not all of her, right?

"I also checked the portal. It is still decidedly closed."

She gazed at him with wide eyes.

"Oh—and what would you have done if it were working?"

He opened his mouth to speak and then shut it again. Shrugged.

She padded over to the empty fridge. They were going to have to go grocery shopping too.

Poor Sebastian. He was in for a serious crash course on twenty-first century life today.

An hour later, Sebastian stood in the kitchen, dressed in James' clothing.

An awkward silence hung between them.

"I look ridiculous."

It wasn't a question.

Georgiana pursed her lips together, determined not to giggle.

James was a fairly casual person, particularly when it came to twenty-first century dress. Sebastian, however, could not carry off jeans and a t-shirt with such easy aplomb. At least, not when the clothing in question was two sizes too small.

Pulled down firmly over Sebastian's boots, the jeans drifted a full five inches off the ground. More capris than pants. And the t-shirt hit just below his belt, far too short.

She was quite sure if he raised his arms, the shirt would drift up to his armpits. Though pulled taut across his chest, it did marvelous things to his broad shoulders.

All in all, he was being a *remarkably* good sport about the whole situation.

"You could look more ridiculous," she offered, now biting her lip harder. "I am sure Marc has a Bronco's jersey around here somewhere. It's bright orange and—"

"Go on. You know you want to laugh."

Her lips twitched. "No—not really."

But, really, she did.

He shook his head slowly, eyebrows raised in disbelief.

"I mean, some would say you even look *dashing*—" She broke off, laughter bubbling.

With a pointed look, Sebastian placed his hands on his hips, causing the shirt to lift dangerously into midriff territory.

"Let me go see if I can find you a jacket." Georgiana hurried toward the staircase, muffling her giggles in her hand.

An oversized military-style jacket helped. A bit. The sooner they got him clothing, the better.

The car required a little longer for Sebastian to settle into. It took an hour of driving before he stopped violently recoiling every time they passed an oncoming car. However, given that flinching was not unusual when she had a passenger with her, she didn't think too much of it.

Shatner texted her as she drove. He wanted to see her.

Actually his exact words were something along the lines of 'hey, how's your beautiful face?' but she read enough between the lines to understand the sentiment.

She ignored it because, well, she knew better than to text and drive.

Shatner texted again an hour later as Georgiana sat waiting for Sebastian to model another outfit for her. She meant to respond to Shatner, truly she did, but then Sebastian walked out of the fitting room in a sculpted, immaculately tailored three-piece Italian suit.

Georgiana forgot to breathe.

Honestly! How was a woman to function when large men with charming smiles blithely modeled designer clothing in front of her? She was only human after all.

Shatner texted for a third time during dinner. Georgiana glanced at it and quickly typed back that she would call him tomorrow.

She tried to care about Shatner, really she did.

But Sebastian kept drawing her attention.

They were seated at a restaurant in an old warehouse rehabilitated with industrial fixtures and modern furniture. The kind of place that dismantled traditional British food and put it back together in interesting ways.

They had completed their shopping for the day as the car was nearly full and Georgiana was quite sure she was near the limit on her credit card. Fortunately, James had authorized any and all expenses, and his pockets were more than deep enough.

It was all worth it. Every penny.

Who knew Sebastian would have such excellent taste?

He sat across from her in a fitted white button down shirt tucked into designer jeans that clung like a glove. All topped with a gray-blue tailored suit coat with just the right amount of sheen. His Caesar haircut had been trimmed and gelled and his side whiskers were thinly sculpted on his cheeks.

When had he become so impossibly handsome?

Georgiana gave a happy sigh just drinking him in.

He looked not unlike a young Daniel Day Lewis. *Last of the Mohicans* Daniel Day Lewis, which she had watched more than once while in the hospital recovering, right along with just about every period film ever made.

There had been little else to do.

And Daniel Day Lewis *had* been a particular favorite.

Over a dinner of deconstructed shepherd's pie, she and Sebastian plotted their strategy for research. She explained concepts like photographs and the Internet.

As they talked, unbidden, her eyes drifted to his lips. How would they feel?

She sucked in a deep breath, trying to clear her thinking.

Shatner. She had Shatner.

But did she really want Shatner?

That was a treacherous thought.

She was *such* a terrible girlfriend. Shatner had always been kind and good to her. This was a horrid way to repay him. Tomorrow. Tomorrow she would call Shatner and arrange time to see him. Talk to him. Assess the state of her heart.

Sebastian opted to snooze on the ride back to Duir Cottage, saying that keeping his eyes closed was better for his sanity.

Once home, Sebastian pulled off his suitcoat, rolled up the sleeves of his fitted shirt and built another fire. Georgiana made tea and then curled up next to him on the couch. She couldn't help it. Her toes were cold, and he was so warm and the fine cotton of his shirt so soft. Besides, now he smelled like wool and the expensive cologne she had insisted on buying.

It was a combination impossible to resist.

She nestled into his arm for a bit, just breathing him in, Sebastian wrapping his hand around her toes again.

Wanting to broaden Sebastian's understanding of the twenty-first century, she flipped on the flatscreen TV next to the fireplace and made him watch *Sherlock*, digging Godiva chocolates out of the pantry.

Cuddled up against Sebastian Carew, watching Benedict Cumberbatch and eating mocha dark chocolate truffles.

Ah, yes. Now *this* was bliss.

On Tuesday, Sebastian decided showers were manna sent from the gods.

It had only been a day, but he could not see living without them from this point on.

Surely as an earl, he could find a way to have such a thing constructed in Stratton Hall. He would have to ask his steward about it.

Georgiana had laid out what she wanted him to wear, bless her. The clothing made no real sense. Trousers she called blue jeans and an incredibly soft knitted maroon tunic that the silky label along the neckline called cashmere. It felt marvelous against his skin. He tucked the tunic into his jeans, which sat perilously low on his hips, and secured it all with a worn leather belt.

What was it with the twenty-first century and this habit of making new things look like they had already seen a lifetime of use?

Pushing the sleeves of the tunic up his arms a bit, he surveyed himself in the bathroom mirror.

It wasn't half bad. Definitely more casual than a nineteenth century gentleman but infinitely more comfortable.

He strolled downstairs and then kept right on going down to the cellar. He figured if he checked the portal every day, eventually it would let him through. Back to the world he knew. Away from the confusion that was life with Georgiana.

However, just like the previous day, he could feel the electric current of the portal, but nothing pulled him forward. It was still shut.

Georgiana was in the kitchen fixing breakfast, hair hanging practically to her waist. From what he had seen the day before, most twenty-first century women wore their hair down, regardless of their age. She had on a flowy, lacy, rose-colored shirt but, instead of a skirt, today she wore jeans too.

Tight jeans that hugged her legs and made him swallow. Hard.

She smiled at him from the stove where she was stirring what smelled like eggs and sausage, surveying his clothing.

"Nice," was all she said before turning back to dish food onto two plates. From her tone, he assumed that meant he passed muster.

They sat at the table, eating eggs and drinking fresh orange juice. An almost surreal luxury. Who had so many oranges that they could actually juice them and toss the remainder?

But then the chocolate the night before had been a revelation too. Solid and yet impossibly smooth.

No wonder Georgiana was so tethered to the twenty-first century. What could life in the past possibly offer her? Most certainly not solid chocolate and liquid oranges.

Nor a relationship with her beloved brother.

For not the first time, he pondered why Fate demanded his life be so tethered to hers. It seemed he had spent nearly a decade as a satellite spinning in tight orbit around her star. Helplessly pulled to her, unable to set his heart free to chart its own course through the universe.

Why? What did Fate want from him?

"So today, I thought we could start by seeing what we can find on Blackwell and Lady Ambrosia online. Also, if it's all right with you, I thought to phone Stratton Hall and see if I could arrange a meeting with their curator. Perhaps we will find something there."

Five hours later and Sebastian had the beginnings of what would surely be an impressive headache.

They had come up with nothing.

The laptop crashed, as Georgiana described it, every time they tried to pull up information on Lord Blackwell. Lady Ambrosia seemed to have never existed. And Stratton Hall had yet to return their numerous calls.

"Emme warned us this would happen," Georgiana sighed, as they sat at the kitchen table. Shifting, she tucked a jeans-clad knee under her, chewing on the end of a pencil. Her toes were, again, bare.

Did the woman ever wear stockings?

Did he *want* her to wear them?

Part of him was proud that he now knew her big toenail turned purplish when cold.

Sebastian drummed his fingers against the table.

"It is a bit discouraging," he admitted.

"I'm not sure what to do next. And I'm worried for you."

"For me?"

"Well, yes. You do still have to get married, you know."

Ah, yes. There was that.

He pressed his fingers against his forehead, hoping to ease the tension in his skull before the pain moved into the pounding stage.

"Do I?"

She blinked at him, obviously surprised. Rain tapped against the windows, autumn weather settling in.

"Don't you? You stand to lose sixty thousand pounds, Sebastian. That is an absurd sum of money. Millions of pounds by 2013 standards."

Sebastian nodded. "True, but a third of the money goes to the gooseberry society run by the late earl, essentially staying in my keeping. So technically, it is only forty thousand pounds I stand to lose."

"Ah, well, that makes everything better." He didn't miss the sarcasm in her tone. "Who will you marry?" She studied him, blue eyes intent.

Sebastian shrugged. "Probably one of the Miss Burbanks, I suppose."

"You *cannot* be serious."

"Lady Ambrosia, then?"

"Sebastian, this isn't a joke."

"Who said I was joking?"

He would sooner die a pauper, but Georgiana didn't know that.

And—dash it—there she went staring at his mouth again. His lips tingled unbearably under her scrutiny.

Would they ever get back to that place?

The one where she moved into his arms and rose on tiptoes, reaching for him, dressed as lord and lady. Simpler times.

Just the thought caused a sharp ache.

None of which helped his throbbing head.

He massaged his forehead. The pain seemed to be creeping toward a spot between his eyeballs.

She regarded him for a moment longer and then stood and wandered into the kitchen, rummaging through a cupboard.

Sebastian threaded his fingers through his hair, trying to ease the pounding in his skull.

"Here, looks like you need this," she said at his elbow. Looking up, he saw a glass of water and two small blue pills resting on the table. "Swallow them without chewing. They should help your headache. And then come here."

She drifted over to the sofa and sat at one end. He swallowed the pills down and followed her. She placed a small pillow in her lap.

"Lay down and rest your head." She indicated toward the pillow. "Emme's friend, Jasmine, taught me how to do some massage to help with scalp tension."

Lovely. Her fingers rubbing his head. The scent of roses which enveloped him when she was near.

Twenty minutes later and his headache was a thing of the past. Her fingers felt marvelous moving through his hair, massaging his skull and forehead.

She had noticed his pain. And had cared enough to do something about it.

Just as she had explained every unfamiliar twenty-first century thing all day. Patient. Attentive.

Helping him settle in and ease his unease.

New, modern Georgiana was *not* as lethal to his heart as the younger Georgiana.

No. There was really no comparison.

She promised to be much, *much* worse.

Georgiana woke on Wednesday hating every woman in 1813 who thought she could win Sebastian's heart.

She felt particular antipathy for the Miss Burbanks.

They didn't know Sebastian well enough to tell when he had a headache.

That was *her* job.

Well, even if they did, she most certainly didn't want to imagine one of them running her hands through his silky hair to relieve it.

Which, of course, meant she spent a good fifteen minutes imagining just *that*.

Miss Mica—or was it Miss Michaelina?—sidles up to Sebastian. He gazes at her fondly and pulls her closer, nestled protectively against his side. She caresses his head, threading her fingers around his skull. Sending her hands over and over through his hair . . .

Georgiana watched it all unfold, becoming more and more indignant with each conjured sweep of the other woman's hand.

The woman had no right touching him at all. How dare he allow such a thing!

She fumed over it while showering and blow drying her hair. She angrily stuffed her legs into jeans, stashing her phone in her back pocket. Then, still upset, she sorted through Sebastian's clothing in the west bedroom, choosing out a comfy pair of blue slacks, tailored shirt and gray wool suit vest.

Dumb man would probably look devastatingly handsome in them.

Curse him with all his effortless charm and broad toe-warming hands and teasing wit and brooding *fierceness*.

Too caught up in her imaginings, she rapped on Sebastian's bedroom door and entered without waiting for him to answer.

And then stopped short, all the air whooshing from her lungs. Forgetting how to breathe, much less anything else she intended to say.

He stood at the window, watching the rain patter down over the back garden. Jeans loosely fastened and slung low, low around his hips.

His back to her.

His very bare, very muscled back.

"Oh!" Her gasp echoed through the room.

He turned, giving her a raised eyebrow.

Dimly, she was aware of the muscles tensing under his skin, the enormous breadth and depth of his shoulders.

The sheer male *shock* of him.

But that was not what held her attention.

No, it was the history written across his skin.

A puckered scar stretched the length of his right ribcage, purple and angry. Thin, white lines marred his left shoulder. A particularly nasty red indentation sat above his left hip. Eyes surely wider than possible, she lifted her head to see him staring at her.

Quiet. Intent.

"I was a soldier for five years, Georgiana. What do you think happens to soldiers?"

She traced the scars with her eyes. The pain and suffering written— no, carved—into him.

"I don't—I mean—"

He grunted and reached for a white undershirt.

"At least all of me is still here . . . in generally one piece." He studied her. Haunted. "Well, most of me . . . the parts that weren't already lost long ago . . ."

What—?

A pause.

He swallowed, Adam's apple bobbing visibly along his bare throat. Shook his head.

"I watched so many . . . saw so many—" He stopped. Clenched his jaw. "—so many men did not . . . are not . . ."

Shaking his head, he pulled on the t-shirt, shoulders flexing, covering the biography etched into his skin. Placing his hands on his hips, they faced each other.

For once, her imagination failed. Her mind cringed to think of him wounded, bloodied. Without her.

Alone.

Her vision swam.

"Who did this to you?"

He laughed, short and bitter.

"The French, mostly. Though I caught a bayonet along the ribs from a Spanish loyalist in Portugal."

Her heart thumped in her ears, a painful ache tightening her chest. Words failed. She could only nod.

"I am lucky to be here at all, in truth. I should have died twenty times over."

Wearily, he ran a hand over his face. Shook his head again. Gestured toward her, almost helplessly.

"But you see, I have this friend—blond hair, loves mysteries, perhaps you know her?—and I made this foolish promise at a ball once that I would return to her so—"

Something snapped within her in that instant. Some emotion she had been holding back, dammed off.

But with his words, it broke free and thundered through, scoured out every other feeling. Flooding her.

"Oh Seb!"

Hiccupping, she ran to him, wrapped her arms around his waist and buried her face in his chest, gulping back sobs. Hands pressed against the muscles of his back.

His strong arms enveloped her, cheek resting against the top of her head. He shifted after a moment, sending a hand up into her hair, massaging her scalp, easing her tension.

How *pathetic*!

He had a few scars from battle wounds *years* in the past and here she stood, soaking his shirt with tears. What was wrong with her?

But . . .

How could she not have *known* this about him? How could she have left him *alone* to fight and do battle without her?

Sebastian was her *dearest* friend. Surely at some point in the past five years, she could have at least *asked* how he was. Sent his sister a letter. Something.

Anything.

And how close had he come to not being here for her to hold? The thought made her cry harder, clutch him tighter.

After a few minutes, Georgiana wasn't even sure *why* she was crying anymore.

The flood gates had been loosed and now there was too much emotion inside, fighting for a way out.

Sebastian made soothing noises against her hair, rubbing a hand between her shoulder blades. Eventually her sobs quieted, but she still held him close. Sinking into the warmth of his strong arms around her.

She sniffled into his shirt. "That blond friend of yours was an *idiot*. She should have made you promise never to leave."

He didn't reply. But his lips did brush her head. She nuzzled her cheek into his shoulder, trying somehow to get even closer.

To absorb herself into him.

His grip tightened around her.

"Promise me you will *never* go back to war." Her voice muffled against his chest.

"I promise. I have definitely done my part against Napoleon. Besides, I am quite sure he is long dead and gone now." His quiet laugh rumbled under her ear.

"True."

She lifted her wet face from his chest, smoothing his damp shirt with her hand.

He gave her a small smile.

Wiped a stray tear away with his thumb, his touch scalding her cheek, his eyes pools of dark chocolate.

Impulsively, she popped up on her tiptoes and planted a kiss on his smooth cheek.

An affectionate, thankful sort of kiss.

Grateful for his life.

For his warm, beating heart.

Instantly, he went unnaturally still. Turned his head to her, their lips only inches apart.

Georgiana told herself to step back.

She still, *technically*, had a boyfriend. A boyfriend she kept neglecting to text . . . she really *should* step back.

But . . .

Unbidden, she found herself staring at his mouth. Aching.

Wondering. Being here, with him, like this . . .

It was dangerous in so *many* ways.

But . . .

Curiosity had *always* been her downfall. And she had spent so many days now wondering about those lips of his . . .

What if she closed that final inch? Claimed him? Their combined breathing pulsed in the room. She canted toward him, eyes blinking languidly.

Close . . .

And then, *he* leaned down. Brushed his warm mouth against hers.

Feather-soft.

Barely there and then gone again.

So quick and light, she wasn't even quite sure their mouths had actually touched.

Had he kissed her? Or had their faces just been too near?

A loud *whip-woo* cut through the silence.

His head reared back. Like whiplash.

He stepped back from her. Georgiana sucked in a breath, trying to clear her head.

Again. *Whip-woo.*

She grabbed her phone out of her back pocket, head spinning. She squinted. Text. Shatner.

Her boyfriend still. Technically.

Sebastian let out a short breath. "Let me get dressed."

She nodded.

"And I'll make a fire."

She nodded again. Swallowed and then found her voice.

"I'll fix breakfast."

She paused and turned to leave.

Stopped. Turned back to him.

"And then I want to hear every little detail about your time in the army."

Thursday proved another fruitless day of searching, foiled at every turn.

And the portal still wasn't working.

Sebastian was quite sure the universe hated them.

They had spent the day driving from place to place, getting nowhere. Stratton Hall was unexpectedly closed due to a roof leak. The nearby parish couldn't find the records for the particular years they needed. Lady Ambrosia *still* seemed to have never existed. And Lord Zeus was everywhere, but only as a gamer profile and new age religious figure. Nothing linked the name to a nefarious nineteenth century criminal mastermind.

In short, everything was conspiring against them.

Of course, it didn't help that the events of the previous day kept replaying over and over in Sebastian's mind. Nearly haunting in their obsessive hold.

He could still feel her body sobbing against his chest. Over what, he didn't know.

Surely not *him*.

And then he had *kissed* her. The barest brush of lips to be sure. But a kiss nonetheless.

Had she kissed him back?

He relived the moment yet again. That exchange of breath, the softest of touches before he remembered himself and pulled back.

Not that it mattered, really, whether she had returned the kiss-that-was-barely-a-kiss.

Only the worst sort of cad kissed a woman after she cried her pain into his chest.

Particularly a woman who was supposedly involved with another man.

It was *not* his finest hour.

Furthermore, he most certainly did not want to *ask* her about it. Such a question would likely earn him some pretty speech about mistakes and things-that-must-never-happen-again. Making him feel obligated to apologize.

And he no intention of *apologizing* for kissing her.

After she had calmed down, they had spent the day talking about his life as Captain Sebastian Carew.

There were so many experiences as a soldier that he had buried away. Talking about them was *not* on his list of preferred activities.

But she had been persistent, insisting she wanted to know, to understand what he had been through. Asking gentle questions, delicately coaxing the memories from him.

And still reeling from that feather-soft kiss, he had allowed her through his defenses. Had opened up and discussed memories he had never told anyone else. Horror and terror and pain he preferred to forget.

She had listened intently, lacing her fingers through his, putting a hand on his arm. Touching him somehow throughout.

Afterward, he had felt cleansed. Unburdened. Just that much closer to Georgiana.

For herself, Georgiana had recounted more of her travels and experiences in 2013, including a crash course in what she called taekwondo. He had found the dancer-like fighting moves fascinating.

Tonight, they were curled up on the sofa. This time with takeaway pizza and ice cream.

Watching that ridiculous Sherlock Holmes. Again.

"You do realize no one is that intelligent, right?" he stated after an hour of rapt attention, watching *her* watch Sherlock.

The play of emotions over her face—a tiny smile, a widening of the eyes.

"Hush." She swatted his arm without losing her focus on the television.

"Well, he is impossibly intelligent but also improbably dense, at the same time," he had to add.

She held up a stalling finger, again not averting her eyes.

"No. Just no. You are not allowed to malign Sherlock." She wagged her finger.

A pause.

She cast him a coy, sidelong look. "You're just jealous because he is so very *dashing* . . ." She clicked her tongue.

The minx.

He chuckled. "If by *dashing*, you mean good at running away, then I will have to concur—"

"Stop!" She elbowed his ribs. "So help me, I will drive to London tomorrow and buy you one of those overcoats. *And* the hat. Just so you can practice your *dashingness*—"

"Please. I don't need a *coat* to be considered all the crack. You wound me with your supercilious talk of—"

She let out an exasperated huff of laughter, breaking his thought.

"What is it?" he asked.

She turned to him, pressing a button which froze Sherlock mid-speech. Finally pulling her attention completely away from the television.

"How do you do it?" she asked, shaking her head in wonder.

He cocked a questioning eyebrow and rolled his hand. *Go on.*

"You can be so intense one moment and then all charm and ease the next. It's fascinating."

He paused.

Things had taken a decidedly unexpected turn.

"You find me *fascinating* . . . I am interested in the direction of this conversation . . ."

"Sebastian," she said warningly.

"No, no, far be it from me to interrupt. Pray continue."

She nudged his shoulder. "This is precisely my point. This is the Sebastian I knew. Endlessly charming, refusing to take himself or anyone else seriously. But there is now Intense Sebastian . . ."

They stared at each other for an instant.

"Intense Sebastian who looks at me just like *that*." She pointed at him.

"Like what?"

Another pause.

"Like I am the beginning and end of the world. Like he would like to throttle me and keep me safe all at the same time."

He laughed. He couldn't help it.

"Yes, that does pretty much sum it up."

She swatted his leg.

"And who do you like better. Charming Sebastian or his intense older brother?" He had to ask.

She stilled. Locked eyes.

And then leaned into him, curling up on his chest.

Again.

This time he wrapped his arm around her, and she tucked an arm around his back, resting the other on his stomach.

All feeling so much like home.

"Both," she whispered after a moment. "It's like I am suddenly seeing you complete. Whole. The person you were always meant to be."

He absorbed her words. But he heard them differently.

Ironic. After all this time, she finally saw the person he had always been.

Duir Cottage

September 20, 2013

Birthday in minus 18 days plus two hundred years

On Friday, Georgiana woke to a *whip-woo.*

Text from James.

> *Please tell me you have dumped Shatner.*

> Not yet.

> *Mmmmm, interesting not-so-subtle implication that you do intend to break up with him.*

> Yes. I need to talk with him.
> I'm just avoiding the conversation. He's always been so nice, and I feel like such a jerk. It will probably break his heart.

Eh. He'll get over it.
So does Stratton figure into all of this?
Georgie?
Georgie?
Where did you go?

Still here.

With Seb, it's complicated.

I mean, he's wonderful and . . .

Yes? ;)

Stop it, James. You know how Emme feels about emoticons.

Sebastian is wonderful and . . .
Go on.
:})
I've dubbed that emoticon the Sir Henry, btw.

No, you've ruined the moment. I can practically hear you laughing.

Well, if you want my opinion,
(which I am quite sure you do not)
I think Stratton is a lovely human being.

You can't say that about another man, James. It's creepy.

But true.

Are you bromancing again?

Ignoring that. Emme and I are making our way back to you. We should be home on Sunday :}p

Shaking her head, she texted more and then showered, dressed and joined Sebastian in the kitchen.

And spent most of the day trying not to think about him and war and all the horrid things he had seen.

And that kiss. Well, the kiss-that-was-barely-a-kiss.

Was it enough of a kiss to warrant a place on her list? Because if so, that brought her kiss count up to seven.

Which was actually an important thing for a woman to know.

She wanted to ask him about it but doing so would also mean acknowledging that *it* had happened.

Besides, did she want *it* to have happened?

Well, yes, she did. She actually wanted to explore *it* a bit more, if she were being truly honest with herself.

The problem, of course, lay in their current situation. Sebastian was unmoored from everything familiar and decidedly vulnerable. Kissing him without being more sure of her exact affections for him, and his for her . . . knowing they most likely would not share a future in the same century . . .

Well, it just wouldn't be kind. To either of them.

Like the rest of the week, Friday proved to be another day of fruitless searching. The person they needed to talk with at Stratton Hall was on holiday in Morocco until Wednesday. Records from the time period around Lord Blackwell's life were inexplicably missing from the family archive.

They were no nearer to their goal. Nothing made sense. What were they supposed to find here in 2013? Why allow a trip through the portal if they would not be able to see anything?

Georgiana pondered this as they sat on the sofa again.

"I like your toes," Sebastian said suddenly, staring at her feet.

Georgiana blinked. And then laughed.

"You do? Why?"

He shrugged. "They define you. Elegant and long. Expressive. I like this third one"—he touched it— "how it curls a little into its neighbor. Like it doesn't want to miss any of the fun. It wants to be part of everything. I bet it finds mysteries *thrilling*."

He was *right*, curse him.

It *did*.

How had he become such an expert on her toes?

As she had texted that morning to James, she had come to realize Shatner just wasn't for her.

He didn't *see* her. He liked the *idea* of her, just as she liked the idea of him. But that wasn't knowing.

And after spending so much time with Sebastian, she really liked being *known*.

Liked that there was someone in the world, other than a blood relative, who saw her to her very core and accepted her just as she was.

Just as she did him.

Man Sebastian and Boy Sebastian. Charming Sebastian and Intense Sebastian. Somehow they had all merged into the same person—a sweet, considerate, fierce, wickedly charming man she was coming to passionately adore.

It was an unsettling realization.

No. It was *terrifying*.

Because caring deeply for Sebastian would force her hand. Leave her with terrible decisions that no one should have to make.

Too much. It was too much to contemplate.

So she pushed it to the back of her mind.

And still didn't text Shatner.

DUIR COTTAGE
SEPTEMBER 21, 2013
BIRTHDAY IN MINUS 17 DAYS PLUS TWO HUNDRED YEARS

Saturday dawned bright and clear, an English autumn day at its finest.

After a week of chasing clues, they were no closer to discovering any answers about Lord Zeus and his nefarious nineteenth century activities. Instead of spending another day in futile research, Georgiana decided to focus on doing something to ease their minds.

So in that vein, she laundered and pressed the clothing they had worn through the portal. Meticulously dressed herself.

Perhaps a night spent in the nineteenth century would lift their spirits.

Chapter 19

The old guild hall
Herefordshire countryside
September 21, 2013
Birthday in minus 17 days plus two hundred years

Oooooh, Lord Stratton, *such* a pleasure to meet you," tittered Mrs. Withering in her muslin high-waisted dress and mismatched polyester gloves. She shot Georgiana a delighted look and then sank into what could only charitably be called an awkward curtsy.

Ever the gentleman, Sebastian gave Mrs. Withering his most earl-ish bow in return.

Hand tucked around Sebastian's arm and wearing the same white muslin dress and blue spencer she had on when she passed through the portal, Georgiana smiled warmly at her friend.

"Miss Knight, how extraordinarily kind of you to bring an—*ahem*—earl to our meeting." Miss Cartwright said *sotto voce* at her elbow. "He is most *dashing* . . ."

Miss Cartwright peered around Georgiana, stealing a peek at Sebastian, and then gave a happy little sigh.

Honestly, a group of debutantes and match-making mamas at Almack's could not have been more obvious.

Was there a group of women anywhere who did not go into a collective swoon at the sight of a man in tight breeches?

Every. Single. Time.

Sebastian's arrival at the Bosom Companions of the English Regency reenactment group had been nothing short of an earth-moving upheaval. The group had always been slim on male members, particularly those under the age of fifty-five.

The eleven ladies and three elderly gentlemen had spent the first five minutes just gaping at Sebastian in his well-ironed and brushed green coat with its ivory waistcoat. Fawn-colored inexpressibles hugged his legs, disappearing into tassel-topped Hessian boots.

For his part, Sebastian had readily agreed to attend the meeting and had taken delight in dressing as the Earl of Stratton again. Relieved to do something he understood, that didn't feel foreign and new. Georgiana had stared as he tied his neckcloth into a perfect mathematical. So precise and careful.

Tucking all of him back together into this wonderfully complex man.

She had to agree with all the ladies who now regarded him with decidedly starry eyes. He was most definitely swoon-worthy.

Sebastian caught Miss Cartwright's gaze and winked. Georgiana nearly poked him in the ribs.

Impossible man.

Though she did clutch his arm tighter. It was in no way a sign of possessive jealousy. She just enjoyed being near him.

Well, there was perhaps the *smallest* amount of jealousy involved—a thought she was afraid to examine too closely.

"Well, Miss Knight, thank you for bringing us a most proper gentleman!" Mrs. Withering gave a giggle and clapped her hands in delight, looking around the old medieval guild hall where they met, making sure everyone nodded their heads in agreement.

"Ladies. Gentlemen." Sebastian nodded in their direction. "It is indeed a pleasure to join you this evening. Miss Knight has been most lavish in her praise of your wonderful organization."

And then he did his worst.

He gave them *that* smile.

The one that spread slowly and promised charm and kindness and good humor.

The smile that said *you* are all that matters to me.

His smile hit the room with all the subtly of a lightning bolt. Georgiana saw it instantly reflected on the faces of all those present.

That smile *incensed* her.

Sebastian should know better than to so cavalierly toss it about. Such bone-wilting charm could do some serious damage.

Captain Wilson cleared his throat first.

"Miss Knight has briefly regaled us with your 'history,' your lordship," he said, obviously wanting to put air-quotes around the word *history*. "I understand you were part of the Eleventh Light Dragoons before becoming the Earl of Stratton. Didn't the Eleventh Light Dragoons see action on the peninsula?"

Each member of the society had their own nineteenth century persona.

Mrs. Withering was the widow of a wealthy landowner. ("Imagine Mr. Darcy's mother, were she still alive, bless her soul.") Miss Cartwright was the precocious daughter of a vicar, patterning herself after Jane Austen. Captain Wilson was pensioned military. Mrs. Smith styled herself as Lady Ashton, the wife of a baron. Tonight, she had arrived with a new paid companion in tow—a tall girl with lovely brown eyes. Lady Ashton was the only twenty-first century person Georgiana had met who still employed a lady's companion. It was odd, to say the least, listening to Lady Ashton chastise the girl for not fetching her laptop fast enough. The list went on around the room. Georgiana and Sebastian had opted to just be themselves.

"Yes, indeed Captain Wilson. We did see action on the peninsula. I was unfortunate to catch a bayonet from a Spanish loyalist in Portugal. Ugly wound that. I lay in a field hospital outside Porto for weeks afterward."

Georgiana only barely stopped herself from wincing. Would she ever be okay thinking about him wounded and ill so far away?

"Capital, capital, my fine fellow." Wilson clapped Sebastian on the shoulder, drawing him away from Georgiana. "I should love to swap tales of our adventures."

Captain Wilson—actually Fred Wilson who owned a dry cleaning shop in Leominster—obviously considered Sebastian's tale an excellent piece of fiction. For his part, Wilson was sometimes a captain in King George's navy and, at others, an officer at Waterloo. It depended on his mood and which of his two uniforms he chose to wear. Wilson always found a way to wear his sword.

Tonight, he was naval Captain Wilson, complete with bicorn hat, gold epaulettes on the shoulders of his blue coat and a sword strapped around his waist. Deep in conversation—well, Wilson talking to Sebastian—the men drifted to the side of the room.

Georgiana found herself talking with Mr. Montrose (accountant by day, Regency dandy by night) who had detained her with concern over the care of *his* new rapier. Georgiana didn't have the heart to tell him that wearing swords had gone out of style around 1790 for everyone but the military. But as Wilson wore a sword, Montrose insisted on sporting one too.

As she listened to Mr. Montrose, she watched Sebastian from the corner of her eye, strolling around the old whitewashed room with Wilson. He stopped to debate the age of the ancient ceiling beams with Lady Ashton and her companion and then paused before the flagstone fireplace to compliment Miss Cartwright's embroidery.

Irresponsibly, whipping out that smile of his again and again.

When she had the chance, she grabbed his arm.

"You need to be more careful," she muttered in his ear.

He instantly lifted a quizzical eyebrow. "I beg your pardon? Was I not kind enough about Miss Cartwright's embroidery? The orange and purple roses are not to my taste, but—"

She gave him a decidedly unladylike elbow to his ribs.

"No, it's your smile. You can't just go tossing charm around like that."

He gave a surprised burst of laughter.

"Like what?"

"Like—like its candy. Show some responsibility. Someone could get hurt."

"Get hurt?" His face was now comically confused. "Because of my smile?"

"Yes!" she hissed.

He stared at her for a moment. Chuckled.

"You mean *this* smile."

And then he did it again. That look spreading sweet and syrupy across his face.

The *nerve* of the man.

Georgiana had to clutch his arm a little tighter as her legs suddenly felt wobbly.

What right did he have to stand here and give her knee-liquefying smiles? The kind of smile that turned her insides to mush.

Wait, what?!

Oh dear.

Georgiana nearly gasped as she examined her emotions.

He *did* turn her insides melty. Every. Last. Inch.

Of all the *terrifying* things . . .

Her surprise must have shown on her face, because Sebastian cocked his head questioningly.

The large, guild hall door crashed open.

"Georgiana!" A familiar voice called behind them.

She whirled around to see Shatner closing the door and walking toward her. His stride was all swagger, and he smiled, though the expression seemed a trifle forced.

"Georgie."

"Shatner." She was sure her eyes were wide, wide.

He sauntered up to her. "I knew I would catch you here, luv. I've been trying to get hold of you."

He threw an arm around her shoulders, looking like he always did: tight t-shirt, tailored jacket, designer jeans. Hair studiously disheveled, chin stubbled. Though his scruffy beard seemed perhaps a titch longer than normal, his eyes blood-shot.

"Hey you," she managed weakly, turning her eyes to Sebastian. He stared at them together. In particular, his gaze drifted to Shatner's hand draped around her, eyes unreadable.

"I was hoping we could talk," Shatner said, leaning into her ear. "I've really missed you."

Georgiana still looked at Sebastian. Coming right after the realization of the depths of her affections for him, Shatner's interruption was awkward.

The entire *situation* was awkward. Particularly as her knees were still decidedly wobbly.

And how was it Shatner seemed so much smaller. Thinner. Was it possible for a man to shrink in just a matter of days?

She wanted to send Shatner on his way, slide her hand into the crook of Sebastian's arm and spend the rest of the evening basking in his bone-melting charm.

She knew she needed to break up with Shatner. Just to make it official. Her affection for him seemed so paltry now that Sebastian had taken up residence in her heart. Her heart pulsed in fast agreement with the thought.

But she had watched enough television to know the process probably wasn't going to be quick. And she really didn't want to spend the entire Bosom Companion meeting huddled outside in Shatner's car listening to his (deserved) recriminations, all the while wondering if Miss Cartwright was succeeding in her flirtation with Sebastian.

Shatner apparently had other ideas. "Georgie, c'mon. We need to talk."

With a hand on her shoulder, Shatner turned her around, drawing her toward the door.

"Shatner, this really isn't a good time." Georgiana tugged away from him. "I'm so sorry. Can I call you tomorrow—"

He whirled on her, his good humor slipping. "I've had enough of this little game, Georgiana."

"Shatner—look—I'm really sorry. I'll call—"

"Call me? You've been saying that for weeks now and I haven't heard one single damn thing—"

"I know, I know—I'm really sorry. Things have been a little . . . complicated and—"

"And what, Georgie?" Shatner closed the small space between them. Grabbed her arm. "I thought we had something. I thought you cared—"

Someone cleared his throat loudly behind her.

"Are you in need of assistance, Miss Knight?" Sebastian's deep bass sent goosebumps up her spine.

"No, she's fine." Shatner's eyes did not leave her face. "She and I were just leaving—"

Georgiana pulled on her arm. "Shatner, seriously, this is really a bad time—"

She felt the strength of Sebastian's body behind her finally drawing Shatner's attention. Shatner raised his head and gave Sebastian a good long look.

"You!" Shatner nearly spat the word, moving past Georgiana to stand in front of Sebastian, hands on hips. "You again. You've been keeping her from me, haven't you?" Shatner asked, voice taut.

Sebastian inched an eyebrow upward. Every line of him pure, carved aristocratic hauteur.

Intense Sebastian.

"I do believe Miss Knight is mature enough to know her own mind. If she has chosen not to contact you—"

"Who are you? Do you ever wear *normal* clothing?" Shatner raked him up and down with a derisive look.

Fluttering, Mrs. Withering intervened, ever the conscientious hostess.

"Mr. D'Avery, what a pleasant surprise." Her tone indicating it was anything but. "May I introduce the Earl of Stratton—"

Shatner rolled his eyes heavenward. "Again with this *earl* nonsense. Do any of you take reality seriously?" He swept his arm to indicate the group of people now surrounding him. "I mean, you are grown-ups, but you traipse around in ridiculous clothing wearing damn swords. Why don't you try living in the real world instead of some fantasy make believe?"

Shocked gasps echoed through the room.

"Really, D'Avery, a gentleman could demand satisfaction for such insulting words." Captain Wilson strode forward to Sebastian's side.

"Satisfaction?" Shatner stared at Wilson as if he had sprouted wings. Wilson drew his sword with an illustrative sibilant hiss.

"Are you kidding me? What in the bloody hell are you suggesting?" Shatner looked sufficiently outraged.

"Mr. D'Avery," Sebastian said in his most repressing of tones. "As there are ladies present, I would politely ask you to moderate your language—"

"Language?" Shatner let loose a string of profanity that was decidedly educational in its depth and creativity.

Even Sebastian's eyes widened in shock.

"Now see here, Mr. D'Avery," Mr. Montrose said, joining them, sword tangling awkwardly with his coattails. "As Lord Stratton has said—"

"*Lord* Stratton can kiss my—"

Shatner bit off his sentence and lunged for Montrose's rapier, whisking it out.

Everyone gasped.

"So what is this *satisfaction* you demand?" Shatner growled.

Mrs. Withering and Miss Cartwright clapped excitedly.

"Ooooooh, Miss Knight, how thrilling! You didn't tell us you had arranged a duel too." Mrs. Withering seemed poised to go off in raptures.

And then she let out a little scream of horror as Shatner swiped the sword at Sebastian's head.

With thinly concealed contempt, Sebastian backed up a few paces. Casually, he shrugged out of his green coat and handed it to Miss Cartwright to hold. He then ran a finger around his neck, loosening his cravat. Even in his shirtsleeves and waistcoat, he was a magnificent figure. Captain Wilson immediately handed his own sword to Sebastian.

Swishing their respective swords, the men faced each other.

"You should know, *Lord Stratton*,"—a world of sarcasm in that name—"that I spent nearly a term in the fencing club at Oxford. My mates said I had real talent."

Sebastian cocked his brows at Shatner's arrogance. "Indeed. How fascinating. I, however, did not learn sword fighting at university—"

"Ha! Exactly. Probably couldn't even get your sorry carcass accepted—"

"I learned fencing the old-fashioned way. Through actual fighting."

Shatner let his sword point dip and shook his head. "You have *got* to give up this ridiculous ruse—"

"Eleventh Light Dragoons, I say," Captain Wilson inserted, popping his head between them. "Lord Stratton served with the Light Dragoons. Said he took a bayonet on the peninsula fighting those Frenchies—"

With a grunt of disgust, Shatner feinted toward Sebastian, testing him. Sebastian stepped out of reach with an almost casual air.

Having seen enough of the two men at each other's throats, Georgiana ran between them.

"Enough, both of you. I don't want anyone to get hurt." She held out her hands.

Shatner snorted. "This enormous idiot has been trying to steal you away from me—"

"I have done nothing of the sort." Sebastian shrugged. "Miss Knight is fully capable of knowing her own mind. But far be it from me to deny you satisfaction."

Shatner held his sword high, strained, aimed toward Sebastian's chest. For his part, Sebastian held his own sword loose and low, the casual stance of a man used to weapons and combat.

Grunting, Shatner lunged, intent on ramming the sword into Sebastian's heart. Georgiana squeaked and stepped back.

With striking economy of effort, Sebastian smoothly sidestepped and with two well-placed taps of his own sword, flicked Shatner's weapon out of his hands, sending it clattering to the flagstone floor.

"What?! How did you—"

Magnanimously, Sebastian gestured for Shatner to pick up the sword.

"Try again," he said, dryly. "This time, keep your weapon a little lower. Had this been an actual fight, I would have run you through the heart by now."

With a grunt, Shatner picked up his sword and instantly lunged.

Georgiana watched the men parry back and forth. Sebastian clearly had Shatner well in hand. Despite his size, he moved quickly, deploying strokes with military precision.

She could clearly see him as a warrior in red regimentals, commanding his men, fighting the French with lethal brutality. Bold. Relentless. He would have been a formidable enemy on the battlefield.

Forget Mrs. Withering—she might go off in raptures herself.

As it was, Shatner posed little challenge. Sebastian sent the smaller man's sword skittering across the floor again two seconds later.

"I warned you to hold it lower," Sebastian said helpfully.

"You—you—" Picking up the sword, Shatner let loose an ear-sizzling stream of profanity most of which focused on Sebastian's manliness. Or the lack thereof.

Sebastian gave a patronizing *tsk tsk*—nonchalant and calculatedly pitched to be enraging.

"How disappointing, D'Avery. A true gentleman does not need to resort to profanity to give a cutting retort."

Shatner responded by slashing at Sebastian's head. Easily, Sebastian deflected the blow.

"Allow me to illustrate." Sebastian looked upward for a second—thinking—and then made a sweeping gesture. "'Pon rep, I heard tell a half-wit gave you a piece of his mind, and you, sirrah, have been dashed desperate to hold on to it.'"

Miss Cartwright giggled. Georgiana kept her lips pressed firmly together. Smiling would *not* help this situation.

With a particularly violent oath, Shatner rushed at Sebastian again, who neatly parried and danced away. Cool and collected, eyes intent.

He was obviously enjoying himself immensely.

Shatner continued to swear. "You obnoxious—"

"Well, if you must profane, at least be creative about it," Sebastian said.

Shatner lunged. Sebastian flicked the blade away.

"For example," Sebastian continued, "His lordship said you were a great asset. I informed him that, alas, he was off by two letters."

Captain Wilson let out a loud guffaw.

Still swearing, Shatner darted toward Sebastian.

"No? That one *did* perhaps require a little too much thought." Sebastian danced away. "Allow me to be more direct: I once considered you a pain in the neck. But now I find my opinion has sunk *much* lower."

Mrs. Withering tittered behind her hand.

Shatner paused, breathing heavily. Glared.

"Another?" Sebastian offered. "I understand you enjoyed playing horse as a child. Your friends portrayed the front end, but you were just yourself."

Sebastian gave an encouraging sweep of his sword.

"You see, D'Avery, that is how it is done. Now you try."

Suddenly, Sebastian grinned. Slow and decidedly wicked.

Terrible, awful, magnificent man.

How could she *not* adore him?

Shatner grunted again, panting heavily. "Yeah, well, calling you dumb would be, uh, an—an insult to—to . . . stupid people," he said.

Sebastian nodded, condescendingly encouraging.

"A decent effort. Though a little sluggish on the delivery and not terribly creative." He gestured with his rapier as if thinking. "I prefer something like 'I say, old chap. I hear you were shot through a forest of stupid and didn't miss a tree.'"

Georgiana giggled. A little too loudly.

Shatner whirled to glare at her.

She swallowed her mirth, slapping a hand over her mouth.

Sebastian tapped Shatner's blade, drawing his attention back.

"Careful, steady now. T'would be a terrible disappointment if your brains went to your head."

With a roar, Shatner lunged again, swinging wildly. Sebastian created a net of arcing metal around himself.

"I hear tell you are nobody's fool, but perhaps someone will take pity and adopt you."

"You immature piece of—"

"I fail to see why you are so angry with me, Mr. D'Avery," Sebastian said, parrying again and again, his blade flickering, holding Shatner at bay.

Grinning impishly.

"You have taken my girl and—"

Shatner lunged, blade slashing, which Sebastian, again, sidestepped, extending his boot as he did, sending Shatner sprawling spread-eagle to the floor. His sword skittered well out of reach.

Biting her lips to keep from laughing, Georgiana rushed into the fray.

"Enough! Enough, both of you." She looked at Sebastian

warningly—a look marred by her smile—and then knelt beside Shatner who had rolled onto his backside, still winded, glaring up at Sebastian.

Sebastian studied them, sword held loosely at his side.

All mischievous grin and effortless charm.

Tall, imposing. A fortress of strength.

Every inch the complete darling man she adored.

"We're leaving. I have had *enough* of this—this farce," Shatner said, scrambling to his feet and clutching Georgiana's hand in his clammy one. "C'mon."

Georgiana tugged her hand free from Shatner's.

"No," she said. "No, I will not be leaving with you Shatner. Not now. Not ever."

Still breathing hard, Shatner regarded her with wide eyes. Terrified. Panic-stricken.

"No—no! You can't do this to me, Georgiana." He ran an anxious hand through his hair and grabbed her wrist again.

"Shatner, I'm breaking up with you."

"C'mon, *please*. Do you *want* to kill me?"

"Kill you? Please."

"No, you don't understand. I will *die* . . ."

"Don't be so melodramatic—"

"You're *killing* me, Georgie. I will be hunted down and killed—"

"Shatner, that makes no sense whatsoever—"

"No, no! Please. Just talk to me. Let's work this out—"

"Shatner, people break up all the time. I'm sorry but we both need to move on."

"Georgie, c'mon, please." He pulled her toward the door, away from Sebastian and the rest of the room.

She grimaced and looked down, intending to tug her wrist away from his moist hand.

And then froze, gasping in surprise.

There. Just above his wrist. The mark of Lord Zeus, tattooed into Shatner's arm.

Branded into his skin.

Stark and severe in black ink. Unmistakable.

For once, every single hair on her body stood on end. Shock. Horror.

Shatner noticed her noticing.

She brought her eyes back to his. Huge and stunned.

Yanked her hand away.

"We're through, Shatner. Done."

She turned her back to him. Walked back across the room to the fire-place, hugging her shaking arms with her hands. Any lingering doubts or sense of remorse evaporated.

"Georgiana, please. Let me explain," Shatner's voice pleaded from behind her.

And then Sebastian's low rumble. "I believe the lady asked you to leave, D'Avery."

The blood rushing loudly through her veins drowned out the rest of the conversation.

Shatner? And Lord Zeus? How was that even possible? Her mind boggled with unanswered questions.

Dimly she heard Shatner say, "Tomorrow, Georgiana. I'll call you tomorrow. We can work this out," before the door slammed shut.

"What an exciting meeting." Mrs. Withering fanned herself. "Lord Stratton you must really come more often."

Chapter 20

IN THE CAR
HEREFORDSHIRE COUNTRYSIDE
LATER ON SEPTEMBER 21, 2013
BIRTHDAY IN MINUS 17 DAYS PLUS TWO HUNDRED YEARS

Georgiana was upset.

Tremendously, entirely overset.

Sebastian watched the dark lights flash along the highway as she drove. She had yet to speak more than monosyllable words to him.

Tonight had not been his finest hour. Baiting D'Avery like he did, mocking him, toying with him.

All week, he had been floundering in a sea of pounding emotions: frustration, loss, heartache, despair, anger. Seeing Georgiana in the twenty-first century and realizing all hope was truly gone, that she would never be his. And, then, losing his heart even *more* fully to her.

Just when he thought Fate could not be any more cruel, it somehow found a way to up the ante.

But tonight . . . it had just felt so blasted good to be himself again. To be properly dressed and in a situation where he marginally understood the rules.

And then D'Avery had arrived. The man who had practically been Georgiana's betrothed—someone Sebastian should respect out of good manners, if nothing else. A decent man who Sebastian had taunted and mocked and publicly shamed.

It was not Sebastian's finest moment.

She was withdrawn, obviously thinking. Trying to sort out some emotional upheaval.

Had his behavior contributed to Georgiana's decision to break off with D'Avery? Was she angry with him for portraying D'Avery in such a poor light?

Or was she just sad over the end of the relationship?

Regardless, it cut him to see her so upset. Particularly knowing he was partially to blame.

He wanted to hold her, cuddle her up against him, warm her toes and let her pour out her hurt and anger into his chest.

Let her grieve for the loss of a man who was not himself.

Come here, Georgiana, let me hold you and kiss away the memory of that other man . . .

What a despicable *cad.*

He leaned his head back against the seat, trying to breathe normally.

It was no good. The pain pressed in on his chest.

They turned down the now familiar lane, and Georgiana parked the car in the gravel driveway. Duir Cottage loomed in front of them, windows black. The enormous oak tree in the garden moved slowly in the cool night air.

Darkness engulfed them.

To his right, she sighed. A sad, lost sound.

He angled toward her in his seat, her face an inky silhouette against the window.

"I'm sorry," she whispered, soft and low.

He had expected many words from her.

Yelling, ranting. Helpings of much deserved guilt on his head.

But an *apology*?

No. That he had not anticipated.

He let out a gust of air.

"Whatever for?" he asked.

Turning sideways, she reached for him, instantly twining their fingers together, pulling his hand onto the center console between them.

"For the scene with Shatner, for being such an idiot, for dragging you into this mess . . ."

He nearly laughed at the irony of it.

"It should be *me* saying those things to you—"

"Really? What on earth do you have to apologize for?"

Even in the dark, some thread of light caught her golden hair, giving her head a faint aura. He could see her puzzled expression.

"I—I was hardly kind to Shatner tonight and for that—"

She gave what could only be described as a grunt.

"Ugh! Shatner."

"I am sorry for the way I treated him—"

"Please don't apologize, Seb—"

"I am sure the entire evening proved a shock and—"

"*That's* an understatement."

Staring down at their hands hidden in the darkness, she gently rubbed her fingers along the length of his palm.

Sending gooseflesh skimming the back of his neck.

After a moment, she nestled her smaller hand into his larger one, holding it tightly.

Sebastian took in a shuddering breath.

"Georgie . . . I'm sure in time you will move past this loss—"

She laughed. Shook her head.

"No—no, that's not the problem."

She let out a gust of breath, still shaking her head.

Sebastian waited for her to continue.

"He had the Zeus mark on his arm." Words said stonily. Toneless. "No, not just *on* his arm. Tattooed into it. Like a branding iron."

Sebastian reared his head back, a hiss escaping him.

"What?! How is that even possible?"

Georgiana gave a mirthless laugh.

"My thoughts exactly."

"Heavens, what a twist—"

"I know it's supposed to be thrilling—I mean, how could such a thing *not* be thrilling—but instead it's confusing and troubling. How is he involved in this?"

"Oh, Georgie . . . that's terrible. And from Shatner, no less." He squeezed her hand, trying to give some comfort. "I am sure in time your heart will heal, that you will not feel this . . . betrayal so keenly—"

She grunted, still shaking her head.

Back and forth, back and forth. Rubbed his hand again.

"I am so . . . *so* sorry. So terribly sorry I have involved you in this muddle—How can you ever forgive me?"

"Forgive you?"

She shrugged.

"Without this mess, you would probably be back in 1813 pursuing some perfectly normal woman and resolving the issue with the old earl's will . . ."

He trapped her hand in his. "No, no Georgie—"

"I am so confused, Sebastian. There is so much I don't know . . . So much—"

She stopped.

Something touched his face in the dark.

Her hand. Caressing. Tender.

Her fingers threaded into his hair.

"Georgie," he managed to say. Hoping his voice didn't sound whispery and faint.

It did.

Funny how difficult it was to speak past the yearning ache spreading through his chest.

A second hand followed her first, until both her hands were running through his hair, caressing his cheek. Long, languid strokes.

"What am I ever to do?" she choked. "So impossible . . ."

She leaned toward him.

He felt her breath against his ear, his temple.

Her lips brushing feather-light against his cheek.

So *impossible*.

The air stampeded from his lungs in a violent whoosh.

She didn't stop.

His eyelids. *Kiss.* His nose. *Kiss.* His chin. *Kiss.*

And then . . .

And then his mouth.

Ah!

Her lips were a wonder.

Pillowy. So unutterably soft. Moving gently over his.

Beseeching. Asking.

Lovely.

With a groan, he wrapped a hand into her hair and pulled her mouth more firmly into his. Demanding more. Needing more.

He was only human, after all.

Georgiana returned his kisses, measure for measure, hands clutched around his neck.

Somehow in all his imaginings—and there had been *many* of them over the years—he had never stopped to consider how she would taste.

But it hit him now with startling force.

Honey sweet. Liquid.

Sunshine and warmth and happiness.

She tasted of every hope, every want.

He framed her face in his hands, angling his head to drink more of her.

More of her sweetness. Her courage.

Her spirit.

All the while, a part of his mind danced with glee. He was actually kissing *her*. Finally.

Hallelujah!

Afterward, he could not recall how long their kisses had lasted. A minute? An hour?

He only knew it was not enough. A lifetime of kissing Georgiana Knight would scarcely be enough.

She pulled away, trembling.

Heaven knew he would never have been able to end the embrace on his own.

She let out a long, shuddering breath and sat back into her seat. Reclaimed his hand in hers.

He brought her hand to his lips. Kissed her knuckles lingeringly.

He refused to examine *why* she had kissed him. From shock? Loss? Or was it—finally, *at last*—something more?

No, those were questions he did not want to ask.

Ambiguity provided emotional safety.

And given the battering his heart had taken over the past week, he preferred to just let things *be*.

Georgiana lay in bed, replaying the events of the evening.

Sebastian fighting Shatner, so poised and calm. Fiercely charming in his witty repartee. Finally telling Shatner that they were done. Shatner and his startling tattoo.

Those *should* have been the events keeping her awake.

They weren't.

It was the memory of *his* kiss.

Of his warm mouth on hers, coaxing, demanding. The coiled strength of his hand in her hair.

The inexplicable *rightness* of it all.

As if she had been waiting her entire life for that one kiss. Her heart sang hosannas through her veins. But a thousand questions lingered.

Well, that wasn't quite true.

It was one question, and one question only, that plagued her.

Why had he kissed her?

Okay, so she had technically kissed him first. (Which made it decidedly seven men that she had kissed. No doubting the kiss this time.)

And she knew why she had kissed him. This new *awareness* of him demanded no less. She ached to be closer, to learn him. Like an explorer charting a new country, she wanted to get a stronger lay of the land. Understand the natives and how they viewed her.

But what had motivated him? Because he was a polite man? And when kissed, polite men generally returned the affection?

Though, he had definitely, *enthusiastically* kissed her back, a little more ardently than mere politeness, despite being quiet and reserved before and after said kiss.

What did it all mean? Had he wanted to comfort her, just as he had a few days previously when she had cried into his chest?

Or after all this time, could there perhaps be truth in all his teasing, that he saw her as substantially more than just a friend?

Her breathing went all fuzzy at that thought.

She had no answers.

She knew one thing only . . .

She ached to kiss him again.

After an hour of staring at her ceiling, she gave up. Maybe some ice cream and late night television would calm her.

Padding downstairs in loose pajama bottoms and t-shirt, she absently twisted her hair into a knot on her head, flipped on the light in the kitchen and then froze. Surprised.

Sebastian was there, leaning back against the island, a carton of ice cream in one hand, spoon halfway to his mouth in the other.

Dressed just like her: loose pajama bottoms and a t-shirt that hugged his shoulders.

Hair rumpled, side whiskers a little ragged. Dark eyes gleaming as they raked her from head to toe.

He looked so young, like a university student just down for the term. Not a weathered soldier turned earl and parliamentary lord.

The contrast made her knees weak.

He was utterly delicious.

Shooting her an appreciative look, he popped the spoon in his mouth.

"You willing to share that?" she asked, sauntering over, leaning against the island next to him.

He nodded, digging out another bite. Offering it to her from his spoon.

"I couldn't sleep," he explained.

She sighed, relishing the smooth chill of the ice cream.

"Me either." She took another offered bite. "What's bothering you?"

He ignored her question.

"Why does chocolate ice cream make everything instantly better?" He shook his head in wonderment, taking another bite for himself before gouging out a spoonful for her. "It's the most amazing thing."

"Seb, you are avoiding my question. What's wrong?" She fixed him with a stern stare. But still readily opened her mouth for another spoonful of ice cream.

He dug back into the carton. Shrugged.

"I have this friend. A very old . . . very dear friend, mind you. And as best I can tell, she broke up with a man she cares about . . ." He lifted his gaze and fixed her with his chocolate brown eyes. "And then, adding insult to injury, another old friend took advantage of her downcast spirits . . ."

His eyes flicked down to her mouth.

Oh!

He shrugged again. Turned slightly away. Head bent, digging out the last bits of ice cream from the bottom of the carton.

"How about you?" he asked, a little too casually.

Georgiana sighed. "Well, I have had an interesting evening myself. I realized my *former* boyfriend—who I have been meaning to break up with for several days now—is most likely in league with some nefarious underworld organization. But, surprisingly, that wasn't the most shocking revelation of the evening."

Sebastian instantly stilled, lifting his head. Offered her the last bite of ice cream. She licked it, leisurely, off the spoon.

"No? So what was most surprising?"

His voice sounded nonchalant. But the tension in his shoulders gave him away.

"Well, you see, I have this friend too. A very old, very dear friend. Really like a *brother* to me . . ."

He deflated, just like that.

A popped balloon.

His eyes shuttered and then he instantly turned away, walking over to drop the empty carton into the recycle bin.

Well.

That had been unexpected.

Apparently, he did not appreciate references—even ironic ones—to the once filial nature of their relationship.

Happiness burned through her like fire.

Giddy.

"I find I am exceptionally tired after all," he said, coming back around the island. "So I believe I will bid you good night."

He made her a small bow, which looked absurd in his flannel pajama bottoms and t-shirt. He moved to walk past her, but she stopped him with a hand to his chest.

His exceptionally firm, *warm* chest.

She could feel his heart beating fast under her fingers.

"You didn't allow me to finish," she whispered.

"Georgiana, it's late and—"

"Hush." She placed the fingers of her other hand over his mouth. "You see, I had always considered this friend to be more like a brother to me. But then . . . something happened. Well, it's been gradually happening over the last couple weeks."

He quit breathing. His chest just stopped moving under her touch. A light kindled in his eyes.

She continued. "Tonight, I—I realized when this excessively *dashing* friend of mine smiled, that slow, spreading smile of his . . . Yes, just like he is right now, in fact . . ."

With a wondrous laugh, Sebastian turned his head into her hand. Kissed her palm.

Wrapped his arms around her waist and pulled her to him.

He blazed with light. Like a beacon suddenly lit.

Popping up on her tiptoes, Georgiana whispered against his cheek, "Well, tonight I realized his smile turns my insides all *melty* and—"

Whatever else she intended to say vanished as his mouth captured hers.

Achingly tender, lips lingeringly cold from the ice cream.

She threaded her hand into his hair, somehow needing to be even closer. Her other hand slipped around to his back, reveling in the heat of his muscles radiating through the t-shirt.

He enveloped her in his arms, kissing her like a man in a desert.

Like he had been thirsty for far too long, and she was the only one who could quench it.

"So help me," he growled after a long while, "if you ever mention *brotherly* affections to me again . . ."

He emphasized his statement by giving her a decidedly *non-brotherly* kiss.

Georgiana laughed. A cascade of pure joy.

He groaned, hugging her to him. "Ah, darling, that laugh," he whispered. "That amazing, glorious sound . . ."

She laughed again. How could she not?

A while later, Georgiana found herself snuggled against him on the sofa, his arm wrapped around her.

His hand was large and warm on her hip, thumb moving in lazy circles that did tingly things to her insides. She had her head on his chest, the slow thump of his heart soothing her to sleep.

How could she ever bear to be parted from him?

It was the last thought before sleep took her.

Chapter 21

Sunlight pricked Sebastian's eyelids. For a moment, he floated in nothingness, disoriented, and then all the memories of the previous evening rushed back.

The sword fight, Shatner, ice cream.

Georgiana!

He had *finally* truly kissed Georgiana.

And, even more, she had kissed him back. Shyly admitted he turned her insides melty.

He nearly groaned from the sheer, dizzying happiness of it all.

It lapped through him. Relentless waves.

Kissing her had been . . . so . . . indescribably wonderful.

The taste of her, the feel of her in his arms. All impossibly right.

Grinning, he realized they were still on the couch, Georgiana's warmth snuggled up against him.

He had a terrible crick in his neck and his arm ached, but the comfort of just holding her, of feeling her arms around him, trusting, loving . . .

Eyes still closed, he sighed and gathered her a little closer to him, bending down to kiss the top of her head, rubbing his hand on her hip—

"So help me, if your hand moves even an inch higher . . ."

A cool, aristocratic voice knifed through Sebastian's consciousness.

With a gasp, Sebastian jerked fully awake. James Knight sat not three feet away in one of the wingback chairs, nursing a cup of coffee, legs crossed, foot bouncing.

Every inch the bristling nineteenth century gentleman, despite his jeans and t-shirt.

Ruthlessly surveying him, James took a leisurely sip of coffee. Slurping nice and loud.

Waiting for Sebastian to explain himself.

"Knight," he gasped weakly.

Georgiana stirred against his chest, nuzzled into him and then became more awake. Locked her blue eyes with her brother.

And practically launched herself away from Sebastian. Ending up on the other edge of the couch, face cherry-red.

Now she blushed.

"J—James," she stammered. "You made it home."

"Indeed." His voice a masterpiece of irony. "As you see."

James calmly regarded them both, taking another languid sip of coffee. Ensuring the noise was rattlingly loud.

Sebastian was quite sure there would come a time when they would all laugh about this.

Do you remember when James arrived home early and found Georgiana and me in the most compromising situation?

However, given the icy gleam in James' eye, that moment was still several months away. Maybe a couple years.

Georgiana shot Sebastian a panic-stricken look.

James sipped his coffee. Loudly.

Silence.

"Again, Stratton, I would be interested to know your intentions toward my sister." Only the tight bouncing of James' legs betrayed his anger.

A chuckle came from the kitchen.

Sebastian whirled his head around to see Emme leaning against the island.

"James, give it a rest," she grinned. "Georgiana is a grown woman. She's twenty-four, for heaven's sake. Stop being all nineteenth century, aristocratic weird about this—"

"She's my baby sister, Emme."

"You didn't mind her hanging out with Shatner—"

"Shatner was just, well . . . Shatner. But *Stratton* knows better. He is supposedly a man of honor, and I trusted he would behave in a most gentlemanly-like manner—"

"Yes, and you have had little fondness for Shatner."

"True, but—"

"You *like* Stratton, remember? He's a good egg, as you keep saying—"

"Agreed, but that doesn't give him the right to take liberties—"

"Liberties?" Georgiana found her voice. "Heavens, James, what kind of person do you think I am?"

Georgiana scooted closer to Sebastian, wrapping her hand into his, hair golden and mussed from sleep.

She was unbearably beautiful.

"Georgie, you are in no position to be—"

"Sebastian has been a perfect gentleman all week long—"

"*Gentlemen* do not curl up with well-bred young ladies who—"

Emme laughed.

All heads swiveled back to her.

"This is *not* humorous." James glowered.

"Riiiiiight," she drawled. "There is nothing funny about this *at* all." She laughed again.

James glared mock-daggers at his wife.

"What do you want to do, James? Force them to marry? Make her leave us and return to the nineteenth century with him?"

Sebastian blinked, as if someone had flicked cold water on his face. Right. How could he have forgotten. *That* enormous problem still faced them, no matter how much he and Georgiana enjoyed each other's kisses.

James stared at his wife for a second, scrubbed a hand through his hair. Let out a long breath.

Turned his eyes back to Sebastian and Georgiana.

"Well, what *are* you two going to do about this?"

Georgiana tossed her head.

"There is nothing to *do*, James. This is for Sebastian and me to sort out. So, let's just leave it."

James scowled. Emme chuckled.

Georgiana pulled her hand free of Sebastian's and started combing fingers through her tousled hair. "In other news, Sebastian nearly took a sword to Shatner last night and, obviously given other developments,"—she gestured with her free hand to the space between she and Sebastian—"I finally officially broke up with him, so—"

"Thank heaven! What a relief," James said with slight burst of air.

Georgiana raised her eyebrow, gathering her long hair and twisting it into a knot on top of her head. "I knew you didn't particularly love Shatner, but I didn't realize you were so opposed to—"

"Did you want me to fetch the file, James?" Emme interrupted.

"File?" Georgiana asked.

James nodded.

"Let's just say that things with Shatner were not entirely on the up and up. He was involved in some fairly dodgy dealings." James looked back and forth between Sebastian and Georgiana. "That doesn't seem to have shocked you as much as it probably should have."

"Gah! I forgot the best part!" Georgiana threw her hands in the air. "Shatner has the Zeus mark tattooed on his arm."

James hissed in a breath, eyes instantly widening.

"Well, well, well," he murmured. "*That* certainly makes everything more interesting."

"Doesn't it?" Georgiana bounced a little.

Ah, irrepressible Georgie. Nothing kept her down for long.

"What have you found?" Sebastian asked, grasping Georgiana's hand again. Not wanting to let her go, not caring if James saw the affection between them.

"I knew you were looking into his finances, but didn't realize you were doing such in-depth investigating."

Georgiana ran her thumb over the back of Sebastian's hand.

Over and over. Possessive.

It felt wonderful.

James shook his head. "I didn't intend to go so deep either, but it was like a collapsing haystack. Every time I grasped a straw, five more would poke out."

He stood and walked over to the large table, taking the folder of documents Emme handed him.

Curious, Sebastian and Georgiana followed, hand in hand. James spread papers out on the table, digging through them. He pulled out one, studied it, and then handed it to Georgiana.

"Basically, it turns out Shatner is involved in an organized crime ring."

Sebastian let out a low whistle.

James turned to his sister. "I am sorry to be the bearer of bad news, but dear Shatner never worked with orphanages or anything so noble. Most of his overseas trips involve drug trafficking or arms dealing. He is in deep with some extremely nasty people."

Georgiana stared at the paper for a moment. Morning sun poured through the large bank of windows, flooding the room with light, turning her hair into a halo.

Sebastian studied her, but she didn't show any signs of distress.

"But why chase me?" she asked.

"Well, I had tentatively committed to donate a rather large sum of money to his charitable organization . . ." James' voice drifted off.

Georgiana blinked at her brother, eyes wide in surprise. Sebastian felt momentarily ill. Dearest Georgiana deserved so much more than—

She startled them all by laughing. "That does explain quite a bit." She continued to smile, though a little wistful.

James cocked a questioning eyebrow at her.

"Heavens, James. You were always worried about nineteenth century fortune hunters but, as it turns out, such behavior isn't as old-fashioned as one might think. Poor Shatner just wanted to marry me for the money after all."

James sighed, nodding. "I am afraid that is too true."

She shook her head, laughing again and then leaned into Sebastian's arm. "At least I now understand how you have felt, Sebastian. All those women chasing you . . ."

He chuckled and wrapped an arm around her, pulling her close to him. Sebastian had never considered himself to be anything less than a gentleman. But despite her brother's presence, he wanted to hold Georgiana to him, breathe in roses and sunshine, bask in the wonder of her returned affection.

"All right, but Shatner had the Zeus symbol on his arm. Why that?" Georgiana asked, returning Sebastian's embrace and snuggling into his side.

James pretended not to notice their casual embrace. "The Zeus symbol is a kind of calling card for the organization. As the king of the Greek gods, Zeus represents supreme power and rule. Something the group obviously aspires to. The symbol appears over and over on their documents. It seems to be a title that is passed along, like being the mob boss or godfather of the organization."

James turned back to the kitchen table and dug through a few more items, the papers making a swishing sound.

"It is a puzzle . . ." He paused, examining one paper in particular. "Though, then again, maybe not. Look at this."

He thrust the paper at Georgiana and Sebastian. The letterhead made so much immediately clear.

GLIB was stamped prominently atop it.

"The Gooseberry Brotherhood seems to have been the front for the group."

"Heavens!" Georgiana gasped, turning to stare at Sebastian. "That is certainly . . . well . . ."

Sebastian nodded slowly. "That does explain quite a bit."

"It was the Gooseberry Lovers International Brotherhood all along then?"

"That society started by Lord Tangert," Sebastian murmured. "The fourth original member of the Royal Gooseberry show with the old Lord Stratton, Sir Henry and Blackwell. Though he was tossed out of the organization for being a cheat."

"Was he?" James asked. "My people have found hundreds of pages of documents, some of which go back over two hundred years. Many bear the Zeus symbol. It seems as if there was a Lord Zeus at least by Lord Tangert's time, if not even before."

They all stood, staring at the pile of papers.

"I have a meeting tomorrow in London with investigators," James said. "They will have warrants for the arrest of all the higher ups in the organization, including Shatner."

Georgiana nodded. "That is good. And this does help us know where to look in the past too, I suppose."

"Exactly," Sebastian agreed. "Though if I remember correctly, Lord Tangert and his younger son were lost in the wilderness of Labrador several years ago . . . well, according to my reckoning of time, that is."

James nodded, "True. And records going back that far have been vague and short on details. I still have no idea who is behind the threats in 1813."

"Yes, but now we at least know where to start looking in the past. We start with GLIB," Georgiana said.

"Who runs GLIB in 1813?" James asked.

"The current Lord Tangert, I believe," Sebastian answered. "The oldest son of the Tangert who was lost in Labrador. I think I've met the man once or twice in London. Seems basically a decent sort—"

"Yes, but then so did Shatner," Georgiana noted.

They all grumbled in agreement.

"Why does everything come back to gooseberries?" Sebastian asked.

"Wicked little fruit." Georgiana gave a small laugh.

They all looked at each other for a moment.

"So now what?" James asked.

"We know where to look." Sebastian shrugged. "Until the portal allows me to return, we hunt here for what information we can find. The Tangert family is a good place to start."

Chapter 22

Sebastian stood in the back garden of Duir Cottage. Alongside the rustling of the old oak tree, he could hear the far off rumble of the motorway, the hum of a car or two along the lane to Haldon Manor.

The sounds of twenty-first century life were ever present. But the sunlight was still the same. Early morning rays slanted across the garden, turning the trees beyond into a golden haze.

James and Emme had left early, heading to London to meet with investigators. Sebastian had come downstairs to see them off. He assumed Georgiana was yet abed.

They had managed to do some internet research yesterday. The Tangert family line had died out in the early twentieth century, so there was little there to help them. Returning to 1813 would probably be the best way to continue the investigation. At least in the nineteenth century, Sebastian had hopes the universe would no longer put obstacles in his way.

After their bit of research, he and Georgiana had stayed up late talking with James and Emme. The affection and closeness between Georgiana and her brother were obvious.

If the portal would allow him to return, would she consider going with him? Could he ask her to give up James and this modern world? Would her deepening affection for him be enough?

Sebastian couldn't even imagine summoning the words. Deciding she cared for him as more than just a brother, that he turned her insides melty, didn't mean she was ready to walk away from her life here, from the people she loved most in the entire world.

It didn't mean that she chose *him*.

The more he thought about it, the more glum he became.

How could he stay here with her? How could he leave the earldom and everyone in 1813 who depended on him? Sure, another distant relative would take over, but what about his mother and stepfather? His sisters? What about his own sense of satisfaction in making a difference?

But after having had the barest taste of Georgiana, the shattering vibrance that her love would be, how could he ever walk away from it?

He stood, watching the sun rise higher. The yard itself wasn't too large, an overgrown space with raised flower beds that had once functioned as a kitchen garden. A worn picket fence ran behind. But the fence backed the golf course of the Haldon Manor Hotel and Spa, so the garden seemed to stretch into the endless green behind Duir Cottage. Golden light spilled through the trees beyond the back gate, only marginally warming the autumn crisp air.

"Mmmmm, I looked out my window this morning and thought, who is that *dashing* man standing in my back garden . . ."

Turning, Sebastian chuckled as Georgiana shut the kitchen door, wrapping a shawl more tightly about her shoulders and knotting its long length in front.

Smiling, she joined him overlooking the trees, slipping her smaller, colder hand into his. He clasped his fingers around hers possessively.

It wasn't enough.

He drew his hand, still entwined with hers, around the small of her back and pulled her to him, snugging her body firmly against his chest. With a sigh, she twisted her hand free and wrapped her arms around him, returning the tightness of his embrace, measure for measure, pressing her head into his shoulder.

Sebastian slid a hand into her silky hair, threading his fingers, letting the morning light filter through it. Gold on gold.

"It was a morning just like this, you know," he said after a moment.

She pulled back slightly, eyes questioning.

"When I first met you. It was a crisp sunrise and you rose like a nymph out of the mist. You were twirling, your hair down . . ."

She continued to gaze at him, brow furrowed.

"The first time we met? When I was thirteen?"

"Yes. You laughed. I thought it was the most amazing sound I had ever heard."

She laughed.

"Exactly," he smiled. "Just like that. You were so lovely. I *had* to get to know you."

She blinked, obviously somewhat taken aback. And then smiled.

"Why are you telling me this, Seb?"

He shrugged.

"I've been standing out here trying not to think about what the future may hold," he said. "Which, of course, means I have been thinking nonstop about the past."

She sighed and cuddled back into his chest.

He breathed in deeply, letting the smell of roses wrap around him.

"I don't want to live without you, Georgiana," he murmured against her hair. "The timing may be difficult but, without you, I have no hope—"

With a small grunt, she pulled away from him, hugging her arms across her chest.

The abrupt withdrawal surprised him.

"Whatever is the matter?"

She regarded him for a second.

"This is back to that stupid clause in the stupid old earl's stupid, stupid will, isn't it?"

The *will!*

He had totally forgotten about that. The shock must have shown on his face.

"Seb, I know you need to get married and all—"

He laughed, a short, quick sound. Felt the emotion of her words jolt through him.

How could she doubt his love? But, then, he had never completely confessed his adoration either.

So he did the only thing he could do. The only thing he wanted to do.

He kissed her.

Hard.

Fierce and demanding. Pouring a decade of fruitless hoping and yearning and despair into that one kiss.

No mere touching of lips. But a siege.

She didn't stand a chance.

Her knees buckled—he held her tightly. Kissing her over and over.

"Enough, Georgiana," he murmured against her mouth, both of them breathing hard. "I could care less about that blasted will. I haven't thought about it even once in the past week. It doesn't matter—"

"But, Sebastian, you *have* to marry, we have been through this—"

"I do not *have* to do anything. The only thing I have ever wanted to do is marry *you*, you maddening wretch."

"Oh!" Her small gasp puffed against his lips.

He pulled back to cradle her wide-eyed face in his hands. Gazed into those blue, blue eyes.

"I love—" His voice cracked. He swallowed and tried again. "I—I love you, Georgiana . . ."

She traced his face with a hand, soft, wondering.

"Truly? It seems terribly convenient that you—"

He gave a bitter laugh. Stared at her with all the intensity of his soul.

"You are not hearing me, my love. I have always—*always*—loved you. From the first moment I saw you standing in that meadow, I have loved you."

He gave her head a little shake, just to emphasize his point. Like a burst dam, he couldn't stop the tidal rush of emotion.

"I love your curiosity. I love your laugh. I even, yes, love your absurd obsession with mysteries."

"Oh Seb!"

"As a soldier, I would hold the image of you at the ball at Stratton Hall all those years ago. Do you remember that night? Your golden head shimmering in the candlelight. It was your name on my lips as I charged into battle."

Her eyes shimmered in the morning light.

"I swear there were times when I felt I would give up my immortal soul just to spare you a moment's grief—"

He slid his arms down her back, pulling her closer to him.

"I never dared hope—I was the stepson of the vicar with supposedly distant ties to the Earl of Stratton. I knew you only ever saw me as a brother. I told myself it was enough. Enough to have your friendship. Enough to hear your voice, to know we both lived and breathed on this planet. I was such a liar. It was *never* enough."

He kissed her forehead.

"But then my fortunes changed and that dratted will gave me the perfect excuse to hunt you down. To find you and do what I could to ease your illness. I loved you so much—so very much—I wanted to give you whatever bit of happiness I could. To claim even the smallest part of your life as my own."

Chest heaving, she wrapped her arms around him again, holding him tight. Sebastian wrapped his hands into her hair, trying somehow to close the infinitesimal space that still remained between them.

"Do you think if I spend every day between now and eternity worshipping you that you will finally understand? Believe it deep in your soul that I *adore* you?" he whispered into her ear.

She pulled back to look at him.

"Seb, I—"

He stopped her with a finger to her lips.

"Hush. I know you don't love me as I love you. It is enough to think you might try. I am not going to ask you to marry me. Not now. I intend to have you for forever and do not want you to ever doubt *why* I begged you to marry me. I know the will stipulates I must marry before my birthday in less than two weeks, but I will not jeopardize your future happiness for a little money. The earldom will survive. The only thing I want—the only thing I have *ever* wanted—is you at my side."

She took another step back. Dazed. Blinking.

He ran a thumb along her cheek, so soft. So beloved. "My darling, I have waited ten years for you to finally *see* me. I will wait another ten if I must. If it means, in the end, that you spend the rest of your life with me."

"I—I don't know what to say," she whispered. "I adore you, Seb. Truly I do. But moving from adoration to love to marriage is still quite a series of steps. And just *thinking* about marriage brings its own set of problems. Where would we live? In which century?"

She gazed past him to the garden beyond. "It's just that with James here . . . Would you be willing to stay here? To give up on trying to force the portal to allow you to return?"

The very question he had been dreading. He dropped his hands to her waist, keeping her close to him.

"I don't know," he answered truthfully. "So many people depend on me back in 1813 . . . I made a commitment to God and country when I became an earl . . . Besides, what would I do here? I have no money—"

"James has money—"

"Yes, but I could hardly live the rest of my life on your brother's largess."

They contemplated each other for a minute.

"I am not sure this century is right for me," he confessed.

"But think of all the advantages. The medicines, the amazing machines . . ."

He smiled. "Yes, but I keep coming back to all the people who depend upon me. As an earl, I touch so many lives. I am a direct participant in government. I have influence. I have spent my entire life in anonymity, watching others have a purpose. I feel I have been given this amazing opportunity to make a difference, to live a life that truly matters . . ."

"Yes—but to live knowing that your child could die of an easily preventable disease, dealing with so many horrid things that aren't a factor in modern—"

"True, Georgie, but . . . how do I explain this? Every generation, every time and period in history, has its good and bad. Its highs and lows. Yes, this century offers distance from death. It offers equality unheard of in 1813. But those things only have come about because people in 1813 wanted change. Someone had to care first, someone had to fight in order for the world of 2013 to exist. And you know me. I have never been afraid of being on the front lines."

She chewed on her cheek, regarding him thoughtfully.

He ran a finger along her jaw and continued. "I was born and raised in the nineteenth century. I accept the reality of life then. Death will come to us all, regardless of when we live. I am sure people in 2213 will be appalled by the risks and squalor of life in 2013. And yet people here seem to get along just fine with the lot they have been dealt. That is the nature of each generation. Each time has limitations. We accept those we cannot change and fight to right those we can."

Sighing, she leaned into him. "True, but Seb—"

"Just a moment. Let me finish. When it comes to change, my reach is so vastly larger in 1813 than it is here. I want to live my life with you, but please consider living it with me in the nineteenth century. Come. Be my countess. Use your imagination and creativity to better the lives of the thousands who depend on me. Make the world—then *and* now—a much better place for your having passed through it."

His eyes pleaded, begging her to see.

Confusion warred within her.

"But James . . ." she whispered. "It would kill him to have me leave. And though he could maybe one day know what my life had been, I would never know his. I don't know, Seb. I do adore you, truly I do. It actually terrifies me. I recognize I could come to care for you with such an intense passion—"

Her voice broke. Shaking her head, she buried her face in his chest.

"There is time yet," he murmured, stroking his hands up her back. "The portal hasn't allowed me to return and who knows when that will change. Besides, I don't need to return home today or even tomorrow. We can wait it out. Talk with James. Examine everything. Besides, with

Lord Zeus in 1813 perhaps looking for you, it's probably best if we lay low here for a while anyway."

He held her, letting the happiness of her affection run through him. The *hope* of her love.

Time. He would give her time. All the space she needed to chose him. He had already spent a decade being patient. Another month or two hardly mattered.

He bent down and kissed the top of her head. Her forehead. Her eyes.

She let out a soft little breath. What else was he to do?

He kissed her mouth.

Like sinking into a feather bed, an infinity of give. Where he just kept falling and falling and falling.

Every hope, every longing focused down to that one solitary point.

How had he survived this long without her kiss?

As usual, when kissing her, time stilled. When he finally pulled his head back, the sun had risen considerably higher in the sky. She shivered and he hugged her to him.

She sighed contentedly into his chest. Dressed in those same loose pajama bottoms with the shawl drawn over her t-shirt for warmth, her feet—

"Georgiana Elizabeth Augusta Knight!"

She looked up at him.

"Do you *ever* wear stockings?"

She looked down at her extremely bare, decidedly purple toes. Wriggled them. Laughed.

"They don't feel cold. Someone has been doing an excessively good job keeping them tingly and warm." She gave him an arch look.

"Impossible woman," he muttered against her mouth and then, quite literally, swept her up in his arms, carrying her back into the house.

Georgiana laughed as Sebastian set her down in the kitchen of Duir Cottage. She did not know what the future would hold for them, but for now, it was enough to just *be*.

To laugh with him, to revel in the incredible rightness of being in his arms, to wonder at the miraculous gift of his love.

He *loved* her! This magnificent, amazing man had chosen her.

Shaking his head at her, he stomped over to the kitchen table and pulled out a chair. Dressed in a dark forest green cashmere sweater and jeans that made her heart skip. Though, honestly, the man would look devastating in anything. He kicked off the slip-on leather shoes he wore and then stripped off his thick socks.

He patted his lap.

"Sit." It was not a request.

Grinning, she walked over and sat primly on his knees.

"Foot." He held out a hand.

Wryly, she curled her leg up, sighing as he wrapped his warm hand around her blue toes. Poor things. Clucking his tongue, he put his sock on her foot.

"Other foot," he commanded, repeating the process. Georgiana wiggled her toes for him.

When he was satisfied, he tugged her to him for a lingering hug and kiss.

"Better?"

"Better," she agreed. "Thank you."

He rose, setting her on her newly-stockinged feet.

"Good."

"Breakfast?"

"Please."

He padded toward the fireplace, looking to put another log on the fire.

She pulled a frying pan out of the cupboard and grabbed eggs from the fridge.

She heard him move through the kitchen and down the hallway. Open the door to the cellar.

"Honestly, Seb," she called. "You check that thing every day. What would you do if the portal did work?"

Silence.

"Sebastian?"

Nothing.

She ran across the kitchen—slid, actually, in his thick socks—and into the closet.

Paused on the stairs.

The portal hummed, pulsed with electricity.

"Sebastian?"

But he was gone.

Chapter 23

Duir Cottage
September 23-26, 2013
Birthday in minus 15 thru 11 days plus two hundred years

Georgiana spent the rest of Monday pacing in front of the closet door.

She didn't dare go into the cellar. James wasn't home, and if she went into the cellar and was sucked through the portal, she might never see her brother again.

But *Sebastian*!

To not see his smiling face, to not feel the slow thump of his heart under her cheek, to not relax into his strength and courage.

To not have *him* . . .

She was sobbing in the hallway when James and Emme returned. Through hiccups and long pauses, she managed to tell them what had happened. James held her, and Emme listened as she cried out her fears and worries and heartache. Apparently, Sebastian's reason for coming through the portal had been fulfilled. He had discovered the origins of Lord Zeus, and Georgiana had learned the truth of her affections for him. And so the portal had taken him home.

But what about her? She and Sebastian were destined to be together, their circles completely linked. Of that, she was sure. The portal would most likely allow her to pass through. But knowing this, if she returned to 1813, the portal would probably be closed to her from that point on. There would be no coming back, no visiting James in the twenty-first century. She would be cut off from her brother forever.

What to do? She felt hopelessly trapped between the centuries, aching for both. James had been her past. But Sebastian was her future.

How could she live without *him*?

Tuesday dawned dismal and dreary. A description which encompassed more than just the gloomy, autumnal weather. It was if all the world felt her distress and decided to join in the melancholy.

He *loved* her.

He had *always* loved her.

She spent the entire day curled up on the couch, Staring at the fire and eating far too much chocolate ice cream. Digging up every memory she had of him. Sebastian defending her to the village boys, sitting by her bedside when she was ill. Waltzing with her at Stratton Hall. Begging her to marry him over and over. She had been such a blind fool.

James or Emme sat patiently next to her throughout, James rubbing her hand. Even Marc called from Bangkok in an attempt to cheer her up. They were so incredibly sweet and supportive.

Good, kind James. The person who, up until a month ago, had been the closest to her in the whole world. The man who was part brother, part father. The person who had taught her how to ride a horse, how to drive a gig, and how to shoot a rifle—much to Arthur's dismay. The brother who searched tirelessly to find a cure for her consumption.

How could she live without *him*?

On Wednesday, Georgiana determined to at least take a shower and change into clean clothes. But she walked by *his* room. Which led to her walking *into* his room.

Four hours later, James found her curled on Sebastian's bed, cuddled up with a pile of his clothing, his nineteenth century green coat wrapped around her. Breathing in the lingering remnants of wool and leather and Sebastian.

Her heart so heavy she could hardly speak, much less eat. Her toes were cold. She had forgotten to put on socks.

How was she to live without someone to keep track of her toes? She was completely toe-irresponsible.

Her future stretched before her, bleak and empty. Devoid of melting smiles, fierce protectiveness and toe-warming hands.

By late afternoon, Emme finally convinced her to take a much-needed bath. After which Georgiana huddled in one of the wingback chairs in front of the fire and cursed the fact she had nary a photo of Sebastian. Which lead to another violent bout of crying.

What kind of terrible person was she to not have a single real *thing* from him?

How could she live with *herself?*

On Thursday, James and Emme staged an intervention.

"Enough, Georgie," James said as she lay on the couch, staring listlessly at the fire. "Stratton hasn't died. He loves you and wants to marry you. You can join him."

Georgiana's bottom lip quivered. She licked a tear off her lip.

"But—but having him means losing *you*," she whispered.

Heaving a sigh, James wedged himself next to her on the couch, drawing her into his arms. She nestled into his shoulder.

"Then stay."

Georgiana cried harder.

"B-b-but that means leaving *him*," she gasped.

James held her, fingers stroking her hair, gazing sightlessly into the flames.

"There is no way to make this better for you, sister dear," he sighed. "Stratton is an earl now and justifiably tied to his life in the nineteenth century. He wants to make a difference, and I deeply admire him for it. He's a good man, Georgie, and will do great things with his life."

Georgiana heaved a terrible sob and then swiped at her tears. Hiccupped. "Wh-Why must this be so difficult? I've turned into the sniveling heroine of a gothic novel—"

"Hardly, my dear. You only *wish* to be the heroine—"

"James—" she warned.

"It's true. As much as you want this to be a melodrama, it's not. The decision is really quite straightforward."

"Please. There is nothing straightforward about this." She thumped his chest for emphasis. "It's an awful dilemma, full of heartache no matter what I decide."

He rested his head on her hair. "Life is full of hard choices, my dear. Life's greatest joys are often tied to life's greatest sorrows. Joy and pain are just two sides of the same coin. You can't have one without the other."

James took in a deep breath.

"I can't believe I am actually going to do this. I have a confession to make," he said after a moment. "Something I have never told you. Are you sure you want to hear? It's not my finest hour."

Mutely, she nodded her head against his chest.

"Right before Papa died, I intended to leave. I had been saving my allowance for months and managed to purchase a berth aboard a clipper bound for India."

Georgiana stilled.

How had she not known this?

"But then Papa died, and I found myself faced with the daunting task of being scarcely twenty years old and suddenly head of the family. Mama was beside herself with grief—"

Georgiana wiped a tear from her cheek. "I remember. It was terrible. All the wailing . . ."

"Exactly. So I sent you to live with Grandmama, as I was overwhelmed and could scarcely hold things together myself—"

"Which was a wonderful choice. We moved through our grief together and—and I met Sebastian . . ." Her voice wavered.

James nodded.

"I didn't bring this up to remind you of the past. I just wanted to help you understand what happened during those years."

Georgiana sniffed.

James continued. "After Papa died, I didn't give up on the dream of leaving. I worked toward slipping off on some adventure a few years later, figuring I could leave things to Arthur's care, but then Mama died. And we both remember what a difficult time *that* was . . ."

She did remember. She had been all of sixteen and so much in need of a mother's care. But James had shouldered the burden even then, helping her learn to navigate social situations. Helping her to move between being a girl and becoming a woman.

"I still wanted to leave. But then, a few years later, you fell ill. I committed to being with you until whatever end God saw fit to bestow. If you had recovered in the nineteenth century, I planned on seeing you happily married, and then I would head off on my grand adventure. Leaving was always in my plans."

"But you didn't leave, James. Well, at least, you didn't leave me. You could have, but you always chose to do the honorable thing and—"

"Hush. Let me finish. I am eternally grateful for your health. For the chance I have had to see you whole and well and so—so *happy*. You have always been a cheerful sort of person, full of energy and sunshine. But when Stratton walks into the room, you become incandescent. Lit from within in a way I can barely describe . . ."

Something wet hit her hand.

Instantly, she pushed herself up to sitting. Seeing his liquid eyes.

"No! Nononono . . . James, I cannot bear to think of being parted from you—"

"Georgie, I never expected you and I would spend the rest of our lives in each other's pockets." He touched her cheek. "That's what I am trying to tell you. I had always seen us apart. I suppose I have been fighting the reality of our separation, selfishly pulling you back to me."

He gave a wistful travesty of a smile.

"I love you, Georgie. You have been one of the best and brightest parts of my life. But"—he held up a silencing hand—"despite my great love for you, it is *not* the same kind of love I have for Emme. Nor should it be. There is a reason why we leave our parents and siblings to join with our spouse."

"Oh James . . ."

"We will be okay, both of us. It is enough for me to know you are happy and cared for and deeply, deeply loved. Stratton is a marvelous man. I could not give you up to anyone less than what he is."

James brushed a tear off of her cheek. Georgiana sniffled and reached up and did the same for him.

"Besides," he continued, "I think you have a love letter in 1813 you need to write. I would hate for you to mess up the space-time continuum somehow—"

"Oh my! I had almost forgotten about that ridiculous love note. You're right. I *do* need to write it."

Sebastian. How she adored him.

Beloved keeper of my soul . . . wrap me in the light of your love.

She would mean every single word.

Of course, just thinking about that letter brought home the reality of her decision. Choking, she buried her face in James' chest again.

"Be free, sister of mine," James whispered into her hair. "And think positively. We do have another brother. Imagine Arthur's joy in being able to casually drop '*My sister, Lady Stratton, said the other day*' into every other conversation."

Even through her tears, Georgiana managed a good, long chuckle.

Chapter 24

Sebastian was gone.

Georgiana had arrived at Haldon Manor in the rain, dripping wet, wearing the same muslin dress and blue spencer she had on when she left. Aching for Sebastian's embrace, straining for that first glimpse of him. For that moment when their eyes would meet, and he would know she had chosen him.

Over everyone and everything else.

But she arrived home to find Sebastian had just left.

Furthermore, final preparations were underway for a ball to be held that evening, thrusting the entire house into chaos. The great hall had been transformed into a ballroom with greenery and flowers festooning the walls.

Marianne squealed in delight over her return but had immediately been drawn back to directing footmen moving furniture around in the drawing room. Arthur emerged from (hiding in) his study, giving her an affectionate embrace and kiss upon the cheek, cheerfully welcoming her home. Despite everything, she did love her stodgy brother too.

She should have been desolate. She had rushed to Haldon Manor, expecting to find Sebastian here, waiting for her. To not find him was unsettling.

But being back home felt peaceful, calm. Right. Even with Sebastian's departure.

After greeting everyone, Georgiana had stolen to her room for a warm bath and even warmer set of clothes.

Her leave-taking from James and Emme had been heartbreaking. The goodbyes had gone on for hours, days really. It had taken her a week to reach the emotional point where she could go through with it, to pack all the last vestiges of twenty-first century life and say adieu. Marc had finished up filming and even arrived in time to watch one last Broncos game with her. They were all headed off to the United States next. First to visit Emme and Marc's mother in Denver and then on to Utah for some red rockin', as Marc called it. Whatever that meant.

James was still decidedly worried about the whole Lord Zeus intrigue and wanted to give Sebastian a little time to investigate. He had made Georgiana promise to keep a stun gun and mace on her person at all times.

But in the end, coming back had felt unbearably right. Without Sebastian, life in 2013 stretched before her with numbing sameness.

True, she didn't know what life in 1813 held for her, but she felt alive with hope. Hope that with Sebastian, her life would be full of purpose and belonging.

Now if she could only *find* him. Sebastian had left just hours before her arrival.

". . . and I am not entirely sure where," Arthur said. "I was out hunting early this morning—anything to escape the chaos of ball preparations—and returned to find that Stratton had received a letter and been called away."

They sat in his study, the bustle of servants, running to and fro, a thrum of noise in the background. The steady rain had eased, and now sun peeked through the racing clouds. The light in the room swiveled between gloomy dimness and sunny cheer.

"Thank you for concealing our absence, by the way. The trip through the portal was most unexpected."

Arthur waived his hand. "Well, I could not allow the entire affair to reflect poorly on your reputations. I put it about that you rushed off to Aunt Maud in Shropshire, helping her recover from the putrid sore throat. While I believe Stratton left to attend to business in London. Of course, when Lady Ambrosia and Lady Michael pressed me for the particulars, I did not have any. I am hardly in Stratton's confidence, am I?" He winked good-naturedly.

"Ah. Are the ladies still in the neighborhood?"

He shrugged. "Lady Michael and her daughters left not long after Stratton. Lady Ambrosia has remained, though I believe she has taken to plaguing Linwood and Blackwell at Kinningsley. You should see them all tonight at the ball."

Georgiana smiled. "The ball looks to be lovely. I am sure Sebastian will be sad to miss it."

"Yes, Marianne is quite put out over it actually. She had planned the ball for tonight, as it is the full moon. A festive evening to honor Stratton's continuing presence in the neighborhood. He was to have been the guest of honor. Though you will be true guest of honor, now that you are here to stay."

"Thank you, brother. It is wonderful to be home."

They sat in companionable silence for a moment.

"Stratton waited for you, you know. He has been here for the last two weeks, constantly sending out letters and closeting himself with Sir Henry or Lord Blackwell. Or both. Though I am not privy as to why. He confided in them but not me. Most likely, they have been sorting out this mess with the late earl's will."

She nodded. That was probably *not* what Sebastian discussed with

Sir Henry and Blackwell. Undoubtedly, he was working to uncover Lord Zeus.

Knowing that Zeus was blackmailing Lord Blackwell, Sebastian most likely confronted him, letting Blackwell know they were aware of his problems. She would have loved to see Blackwell's reaction when faced with his involvement with Lord Zeus. Bringing in Sir Henry was probably a good idea, as they knew Zeus had some ties to Tangert. Both men knew the former Lord Tangert and his gooseberry society. Pity no one knew what Lord Zeus looked like.

But she was comforted to know Blackwell and Sir Henry would be around to help. Now that she had a hope-filled future to look forward to, she preferred to get her thrills through books, not real-life cloak-and-dagger.

"Stratton most certainly didn't seem too concerned about his birthday, which is now only two days hence." Arthur shook his head. "Anyway, a letter arrived via courier at first light this morning, and Stratton headed off post-haste to parts unknown."

The sun burst through the clouds, flooding the room in brilliant light for a moment or two. Then retreated again.

"Did he leave a message for me?" she had to ask.

Arthur pondered her for a minute and then shook his head.

"No, not with me. But there is a chance Captain Phillips knows something."

"Captain Phillips is here?"

"He hasn't been seen these past few weeks, but he arrived this morning right after Stratton departed, frustrated to have just missed him. Though I am not sure where he has got to now."

Georgiana nodded. She would have to corner Phillips when he returned. She was desperate for any news.

After nearly two weeks, she ached for Sebastian. It was a visceral, gut-wrenching sort of need.

"I will be honest, Georgiana. Stratton did seem of the opinion that you and he had finally come to an understanding. Am I wrong to assume your presence here implies as much? In fact, I had faintly hoped the ball tonight would be a betrothal celebration, as well."

She smiled—a dizzy, happy smile.

The smile that said one's heart was no longer one's own.

Looking at her face, Arthur chuckled.

"Well, well . . . my sister . . . Lady Stratton . . ."

Georgiana laughed. She couldn't help it.

After chatting with her brother, Georgiana slipped out of Arthur's study and climbed the stairs to her room.

"Pardon, miss." Fanny's voice called behind her. Turning, Georgiana gave her maid a questioning look. "I'm dreadful sorry to bother you, but I thought you might want to see this."

She handed Georgiana a folded letter.

"'Tis Lord Stratton's. I were watchin' his lordship give his valet instructions as he left the great hall this mornin' and this letter slipped from his coat pocket. I snatched it up and tried to reach his lordship, but he was in a terrible hurry. I didn't want Mr. Knight to think I had taken the letter on purpose-like. But *you* know I would never do such a thing." Fanny stood twisting her apron nervously.

Georgiana glanced at the address:

Lord Stratton
Haldon Manor
Herefordshire

"Indeed, it is Lord Stratton's. Thank you, Fanny. You did the right thing. I will ensure this is returned to him. Please come to me in an hour to dress my hair for the ball." Georgiana smiled and then continued on to her room.

Standing inside the door, she contemplated the letter.

She knew reading another's personal correspondence was *not* proper. Even the letters of one's (almost) betrothed.

But . . .

Perhaps this was the letter which had sent Sebastian away on business. Maybe something had been discovered about Lord Zeus. Such information could be useful. And were Sebastian here, he would surely share its contents with her.

Besides, the handwriting seemed vaguely familiar now that she studied it some more. She ran her fingers over the address again. And then frowned.

Wait! No!

No, no, no!

It couldn't be!

She turned the letter over and with shaking hands, opened it. Covered her mouth with her palm.

Impossible!

And yet . . .

The parchment quivered as she read:

Lyndenbrooke
October 3, 1813

Beloved keeper of my soul,

Oh, my darling love! I have been so blind, so unseeing of my own affections. You and only you rule my heart. Can you forgive me? As I sit writing this, there is a hole in my heart the shape and size of you. Your beating heart might as well be my own.

I came to Lyndenbrooke, hoping to call on you at Stratton Hall, only to find you departed. Wretched, wretched fool that I am, longing for your love. Please come to me, comfort me with the warmth of your embrace. Whisper those words of adoration I so long to hear from your lips. If you will have it, I offer you the profound love that comes from deep within a woman's soul. Darling, suffer me no more to pine for you. Come to me. Wrap me in the light of your love.

With a heart ever your own,
Georgiana Knight

Gasping, she sank to sit on the edge of her bed.

How—?!

The shock hit, making her breathing tight.

It was her handwriting. Or, at least, a fair approximation of it. Rushed, hurried.

But as she studied it more closely, she noticed some of the letters weren't exactly right. She didn't swoop her 'L's like that or close her 'P's so tightly.

It was her handwriting but not quite. Close enough that with the distance of two hundred years, she had never doubted its authenticity.

It had to be a forgery.

She sat motionless, too stunned to process more than the air moving in and out of her lungs.

What an unexpected twist.

She scrutinized the letter again.

Gah! She was *such* a dimwit!

It was so obvious now. Despite all of her lists and theorizing and studying, she had missed the most glaring clue of all.

The letter was signed with her first *and* last name. Who would ever sign a deeply personal confession of love so formally? *Idiot!* It was a dead giveaway.

And now that she really considered it, the letter was far too impersonal. Not a single reference to mysteries or toes or melting in the entire thing. Hardly the love letter she would write to Sebastian.

But who *had* sent it?

The answer seemed more evident with each breath.

It could only be Lord Zeus.

Turning the letter over, she examined the address on the front again. The Zeus symbol was nowhere to be found on the paper.

Surely this was the letter Sebastian had received that morning, the one which had sent him hurrying off. Upon receiving the letter, his thought process would have been as follows: Georgiana had come through the portal and, instead of looking for him at Haldon Manor, had immediately returned to Lyndenbrooke and Stratton Hall. And so he hurried after, eager to see her.

It seemed somewhat silly that he would believe she had straightaway left Duir Cottage for Stratton Hall. But, when faced with the letter that he had seen with his own eyes in 2013, why would he doubt? No, he would have thought it came from her, that it was a grand gesture of her love for him.

Which she *would* absolutely do, by the way.

But why would Zeus write such a letter in the first place?

The answer was immediately obvious. To lure Sebastian away from Haldon Manor before she actually *did* arrive home.

Which begged the next question. What did this mean for her, now that she *was* home?

The clouds continued to clear, and, as the first carriages pulled up the gravel drive, the night sky was bright with light from the full moon.

Being a daughter of the house, Georgiana stood in the receiving line with Arthur and Marianne greeting their guests. She curtsied and smiled to an endless stream of people.

As relatives, Lord Linwood and Lord Blackwell arrived first, Blackwell ostentatious in a deep red satin coat peppered with embroidered flowers. Linwood dutifully kissed his sister and stoically followed Blackwell, who minced his way into the great hall.

Lady Ambrosia arrived a short while later in a rose pink dress which, as usual, hid few of her charms. She threatened to tumble out of it as she sank into a polite curtsy. Sir Henry arrived right after the vicar, giving Georgiana an exceptionally fond kiss on the cheek. Or at least what seemed like a kiss despite the bristle of his mustache.

To one and all, Arthur made excuses for Sebastian's absence. Though he hinted over and over there would soon be a stronger 'connection' between the Knight family and Lord Stratton.

It was clearly one of the best nights of his life.

For her part, Georgiana wore an ice blue ball gown of duponi silk with tiny puffed sleeves. An embroidered sheer overdress, studded with rhinestones, flowed behind her. It was her favorite dress; she and the costume designer from Cosprop had worked for nearly a month to get it just right.

Though fashionably low-cut, the bodice was just loose enough to accommodate a small can of mace; the forged love letter and a stun gun rested in her reticule. Though danger seemed unlikely tonight. Thankfully. With pearls threaded through her hair and fashionable curls framing her face, she felt in her element.

If only Sebastian were at her side, the evening would be complete.

The fake love letter consumed her thoughts. How bitterly disappointing to find it was a forgery. She had so been looking forward to writing it for Sebastian.

Were it not for the ball, she would have set out immediately for Lyndenbrooke and Stratton Hall. She was positive that was where Sebastian had gone.

Well, maybe.

If the letter was the one he had received that morning.

But what if he had received the letter several days earlier? What if he had already sent word to Lyndenbrooke and ascertained the letter was a fake? Though the letter was dated October third, which meant it had been 'written' and posted only a few days ago . . .

Where *had* Sebastian gone?

It was so maddening to just sit and do nothing. But with Lord Zeus still obviously about, doing anything else would be foolishly stupid.

Georgiana loved mysteries, but even she knew when to stay put.

And so with a smile on her face, she danced the opening set with Arthur, who was in high spirits over the success of the evening. Linwood claimed the next set and was taciturn as ever, giving monosyllabic answers to all her questions.

Thankfully, Captain Phillips, who had arrived late, claimed her hand next.

"It is a pleasure to see you again, Captain," she said as he twirled her in a waltz.

He smiled amiably. "Thank you, Miss Knight. You look lovely this evening. I overheard your brother speaking with the vicar and, unless I am being impertinent, I believe congratulations are in order." He gave an arch grin.

Georgiana laughed. "Congratulations might be a bit premature, Captain, but I shall be most glad to see Lord Stratton again. Arthur said he left in such a hurry this morning. Would you happen to know where he went or when he might return?"

Phillips shrugged. "It is so hard to say with Stratton. I arrived after his departure, and he made no mention of a trip in his letters to me."

"Oh." Disappointment must have shown on her face.

"But I do know a few things," Phillips began hesitantly. "Perhaps between what you know and what I know, we could make a whole of it?"

"What a perfect suggestion, Captain—"

"Of course, a dance floor is hardly the best place for such a conversation. Perhaps you would be willing to meet me out in the garden in, say, fifteen minutes?"

"The garden?" Georgiana laughed. "Heavens, you have not been back from war long enough, Captain. Meeting in such a secluded place would surely leave us open to gossip." She thought for a second. "Arthur's study should be fine. I believe Marianne had the fire lit, and we will leave the door ajar. Fifteen minutes did you say?"

Phillips nodded, a smile teasing his lips. "Fifteen minutes."

Georgiana was in the study five minutes early, seated and studying the mysterious forged letter by light of the candelabra on Arthur's desk. Only her finger twining around and around the strings of her reticule on the desktop betrayed her impatience. A knock on the open door caused her to jump, dropping the letter to the desk surface.

"Beg your pardon. You were expecting me, were you not?" Phillips said impudently, walking into the room. He gave her a short bow and solicitously set the door to be slightly ajar.

"Miss Knight, I am so glad you have finally returned. I can only imagine Stratton's dismay when he discovers how narrowly he missed seeing you." He studied her for a moment. "To be honest, when you first disappeared, I thought Stratton had spirited you away, taken you off to Gretna Green or some such."

Georgiana gave a small laugh, placing her hand over the letter. "Yes, that would have been quite the scandal. As I am sure my brother mentioned, I was called away to tend to a sickly aunt in Shropshire."

Phillips nodded. They studied each other for a few moments, his eyes flicking to her hand over the letter. A few candles danced around the perimeter of the room, but after the blazing light of the ballroom, the study was dim.

"Well, Captain, let us compare notes." She indicated the seat across the desk from her.

He nodded again, thoughtfully, folding himself into the chair opposite.

"I must be honest, Miss Knight. Stratton is my particular friend, and I want what is best for him," he said, casually tugging on the sleeves of his coat. "Though I know he thinks most highly of you, I wonder if you are worthy of his trust."

The air in the room shifted slightly. He leaned back in the leather chair, arms folded across his chest, face suddenly devoid of any good humor. Every inch of him a military man of action.

"We both know the sickly aunt in Shropshire is a lovely fiction." His eyes studied her. "Stratton is a good man, and it sickens me to see someone toying with his affections. What precisely is your game, Miss Knight? Where *have* you been the last three weeks?"

Georgiana studied Phillips for a moment. According to Arthur, Phillips had been absent from Haldon Manor ever since Sebastian had returned. Had Phillips and Sebastian corresponded during that time? Had Sebastian confided in him? And if so, why was Phillips acting so severe toward her?

"Really, Captain. Such accusations are not worthy of you. Why would you doubt the veracity of my story—"

"I doubt the truthfulness of everything, Miss Knight. I doubt you even *have* an aunt in Shropshire. I doubt you had consumption last year. If I did not know for a fact that you were indeed Miss Knight of Haldon Manor, I would doubt even that."

Georgiana sighed. This conversation was not going quite as she would have hoped.

Again, how much did he know?

"Your loyalty to Lord Stratton is to be commended, Captain. But I assure you, I also have his best interests at heart. In fact, I was hoping we could pool our mutual information—"

"Why should I tell you anything, Miss Knight?"

She blinked.

Phillips shifted in his chair. "You give me no explanation and yet expect *me* to offer information—"

"Please, Captain, questions about myself are moot. Lord Stratton knows everything about me and my history. If he wished you to know, he would have told you."

"Ah." The word hung between them. "So you admit there is more to your tale than you let on. Again, what is your game, Miss Knight?"

They studied each other for a few heartbeats. Georgiana glanced down at the letter she held. Perhaps there was a simple way of knowing how much Sebastian had confided in Phillips.

Calmly, she reached for the quill sitting in its inkwell. It only took a second and two swipes with the pen to create the Zeus symbol.

There, on the edge of the letter.

She replaced the quill and edged the letter toward Phillips, allowing him to see the mark she had drawn, observing him carefully.

His reaction was subtle. A slight tensing around the eyes, his smile a little too forced when he sat back in his chair.

"You write me odd symbols, Miss Knight? Is it a game you and Stratton play?"

"No. It is not a game, Captain. Far from it."

Georgiana's mind played through all the possible reasons for Phillips' reaction.

He had clearly recognized the symbol, of that she was sure. But if Sebastian had told him about it, why not admit it? Her writing the symbol would indicate she knew about Lord Zeus too, that she was in Sebastian's confidence.

Unless Sebastian had *not* confided in him about the symbol.

Which meant Phillips knew about it some other way.

But how else would he know about the symbol?

Something crystallized within her. A sharp moment of revelation.

A terrible, horrible suspicion. A possibility she had not foreseen.

None of them had.

Phillips seemed so genuine.

But . . .

Wasn't that what they said about all criminal masterminds?

He still seemed nice, sitting there calmly across from her. However, small things betrayed his tension. His hands gripping the chair too tightly, his posture a little too erect.

Despite her attempts to keep her face emotionless, a startled gasp escaped her. Was she truly sitting across from a vicious villain?

The atmosphere changed, becoming instantly charged.

Amiable Captain Phillips suddenly disappeared, all smiles gone. He became a menacing, hard-eyed man, the whites of his eyes a little crazy around the edges.

Voices from the great hall buzzed in the background, the strains of the orchestra underlying it all.

She swallowed and casually picked up her reticule, the stun gun inside a comforting weight. Proud of how little her hands shook.

"I believe I have found out all I need to know." Georgiana stood and walked swiftly around the desk, intent on the doorway and escape.

He quickly stood as she rounded the desk and grabbed her arm. Holding her tight, eyes flinty and implacable.

"Oh no, Miss Knight. You will not be leaving so readily."

Chapter 25

Georgiana lifted her chin and gathered bravado around her.
"Captain, this is absurd. You are a guest in my brother's house.
How dare you threaten me—"

With a harsh laugh, he shook her arm and pushed her—none too
gently—into the chair he had just vacated.

Stripping the reticule out of her hand in the process and tossing it
back on the desk.

He placed himself between her and the door, so close his legs nearly
touched her knees. She had to crane her neck to look up at him.

"I admire your spirit, Miss Knight. Or may I call you Georgiana?"

"Miss Knight will do." She tossed her head, trying not to stare longingly at the reticule now lying out of arm's reach. "Shall I call you Lord
Zeus?"

He shrugged. "Many have gone by that name over the years. Let us
just say it is a title I . . . inherited."

Trying to match his insouciance, she rose from the chair. The door was tantalizingly close.

He pressed her back into the seat with a rough, firm hand.

He *tsked* and made a shushing sound.

"No, that will not do, Georgiana. You play a dangerous, deep game. I think you are in far over your little head." He leaned over her. "Such a pretty head it is. I would hate for anything to happen to it."

Her reticule with the stun gun lay tauntingly on the desktop. The mace can pressed into her chest, buried in her stays. At least she still had *that* on her person. It wasn't much protection, but it would be some. How to get it out?

He regarded her with dark, hooded eyes. His presence threatening.

Now terrified chills raced down her spine.

The sensation *should* have been thrilling.

It wasn't.

Why had she *ever* thought being held captive by a madman would be exciting?

He glanced at the desk and lifted the letter off of it.

Could she reach the stun gun in her reticule? If she had the right distraction . . .

"Why not have me break off with Sebastian? Why go to the trouble of a love letter?" She gestured toward the paper he held.

Mace and a stun gun. Both were in the room. Though there was always her taekwondo training too. Granted she was in a heavy ball gown.

"What? And have Stratton chase one of those wretched Burbank chits? Some pale London miss? No, thank you. My intentions are to ensure Stratton is convinced of your affections until *after* his birthday has passed."

He regarded her with a leering smile that made her flesh crawl.

Again, not in an exciting way. Unfortunately.

"Let me be clear, shall I, my dearest Georgiana." He ran a finger along her jaw. "From this point on, your future will be tied to your ability to make yourself . . . useful . . . to me. And we both know what happens to foolish women who stop being . . . useful."

"Like poor Miss Franklin?" Georgiana was proud her voice didn't quiver like her knees.

"Precisely like Miss Franklin. She proved most helpful for a while. I always like keeping a talented artist on hand for . . . projects." He waved the forged letter. "Fortunately, Lady Ambrosia has been an excellent replacement. She has truly captured your handwriting, I think."

Clenching her hands into fists to stop their trembling, Georgiana swallowed.

"Something tells me you were never actually a captain in His Majesty's army." His head reared back, indicating she had scored a hit. It was strictly a guess on her part, a delay tactic.

"Forgery has all sorts of uses. Letters of recommendation from a dead Canadian general, which gained me entry into any number of officer's billets—"

"And thereby enabling you to meet leaving officers who you could either extort or befriend, becoming a sycophantic hanger-on."

He studied her for a moment. "For being military men, soldiers are far too trusting of their own kind. Of course, forging love letters is decidedly more diverting."

He smirked, folded the letter and slid it into his coat pocket and regarded her with another of his sneering smiles. "I am always happy to have a new recruit."

"And if I refuse?" Georgiana said, voice resolute.

Phillips chuckled.

An ugly sound.

"Ah, Georgiana. You are indeed a lady with pluck. It is obvious why Stratton is so smitten with you."

She stared at the door beyond him. It was still slightly ajar. She only had to distract him long enough to make a break for it.

Despite all their precautions, she had landed in a dreadful fix.

But was she really . . .

Half the county *was* within earshot.

And heroines in gothic novels were invariably stupid. Which she would like to think she was *not*. Stupid, that is. Heroine, definitely.

Summoning her courage, she shrugged and made to stand up. Phillips pushed her back down in the chair.

She raised her eyebrows haughtily.

"Need I remind you, Captain, we are in *my* home. Surrounded by scores of people who will come running to my rescue should I scream—"

"And that is why you will not raise any alarm—"

"Why? Why would I keep silent?"

Phillips blinked. "We are alone together. The scandal of being caught—"

"Pfft! I am practically an engaged woman, and I do not think Sebastian will care overly much. Particularly once I reveal your identity—"

"You are truly a foolish woman." He leaned over her again, shaking his head. "I could wring your neck before a single cry could pass your lips—"

"Are you so sure? I am not much use to you dead—"

"This is what will happen." He bit off each word, enunciating it clearly. "You and I are going to walk out of here. You will plead a headache to your brother and then retire to your chambers where I will meet you. You will then accompany me—"

"Why?! Why in heaven's name would I do that?"

"Because . . . I will kill you if you do not." He cocked his head, as if explaining something to a remarkably stupid child.

Mimicking his look, she leaned toward him. "Really. And accompanying you into the night *will* save my life? I would rather take my chances in your speedy ability to, as you put it, wring my neck. Or, even better, put a bullet through me in my brother's ballroom if you must—"

"Ah, but I am currently holding Lord Stratton as a hostage. My men accosted him as soon as he left Haldon Manor. Will you risk his life too? A bullet could just as easily find him."

She froze. Gasped. Terror raced down her spine, choking in its ferocity.

No! Not Sebastian.

"Exactly, my dearest Georgiana." Phillips' lip curled, noting her reaction. "You see the seriousness of this situation. One word from me and *boom*. Lord Stratton is no more, lying dead in a puddle of his own blood."

No! The room swam before her eyes. She would do anything—

He took her distressed silence as agreement. "Excellent. I am glad that we are in agreement here. I trust I now have your full cooperation?"

She swallowed, staring at him. Phillips was all smug confidence.

If he had Sebastian . . .

But, as she thought about it more, she wondered. *Had* he captured Sebastian?

Emotional manipulation like this was *exactly* what made gothic heroines so dimwitted. She forced through her panic and looked at the situation rationally.

Threatening a peer of the realm was an extremely serious, hangable offense—one that Phillips had just confessed to her—turning her into a disposable witness. Leaving with him would be unbelievably stupid.

And if anything happened to Sebastian before his birthday, the earl's will would become null and void. All of Phillips' scheming would be for naught . . .

So even *if* Phillips held Sebastian—which she was starting to doubt he actually did—she still had at minimum two days to find Sebastian and free him. Something she could hardly do as Phillips' captive.

Phillips eyes narrowed, noticing the change in her.

"You're bluffing." She gave her head an calculatedly careless toss. "You don't have Sebastian as your captive. And even if you did, you would not risk his life. He is far too valuable to you alive. I, on the other hand, have no such protection. You will let me go—"

She pushed him again, trying to rise out of the chair. He was a large man, taller than James but not nearly the height and size of Sebastian. Even so, his chest was a solid wall. He shoved her back down.

What to do? She ran through her options.

She could scream. But how much of a scream could she manage before he choked her? He was less than an arm's length away.

The stun gun was on the desk, out of reach. The mace was in her stays, but he would stop her before she could retrieve it. Taekwondo was less effective when seated in a ball gown. But at the moment, a physical attack was probably her best option.

First, however, she needed to be free of her skirts. She rose again, acting like she wanted past him, but using the forward motion instead to lift her skirts up to her calves, loosening her legs.

With a low chuckle, Phillips pushed her down again.

"We can play this little game all night, Georgiana. You are going nowhere."

She quickly ran through all the *paegi* options in her head, trying to decide which freeing technique would be best for this situation.

Did she want to go with a cat stance or walking stance? Both were difficult when seated, but if she scissored her legs—

Oh, forget it.

With a quick jerk, she feinted to the right and used the slight distraction to plant a hard, solid kick to Phillips' groin. A satisfyingly direct hit. Simultaneously, she swept his body with her right arm, giving him a jarring knock to the skull.

As Phillips fell, she darted up, intent on the door. A scream ready in her throat.

But Phillips was faster. Moaning from her decidedly well-placed foot, he snagged her leg, sending her tumbling. Knocking the wind out of her, turning her scream into a muffled *oomph*.

Gasping, she flipped to her back and attempted a sweeping kick at his head. But the heavy fabric of her dress hampered her movements.

Stupid dumb dress.

With a snarl, Phillips crawled up her body—still panting—pinning her legs at the knees.

"You bloody little—"

Sitting up, she chopped his neck with the edge of her hand and scissored her legs, loosening his grip. She managed to free her right leg and delivered a solid foot to Phillips' solar plexus, freeing her other leg.

Rolling away, she tugged the mace free of her bodice and was nearly on her feet, when Phillips bear hugged her from behind. Her hands were still at her bosom, elbows bent. His tight grip trapped her hand with the mace at the level of her shoulder.

Thank goodness he had no clue what the black can contained. Holding her breath and closing her eyes, she twisted the nozzle so it pointed at his face behind her and sprayed the mace at point-blank range. The angle was awkward, so only a small amount of the pepper spray deployed, but it was enough.

With a howl, Phillips' hold loosened. Forcefully, she slammed the back of her head into his nose and delivered a sharp elbow to his ribs. He staggered back, coughing uncontrollably.

Without looking around, Georgiana dashed for the door and escape. Only to run into the rotund chest of Sir Henry coming through it—Blackwell right behind, moving as quickly as he could in his high-heeled dancing shoes.

"I say!" Sir Henry gasped, grabbing her arms, taking in her disheveled appearance.

"Thank heavens!" Georgiana gasped, clutching at Sir Henry.

Both men looked past her to Phillips, still coughing violently, rubbing his eyes.

With a flourish, Blackwell pulled a hefty pistol from inside his elaborate coat, cocked it and pointed it at Phillips' head. Hearing the noise, Phillips froze and lifted his face, nose bleeding, eyes red and swollen.

"A pistol, Bertie? And in a full evening kit, no less?" Sir Henry chuckled.

"They don't make clothing like they used to, Henry." Blackwell shrugged. "Dratted newfangled coats are far too tight to hold decent weaponry. Are you unharmed, Miss Knight?"

Georgiana nodded, noting a slight irritation from the pepper spray still lingering in the room. Phillips was coughing uncontrollably again, palms pressed to his eyes. He was obviously having trouble seeing.

Sir Henry patted her back. "Stratton said we were to keep an eye on you, m'dear. I am grateful we came looking—"

"He is Lord Zeus." Georgiana gestured toward Phillips.

Both men froze, staring at her.

"Why do you believe him to be Lord Zeus?" Sir Henry frowned. "He has always seemed most amiable to me."

Coughing a bit herself, Georgiana stepped back from Sir Henry and held up a staying hand. *Just a moment.*

Crossing the room, she skirted the still incapacitated Phillips and opened the large windows behind the desk to air out the room. The relief was almost immediate.

Feeling the fresh breeze, Phillips turned toward the window, still coughing.

"I would recommend staying where you are, Captain." Blackwell said grimly, his pistol trained on Phillips. "Keep your hands where I can clearly see them." Phillips shifted and Blackwell stiffened. "Or not. I should dearly love an excuse to shoot you."

Phillips instantly stilled.

"So you were about to explain, Miss Knight, why you believe Phillips here to be Lord Zeus," Sir Henry said as she rejoined him at the door.

She shrugged. "Check his arm."

"Ah, clever girl."

Blackwell motioned with his pistol. "You heard the lady. Show us your arm."

Phillips glowered at them, jaw obstinate.

Blackwell gestured again with his pistol. "As I said, I should dearly love an excuse to shoot you . . ."

With a cough, Phillips yanked up his sleeve. The Zeus symbol stood out in black isolation on his forearm.

"Well, well, well," Sir Henry murmured.

"How *did* you get yourself involved with this mess, Captain?" Blackwell said almost to himself.

Eyes swollen and still not quite focusing, Phillips jerked down his sleeve, his face taut. And then broke into another fit of uncontrolled coughing.

"Makes no sense, really." Sir Henry stroked his whiskers for a second. "Lord Zeus is linked to GLIB, but Phillips here was supposedly an army captain in Canada—"

"Phillips admitted he was never actually an army officer. He forged all his papers and letters of recommendation from Canada—" Georgiana snapped her fingers. "Wait! The giant golden gooseberry of Labrador!"

Sir Henry's mustache bounced. "Jack Tangert, old Lord Tangert's younger son—"

Blackwell hissed through his teeth. "Of course. I only met Jack Tangert once. He was barely a lad of seven at the time but . . ."

Both men paused, studying Phillips as he continued to wheeze.

Phillips sat on the floor, back against the desk, shooting them all angry looks when he could muster them.

"The resemblance is still there, in the eyes and cheekbones. Would not have thought to look for it, however," Blackwell said.

Georgiana surveyed Phillips, he seemed to be getting himself under control, though his eyes remained unfocused.

Wasn't this the point where the criminal mastermind told them his story?

But Phillips sat stonily on the floor, staring sightlessly straight ahead.

He was *such* a disappointment. In so many, many ways.

She grimaced. "Well, this has been a delightful evening, Captain Phillips—Lord Zeus—or whatever you would like to be called—"

"Jack," he said shortly and then coughed.

"Jack," she repeated. How . . . ordinary. Even his *name* was a letdown.

She tapped a foot on the floor. "First of all, you are not holding Lord Stratton hostage, correct? Because I am sure Lord Blackwell here would be happy to torture that information—"

"No!" Phillips eyes widened in alarm at Blackwell's wicked grin. "Stratton is . . . not in my custody."

A wave of relief rushed through her. Sebastian was safe!

"So . . . aren't you going to tell us why you did it?" She waited expectantly.

He said nothing. Just swallowed and rubbed his eyes.

"Would you like me to help you get started? Let's see. You clearly survived the trip into the Canadian wilderness that killed your father. Your father *is* dead, right?"

He stared beyond her. She took that as an affirmation.

"And then . . ." She made a rolling motion with her hand. *Go on.*

He shrugged again.

"Really, *Jack*, you could be more forthcoming." She pursed her lips. "You clearly do not appreciate the cathartic power of monologuing. All the best criminal masterminds do it. Chronicling your clever plot dulls the sting of being caught."

Phillips turned his head, obviously not interested in being cooperative.

Georgiana sighed. Just *such* a disappointment. "Very well, allow me to continue to fill in the gaps. I assume, based on what you said earlier about inheriting your title of Lord Zeus, that your father was Zeus before you. With his death, you took over the mantle. I'm guessing you had some sort of interaction with General Brock in Canada, enabling you to forge letters of recommendation. So, you made it back to England sooner rather than later, probably lying and blackmailing along the way. Gathering secrets. I'm guessing poor Miss Franklin last year was just another of your victims. You were blackmailing her and then killed her when she was no longer useful. Did her death force you to lay low for a while? Take your forged letters of recommendation and set off for the Channel Islands?"

Phillips sat stonily, coughed twice again. Saying nothing.

"And then you met Lord Stratton in the billet in Jersey. But why attach yourself to him?" Georgiana tapped her lips, thinking. "Obviously, you wanted money. And Stratton's need to marry would have been a good opportunity. No, but I'm wondering if there isn't more to it—"

"Revenge," Blackwell interrupted.

"Ah yes, Bertie, it was definitely revenge," Sir Henry agreed. "Knowing that GLIB was involved, we knew it must have something to do with old Lord Tangert. We spent most of this week discussing the matter with Stratton."

"Precisely," Blackwell agreed. "Tangert hated us—me, Sir Henry and the previous Lord Stratton, John Carew. We called him out for cheating, for injecting water into his gooseberries. Saw to it that he was banished from the Royal Gooseberry Show. Tangert was the type to seek revenge, even beyond the grave."

Phillips sniffed and shifted to stare at the door beyond them.

"Ah, that makes more sense," Georgiana agreed, gesturing toward the Captain and drawing his still-glazed eyes to her. "Clever, Phillips. Getting both money and revenge. Always a winning combination. What was the nature of the revenge?"

"Horrid," Sir Henry rumbled. "Two weeks ago, Stratton sent his Bow Street Runner after the case. The Runner turned up evidence that Lord Harward's death was anything but accidental. The carriage axle had been cut through causing it to snap, sending the carriage careening and killing Harward and his family."

"How dreadful!" Georgiana gasped.

Phillips glared at them in hostile silence.

"So he then hunted down Sebastian as the heir?"

"No. We still think that was a coincidence. Phillips was just fleeing the nastiness of Miss Franklin and Lord Harward."

Georgiana nodded. "Do you have anything to say for yourself, Captain?"

Phillips merely clenched his jaw and narrowed his eyes.

She shook her head and gestured toward him. "So let's continue this story. You ferreted out some indiscretions in Lord Blackwell's youth—we don't need to know them, by the way, your lordship"—said as an aside to Blackwell—"and used that leverage to force him into helping you and Lady Ambrosia prevent Stratton from marrying. Once Stratton failed to meet the criterion outlined in the will, twenty thousand pounds would go to Blackwell and then on to you. Further avenging your father and giving you a nice nest egg."

Still nothing from Phillips.

"And then you bludgeoned the Prince Regent to death and stole the royal jewels—"

"What the blazes?!" Phillips interjected, instantly sitting taller.

"Just wondering at what point you would contradict me. I take it everything else is true."

Phillips ground his teeth, his pointed silence her answer.

"Well, this most certainly has been an entertaining evening," Blackwell said. "We will need to bring Linwood and Knight into this matter. As magistrates, they will head up the rest of the investigation and prosecution."

Sir Henry nodded. "Agreed, Bertie. It has been nice to finally get some answers and understand how Tangert has been involved with this mess."

"Indeed, Sir Henry." Georgiana shook her head. "Imagine it. Gooseberries were part of this whole mystery from the beginning. Who knew such an innocent little fruit could be so nefarious?"

Sir Henry gave his characteristic booming laugh, mustache twitching.

"Ah yes, m'dear," he said affectionately, patting her arm. "Now you finally understand their captivating appeal."

Chapter 26

The fire had died low, casting the library into deep gloom. Only the candelabra at Sebastian's elbow provided a small pool of light. After days of rain, the weather had finally lifted, leaving the night air chill, hinting at winter. The firelight flickered, casting weary shadows on the books and dark wood.

A large window to the left of the room rattled.

Sebastian had arrived only that afternoon. In his haste to rush to Lyndenbrooke, his horse had come up lame, forcing him to spend the previous night in a cramped inn.

Once arriving, he had gone first to Lyndenbrooke only to find

Georgiana was not there. And, even worse, she had not visited Lynden-brooke for years, since before her illness.

After his desperate, mad dash to reach her, the devastation—the depth of the deception—left him speechless.

The housekeeper at Lyndenbrooke must have thought him a little crazed, as he stood in stunned silence, dripping wet in the front vesti-bule, looking all too much like a fool. The pity in her eyes had *not* been flattering.

He had then ridden the two miles to Stratton Hall nearby. But with the late hour, returning immediately to Haldon Manor was not advisable. He would wait for first light.

He had come to the conclusion that the love letter was a dupe, obvi-ously a decoy sent by Lord Zeus, luring Sebastian away from Haldon Manor before Georgiana 'returned' from Shropshire. Part of him was relieved she was still in the twenty-first century. At least, she was safe.

But . . . it also meant that Georgiana had not, in fact, returned.

The despair sat bitterly in his throat as he stared into the fire. For nearly thirty-six hours he had believed. Had thought she had returned to be with him. And then that letter . . .

That remarkable love letter—the one he had read in Duir Cottage, tucked into its plastic sleeve—to believe it had been meant for him all along.

The searing joy of it had been . . . indescribable.

Like a sunburst in his chest.

It had taken a while to resume breathing after reading it.

He had tucked it into his greatcoat pocket and then hurriedly packed for Stratton Hall and Lyndenbrooke. But when he had arrived, neither the letter nor Georgiana were to be found.

And so here he was. Staring into the fire in his library.

Alone.

Georgiana-less.

Aching to hear her voice, the tripping sound of her bare feet. Still vainly hoping that the portal would work. That she would chose to leave James and the twenty-first century to share a life with him.

He leaned his head against the wingback chair, trying to relax into its comfort.

He would wait for her, would return to Haldon Manor and keep his vigil, all the while trying to track down Lord Zeus and unravel the conspiracy.

He hoped Lord Zeus would not remain a problem for much longer. It was his birthday tomorrow and, as Georgiana Knight was still centuries away, the money would likely go to the gooseberry societies. Sebastian needed to return to Haldon Manor, if only to monitor the circumstances.

Though, it had been nice to see his parents and sisters this evening. They had gathered to greet him soon after his arrival, his married sisters bringing husbands, nieces and nephews with them. Everyone had begged him to stay for his birthday, at least, before leaving for Haldon Manor. Perhaps he would consider it.

The heavy ache would not leave. He knew Georgiana cared, but did she care enough? Would she choose him?

Over everything and everyone else?

And even if she *did* choose him, would the portal let her through? Were their lives truly linked?

Sighing, he settled farther into the chair, pinching the bridge of his nose. Dressed comfortably in fawn-colored trousers and loose shirt-sleeves underneath a heavy blue brocade banyan. The nineteenth century forerunner to flannel pajama bottoms and a soft t-shirt.

The window rattled again.

His subconscious registered the sound first, dismissing it. But then he remembered there was not a breath of wind outside.

What?

Warily, he stood and walked over to the window, intending to latch it more firmly. Only to see a familiar shape standing in his bushes, waving at him.

An impossibly beloved figure.

His heart stuttered to life.

Grinning widely, he opened the window and stared at Georgiana. Dressed in jeans, t-shirt, moto jacket and black beanie.

Despite the darkness of the night, it was like seeing the sun.

Hope flared through him, choking, effervescent.

"Good evening, sir," she said, giving him a bow.

"Georgie! You scapegrace!"

"I was hoping to have a word with his lordship, the most *dashing*, devastatingly handsome Earl of Stratton and was told he might be in residence . . ."

"Horrid woman! Get yourself in here before you freeze to death."

Chuckling, he reached down and helped her climb through the window, her hand decidedly chilled.

She was *here*. But how? When?

"I thought we agreed you would curtail your nighttime prowling." He shook his head as he latched the window shut.

"True." She gave him a decidedly unrepentant smile. "Consider this one last hurrah before I turn in my prowling sneakers."

She had chosen to return. Did that mean she had decided to . . .

His train of thought abruptly fled. Georgiana had reached up and pulled the cap off her head, her glorious golden hair tumbling down her back.

Sebastian forgot how to breathe, much less anything else.

Lovely. So lovely.

Had it really only been two weeks since he had last seen her? It felt like a lifetime. Far too long.

His arms acted without conscious thought, tugging her to him. Georgiana clutched him instantly, pressed her cheek against his thin shirt. She sniffled, kneading his back with her hands.

It took a second for him to realize she was shaking. Hard.

"I have missed you so." Her voice trembled.

"Georgie . . . darling . . . sweetheart," he choked, gathering her closer, kissing her head.

And, suddenly, her hands were on his face, in his hair. He saw a flash of her tear-stained face before her mouth claimed his.

Hot, needing.

Desperate to somehow hold him closer.

She tasted of tears and hope. Loss and joy.

"Seb—oh, Seb—I—" she whispered. Kissing his mouth, his jaw, his eyes, his cheeks. Over and over.

She was here! Georgiana Elizabeth Augusta Knight was here, in his arms, kissing as if she never intended to leave.

Happiness scoured him, seared with its intensity. Champagne bubbles in his blood.

Holding his head between her hands, she pulled back to gaze at him. Eyes luminous pools, brimming with such wonder, such happiness.

With his thumb, he brushed a lingering tear off her trembling cheek. She still shook like a leaf.

"Can we move over to the fireplace? I am quite frozen," she chattered.

"Poor darling!" He laughed and instantly swung her into his arms, carrying her over to the fireplace and setting her down. He turned and snatched a blanket from a corner cabinet as she crouched, warming her fingers. Face bathed in flickering amber light.

Smiling, he wrapped the blanket around her shoulders and grasped her chilled hands in his, pulling her to her feet. Shamelessly using it as an excuse to pull her back to him. Again. He had been far too long without her in his arms.

"I can think of much more effective ways to warm your fingers," he murmured against her hair.

Sighing, she slipped her hands inside his banyan and wrapped her arms around his waist, burying her face into his chest. Her frigid palms burned like two firebrands on his back.

He returned the favor, engulfing her. Pressing one hand between her shoulder blades and sending the other into her hair. Breathing her in.

"Ah, Georgie." Whispered in her ear. "My love." Brushed her cheek. "Georgiana."

Soft, so soft. Her lips were chilled, but Sebastian felt up to the task of warming them. He kissed her slowly, tenderly. Adoring how readily she kissed him in return. Savoring the rightness of her in his arms.

"Dearest, I was so worried. I got that letter and came rushing to Lyndenbrooke but—"

"Oh! That ridiculous love note!" She pulled back to look him in the eye. "Sebastian, I am so sorry you had to deal with that letter. Turns out, it was—"

"A forgery," he readily finished. "Yes, I suspected as much when I didn't find you here."

"I was so stupid! I should have realized from the very beginning it was a forgery."

"Darling, there is no need to berate yourself over it. It was an excellent mimicry of your handwriting—"

"True, but it was signed with my *full* name. Who signs their last name to a deeply personal love letter?"

Sebastian gave a startled chuckle. "Most certainly not you, my love."

"Exactly!"

She laughed. That one sound dearer than all others. The melody that promised sunshine and stars and earned her another bone-melting kiss.

"Georgie, darling, I want to know everything. Can you go back and start from when I left Duir Cottage? Catch me up to the present?"

With a laugh, Georgiana did just that. Telling him about her (sort of) emotional break-down after he left. Her conversation with James and saying goodbye to him in 2013. Arriving just yesterday to find Sebastian gone and then realizing the love letter was a forgery.

The entire scene with Phillips nearly stopped his heart. While listening to Georgiana describe the danger she had been in, he released her and paced in front of the fire.

And then there was Phillips himself . . .

How could Sebastian have been *so* deceived?

Phillips had been a good friend. The best of friends.

The feeling of betrayal was raw. Visceral.

Even after nearly an hour back and forth talking with Georgiana about it, the pain still lingered. The wound would take time to heal.

For now, he was just eternally grateful she was finally safe.

And knowing that Phillips was Lord Zeus did clarify quite a bit.

It explained how Lady Ambrosia had always known where to find him, why the ladies who surrounded him were completely unsuitable. Anyone who could potentially attract his attention had been kept away. Everything hindering him so he wouldn't have time to form a relationship before the deadline expired.

Even worse, looking back, he was sure Phillips had deliberately prevented Sebastian from hunting for Georgiana sooner. It had all been skillfully done. Phillips had just underestimated the depth of Sebastian's attachment to Georgiana and, of course, Georgiana's own prodigious sleuthing skills.

Now, Sir Henry had the matter firmly in hand and had ferreted out a great deal of information. He was a man of many talents, Sir Henry. They would be able to disband a good portion of Lord Zeus' organization.

For tonight, however, Sebastian was just grateful Georgiana was safe.

"So after fretting about you for most of the night, I left at sunrise this morning," she finished. They stood in front of the fire, her arms again around his waist.

"I don't even want to know how you came to be here," he chuckled.

She gave him a decidedly naughty grin.

"Let's just say Arthur will be none too pleased to find his strongest hunter has been momentarily, uh, borrowed from his stables. I left a note, crept out, saddled his horse and rode."

Sebastian chuckled, kissing her forehead. "That's my Georgiana."

She shrugged. "I just couldn't wait another day, another moment without seeing you. I was so . . . angry the letter was a forgery—"

"Angry? Truly? I supposed you might be disappointed, but forgeries *are* mysterious, so why—"

"No, angry. Extremely upset."

He cocked his head at her. Raised his eyebrows in question. *Please explain.*

"Ridiculous Lord Zeus beat me to it. I spent *all* last week excited to return home and compose the most glorious love letter known to mankind. And then, I arrive, and that dastard Zeus steals my thunder—"

"Ha! Pun intended?"

"Yes, thank you—and writes the letter himself. He spoiled all my fun, the wretch."

"Well, I am sure you will find a way to make it up to me—"

"Oh, but I did!" She pulled back from his embrace, digging a hand into her pockets. "I swear it was here . . . I stowed it away this morning before I left—"

"Pardon?"

"A love letter. I wrote you another one. A better one. A *brilliant* one." She had pulled her pockets inside out by now, finding nothing. The pockets of her jeans were empty as well. "No! Argh! How could I have lost it? Of all the terrible—"

"Hush, my love." He pulled her back into his arms.

"I lost it, Sebastian. It was here. How *horrid*! Am I doomed to never give you a heartfelt, romantic love note?"

Tears tumbled down her cheeks again, even through her smile. He brushed them away.

He kissed her cheek. "You could tell me instead."

"Darling, dearest Sebastian," she whispered.

Taking a deep breath, she took his head in her hands, forcing him to stare into her eyes. Swallowed her emotions.

"Sebastian Carew, I traveled two hundred years and rode sixty miles on horseback to tell you that I—" Cheeks glistening wet. "I love you. I love everything about you."

Her words were electric jolts of glittering happiness. Somewhere he forgot to breathe.

"I love the way you look at me like I am the beginning and end of your world. I love your fierceness, your teasing, your goodness."

The joy crashing through his soul stretched on and on . . . A heavenly sort of forever . . .

"I love that you are loyal and thoughtful. In short, I just love you—"

He kissed her.

Right then.

Right there.

Not to silence her. But because the swelling ache in his heart demanded no less.

A long kiss. The kind that dragged forever from one's chest.

"Darling Georgiana," he murmured against her mouth. "Beautiful, clever, sunshining Georgiana."

She kissed him lingeringly and then pulled back, laughing, swiping at her wet cheeks.

"I promised myself I wouldn't botch this." She stamped a foot in laughing irritation. "I had *ten hours* on horseback today to think about it. Gah. Dumb trip would have taken less than ninety minutes by car—"

"One hour," he corrected with a grin. "I've seen you drive, remember?"

Chuckling, she swatted his shoulder.

And then shook her shoulders and straightened her spine.

"Sebastian, I love you. And I have been thinking it would be a most excellent idea if I—well, you and I—were to make our relationship more permanent in nature—"

"Wait—Georgiana Elizabeth Augusta Knight, are you asking me to marry you?"

She paused for a second. And then stamped her foot again, laughing.

"I cannot *believe* I made a mess of that! Ten hours. I had *ten hours*, Sebastian, and I was so determined to do it right."

"Ah, Georgie. 'Tis tragic. And my first real marriage proposal too."

"Sebastian—"

"I mean, other women have strongly hinted at marriage, but you are the first to actually come right out and pop the question—"

"Sebastian, stop!" She was laughing more helplessly now.

"And then, it wasn't even a question, really, was it?"

"Well, it was to be my eighth and final marriage proposal—"

"Eighth? Really? Quite impressive."

"Do I detect some sarcasm in that?"

"Well, after witnessing so many proposals, one would think you would be more experienced. I mean, you should have at least knelt down—"

"Sebastian Carew, you are truly a dreadful man." She punctuated the statement by pulling his head in for a decidedly not-dreadful kiss.

A kiss which lingered for a while.

"Heavens but I adore you," she whispered against his mouth.

"Darling," he murmured in return.

She sighed and leaned back in his arms.

"I have always wondered why men fumble with marriage proposals so," she said "*Now*, I know. It's like a thousand emotions all crowding in, demanding space in your head, and before you can think clearly, words just slip out."

He chuckled and opened his mouth to speak, but she stayed him with a hand.

"No. Let me try again. As I intend this to be the *last* marriage proposal of my life, I want it to be perfect."

She straightened her shoulders. Gave herself a shake. Nodded.

"Sebastian Carew, my sometime investigative wingman, efficient toe-warmer extraordinaire, giver of bone-melting smiles, but most importantly, dearest love of my heart, I would be forever humbled if you would do me the honor of accepting my hand and make me yours. Darling, will you marry me?"

The tears tumbling down her cheeks did nothing to dampen the luster of her smile.

Sebastian was quite sure his face looked the same.

"Georgiana." He cleared his throat. "Darling, dearest girl." He kissed her forehead. "Yes. A thousand times yes."

With a giggle of joy, she threw her arms around his neck, and he swept her up, into his embrace.

After a moment, she pulled back with a start. "The will! I had completely forgotten. Seb, your birthday is tomorrow, there is no way, with the banns to be read and Gretna Greene too far—"

He laughed and kissed her nose.

"Nonsense! I am not an earl for nothing. I arranged last week for a special license from the Archbishop of Canterbury. We can marry at first light, in whatever location you wish . . ."

She smiled.

That wide, wide smile.

Lush.

Impossible not to kiss.

And so he did.

Epilogue

Sebastian Carew reclaimed his heart on his twenty-seventh birthday.

He stood in that same meadow near Stratton Hall—morning light slanting through the surrounding autumn fire trees—where he had first lost his heart.

Watching as Miss Georgiana Elizabeth Augusta Knight walked slowly toward him through the dew-kissed grass. Blond hair hanging loose in waves down to her waist, shimmering like spun gold just as poets described.

The goddess of love come to him.

That precise point which divided his life ever after into two distinct parts.

Before her and *after her.*

When she firmly tethered him to her gravity, finally claiming the other half of his soul.

The special license granted them permission to marry anywhere, indoors or out, and so Sebastian chose this meadow. The place where all his hopes had begun.

As vicar, his step-father officiated the service. His mother wept.

His sisters, their husbands, and all his nieces and nephews cheered wildly as he kissed his new bride.

It was as if some divine angel were smiling down upon them all, bestowing grace and joy.

The quickness of their marriage did not allow Arthur and Marianne to attend, and so Georgiana asked to honeymoon at Haldon Manor, turning Duir Cottage into a cozy love nest.

As was expected, Arthur Knight was beside himself over their union. It is said he shed more tears than anyone when informed of the marriage.

This day found the happy newlyweds curled up together on a sofa in Duir Cottage. It was not the same sofa as existed in the twenty-first century, nor was it in the kitchen (that being the realm of servants, as befitted nineteenth century life), but it was still a comfortable sofa, over-stuffed and situated in front of the fireplace in the front parlor.

Georgiana was curled up beside him, snuggled completely against his chest. For his part, Sebastian had one hand around his wife's waist and the other wrapped around her ever-cold toes.

"You are a countess and, yet, you still cannot seem to keep stockings on your feet," he murmured against her hair.

She laughed softly and cuddled closer to him.

"You are a horrid enabler," she said in return. "You provide me with no motivation to *want* to be toe-responsible—what with your deliciously warm hands. You have only yourself to blame."

She made sure her voice sounded properly prim.

He chuckled under her cheek.

"Impossible woman," he muttered.

Later on. Not on that day, but a week later when the sun shone bright and the leaves clung desperately to that last gasp of warmth, Georgiana stood in the hallway at the closet door.

Clutching a folded bit of foolscap in her hand.

"You have to come down with me and not let me go," she said, turning to Sebastian. "If something goes wrong, there is no way I will be separated from you again."

"Agreed."

Hand in hand, they descended the cellar stairs. The portal hummed, sending electrical pulses through the air.

"This probably won't work, but I have to try," she said into the quiet damp.

Squeezing his hand tightly and keeping him close by her side, she walked forward to the portal. Kissed the note in her hand and pressed it against the stone.

And then gasped, as it was instantly absorbed into the rock.

"Oh! Oh my!" She jumped back, clapped her hands in delight. "Sebastian! Do you think it worked? Do you think James will get my note?" Even in the gloomy darkness, her eyes shone brightly. "I just so wanted him to know about our marriage. That I am happy and whole and at peace."

Sebastian smiled, kissing her forehead. "I am sure he will know, my love, one way or another."

Still hand in hand, they walked back upstairs and spent the rest of the afternoon talking about the foundling hospital they were to build near Stratton Hall, Georgiana's eyes glowing with excitement. For his part, Sebastian eagerly awaited the completion of the new bathing rooms being installed.

Hours later, Georgiana peeked down the cellar stairs. There, resting on the dirt floor, a large envelope gleamed in the darkness.

"Sebastian!" Breathless with excitement. "It worked! He sent some-thing back—"

Sebastian was at her side in an instant. Again, clutching his hand tightly, they descended the stairs. She snatched the envelope and scrambled back up to the hallway.

Georgiana studied the envelope. There was a large post-it note affixed to it. James' bold, swooping handwriting was unmistakable.

Congratulations, Georgie! Emme and I are so happy for you and Stratton. As I said, I could not have let you go to any less a man than he.

I am relieved the portal understands our lives will always be linked, allowing us to send messages to each other. You are so very dear to me, and I cannot wait to hear about the mysteries and scrapes you land yourself in over the years. Just as I am eager to tell you about my travels and life here with Emme. Be happy, darling Georgiana. Know that you have a brother in the twenty-first century who cherishes and loves you.

On another note, this came in the post for you. Or rather, for Stratton.

I love you, sister mine.

James.

Shooting Sebastian a puzzled look, she opened the envelope. And gasped.

Inside was a plastic sleeve—so very familiar—but the letter was different.

Though she *did* recognize it, despite the paper now being yellowed and moth eaten.

Licking a tear off her lip, she wordlessly handed the letter to Sebastian.

Haldon Manor
October 7, 1813

Beloved keeper of my soul,

How I have missed you, my darling! I have returned, never to leave.

I had always imagined true love to be like a gothic romance: the brave, mysterious knight rescuing the swooning heroine, winning her devotion. But I was wrong. True love—true bravery—is a best friend who never gives up. Who waits for you, who comes for you, even through Death and Time, if needed.

Thank you for cherishing my heart, for keeping it close, long before I knew you held it. For indeed, you are my heart, steadily beating, fiery and bright.

I love you, my darling. More than anything and anyone else.

Georgiana

"Oh my love," Sebastian whispered, kissing away her tears.

"—it's just . . . the most divine—"

And indeed it was.

All of it.

Author's Note

As usual, when writing a story set in the past, I have incorporated select aspects of history and then blatantly made up others.

Some facts that I borrowed from reality and/or history:

Gooseberry societies and competitions were an actual craze in early 19th century Britain. The obsession described in this book was rooted in very real historical fact. Gooseberry clubs and competitions continue to be popular today. Also, I use the original meaning of the phrase 'to do gooseberry' or 'to be a gooseberry' in the book. The phrase isn't one that most Americans would be familiar with at all. But nowadays in Britain to be a gooseberry means to be a third wheel, an unwanted interloper. Originally, to do gooseberry meant to be a lax chaperone—someone who was along for propriety's sake, but would turn a blind eye to lovers stealing a kiss or two. The meaning of phrase has just morphed and changed over the last 200 years.

Genealogical Good Samaritan societies do exist, though they usually focus on reconnecting descendants with old family bibles.

Cosprop (www.cosprop.com) is an actual organization which provides period costumes for film, television and theater. My thanks to them and to the Brigham Young University Museum of Art for the amazing Cosprop exhibit they hosted. There's nothing quite like seeing period costumes up close and personal.

Additionally, Major-General Sir Isaac Brock was killed in the Battle of Queenston Heights near Tecumseh, Ontario on October 13, 1812. And from my (admittedly limited) research, the Eleventh Light Dragoons did see action on the Peninsula. Dr. James Carson, who I mention in passing, was an early researcher of tuberculosis working in Liverpool in the early 19th century.

Things I completely made up: the golden gooseberry of Labrador, the town of Marfield and all the estates listed in the book. Also, in several instances, I deliberately chose to use the American word for something instead of the British, just to avoid unnecessary confusion. For example, Georgiana runs around with a flashlight instead of a torch. But given that she is in the past at the time, she very well could have had a torch too . . . so you see the problem. Wherever I could, I chose the most accurate word possible.

As with all books, this one couldn't have been written without help and support from those around me. I know I am going to leave someone out with all these thanks. So to that person, know that I totally love you and am so deeply grateful for your help!

First of all, thank you to all those who read *Intertwine* and sent me excited emails, asking about the next book in the series. Your encouragement and enthusiasm means more than I can say.

To my beta readers—you know who you are—thank you for your helpful ideas and support. And, again, an extra large thank you to Annette Evans and Norma Melzer for their fantastic copy editing skills.

A huge thank you goes to Lois Brown, author extraordinaire, for being a wonderful writing buddy throughout this process and ensuring Georgiana's mystery was satisfyingly tied up at the end.

And I cannot even begin to thank my brilliant editor, Erin Rodabough. She has the amazing gift of being able to hone in on problems and provide solutions. No to mention just being an all-out awesome friend. Thank you so very much.

Thanks, again, to Andrew, Austenne and Kian for your patience and all the nerf gun wars waged outside my office door while I wrote.

And finally, no words can express my love and appreciation for Dave. Really, just . . . no words. Except, maybe, I love you.

Reading Group Questions

Oh yes, this book has reading group questions.

Why?

Well, the English professor in me couldn't publish this book without making it vaguely educational. And obviously your reading group would show excellent taste by selecting this book—reading groups don't always have to be about the classics and Oprah's Book Club. Sometimes you just need a shameless don't-judge-me read. And any book that has reading group questions has to have redeeming literary qualities, right? So you're totally justified in assigning it.

You're welcome.

1. Was Sebastian too obsessive in holding on to Georgiana? Was Georgiana too obsessive in her love of mysteries? Is there a point at which we should let go of something, even if it really matters?

2. From the very beginning, Georgiana is faced with the terrible decision of staying with her brother in a century she likes well enough, or returning to the century of her birth and a way of life that is infinitely more dear to her heart. Throughout history, people have chosen to leave their parents and siblings behind and pursue a life elsewhere with their spouse. How do you feel about Georgiana facing such a decision? Were you content with the resolution at the end?

3. At what point did you solve the mystery? Did you feel like the resolution with the original love letter and the villain were satisfying?

4. For me, writing is only fun when I can incorporate a lot of voice, meaning there is attitude and personality in the narration—so you get a sense of Sebastian or Georgiana's thoughts throughout the book. Do you find this kind of narration more enjoyable to read or do you prefer the writer's tone to be 'invisible'?

5. When writing historical fiction, you face a conundrum. Do you stay completely true to the language of the period or do you allow it to be more modern (and therefore more accessible to readers)? Some argue that the language of the past would sound colloquial to those of the same time period. For example, a gentleman of 1813 might describe a new carriage as 'bang up the mark,' whereas my brother would describe his new truck as a 'sweet ride.' Though the phrasing is different, the words would have the same casual meaning in both eras. Considering this, how should language be used in historical fiction? Should authors use completely modern language, instead of trying to recreate the cadence of older English, in order to more perfectly capture the sentiments expressed?

6. As a writer, I feel the look of words on the page can communicate meaning as well. Therefore, I deliberately used line breaks, non-traditional punctuation, italics and visual cues to help convey tone and cadence. Did you find this helped as a reader, making your reading flow more easily? Why or why not?

7. Alright, let's cast the movie of the book. (Cause hey, we can dream big, right?) Who plays Georgiana? Sebastian? Etc. In the movie version, what aspects of the book should be thrown out, condensed or altered? Also, what should the theme love song be?

8. I chose to self-publish this book and never considered seeking a publisher for it. How do you feel about the indie self-pub book market? Are you more or less likely to read a book that has been self-published? Do you even notice/*care if a book is self-published?*

House of Oak Series

Divine is the second book in the House of Oak series, which will eventually feature four books (and perhaps a prequel novella showing how the locket was sent on its way to the US, but I haven't firmed that up yet).

As of this writing, the books in the series are/will be:

Intertwine (James and Emme)
Divine (Georgiana and Sebastian)
Clandestine (Marc and Kit)
Refine (Linwood and, yes, Jasmine—coming Summer 2015)

Turn the page to read the prologue of *Clandestine*, book three in the House of Oak series.

Clandestine
HOUSE OF OAK, BOOK 3

PROLOGUE

EXCERPT FROM THE JOURNAL OF GARVIS SAMUELSON

LONDON
APRIL 14, 1828

*T*his was the one—I was sure of it. The wound that would finally kill him. I watched the knife sink deep into my employer's shoulder. I fired at the assailants, but they melted into the London mist. My master collapsed in the dark alleyway, blood rapidly darkening his greatcoat.

I was part of his crew, as he sometimes called us—the group of men who protected and served him. For our part, we simply called him W.

W had survived so much, but as I turned him over, I feared the nasty wound would turn inevitably gangrenous. All the money in England would not be enough to save a man from such an injury. Not even the infamous W, who owned a good percentage of that money.

"Garvis," W said to me between clenched teeth, "in my coat pocket . . . there is the information Wellington seeks. Ensure he receives it."

I nodded my agreement. More men than just W had bled for the information those documents contained. The fate of the British Empire hung in the balance.

How I got W back to his townhouse, I cannot remember. Once there, I handed off the blood-stained letter with strict instructions to place it directly into the Duke of Wellington's hands.

Two footmen carefully lifted W into a clean bed. Lean and tall, W still had the vigor of a man ten years younger, despite the gray creeping in at the edges of his dark hair.

"You know the drill." W fixed me with his pale eyes as a valet cut away his gory clothing. "That special poultice I discovered while in Brazil. Flush the wound with my best brandy before stitching it closed, and do not let anyone—on pain of death—come near me with a leech or bloodletting lancet."

These instructions were not new. W had this same odd ritual around all his wounds. The valet and I flushed and stitched the wound, applying the poultice of herbs and honey. All the while, W mumbling strange sentences, like 'Hope tetanus vaccine is solid' and 'What I wouldn't give for an antibiotic.'

But this, also, was nothing particularly unusual. W occasionally said inexplicable things like 'whatever, man,' and he had a strong affinity for the word awesome. By this point, I had given up making sense of it.

As we were wrapping the wound in clean muslin, W grabbed my hand tightly. "If I end up delirious, do not believe a word I say."

W did well that first night, sleeping fitfully. But despite all our precautions, a fever set in the next morning. W descended into delusional ramblings.

Naturally, I had been through this before with my employer, but usually W's mutterings were quiet and indistinct. This time started like all the others with W murmuring phrases like 'mustn't go back' and 'she's well.'

However after a day, W became more agitated. I woke from dozing in a chair to find him thrashing about. Jumping to my feet, I instantly tried to still him before he reopened his wound. W continued to toss his head back and forth.

"Please, sir, you must calm yourself," I pleaded.

W hissed and opened his eyes, scanned the room and then focused on me. His eyes narrowed in confusion.

"Who are you? Where am I?" he whispered.

"You are in your townhouse, sir. In London. I am Garvis—"

"This isn't my house." W opened his eyes wider, darting a glance around the room again. Staring at the bed hangings, the candles burning, the fire flickering in the hearth.

"No!" W heaved his body, nearly breaking my hold. His eyes rolled back into his head. "No, this isn't right. It can't be."

I needed to calm him. "Everything will be all right, sir. You just need to compose your—"

But W continued to thrash his head back and forth, muttering.

"No! No, I was there. In the cellar of the house . . . falling . . . so long ago . . . cottage . . . Duir Cottage."

"Sir, calm down."

W fixed me with a terrified look. "What is the year?" he asked, licking his lips.

I paused. How gone was he into his delirium? "1828, sir—"

"No! Oh heavens, no!" W groaned. "No, that's not right. It makes no sense." He grabbed my arm with his good hand, holding fast. "Tell me you lie. Tell me the year is 2014—"

Horror flashed through my soul at those words.

"Sir, you are fevered—" But my words fell on deaf ears. W had closed his eyes, murmuring again.

"It was there—there in the cellar. The portal." He started thrashing about again. "My name. What is my name?"

"Please, sir, calm down. You mustn't be so wild—"

"Wild!" W suddenly laughed—a crazed, maniacal sound. "It's all wild, wild, wild! Marcus Wilde!"

Visit www.NicholeVan.com to buy your copy of
Clandestine today and continue the story.

About the Author

Nichole Van is an artist who feels life is too short to only have one obsession. In former lives, she has been a contemporary dancer, pianist, art historian, choreographer, culinary artist and English professor. Though Nichole still prefers the label 'adaptable' more than 'ADD.'

Most notably, however, Nichole is an acclaimed photographer, winning over thirty international accolades for her work, including Portrait of the Year from WPPI in 2007. (Think Oscars for wedding and portrait photographers.) Her unique photography style has been featured in many magazines, including *Rangefinder* and *Professional Photographer*. She is also the creative mind behind the popular websites Flourish Emporium and {life as art} Workshops, which provide resources for photographers.

All that said, Nichole has always been a writer at heart. With an MA in English, she taught technical writing at Brigham Young University for ten years and has written more technical manuals than she can quickly count. She decided in late 2013 to start writing fiction and has loved exploring a new creative process.

Nichole currently lives in Utah with her husband and three crazy children. Though continuing in her career as a photographer, Nichole is also now writing historical romance on the side. She is known as NicholeVan all over the web: Facebook, Instagram, Pinterest, etc. Visit her author website at www.NicholeVan.com to sign up for her newsletter. You can see her photographic work at http://photography.nicholeV.com and http://www.nicholeV.com

If you enjoyed this book, please leave a short review on Amazon.com. Wonderful reviews are the elixir of life for authors. Even better than dark chocolate.

www.ingramcontent.com/pod-product-compliance
Lightning Source LLC
Chambersburg PA
CBHW020404260626
47156CB00007B/2230